TAMIKO

AND THE
TWO JANITORS

BY FORTHRIGHT

FORTHWRITES.COM

Amaranthine Saga, Book 3
Tamiko and the Two Janitors

Copyright © 2019 by FORTHRIGHT
ISBN: 978-1-63123-065-3

TWINKLE PRESS

because I like it when you laugh

TABLE OF CONTENTS

Tamiko

AND THE
TWO JANITORS

1

CATS PAW

While Tami waited for their town's lone stoplight to tick through its cycle, she bumped up the volume on her car radio.

"... encouraging people to check in with their county's Office of Ingress, where a team of Betweeners will be able to quickly set your mind at ease."

The talk show host cheerfully played devil's advocate. "Is this assessment an invasive procedure? Because I'm no fan of needles, let alone *fangs*."

With a polite chuckle, his guest assured, "We may ask a few questions about family history, but identification takes mere moments. All we need is cooperation."

"I'm sure you've heard the latest rumors."

"Oh?"

"The feeds and forums are plastered with warnings against

the very testing you're promoting, saying that the government is rounding up unregistered reavers *for their own good*."

He made that last bit sound unnecessarily ominous. Tami found the hype distasteful.

The guest, who must be a reaver, patiently explained, "Many people are curious if they have ties to the In-between, and we are able to provide answers."

"For a hefty price?"

"No, there's no charge."

"Can't argue with that. Maybe you should give us that list of names again."

"Certainly. In America, the most common surnames that point to a possible kinship to Betweener bloodlines are Reaver, Reaves, Reeve, Eaves, Eaver, Everson, and so on. Or surnames related to specific reaver classifications, like Ward, Warden, Barr, and Battle. A full multilingual, international list can be referenced at any Office of Ingress."

Tami smiled at that. She was freshly returned from an educators conference, and more than once, people had mistaken her for a reaver, based entirely on her nametag.

After the commercial break, they spun off into a discussion of the reaver practice of allowing successive generations to choose their own surnames, often based on their specialization, ranking, or birthplace.

"That's more like it," she informed the radio. Interesting facts would do far more to further the peace process than drumming up suspicions and drowning in sensationalism.

Turning into the dinky back parking lot of Landmark Elementary, Tami claimed her usual spot. They didn't have designated parking, but ever since starting in June, she'd been the first to arrive each morning ... with one notable exception.

An old jeep sat in the far corner of the lot.

Again.

She'd always been the early bird—and a competitive one at that. Tami had left an hour earlier than usual, just to be the first one into the school, only to be edged out by an earlier bird. Clearly, she needed to size up her rival.

Tami didn't know the first thing about cars, but the offending jeep had vintage appeal. Outdated but in good repair, with an open back and sides. Craning her neck, she spotted a couple of plaid blankets that showed signs of a shedding pet, a locked toolbox, a bale of straw, and a fifty-pound bag of sunflower seeds. Which probably added up to a handyman with a dog and several birdfeeders.

"Elementary, my dear Landmark." Aiming for the entrance, she surmised, "The janitor did it."

The side entrance was already unlocked, and the heavy security door swung smoothly despite its weight. This early, the lights were off, leaving a gray hush in hallways that had been welcoming students for generations. Gleaming terrazzo, glass trophy cases, metal lockers, and thick corkboard. It was like stepping back in time.

Tami's girlhood had been spent in these very halls. Dad and Grandad had attended Landmark Elementary, too. Three generations. And according to her mother, high time for a fourth.

She wiped her feet on the mat, and not merely for the benefit of the man coming along the hall toward her, pushing a wide dust mop. He was taller than average and a bit boxy in his shapeless gray-green coveralls, the kind of guy who'd probably played football in high school. His most distinguishing feature was definitely his hair—long and shaggy and vividly red, gathered into a ponytail at the back of his neck.

"Morning, ma'am!" he called amiably. "You're here earlier than usual."

"So it's *your* car I'm always seeing." She fished for his name. "Wasn't it … Mr. Kipling?"

He grimaced. "Yes, ma'am, but everyone calls me Kip."

"Kip," she acknowledged. "Please, just call me Tami."

Brown eyes softened. "If you don't mind, I'd like that. And yep, Coach is mine."

"Coach?" It took her a moment to catch up. "You named your jeep?"

"Seemed the friendly thing to do." Kip leaned against the broom handle. "And we like to get things squared away before things get busy."

"We?" She'd met most the staff in June, but those were informational meetings in preparation for the big conference, and attendance hadn't exactly been mandatory. "Who's the other half of your *we*? Or are you referring to Coach?"

He grinned. "Nah, I'm talking about me and Ash. We're about as *we* as a couple of guys can get. Childhood friends, I guess you'd say."

"Local?" Some days, it seemed like she knew everybody in Archer, but his was a new face.

"Close enough. Grew up in Fletching, but now I live up past

Nocking." He waved for her to continue and accompanied her along the hall. "How was the conference?"

Tami's heart skipped with nervous excitement. "Amazing. And intense. We had classes from morning to night, but they were all so *interesting*. And I was able to meet real Amaranthine!"

"Look at you, snubbing the slang!"

"Our first lessons were in etiquette." Tami shook her head. "Everyone's always saying *Rivven*, even on the news. Most of the attendees didn't even know there was a proper term."

"But they set you straight?"

"Kindly." She patted her satchel. "I brought back so much literature, and some of the information packets are thick as dictionaries. Even if we're not selected, I'm going to read it all."

Kip propped his broom beside the office door and folded his arms over his chest. "Seems good. No regrets."

"Not yet." Tami's smile wavered. "When I stop to think about it, I get nervous."

"When are you supposed to hear who got picked?"

"This week. The reavers said that they'd take their recommendations to the Five, and a decision would be made quickly."

The janitor's gaze drifted to a point over her shoulder. "And how would that decision be relayed?"

"*Official means*—that's all they said."

"So a herald, yeah?" Kip pointed.

Outside the glass double doors, a uniformed individual stood waiting.

"Oh, gosh." Tami grabbed Kip's arm. "Oh, wow. Do you think?"

"How about we ask the nice herald if he has good news?" Pulling a jangling ring of keys from one of his pockets, Kip unlocked the main door and swung it wide.

The person who stepped inside wasn't human. He was slender and pale, with snow-white hair fluffing around pointed ears. By contrast, his eyes were liquid black and bright. "Tamiko Reaverson, Principal?" he asked in a light voice.

"Yes. That's me." She cautiously offered her hands. "And you are?"

With a soft smile, the Amaranthine rested his palms on hers. "I am Remill of the Whistledowns, one of the dove clans. We have always worked closely with reavers and are currently attached to the Office of Ingress here in Perch County."

"You've always lived here?"

"Your home has long been my home," he assured. "Lovely, is it not?"

"It *is*," she murmured.

Withdrawing a heavy packet from his messenger bag, Remill said, "I am here because a communique arrived for you at our offices. And because I enjoy being the bearer of good news."

Kip whistled between his teeth. "That's the real deal, all right."

Tami's fingers trembled as she prodded at wax-sealed string. The impression was of a striking cat's paw—Hisoka Twineshaft's own crest.

"Here," offered Kip, pulling a multi-purpose tool from one of his many pockets and unfolding a slender blade. He worked it under the seal, lifting it away. "That'll do it."

Hands shaking even worse, she pushed the packet into Kip's chest. "I can't. You open it for me."

"If you want." He gave her a dubious look. "Isn't this your big moment."

6

"This moment's too big for one person." Tami flapped a hand at him. "Share it with me."

"Yes, ma'am," he said with a jaunty salute. "Okay. There's a cover letter. Signed with a pawprint."

Tami's brow furrowed, and she leaned in to see. "You can't be serious."

"I'm *totally* kidding."

She cuffed his shoulder. "What does it say?"

The janitor straightened up, and with all the grandeur of a presenter at an awards gala, he read off the message. "Principal Tamiko Reaverson, it is with great pleasure that I am able to inform you that Landmark Elementary has been selected for the Twineshaft Initiative, alongside Archer Middle, West Branch High, and Bellwether College."

Her heart leapt. Good news, indeed!

Kip winked at her over the top of the page and read on. "My committee members were favorably impressed by your passion and by your group's ingenuity in proposing an integration program that stretches from kindergarten through graduate school. We are prioritizing a similar strategy in every state, with your schools serving as a flagship for peace. I look forward to meeting you in person." Kip tapped the page. "And while there's no pawprint, it *is* signed by Spokesperson Twineshaft, on behalf of the Five."

And then she was squealing and bouncing, and Kip was bouncing right along with her. He brought Remill into their celebratory circle, and Tami hugged the herald and kissed his cheek. The dove gave a soft, twittering laugh, so she kissed his other cheek, as well.

The blushing herald excused himself with a graceful gesture

and the hope of future meetings.

Kip asked, "What can I do to help?"

Tami impulsively suggested, "Be on my planning team?"

He thumped his chest. "I'm there."

She doubted a janitor could contribute much, but Kip's enthusiasm was contagious.

True to her assessment, he caught her hands and spun her into an impromptu waltz. He was broad in the shoulder and bulky about the middle, but light on his feet. She laughed, and he beamed as if that had been his whole goal.

"I hear the door," he sang out.

And then Mrs. Dabrowski was there, hand on her hip. "Kip, you rascal! Unhand Principal Reaverson!"

He guided them closer, gave Tami a final spin, then claimed her spluttering secretary for his next partner. Switching to an energetic polka, which Flootie Dabrowski had no trouble matching, he announced, "We're celebrating."

Mrs. Dabrowski stopped and swung around. "We got it?" she asked Tami.

Tami flung her arms wide. "We got it!"

More squeals and hugging, and Tami was surprised by a few tears. She'd worked so hard for this, wanted it so much. And it was *actually* going to happen. "The Amaranthine are coming *here*, to our little town. Oh, I hope they like it."

"Why wouldn't they? This is just as pretty a piece of countryside as you'll find!" Flootie patted her shoulder and staunchly declared, "We'll give them what they haven't always found—a warm welcome."

2

ELDERBOUGH INITIATIVE

rowning at the single, shimmering paper that held Melissa's assignment, the head of Perch County's Office of Ingress asked, "What's all this?"

And even though the formidable woman—Reaver Courtney Barr, according to the brass plate on her desk—had the information in front of her, Melissa stiffly explained her sudden arrival.

"Under the auspices of the Elderbough Initiative, I've come to make an initial evaluation of the Reaverson household in Archer. They're relatives, and at my biological father's request, they've opened their home to me. I'll be staying with them while commuting into Fletching, where I'm enrolling at Bellwether College."

"I can see that." The stout woman with steel gray hair lifted the sheet and her eyebrows. "But the timestamp suggests a plan made in haste. Why?"

"Miss Tamiko Reaverson, age twenty-nine, attended the recent

9

New Saga conference for educators as an applicant for Hisoka Twineshaft's school revitalization project. While there, she caught the attention of one of the organizers, who flagged her name in the system."

"She's an unregistered reaver?"

"If so, I'll protect her."

Courtney asked, "Your classification, Reaver Armstrong?"

Melissa squared her shoulders. "Battler."

The woman lifted a bony finger, pushed back her chair, and left the room.

Alone again, Melissa dragged in a shallow breath. She wasn't very good at this sort of thing. It didn't help that Reaver Barr was such a dour woman, utterly lacking in the usual brand of diplomatic charm. Melissa shifted in her seat and fiddled with her unaccustomed attire. The jeans were all right, but she missed the close fit of her tunic and the weight of her weapons belt. Her training group had been working in light armor for weeks, and she felt naked without it. Worst of all were the sandals. She might be a California girl—born and bred—but reavers did *not* wear flip-flops.

Courtney returned with three sheets of paper. Sliding the first across the desk, she said, "Bellwether has a reaver track. You won't need to enroll in any general studies unless they interest you personally."

Melissa scanned the course list with increasing amazement. "I thought Bellwether College was open to the general public."

"It is. The college is one of the earliest academic institutions in America. It is also one of the first enclaves in this region." With a stern look, she added, "Undisclosed."

Perusing the section of courses and apprenticeships available to battlers, her gaze caught on a single line. "They match Kith to battlers?"

"One of the three founding clans of the Bellwether Enclave is the Nightspangle pack. Theirs is the foremost wolf-partnering program in North America." A steady look. "You didn't know?"

Melissa could only shake her head.

"Nice to know Christopher Armstrong takes his vows seriously." Courtney Barr slid a second sheet of paper across the desk. "He was born here, raised in the enclave, and he's kept their secret. Christopher's Kith partner is a Nightspangle wolf."

"Cove," she whispered.

Partnership between battlers from the mid-ranks was an appealing option for those who wished to distinguish themselves. During her homestays, Melissa always watched her mother train with her partner Magda. The two women had been a formidable team since their academy days, with Mom launching arrows that Magda imbued with crackling energy. Their fierce combination regularly dominated in reaver tournaments, since their bolts could disrupt sigils, sear through barriers, and detonate on impact.

Melissa dreamed of partnership, too, but of a different variety.

During her first year at academy, she'd wandered into an area of campus not intended for small children. Four years old and lost in the armory. But the presence of so many weapons hadn't worried her. The echoing chamber was like her mother's special closet, but on a much larger scale.

Fascinated, she'd explored the various cases, earning a shallow slice on one finger from a dagger and pricking another on a particularly beautiful arrow. She could still remember its fiery

11

fletching, for it had been trimmed with phoenix feathers.

Right about then, she'd found herself nose-to-nose with an enormous feline. The Kith must have been some sort of lynx, for Melissa remembered tufted ears and speckled fur. As well as pale green eyes that shone with intelligence and amusement.

Scruffing her like a wayward kitten, the big cat had carried her like a prize back to the correct dormitory, where the teenaged girl assigned to Melissa had breathed a sigh of relief and held her close. Then taught her how to properly thank the Kith.

The dye was set.

Throughout her schooling, Melissa was most comfortable with her Kith acquaintances or her Amaranthine instructors. Her reserve never confused them. They knew when she was happy or confused or frightened or angry, and they modified their behavior to match her mood. Her awkwardness in expressing herself never mattered. Without a word, she was understood.

So she donned a battler's colors and took her father's name, all to increase her chances of being matched with a Kith companion.

As far as she was concerned, nothing else mattered.

Courtney Barr indicated the second paper. "Christopher Armstrong may not have told you about Bellwether Enclave, but his recommendation has been on file with the Nightspangle pack since your fifth birthday."

"That's nearly twenty years ago."

"The waiting list for whelped Kith is longer than a founding family's pedigree." The woman studied Melissa's transfer papers again, and her lips pursed. "You're not contracted?"

"No."

Reaver Barr gave up waiting for an explanation. "With your lineage, you can't be lacking for offers."

Melissa wouldn't apologize for her decision to prioritize finding a Kith partner over her duty to the In-between. A husband would only complicate things, and an ill-timed pregnancy could undercut her eligibility if a potential partner became available. Mom and Magda had supported her choice to remain single, even though she'd had to pay a hefty fee on her twenty-third birthday.

"I withdrew my name from the register." Melissa quietly stood her ground. "My age, my lineage, and my whereabouts are currently ... undisclosed."

Courtney didn't bat an eye. "Good for you, honey."

"Th-thank you?"

The third sheet of paper crossed the desk. "This is today's threat advisory. Given the founding principle behind the Elderbough Initiative—*pack is pack, care for your own*—I suspect this is the *real* reason Naroo-soh Elderbough hustled you out this way."

"The rogue." Melissa nibbled at her lip as she studied the map and its legend. Clusters of red dots spanned three states without any discernable pattern. "The few reports I've seen describe him as opportunistic ... vicious ... and elusive."

"Three of the rogue's most recent attacks have been blamed on werewolves, which is utterly ridiculous. We've had to withdraw more than half of the Elderbough trackers because the sight of wolves in *any* context sends the public into a panic." Courtney's expression darkened. "Surgeons spent most of last night fighting to save the lives of Kith trackers who ran into the path of a citizen's patrol. Three scraped through. Two died. Shot by silver bullets."

3

RED GATE FARM

Melissa stole a glance at her phone, confirming that she was indeed on the right track ... a literal track. Well, not *quite* that bad, but she wasn't accustomed to bumping along gravel roads. Her relations lived at a place called Red Gate Farm, and a brief phone conversation with her host had ended with the assurance that she couldn't miss it.

"Drive until you run out of road, and you're there," she muttered, creeping along.

She wasn't used to so much green.

Grass carpeted the rolling hills of a pasture on her right, and the trees lining the road created a green tunnel. Very different from sand-skimmed boardwalks and a wide view of the ocean, with the continual rhythm of waves on their beach.

Checking her rear-view mirror, Melissa stopped in the road and put her loaner in park. The faded blue hatchback was already showing a powdery coat of dust from her backroad ramble. She snapped a picture and sent it to Magda, who'd ordered her to stay in touch.

> **Behold, Middle America!**
> **aka middle of nowhere**
> > **A nice place to visit**
> > **Don't stay away too long**
>
> **No promises**
> **They have wolves**
> **If one wants me, I'm theirs**
> > **Lock and load**

That was Magda's way of wishing her luck.

Melissa didn't bother with her seatbelt as she continued along, stones popping under her tires, lazy puffs of dust her only companion on the road. But beyond the wall of trees on her left, she caught glimpses of an orchard and a white plank fence.

A school bus and a van from a Fletching senior center were parked beyond red gates flanked by fluttering welcome banners and barrel-sized pots of geraniums. A big sign announced that it was apple season, with late-summer varieties listed. Melissa hadn't even heard of half of them.

She turned in.

Everything was red and white, from the huge barn with GIFT SHOP painted on the side to the tractor hitched to a long wagon. More signs pointed the way to pick-your-own apples, cider press, petting zoo, hayrides, farm fresh eggs, and a corn maze opening in October.

Coming along the driveway toward her was a young man in overalls. She hadn't even realized people still wore them. Waving a small red flag, he tried to guide her into an open parking place at the gift shop.

Leaning out her window, she explained, "I'm not a customer. Can you tell me where to find the owners? My name's Melissa Armstrong, and they're expecting me."

"This way." He turned and walked away.

Not sure what else to do, she rolled slowly after him. Right before the barn, the drive turned a corner, and a farmhouse hove into view, complete with picket fence, green shutters, and a porch swing. The young man went into his traffic directing routine again, pointing her into the open spot beside a station wagon in front of a detached garage.

She called her thanks and popped the hatch to get her luggage.

Instead of heading back to work, he silently stepped forward to take her suit case.

"Do you work here?" she asked.

"Every day."

He led the way up the porch steps and didn't bother knocking before walking into a big kitchen. A man turned from the sink with a wide smile, and Melissa immediately relaxed. He was at least a decade older than Chris Armstrong, but he looked enough like him to assure her that she was in the right place.

"Melissa!" Making hasty use of a dishtowel, he held out a hand. "Abel Reaverson. I guess we'll go with Uncle Abel, okay?"

She matched his grip. "Hello. Thank you for taking me in on such short notice."

"Don't mention it." Nodding past her shoulder, he said, "You've met my son."

Turning back, she realized that the young man in overalls was still there, staring at his feet.

She flushed in embarrassment. Her whole family was cut from the same cloth—tall, strong, blue-eyed, and fair-haired. By contrast, her guide's features had a distinctly Asian cast.

Melissa said, "I'm so sorry. I didn't realize."

Uncle Abel laughed. "You'll have to pardon Joe. He's a little shy. Tami makes up for it though. She'll be back in another hour or two. She's principal of the elementary school in town. You probably passed it on your way here."

"I did."

"Hiro, that's my wife, she's working in the gift shop right now, so I'm on salad duty. I'll take you out to meet her, but first we should let you set your stuff down and freshen up." He beckoned for her to follow him. "Everything's ready. We put you upstairs, right across from Tami. Joe's room is at the other end, little bigger than a closet, really, but he doesn't seem to mind."

Pausing at the door, she looked back to where Joe was still watching. Her cousin offered a bashful smile and a tentative wave, then escaped out the front door.

When she caught up to Uncle Abel on the stairs, he asked, "Long day?"

"Yes."

His smile widened. "I get the impression that you're a little shy, too."

"I guess so?"

"No problem. You'll see how it works around here. Plenty of room in the world for all kinds of people." He opened a door, saying, "For you. Bathroom's there. I'll be in the kitchen!"

And he left her alone.

She eased into her new room, closing the door behind her. The lock was old-fashioned in the extreme, but with a jiggle and a twist, she managed to turn the skeleton key. After a brief reconnoiter, she crossed to the room's one window and inspected the casement. Flipping the catch, she raised the sash and gave a quick pinch and pull, relieving her window of its screen. With practiced ease, she slid out feet-first and crouched barefoot on the sloped roof outside.

Not a bad vantage point, though it only gave her a view of row upon row of trees. Fortunately, this side of the house was shaded by a pair of elms. She suspected that the grit-and-tar shingles would be too hot in full sun. Boots were definitely at the top of her shopping list.

Keeping low, she scaled to the peak to get the lay of the land—a second barn, tractor shed, animal pens, chicken coop, corn crib. Beyond the second barn were stacks of pallets and wooden apple crates. And she could see a field thick with broad green leaves. Undoubtedly the pumpkin patch.

With no people in view, Melissa straightened to her full height and slowly relaxed the hold she'd been trained to keep on her soul. Maybe not the wisest course, but certainly the quickest expedient.

Thirty heartbeats later, and she was back under wraps, hiding herself from the telltale flit and drift of Ephemera. These low-level Amaranthine rarely gathered without certain inducements, the most basic of which was a reaver's presence.

That settled it for Melissa. Someone at Red Gate Farm needed her.

4

THE OAK GLEN

Joe probably should have rejoined his family in making their guest welcome, but as soon as he closed the gate behind their last customer and stowed the OPEN sign, he struck out through the orchard.

It wasn't that Melissa wasn't nice. But why was she even here?

Grandad's mother supposedly had an Armstrong connection, which meant that Melissa was Dad's second cousin's daughter. Or something. But no matter how Joe turned it around in his head, she was so distant a cousin, they might as well be strangers.

Joe didn't mind dealing with strangers when they were customers. All you had to do was sell them a bushel of apples, a carton of eggs, or a gallon of cider, and they went away. Melissa was a stranger who was moving in. Mom had promised him up and down that a busy college girl wouldn't be around much.

But he *knew* she was here. And that was weird.

Usually, he was only aware of Tami, something they'd always been told was a part of being twins. Joe liked the connection they shared. It was unique.

His sister was all the things he wasn't—confident and charismatic. She worked toward big dreams and fought for big ideals. He couldn't begin to compare, so he didn't try. Tami was Tami. As far as Joe was concerned, the world was lucky to have her. And so was he. But he was himself. And he was *most* himself out here, on their land, among their trees. And especially in the oak glen.

Joe slipped into his favorite retreat. The wide ring of oak trees had been planted by Grandad some sixty years ago, back when *he* was a boy, and the orchard fanned out around it, hemming it in on every side. Over the decades the oaks had put down their deep roots and climbed skyward, sending out beamlike branches until their leaves touched. And in the very center, stood a tree unlike any other.

It was by far the largest tree on the property, visible from the highway if you knew right where to look. If people noticed it at all, they probably assumed their tree stood on a hill, but it was actually tucked down in a little hollow all its own. As if the person who planted it was trying to hide it. The oak glen was a shady vale of mossy stones and twisting roots where he and Tami had picnicked and played as children.

Joe settled among a dramatic swirl of roots that surrounded him like smooth walls, curving up and away from his niche. This spot had always felt like a throne to him when he was little. On the flat stone nearby, Tami used to set up a pretend kitchen and fix him meals of flower petals and grass blades, wild berries and green apples. And he'd lean back and count air ribbons or potter around in the dirt, boring the holes into which he planted his apple seeds.

Tami didn't make it out here so much anymore.

Grandad did, even though the distance made it tough. But Joe figured this was a special place for the old man. He hadn't picked the spot and planted the trees for no good reason. Dad had once told him that Grandad was a twin, too, but his sister had died young. Maybe this was all for her. Maybe Grandad came here to remember.

Once, just a couple of winters back, Joe had heard Grandad refer to this place as a "song circle." When Joe asked about it, the old man brushed it off in his usual gruff way, but the term stuck with Joe.

Maybe Grandad's sister had liked to sing?

Joe doubted he'd ever get around to asking.

The day was getting on toward dinnertime when Joe heard the tractor engine cut out. Minutes later, Grandad was picking his way down the gentle slope. Probably sent to fetch him.

"Found you." The old man grunted as he eased into a neighboring nook among the roots. "You're a mite young to be so set in your ways."

Joe couldn't help smiling. "I take after you."

"Might be," he agreed.

Grandad pulled an apple from his pocket and passed it along, then extracted another for himself. They munched in companionable silence, but Joe guessed there was something on the old man's mind. Was he worried about sharing their home with a stranger, too?

But when Grandad spoke, it was to ask about the tree. "Notice anything different about her?"

"Can't say for sure. I don't see any fruit."

This past May, for what Grandad assured him was the first time, there had been flowers in the uppermost branches of their lone tree. Tiny white buds that opened into creamy flowers. To Joe, they seemed to shimmer, as if catching sunlight and sending it into the shadows. Best of all had been the scent. Every afternoon, when the sun-warmed flowers were at their most intoxicating, they'd come to doze under the tree. Him with an old army blanket, and Grandad with his cushion from the seat of the tractor.

Joe missed that scent enough to long for spring again. "I'll bring the ladder next time. Maybe there are seed pods or nuts."

"Unless she can self-pollinate, she won't have anything to offer."

"Cross-pollinators?"

Grandad hummed skeptically. "Special tree, special case."

"I asked Tami to look into it for me."

"How do you mean?"

Joe explained, "Gave her some leaves. She thought she might be able to find out something online."

Grandad grumbled, "Wasn't no need to do that."

"I know, but our tree wasn't in any of the books at the library." He reached for a leaf that had fallen early—perfectly round, thin as tissue paper, edged in the gold that would soon sweep through the entire canopy. "I wonder how it got here."

But Grandad pretended not to hear.

Joe sighed and lifted his hand. A tiny bird, no bigger than a walnut and just as deep a brown, alighted briefly on his fingertips.

Its speckled throat puffed out, and it warbled three notes, like liquid crystal, piercingly sweet.

They were one of his favorites.

He'd always wondered why no one else seemed to be able to see them.

5

FRATERNAL TWINS

Melissa liked Abel's wife, who asked to be called Auntie or Hiro or any combination thereof. The lady of the house spoke with a slight accent that made it obvious she wasn't from these parts. While pulling together the evening meal, she gave an abbreviated version of her story, how she and Uncle Abel had met at college and married thirty-five years ago. Aunt Hiro occasionally returned to Kyoto to visit her parents, but this was home now.

Her aunt's and uncle's easy camaraderie made Melissa homesick, but it also gave her a fresh avenue of inquiry to bring up to the genealogical division. Many strong reaver bloodlines traced through Japan. Had the archivists checked for a maternal connection to the In-between?

Tami returned late that afternoon, bubbling over with news about the selection of her school by Hisoka Twineshaft. Melissa hung back, not wanting to interrupt, content to gather her own impressions.

But Tami curtailed her news and turned on her with eyes sparkling. "Cousins?"

"On my father's side." Melissa found herself admitting, "Your dad reminds me of mine."

"There's more like him?" Tami smiled teasingly at her father. "Maybe we should sneak in at the next family reunion. How are we related again … through one of Grandad's cousins?"

"Not quite sure," Uncle Abel said apologetically. "Maybe one of the Reaverson girls married an Armstrong?"

Melissa wasn't sure what to say. Reaver bloodlines didn't always involve traditional marriages, nor did siblings always choose the same surname. She'd seen the pertinent section of the family tree used to invoke the Elderbough Initiative. Melissa's biological grandfather was Tami's biological grandfather's half-brother. By arrangement. Perhaps there had been an effort to revive a fading bloodline.

But it must not have worked. According to records, Uncle Abel's grandparents had vowed out, relinquishing their reaver status. They'd left the In-between, but Tami could still be a throwback.

"You're going to be attending Bellwether College?" Tami asked. "You'll soon have classes with Amaranthine. I'm sure it'll be in tomorrow's news."

"What?"

"We were selected! My elementary school and our middle school, one of the high schools, and Bellwether College were chosen by Hisoka Twineshaft for his big school revitalization program."

Tami's father was all celebration, but her mother wanted more information. "What happens next?"

"A little extra funding, which we'll put into renovations and salaries. But most exciting, we'll soon have Amaranthine living in our community!"

"Rivven kids at your school?" asked Uncle Abel.

Tami shook her head. "Not at Landmark. The Amaranthine don't send their children to school like we do. They stay with their clan, so they're essentially homeschooled until they're old enough to take an apprenticeship. West Branch High will see some student integration, but at the elementary level, we'll be given a choice of Amaranthine faculty or staff."

Aunt Hiro asked, "You're replacing teachers?"

"No, no! Not unless or until someone retires. We're focusing on supplemental staff." Tami's enthusiasm seemed to multiply. "For instance, we haven't had a school librarian in six years. And budget cuts meant curtailing arts and music. This is a *huge* opportunity! Our new staff will be enriching our students' lives, all while showing them that Amaranthine are valued members of the community."

"They're a wily bunch," said Uncle Able.

Tami bristled. "What do you mean?"

"Rivven have long lifespans. They may never win over their detractors, but they can outlive them. If the next generation grows up with inhuman mentors and peers, the stigma will fade to nothing."

"Is that so bad?" Tami asked softly.

Her dad gazed thoughtfully at the ceiling. "Nope. They're wiser than we've been, on the whole. And more patient than many folks deserve. When will you get your Rivven?"

Melissa cringed inwardly. She'd never understood why the Amaranthine so easily accepted the label, but in America, they were almost universally referred to as Rivven. It bugged her that the media had slapped their own label on a culture that predated theirs by millennia.

Yet the Amaranthine offered no protest. Under Hisoka Twineshaft's leadership, the clans prioritized peace over pride. If anyone pushed for the more respectful use of proper terms, it was nearly always a reaver speaking up on an Amaranthine's behalf.

Tami eagerly answered her father. "Assignments will be finalized by Christmas. Something to do with the winter solstice. They make big decisions and big announcements during the longest night of the year."

Melissa wasn't surprised. The Amaranthine might be willing to let some things go, but they observed Dichotomy Day without fail.

"My girl's changing the world!" boasted Uncle Abel.

Aunt Hiro murmured, "To think, Amaranthine here. And all because of you."

Which wasn't true at all. Not only had Amaranthine settled in this area first, their community had been carefully crafted to foster a human one. Melissa kept her eyes down and tried not to get angry over simple ignorance. Let the lady principal think what she wanted.

But then Tami surprised her.

"I'm not so sure, Mom. You know, I met an Amaranthine today from a dove clan. He said he's been in Perch County all his life.

27

That he loves it here as much as we do. If this is his home, he can't be alone. Maybe there have been Amaranthine here all along."

Her father said, "If there are, I've never seen hide nor hair of them."

"Why should we?" asked Tami. "It's not as if they have any incentive to come out of hiding."

Uncle Abel was nodding. "The latest proposal involves registry before granting basic rights. And a few states are arguing hotly for tagging."

"No politics during dinner." Aunt Hiro began ferrying serving bowls to the table.

Tami accepted the change of subject and asked, "Where's Joe?"

"Some quiet corner, I'm sure," said Uncle Abel.

"I sent Grandad after Jiro." The woman tilted an ear toward the door. "There's the tractor now."

Turning to Melissa, Tami asked, "Have you met my twin?"

"Yes." And again, she found herself adding more. "I didn't realize you were twins."

"Fraternal, of course." Tami lingered beside the kitchen door as if she'd had enough of being apart. When Joe entered on the heels of the old man who was obviously their grandfather, Tami slipped under Joe's arm, earning a lopsided hug.

Now that they were side-by-side, Melissa could see obvious similarities. The shape of their eyes, their noses, their cheekbones— these they'd inherited from their mother. But Joe had his father's forehead and chin, and Tami's eyes were the same blue as Uncle Abel's.

The old man cut straight to the corner console and picked up the remote.

"We have a guest," protested Aunt Hiro.

"She's staying, but this won't wait. It's a live broadcast."

Uncle Abel sheepishly explained, "My father's a bit of a Rivven fanatic, and tonight's a big deal. Have you been following the Starmark courtship?"

"Not especially," she lied.

A commercial was running for some new drama in the fall line-up. The old man kept it muted, but his gaze never left the screen. He was long and lean like the other Armstrongs she knew, but his hair was pure white, and his blue eyes were partially obscured by reading glasses.

"You see that?" he asked.

She shook her head in confusion, then realized he wasn't looking. "No, sir?"

He pointed with the remote. "Pim Moonprowl. First openly Amaranthine actress on primetime. Get this ... she plays a wolf."

Melissa stared blankly at the clip. The actress was clearly meant to be part of a team of investigators. A tracker with bare feet and baubles at her throat and ankles, clad in a form-fitting corset and a furry miniskirt the same color as her tail.

"Ever seen the like?" he demanded.

"She's very beautiful," Melissa managed as she watched that tail flick and curl.

The old man gave her a disappointed look, then harrumphed. "She's very *feline*."

Uncle Abel asked, "Does it really matter? Rivven all look the same to me."

"Next time you ask for a puppy, you're getting a kitten," groused the senior Mr. Reaverson.

"Dad," his son sighed. "Meet Melissa Armstrong, who will be boarding with us while attending classes at Bellwether."

"George Reaverson." His handshake was firm, his gaze keen. "You look like family. All of us are long in the leg. Make yourself at home."

"Thank you, sir."

"Just George. Or Uncle George, if you care to claim me."

Then the commercial break ended, and he unmuted the television. A five-person panel of news anchors and color commentators welcomed the world to Kikusawa Shrine in Keishi, Japan for the next phase of the Starmark courtship.

Aunt Hiro gave in with grace. Joe helped her add another leaf to the table, and Tami rearranged the place settings so they could all see the television while they ate.

Melissa tuned in to the panel's discussion.

" … made all the more dramatic by yesterday's announcement."

"Spokesperson Twineshaft has shown impressive foresight. By acting as Eloquence Starmark's go-between for the duration of the courtship, he's gained the world's attention. Today's entertainment isn't just a celebration of the upcoming Miyabe-Starmark union, but of the Five's long-anticipated announcement that they've expanded their membership to seven."

"That's right," jumped in their color commentator as the cameras switched to Kimiko Miyabe and her entourage. "Suuzu Farroost, the representative for the phoenix clans, is the first avian spokesperson on the council. We received word earlier that in celebration of the appointment, the clan will honor the couple's

30

continuing courtship with a phoenix fly-over."

"Cameras will be trained on the skies!" The anchor turned to the Betweener on their panel. "Reaver Hinman, am I safe in assuming that this is a great honor?"

"Oh, no doubt. Both an honor and a blessing, since …."

Tami leaned closer to Melissa and asked, "Aren't they a cute couple?"

Melissa tapped her heart. "He adores her."

"*Everyone* does. Have you seen Kimiko's book group on Goodreads? She and a friend run it, and they know *all* the best novels inspired by the Emergence."

Melissa only smiled. She was more interested in the unfolding scene on television. Some things weren't obvious to casual observers, but whenever the cameras lingered on the courting couple, it was possible to pick up on their body language. They sent little messages to each other—teasing, tender.

After dinner, they lingered at the table, watching the pageantry unfold. Reaver Hinman proved an excellent translator as he narrated the graceful movements of the dance performed by a dozen deer clan members. Their festival attire honored both the courting couple and the appointment of Tenna Silverprong to the Amaranthine Council.

" … might interest you to know that the Silverprong clan were part of the first enclave to welcome reavers into their community, pre-dating the founding of Wardenclave by nearly a century."

"And today, they add their blessing to the upcoming union of a reaver to the grandson of one of Wardenclave's founders. Truly a historic event!"

Aunt Hiro took advantage of another commercial break featuring the miscast Miss Moonprowl to chase everyone out of the kitchen and into a shabbily comfortable family room. As Melissa accepted a chair across from Uncle George's, Tami and Joe crowded together on a couch built for two.

As the commentators rambled on about the preservation of old forests and the intricacy of Silverprong woodcarving, Melissa felt a subtle shift in the atmosphere. When she searched for its source, she noticed that Tami now sat with her arm tucked through Joe's, her head resting on his shoulder.

Joe finally looked comfortable, and Melissa was glad for him. But that couldn't be the source of this sense of … of *haven*. It reminded her of being inside the heavy wards of their cove. Carefully tuned. Perfectly balanced.

Uncle George noticed her distraction and caught her eye before solemnly tapping his heart.

She blushed, realizing she'd inadvertently done the same thing earlier. And she knew that he knew that she knew the meaning of the simple gesture. And that—in a slightly different way—it applied here as well.

He adores her.

6

FLICKERING

Y ou're quite the morning lark!" Flootie Dabrowski leaned through Tami's door. "What are you up to with all that? Some kind of craft project? Did you see last night's kiss? For pity's sake, what's going on with your light?"

Tami laughed at the sudden barrage. Her secretary was one of the few people who could out-chatter her, and she liked the change of pace. "First off, what's a morning lark?"

"Opposite of a night owl." Mrs. Dabrowski trundled into the room and planted her hands on her hips, her gaze fixed on the humming, flickering light fixture. "Was it doing that yesterday?"

"Not at all." Tami looked up. "I thought if I jiggled the bulbs it would stop, but I couldn't reach, even when I stood on my desk."

"Saints above, don't you dare be risking life and limb when we have a proper crew for that kind of thing. I'll let the boys know it's acting up." Her gaze swung back to the desk. "You're scanning leaves?"

Tami fiddled with the double row on the glass pane of her scanner, fitting a range of sizes and colors together. "They're from one of our trees at home."

Flootie picked up one that was beginning to turn yellow and twirled it by the stem. "These are practically round! What kind of tree do they come from?"

"Not sure." Tami placed a sheet of white paper over the leaves and carefully lowered the lid, punching the scan button. "We call it our mystery tree. My brother and I have been trying to track it down since we were kids, without any luck."

"I don't know the first thing about trees."

Tami said, "I know fruit trees, but that's my limit. I found an arborist's website, though. I'll post these scans and the basic facts on their forum. One of their experts will probably know it at a glance, which will save me from scrolling through endless near-misses and mismatches."

"You're a smart cookie."

Tami switched the white paper for a sheet of black construction paper and took another scan, unsure which background would make the leaves easier to identify. "I'm counting on the smarts of those botanists. It looks like the regulars on the forums include growers and hobbyists and university professors. And they jump on these kinds of questions. I'll probably have my answer in a day or two."

"I'll leave you to it. Good luck!"

Offering distracted thanks, Tami flipped the leaves so she could scan their undersides. In a matter of minutes, she was logging into the forum and prepping her post.

Help us identify our mystery tree.
Horizontal branching, smooth bark, twisting roots,
round leaves, offset placement, delicate as rice paper,
first bloom this past spring, white flowers, nine petals,
highly fragrant, no discernible fruit, nuts, or pods,
autumn foliage is yellow-gold, a beautiful tree,
but lonely, no others like it anywhere in our area.

She signed the post PrinceTam and made a note on her calendar to check back for responses.

A soft rap on her door pulled her attention to the time. Was she late for her meeting? No, it was still early. The buses wouldn't arrive for another half hour. "Yes?"

The door opened a few inches. "Your light?"

"Oh! That was quick. Thanks."

Tami gathered the leaves strewn across her desk while the janitor silently set up his ladder. She tried to focus on the task at hand, but she was curious. This was the *other* janitor, the one she hadn't met.

He had a lean build, high cheekbones, and sharp features. It wasn't often she met someone with hair similar to her own—straight and black. He'd pulled it into a careless ponytail at the nape of his neck, but its length boasted an enviable gloss. Like Kip, he wore drab coveralls in a shade somewhere between gray and green. From this angle, she couldn't quite read the name on the embroidered patch.

"We haven't met," she said.

"Guess not." He ran lightly up the ladder, tool belt jingling at his waist.

"I'm Tami."

35

"You're Principal Reaverson," he corrected.

"I'm Tami to my friends."

Perfectly balanced on the uppermost rung, he spared her a glance. "I'm not really a friendly guy."

His eyes were so dark, they might as well be black, and the way they glittered, she couldn't decide if he was serious or not. Despite the warning, his tone was polite, almost apologetic. It was the strangest case of mixed messages.

Removing the light fixture's cover, he proceeded to ignore her completely. Tami supposed he was accustomed to being ignored as he went about his duties. Or maybe he was shy like Joe. She tried again. "Kip says you're his friend."

"That's what he claims."

Wait, no. This was more like Grandad. Did curmudgeons come this young? She leaned back in her chair to watch him make handyman magic. "Kip's not your friend?"

"Kip's not fussy. He'll befriend anything that moves and a few things that don't."

Tami smiled. This guy was dodging her questions like a champ, but he wasn't actually denying anything. "He told me you two are a *we*, that you were childhood friends."

"Something like that."

"I haven't seen you around."

"You haven't been around." He slid the bulb back into place and tapped it lightly. The light flickered once, then blazed steadily. "Just because you don't notice us doesn't mean we're not here."

Tami watched him whip out a cloth and dust the cover before fitting it back into place. "How long have you worked here?" she asked.

"I forget."

She supposed she could just check his file, but that would be cheating. "I'm new."

That earned her a flat look. "I noticed."

Was this a problem? Tami sat forward. "You don't like change?"

"Nothing wrong with change, so long as it's good."

"I'll do my best."

He locked gazes with her. "I'm not holding you to anything."

To keep him talking, she blurted the first thing that came to mind. "How do you feel about the Amaranthine?"

"Why do you ask?"

"Landmark Elementary is going to become an integrated school."

"Kip mentioned that."

She said, "He was all for it."

"He's enthusiastic like that." Folding his dust rag and tucking it through his belt, he eased down a couple of rungs.

Tami pressed. "You're not in favor of bringing Amaranthine into the school?"

"I didn't say that." He tapped the pads of his fingers on the side of the ladder. "It's probably a good thing to let the kids meet all kinds of people. Let them see for themselves that they have nothing to fear from the clans."

"Kip offered to be on my planning committee."

"Then janitorial services is represented." Another step down.

She countered, "You can balance his enthusiasm with caution."

"I'm not really a committee kind of guy."

"But you're not opposed to bringing Amaranthine into the

open in Archer? Or in Fletching, for that matter?"

He hesitated. "That's a funny way of putting it."

Tami tried to explain how her perspective had shifted. "What if we're not just helping our kids understand and appreciate another culture. What if we're making our home the kind of place where Amaranthine can live openly?"

Easing up a rung, he sat on the top of his stepladder. "That's idealistic."

"I'll admit, I went into this hoping to upgrade our classrooms and add programs, but I don't think Spokesperson Twineshaft is that shortsighted. We have a chance to make a difference on the national level. Maybe even worldwide." Tami's resolve took shape even as she spoke the words. "I want peace. Let's give it a place to take root. That way, it can grow."

"Twineshaft will back you." He cocked his head to one side. "But have you considered the consequences of letting him use this place?"

She straightened in her chair, responding to his stern expression. "In which area?"

"The most important one—the kids." He spread his hands wide. "Do you have a contingency plan for the reporters, the camera crews, the curiosity seekers, the paparazzi, the protestors? There are plenty of people who want to throw obstacles in front of your ideals. Are you ready for bomb scares and vandals and every fanatic eager to make headlines?"

Doubts spun queasily in her stomach. Tami didn't want to think that the worst could happen, but it was her responsibility to plan for it. "This needs to be a safe environment for our teachers, for the children. But I'm not sure it's sending the right message to immediately put up a fence."

"Agreed. But I'm not thinking about chain link or barbed wire." He rested his chin on folded hands. "Betweeners know how to be subtle. Get some of their reavers in here to ward the grounds."

"They can do that?"

"Cinch."

"And it would do the same job as a fence?"

He fingered a band of leather at his wrist. "Barriers aren't showy, but they get the job done. People won't fuss, but the kids will be safe."

Tami was impressed. "How do you *know* all this stuff?"

He missed a beat. "Television."

She supposed that was possible. Plenty of people were as fascinated as Grandad in all things Amaranthine. "Reavers and wards. I suppose I could contact the county offices."

Nodding toward her desk, he asked, "The papers that herald brought ... did they include a contact person? Might be quicker to work through them."

"You're right!" Tami was already riffling through stacks, searching for the reaver assigned to work with her, the other two principals, and Dr. Bellamy. "I should bring this up to the others, too. They may need to take similar measures."

"There you go." He stood and descended, quickly collapsing his ladder. "You're all set."

"Wait!" Tami hurried around her desk and offered her hand. "I'm Tami."

"You're Principal Reaverson."

Resisting the urge to peek at his nametag, she asked, "And you are?"

He hesitated, as if trying to remember his name. "I go by Ash."

"I go by Tami."

Ash ignored her hand. "If you insist."

"*And* you're on my committee."

One side of his lips tilted upward. "Are you insisting on that, too?"

"Adamantly!" She wriggled her fingers, further insisting on the handshake.

His hand was lean, deeply tanned, and work-hardened, but gentle. When his loose clasp slipped sideways. Tami thought for a moment he was going to lift her hand to his lips, but he just stood there, eyes averted as he supported her hand with his palm.

"I'm not much for meetings," he grumbled.

Tami wondered if anyone truly liked meetings. "You can be on a special advisory committee. We'll have informal sessions, on an as-needed basis, perhaps in your office?"

"You want to meet in our closet?"

She frowned. "You don't have an office?"

"We do," said Ash. "In one corner of the Janitorial Closet."

"Is there room for a meeting?"

"I suppose. If you keep your special advisory committee small."

Tami liked the shine in his eyes, the barest hint of a smile touching his lips, the steadiness of the hand under hers. "Three members?"

"Sounds about right." He withdrew his hand and eased backward, snagging his ladder as he made for the door. "I'll tell Kip."

"Thank you, Ash."

"No big deal." Just before the door pulled all the way closed behind him, he quietly added, "Tami."

7

JANITORIAL CLOSET

Did you see the new principal?" Ash asked.

"Tami? Sure." Kip sashayed around the cramped maintenance room with a mop. "We've already had our first waltz!"

He couldn't keep the disbelief from his voice. "What were you *doing*, dancing with the principal?"

His best friend shrugged. "Seemed like a good idea at the time. If it makes you feel any better, I enjoyed a brisk polka with Flootie, and Harrison has had lessons in ballroom dancing. The only thing lacking from our tango was the rose."

"You tangoed with Harrison?"

"Lured him into a foxtrot, too." Kip waggled his eyebrows. "The kids were impressed."

"You shouldn't tease him so much."

"We were just messing around. He's definitely warming to me."

Ash had his doubts, but let it go. "All clear?"

"Yep! Full lock-down. We have the place to ourselves."

"Well, what are you waiting for?"

Kip replaced the mop and leaned against the back wall. "Hey, if you're feeling talkative, I don't want to interrupt the flow."

"I asked one thing."

"And revealed the deepest inner workings of your heart and soul." The redhead folded his arms over his chest. "So much better than your usual range of grunts and monosyllables."

"I talk," protested Ash.

"Not at any great length." Kip raised a hand. "That's probably my fault, though, not letting you get a word in."

Ash cracked a smile. "You even talk in your sleep."

"You would know!"

"Shut up and get comfortable."

"Gladly." Kip dropped onto an olive green camp chair that had been a fixture in the room for eighty years at least. Bending down, he unlaced a boot and eased his foot from its confines. Kip stretched and flexed, wriggling his toes. "Oh, that's good."

Ash merely grunted. This was part of the daily routine.

Kip's feet were long and large, covered in thick red fur, with pink pads and surprisingly sharp claws.

Next, he tackled the snaps and zips of his coveralls. The moment his arms were free, he was hissing and grunting as he unwound a mass of matted fur wrapped three times around his middle. He always looked so pudgy in his uniform, but there wasn't an ounce of fat on him. Shocking, considering how much Kip could eat.

His tail unwound, Kip shed the coveralls entirely and bounced on the balls of his feet. He bent forward, hands pressed to the floor. Straightening, he took advantage of their room's high ceiling to leap into a backward somersault, landing in a crouch. Then a quick tuck-and-roll, followed by three smart shakes, which was all it took to put the puff back into a tail that would be the envy of any squirrel.

Kip was furred from the waist down and freckled everywhere else. When he scratched up under his T-shirt, he partially exposed the blaze on his belly. "So what's all this about Tami?"

Ash summed up her quandary and their committee.

Kip chuckled. "She hasn't changed much. Always leading the charge."

"Huh?"

"Tami. I remember her."

Ash could only repeat, "Huh?"

"She never paid us much attention. Of course, we were a couple of old codgers back then." He helpfully added, "You were always closer to her twin brother. You know the one—sweet and shy."

Twins rang a bell, and Ash covered his eyes. "She's *Joe's* sister? I can't believe I .... I feel like I owe her an apology."

Kip bounded to his side, grinning rakishly. "Is she your type?"

"No!"

"I didn't know you *had* a type."

"I said *no*." Ash hid his misery against a ready shoulder. "That would be horribly wrong."

Kip's claws raked through his hair, catching on the ponytail tie and removing it. With long, slow strokes, he spoke softly. "You do realize that people like us—if we don't choose people like us— can't avoid the whole age difference issue."

"But she was one of our kids." Ash hated himself for even thinking their new principal was interesting.

"And ...?"

"They don't usually come back."

His friend wrapped his arms around him and chirred soothingly. "You don't have to be embarrassed. She grew up. You're allowed to appreciate the person she's become."

Ash muttered, "I never said anything about *appreciation*."

"Who do you think I am?"

"It's nothing."

"I've seen plenty of nothing. Trust me, this is something."

"Doesn't have to be something," insisted Ash.

Kip hummed and kept right on petting. "Tell me something anyhow."

Ash mumbled, "She has blue eyes."

"That she does. Unusual, but understandable, given her mixed heritage. Jiro and Tamiko—their mom's Japanese."

Ash relaxed into Kip, who'd been his best friend forever. "Her father probably has blue eyes."

"He does. I remember him, too. Abel and his apple fritters." The squirrel's belly rumbled, and he asked, "What do you want for supper?"

"Not hungry."

"Classic symptom of a heart in peril. Are your sort known for love at first sight?"

"How should I know?" he grumbled.

Kip lifted his face and kissed his nose. "I'll talk to Tyrone. He's about our age. Or Cyril, if you'd rather."

"I'm not in love!" Ash bit his lip. "Why are you trying to make this a thing?"

"Because you're an idiot, and I love you. But I won't say another word about the state of your heart where Miss Reaverson is concerned. On one condition."

"What's that?"

"Pizza for dinner."

Ash grunted and hoped he could move on half so easily.

8

NOT ENOUGH TO GO AROUND

Roonta-kiv Nightspangle was a rangy she-wolf whose beauty was somewhat marred by an expression of pure boredom. She looked Melissa over, then sniffed. "Yet another starry-eyed whelp who wants a pet to ride."

Melissa's cheeks flamed, but she took the standard receptive stance, showing her new mentor that she was willing to learn.

"Not many prove themselves worth the effort it takes to train them." Roonta-kiv took Melissa's wrist and pushed up the sleeve. "Well, well."

The cuff covering half her forearm had been a graduation gift from Mom. Supple leather enforced by metal plates, it could stop an arrow or turn a blade, and a clever sheath had been worked into the underside. The slim dagger within was meant to be Melissa's last line of defense, but Roonta-kiv's attention had been caught by Magda's addition.

Three sigil-etched stones gleamed softly in their fittings. Personal wards.

"Armstrong, was it?"

"Yes."

The she-wolf lost the affectation of disinterest, but the regret in her tone wasn't any more encouraging. "More than half our Kith are currently overseas, adding to the strength of other packs, safe from the predation of fear. And the ratio of hopefuls to whelps is five-to-one."

A warning she should have taken more to heart.

Reality bit deep as a blade.

Enrollment at Bellwether hadn't put Melissa on the fast-track to a Kith partnership. Her informal apprenticeship to Roonta-kiv was shared by sixteen other students, all as eager as she to distinguish themselves. And Melissa was late to the game. To the chubby, gamboling cubs from this season's litter, she was an outsider. By the time she won the trust she craved, they would already be paired off with one of her classmates.

Her first day wasn't all bad. She brushed the shelter's alpha pair by way of introduction. But her training menu involved freshening the bedding in a long line of unoccupied niches. She suspected the older students of creating busywork for the new rookie. By the end of the morning, she'd spent more time with a pen of visiting goats than with any Nightspangle wolves.

Disheartened, she left the Kith shelter and dragged her way toward the distant commuter lot. If she was going to stick it out in hopes of a match, she needed a long-range plan. Staying with Uncle Abel and Aunt Hiro kept her expenses low, but by midwinter, Melissa would have to pay another sizable fine.

Maybe she should look for work.

Melissa had already memorized the roads and alleys, more out of habit than anything, but now she turned her attention to the businesses. Overwhelmed by the array, she reviewed her options and reluctantly selected the most efficient path to success.

She called her father.

Twenty minutes later, Melissa stood at the corner of Fourth and Founders, staring up at an imposing three-story building. Built from brick and old-fashioned stonework, it took up the entire block. Her father had given her the name and address of the simplest entrance into the urban enclave. Belatedly, she thought she could have found the place on her own. The building's ornamentation was surprisingly revealing.

Scrollwork and oak leaves shaded clusters of acorns, and carved squirrels scampered along ledges or clung to eaves. Pheasants swooped over windows, and wolves crouched in niches. The only thing keeping it from betraying its residents was the fact that all the buildings this close to the campus boasted similar decorations.

The few enclaves she'd visited before had built a way of life around farming, mining, or an assortment of artisan crafts—pottery, carving, weaving, glass-blowing. Urban enclaves were more daring, interacting to a greater degree with the surrounding human community. One enclave had become world-famous as chocolatiers, and she knew of a group of Dimityblest designers whose line of specialty papers could be found in any craft store.

She never would have expected Amaranthine to run a coffee shop.

Pushing through wide, brass-fitted front doors, Melissa paused to marvel at the spaciousness of Founders Coffee Shop. From what she could see, it took up more than half of the building's first floor. Booths, tables, a long bar fitted with charging stations. Along one interior wall, glass doors allowed peeks into private rooms for study groups and tutoring sessions. Dark wood, antique brass, and beveled glass—everything about the décor belonged in a previous century.

It was busy, with the buzz of conversation, the hiss of steam, and the cheerful call of names as orders were filled. Of course, the best feature of any coffee shop had to be the pervasive fragrance.

Melissa found the ambiance at once relaxing and invigorating.

Countertops were marble, and glass display cases featured a tempting array of baked goods. Deep shelves lined the wall behind the front register, where stacks of white ceramic cups encouraged customers to sit and stay, not grab and go. Students had flocked to generously wide tables. The sound of turning pages and tapping keys came from every side. Founders was clearly set up to encourage gathering and study, like an unofficial student center.

One with a secret.

She could feel the wards, and she knew on an instinctual level that there were Amaranthine close by. What surprised her was that all the customers were from the general populace. They had no idea that the so-called werewolves they feared might well be serving their shots of espresso.

Behind the counter, a black gentleman in a crisp white shirt and dark vest added a swirl of cream to a glass of iced coffee. His co-worker, a much younger man with the same bowtie and name badge, was dusting the foaming tops of three deep-bowled cups with powder.

Melissa queued up behind three girls who whispered, giggled, and called out to the younger man. He cheerily returned their greetings, and he knew all their names. Quite the personal touch.

When her turn came, the young barista slowly straightened, as if to prove his superior height—a scant inch or so. This was the sort of posturing adolescent wolves were known to use when meeting. Did that mean he was a member of the Nightspangle pack? If so, the illusion protecting his identity was perfect.

"Well, *hello* there." His ancestry was Asian, but his accent was all-American. The name engraved on his golden badge was Jiminy. "Pardon me." Planting one hand on the counter, he reached for her hair. Even as she pulled back, he retreated, a piece of straw between thumb and forefinger. He took a conspiratorial tone. "*Somebody*'s been behind wards today!"

She made a discreet hand sign, confirming what was apparently obvious. To him. Much to Melissa's consternation, she couldn't tell if Jiminy was a reaver or an Amaranthine. But at least she knew she was dealing with another Betweener.

"May I ask you a personal question?" His tone was soft and light, his smile reassuring. "Your hand."

Melissa belatedly offered her palms, thinking he wanted a formal greeting.

"Just this one." Jiminy took her by the wrist and pulled her closer. His thumb slid over her pulse point, and he leaned in. The light brown fringe of his bangs fell into his eyes, and he shook them aside. "How many ways are you warded? Let me guess—blue, green, and ... feels pink."

"What?"

Another gentle tug, and he was pointing to her forearm or, more specifically, to the cuff hidden by her sleeve. "You're packing crystals. Can I have a peek?"

He crossed a line by slipping his fingers under the cloth, questing upward. A moment later, she had the offending hand twisted and pinned to cold stone. The angle forced him down, and she reinforced her objection by pushing his head until his cheek met marble.

"Ow."

Melissa's face flushed, and she checked to see if anyone had noticed her manhandling the barista. Both Mom and Magda had been thorough and creative in teaching her ways to dissuade unwanted masculine attention.

The other barista stepped up. "I do beg your pardon, miss. Did his antics unsettle you?" Pressing one large hand to the back of Jiminy's head, his voice deepened to a growl. "He *knows* better."

Jiminy whined, "Sorry, Rook."

"*I* am not the one you should be apologizing to."

The young man's eye rolled to the hand still pinning his wrist, then lifted his gaze to Melissa's. With an apologetic smile, he said, "The third stone's a pink, isn't it?"

He co-worker added pressure.

"Sorry!" he gasped. "You have my most abject and piteous pleas for mercy and forgiveness for my thoughtless act of trespass."

Melissa snatched back her hand. "Peace, please. No harm done."

The one called Rook hauled Jiminy upright and gave him a gentle push toward the array of coffee-making equipment. "Make yourself useful. I'll take care of our guest."

Jiminy reluctantly obeyed, casting a longing look at her over his shoulder.

Not sure why it should matter so much, Melissa pulled back her sleeve and raised her arm, showing him the three crystals that anchored her personal wards. They were indeed blue, green, and a rare pink.

His eyes lit up, and he gave a little fist pump.

Rook, who'd been watching closely, rolled his eyes. "Sorry about that boy's nonsense. He's under strict orders to stay on *this* side of the counter. He's too uninhibited, and our only excuse doesn't make much sense to most."

She shook her head. "He has an excuse?"

Leaning forward, Rook whispered, "Raised by wolves."

Melissa was so relieved to be in the right place, she giggled.

"You're new." He offered his hand in the human fashion. "I'm Lou Booker, one of the owners here."

Her gaze dropped to his nametag—LOU. "Jiminy called you Rook."

"In a family like ours, nicknames are a part of belonging. You may call me Rook. And you are?"

"Melissa Armstrong."

"I thought as much. You look very like Chris."

She eased closer to the counter, thrilled to have found people her father probably counted as kin. "Did you know I was coming?"

"I might have heard a little gossip from one of the squirrels next door. Not much happens in this enclave without it putting a twitch in his whiskers or a flick in his tail." Rook searched her face and warmly added, "Your arrival today is a welcome surprise. Do you have a place to stay?"

"I'm rooming with relatives while I train at Bellwether."

"Your classification?"

"Battler."

Nodding toward Jiminy, Rook asked, "Could you take him? If necessary."

"His height and reach exceed mine, but he was quickly subdued. He's no battler."

Rook chuckled. "He's a handful in his own way, but you're right. Jiminy's our enclave's primary anchor. He's a fine ward."

That explained his fascination with her accessories. Melissa *almost* felt bad for taking his interest the wrong way.

"Would you consider working here?"

She tightened her hold on his hand. "Yes."

"Even if it means coming over onto this side of the counter?"

"May I rebuff your ward if he oversteps his bounds?"

Rook's smile widened. "Whenever necessary. You can have whatever hours you need, and we can work around your training schedule. I'll pay more if you can work mornings."

"I can be here as early as you need." Melissa could hardly believe her good fortune. "Are you sure?"

"Trust me, young lady, *you* are the only one who may have second thoughts. And *he's* the one most likely to inspire them."

Rook turned toward Jiminy, who carried over a brimming cup and set it before her. Coffee and foam created the silhouette of a howling wolf against a moonless night sky, a latte art depiction of the Nightspangle crest.

Jiminy said, "My treat."

"Melissa has just agreed to work with us," said Rook. "Don't scare her off."

Dramatically favoring his wrist, Jiminy promised, "I learned my lesson. Best behavior."

When he moved to the other register to help a new customer, Melissa tried to back up and do things properly. "May I ask about your name, Rook?"

"Yes. Soon." He pointed to the latte. "Find a table. Enjoy your drink while it's hot. I'll join you when there's a lull, and we'll lay a better foundation for the future."

9

URBAN ENCLAVE

As if he'd been waiting for her to finish, Rook came to Melissa's booth at the same time she finished her coffee. "Thank you," she murmured as he collected the cup.

"Things have quieted down. Will you join me in the back?" He slid a brass disk across the table. "And if you could hold onto this? We don't want anyone wondering why Mr. Booker is keeping company with a pretty young lady."

Melissa turned the coin, admiring the delicacy of the sigils. Wards like these helped a Betweener move around without attracting notice. "We mostly use ceramic for these," she said.

"We're on good terms with an enclave that works a forge." Rook led her to the big marble counter at the front and through a little swinging door at its side. "You'll come through here whenever you're scheduled for work. We employ several outsiders, so the back rooms are still considered public territory."

He pointed out the time clock, changing room, break room, restrooms, and two cramped offices—his and his brother's. At the end of the short hall, they turned a corner and faced another line of doors.

"Cleaning supplies, paper products, cold room, and my brother's lab. Very locked. He's fussy about his coffee beans, so he keeps all his equipment and experimental blends under wraps."

She nodded, but her attention was fixed on what she assumed was their destination. The end of the hall fairly buzzed with the strength of a barrier.

"Some of Jiminy's handiwork." Rook took her hand. "First time through will get your back up, but once these wards recognize you, they won't give you any more grief."

Stepping through the barrier gave her a head-to-toe tingle, followed by a snap like static electricity. She stopped to check the size and color the anchoring stones, running her fingers through her hair, which did indeed feel as if it were standing on end.

Rook said, "I'm almost positive he found a way to set the barrier against fleas."

"How ... thorough?" Melissa wondered if the Amaranthine found the addition of that particular feature insulting.

"Let's just say the boy expresses his affection in strange ways." He backed along a much wider hall with curving walls, beckoning her to follow. It was like walking through a stonework pipe. "Now we're behind wards. Only Betweeners can enter these passages, which lead down into the enclave's network of burrows and dens. My home is in my brother's den."

He lifted aside a thick drapery of fur, and she stepped into a spacious apartment. Modestly furnished. With windows offering a street-level view of foot traffic on Fourth.

Melissa's surprise must have shown

"We work alongside humans, and we have to pass as humans. The illusion is much easier to maintain if we live like humans."

"But you're wolves."

"Through and through. Which accounts for an unconventional upbringing for the youngsters we've fostered over the years, your father included." With a careless wave, he added, "Away from academy, this was his home."

"He lived with you?"

Rook nodded. "Christopher grew up in our den. He bussed tables in the coffee shop. He worked part-time in the bakery next door. He trained at Bellwether with Roonta, and he pined after every cub in every litter born to this enclave. When Cove chose him, we couldn't have been prouder."

Melissa was still processing this sudden revelation. Rook wasn't just an acquaintance from the enclave where Christopher Armstrong grew up. "You're my father's parent?"

"And you are your father's daughter. See? We're already connected." He offered his palms and asked, "Are you comfortable with tending?"

"Of course," she assured. "I've been through the training, and I know what to expect."

Rook led her to a sofa and perched close by, without touching. "That sounds like more theory than practice."

She hesitated, cheeks coloring. "I've tended many Kith, but I've never had much personal interaction with the High Amaranthine.

Not one-on-one."

"You're not discomfited." A statement of fact, entirely based on scent, no doubt.

Rook slipped a simple bracelet from his wrist, then loosened his bowtie. Melissa wasn't sure how the two items worked together to create an illusion of humanity, but with both gone, she found herself seated beside a wolf clansman.

Short, black hair was subtly shaggier, and his ears came to elegant points. Light brown eyes changed to the deep yellow of amber glass, with characteristic slit pupils. And the hands he offered were graced by claws that gleamed like ivory against the deep brown of his skin. His tail was visible now, too—long and lavish, pure black with a subtle sheen that suggested reddish tips. Rook would be dramatic in his truest form.

"I've worked with young reavers many times. You will find me a patient partner."

Melissa quickly met his palms. "Yes, please. May I ask about your name? Or *names*, since you've given two already."

Rook's grin now showed a flash of fang. "I am Kinloo-fel Nightspangle. In the language of wolves, my name means 'blue moon child.' Can there be peace between us?"

"Yes."

"And trust enough for tending?" he gently pressed.

"Yes, please."

His hands moved into a supportive position, then simply cradled hers. Thumbs brushing her skin, he soothed, "No reason to be nervous. You're sharp and bright, but I'm tougher than I look. You cannot overwhelm me."

"You can tell?"

"Your wards are impressive, but we're touching." Rook explained, "It's similar to my leading you by the hand through our barriers. You've let me through. I'm on the inside now, and your dazzling crystals are keeping us both safe."

Melissa hadn't known her stones had any sort of defensive capability. "I can hide you, shield you, amplify your strength?"

"I think it's possible. With practice." Rook eased a little closer. "I wish Doon-wen could be here. He's a cranky so-and-so, but he has his reasons. Once he's back from his trip, don't let his grumping get you down. He's as soft as he is ornery."

His low tones worked against her fleeting uneasiness, and the more she relaxed, the more he made the little approving noises she recognized from working with Kith. Without much warning, tears sprang to her eyes. She lowered her gaze, but there was no hiding from superior senses.

"Homesick?" he asked. "Lots of students are drawn to Founders because they need the comfort of other people, a warm drink, a friendly smile, a listening ear. They're lonesome, but we can't nestle them all. With reavers, we're allowed to do what comes naturally. No need to hold back, you know?"

Melissa leaned into Rook, who continued speaking in mellow tones, unhurried and uninhibited. Little stories about when her father was a boy. More warnings about his cantankerous older brother. Unstinting praise for the bakery next door, with a brief caveat to remind her that squirrels numbered among the trickster clans.

Rook stroked her hair, and she smiled at the idea that her father had been similarly cuddled and comforted. She asked, "Did my father consider you his dad?"

The wolf stilled.

She glanced up, worried she'd blundered.

But Rook patted her head and offered a lopsided smile. "You'll find out eventually. Might as well be from me. I'm teased for it often enough."

"If you don't want to ...."

"Peace, Melissa. It's fine." He pulled her in so her head rested against his shoulder. Her cheek pressed against the starched white of his shirt, and his cheek rested atop her head. "When Christopher was very small, he called Doon-wen *Daddy*, which was really very brave. And I was *Momma*, which was really very cute."

Melissa giggled.

Rook's amusement was a rumble deep in his chest. With a nudge to her hair that Melissa suspected was a kiss, he asked, "Shall we?"

"Yes." Melissa focused on the person at her side, searching for the connection that would allow him to touch her soul. With Kith, she had to keep a tight rein on her innate strength. Battlers tended to have an offensive aptitude, and a surge of raw power could devastate an Amaranthine. But Rook was no Kith.

Faint impressions sharpened into clarity and left her in awe. The person who held her so carefully was vast. Her stellar ranking was a pebble compared to the mountain that was Kinloo-fel Nightspangle. She whispered, "You're very old, aren't you?"

"Very."

She'd never been this close to any of her academy teachers. Despite the length of their lifespans, their time was limited. They were like parents with too many children eager for attention. Much like the wolf cubs in the Kith shelter, for every apprentice chosen, ten or twenty or fifty were left wanting.

Melissa hadn't truly understood the opportunities that an enclave might provide. Barely an hour ago, she'd been mourning her lack of prospects. "I think I've always wanted something like this," she whispered.

"Friendship? Kinship?"

She nodded. "The Amaranthine at our school were out-numbered, but that didn't stop me from wishing one of them would single me out."

"But you were never chosen?"

"Not even once."

Rook murmured a strange word that felt like an endearment. "May I make an intensely personal observation with regards to the nature of your soul?"

Melissa fidgeted. "Yes?"

"Most Amaranthine of my acquaintance are most comfortable with a pliant soul. They value softness and sweetness, the elation of tending without a thought to the danger." Rook said, "You have a piquant quality."

"I'm ... sour?"

"No. You remind me of strong coffee—alluring, bold, and bitter enough to scald the uninitiated. Commanding a powerful response and assuring a lifelong addiction."

"I'm bitter."

Rook laughed. "Leave it to a female to pick the insult out of a rhapsody of praise. Melissa, I'm saying that you're an acquired taste."

"That doesn't sound good."

He hummed then asked, "What is the difference between a wolf and a dog?"

"The dog clans are more closely aligned with human society. Some say they domesticated themselves."

"In the same way, those pliant, pleasing reavers offer an Amaranthine a nice, tame tending experience." Rook shook his head. "You, my dear, have a wild soul, fierce and fraught with danger. Can you guess what sort of Amaranthine might understand your appeal?"

Melissa peered hopefully into his eyes. "A wolf who likes coffee?"

"If you can track down something so rare, I'm quite sure they'd be smitten."

She hugged him hard.

"There's my girl." He rocked her back and forth. "You may consider yourself *my* apprentice if you like. I can teach you the delicate alchemy of brewing coffee."

An Amaranthine mentor. What would Mom say if her daughter traded her battler classification for a barista's? Right now, it hardly mattered. Melissa sighed and said, "You smell like coffee."

"Everyone who works here does. Except the squirrels. I'd swear they bathe in nutmeg."

"I accept—the job, the apprenticeship, everything." She shyly added, "I'm glad I came."

"Excellent. Next time you come in, I'll show you the entrance to our Kith shelter."

"The enclave has a separate one?"

Rook shook his head. "Ours is private. It's Doon-wen's. Can you come in the morning?"

"Yes."

"That should be enough time for her to get used to the idea."

Melissa wasn't sure what to say to that.

Rook smoothed her hair and said, "Don't worry. She'll like you. Eventually."

"Who ...?"

"True." He chuckled and clarified, "I'm going to introduce you to a Kith named True."

10

SAFETY FIRST

Tami arrived early at work. Not early enough that Coach wasn't already parked in the back corner, but early. She'd been meaning to organize all the literature she'd dumped into a fat file after the Amaranthine conference. All of it had to be important, but she wouldn't be sure which information was applicable to elementary students unless she went through the stack.

An hour later, she had six piles and was waffling on starting a seventh. Only she was waylaid by an interesting set of cribbed notes, purportedly put together by Kimiko Miyabe herself, on the etiquette of non-verbal communication.

Tami frowned as she tried a series of greetings, then expressions of gratitude. The concept reminded her of sign language, but this was nothing like fingerspelling. The diagrams emphasized the importance of posture and expression, which added necessary nuance to the smallest of gestures.

"This can't be right," she mumbled, trying to decide if the notes meant she was supposed to tap or flick her right shoulder.

"Planning to umpire the next staff softball game?" Kip leaned in the doorway, a bemused expression on his face.

"Not quite." She waved a brochure at him. "Just looking over some of the information they gave me at the conference."

"Ahhh. I've seen that sort of thing before." He strolled over, poking through the pile of glossy advice. "Nice to see you making an effort. I'm sure the new staff will appreciate it."

She hummed unhappily. "I'm fumbling around. I can't really tell from these charts if I'm doing this right."

"It's not so hard." Kip leaned across her desk, tapped his nose, then tapped hers in a silent call for attention. "Lots of this stuff is common sense, really. Take this row."

She scanned the line of nuanced greetings.

"Watch," he said, tapping his nose again.

To Tami's amazement, he ran through the entire series of gestures, just the way they were described in the pamphlet, but paraphrasing their meaning into a sort of one-sided conversation. "Hey, man! What's up? We're good, right? No worries, friend. Take it easy. Everything's fine."

And he made them look entirely natural.

"How did you learn all of these?"

Kip shrugged. "Like I said, it's not hard. You can barely turn around these days without getting the run-down from some public service announcement."

"Show me again?"

Kip ran through the basics two more times, both patient and pleased with her comparatively clumsy efforts.

"Now, all I need is someone to practice on."

He shook his head. "Not a whole lot of Rivven showing their faces in these parts."

Tami sighed. "Can you blame them?"

"Can't say I would."

She leaned forward. "Do you think there are Amaranthine in Fletching?"

"Hard to say." Kip's expression turned more serious. "Once the college adopts the integration program, I'm sure we'll see more around. But I get the impression that they don't want to scare people any more than people want to be scared. Why do you ask?"

"I suppose I'm curious."

"Nothing wrong with curiosity."

Tami waved her hand. "But I feel like I'm curious for the wrong reasons."

Kip dropped into one of the chairs across from her. "How so?"

"Well, I want to meet someone because of what they are, not because of who they are." She searched for a good example. "It would be like deciding I want to get to know Ash because I think he's Native American. Or if I'm only talking to you because I've always wanted a friend with red hair."

To her relief, Kip was nodding. "You've really given this a lot of thought."

"As a kid, I was the only Asian girl in town. People made a lot of assumptions about me because I look like my mother. And even though they never meant anything bad by it, I still didn't like being labeled. Somehow, I wasn't a person; I was a category of person. Whenever they generalized, it made me feel like *less* of a person." Tami slouched back in her chair and indicated the fliers and brochures. "I'm upset with myself for doing the same thing to people I've never met."

"But you're still curious."

"Yes."

Kip draped his arms on the edge of her desk, slouching forward to rest his chin on them. "Hey, Tami?"

"Hmm?"

"You're probably over-thinking this whole thing. Making friends starts in lots of different ways, and if curiosity is what gets a conversation rolling, what's the big deal?"

She frowned thoughtfully. While she had no problem— absolutely none—chatting with people around town or parents of her students or customers at the orchard, this was different in her mind. She didn't want small talk and smiles and setting people at ease. She wanted ... more.

Kip was watching her with a little half-smile on his face. "I mean, think about me and Ash. Why would you ever consider hanging out with a couple of janitors? It wasn't *really* because he's half-Native American and you have a thinly veiled passion for red hair."

Tami laughed. "Of course not."

"Thank back, then. Why us?"

"I guess because ... you seemed nice." Was it really that simple? She considered the man across from her and asked, "Why me?"

"Buttering up the boss!" He laughed at her expression and pointedly flicked his shoulder, making the gesture that he'd casually interpreted as *don't sweat it.* "I told you, this isn't really that hard. Why wouldn't I want to hang out with you? You seemed nice."

Kindergarten orientation was already underway when Tami slipped into the back of a classroom packed with youngsters and their parents. Harrison Peck, the school's attendance clerk, made an energetic emcee. He was at his usual natty best, the real wingtip and bowtie sort. At first Tami had taken him for a fresh-faced intern who was trying too hard, but after a few weeks, it dawned on her that he was the genuine article ... and two years older than her.

He belonged in children's television, and they were lucky to have him. Meticulous to a fault, he never forgot a name and was genuinely concerned for every kid that passed through their doors.

Harrison was wrapping up a spiel on Landmark Elementary's check-in procedures and tardy policies, which was all well and good. What Tami couldn't quite figure out was why he was dressed as a crossing guard.

"... of course, one of my most *important* jobs today is making sure you know who to tell when you need something." Harrison raised a hand. "When you're at home, who do you ask for help?"

The braver kids took the cue and answered variously, naming parents, grandparents, babysitters, and siblings. And Harrison let them share, giving them his full attention. Then he took back the reins. "While you're at school, you'll have really nice grown-ups who are ready to listen and to help you. And you'll always know us because we wear special nametags."

Harrison showed the photo ID on his lanyard. "This means I belong to the Landmark Elementary family. I'm Mr. Peck, and you can recognize me easily, because I always wear a bowtie, even to the grocery store."

"It's true!" called out one of the moms. "I've seen him!"

The kids giggled.

"Then there's these guys. They're fixer-uppers and cleaner-uppers, and they love recess."

To Tami's honest surprise, Ash strode purposefully to the front. She hadn't expected someone who made himself so scarce to willingly take center stage. He lifted his lanyard, then tapped the embroidered name on his coveralls. "I'm Ash."

Harrison stage whispered, "You're a grown-up, Ash. That means they should call you Mr. Fowler."

"No, thanks. I'd rather be Ash." He held up three fingers. "Less letters to remember."

"A – S – H," Harrison spelled out, also raising three fingers. "I suppose that does keep things simple. But aren't there supposed to be two of you?"

"Yeah, there are two of us." And putting his fingers to his lips, he gave a shrill whistle.

Heads turned as Kip charged through the door, pretended to trip, dove into a handspring, and came to a stop like a gold-medal gymnast sticking a landing. The class erupted into cheers and applause, and Kip swept off an imaginary hat and bowed.

Tami shook her head in disbelief. They must have scripted the whole thing.

Harrison used his crossing guard whistle to regain everyone's attention. "Are you all right, Mr. Kipling."

"Who, me?"

"Isn't that your name?" Harrison took a sterner tone. "Where is your nametag, Mr. Kipling?"

"It's here somewhere!" While he patted pockets, he said, "And you can call me Kip."

"That's three letters, too." Ash helpfully pulled the dangling lanyard from Kip's back pocket and handed it to him. "K – I – P spells Kip. Nice and easy."

Now properly displaying his photo ID, Kip said, "I never wear a bowtie, but I always have red hair. I'm Kip, the janitor with red hair."

Ash said, "I don't have red hair, and I never wear a bowtie, but I like high places."

"Top of the jungle gym, top of the slide, top of the bleachers." Kip held a hand to his mouth as if telling a great secret. "I've even found him in trees. Weird, huh?"

More laughter. The kids were relaxed and having fun.

Harrison asked, "Do you think you can remember Ash and Kip as part of your Landmark Elementary family?"

Everyone agreed with enthusiasm.

"And I see Principal Reaverson is here." Harrison beckoned.

Making her way to the front, Tami took the time to scan all the eager faces. "Welcome to Landmark Elementary. We're excited that you'll be learning with us this year." Following the established pattern, she lifted her lanyard. "I don't wear a bowtie, and I don't have red hair. I've been known to climb trees on occasion because my family owns an apple orchard, but I think you can still tell me apart from Ash."

"She's shorter," Kip said. "And a girl."

Tami curtsied. "I do have something that's *always* with me, though."

From where it was mostly hidden by the collar of her second most businesslike suit, she withdrew a strand of heavy stones in shades ranging from deep purple to lavender. They looked for all the world like a fortune in amethysts. For all Tami knew, that's exactly what they were. She'd never had them assessed.

Kip hunkered down, studying her necklace with obvious fascination. "Principal Reaverson, are you secretly a princess?" he asked in awed tones.

She laughed. "I don't think so. This necklace is a family heirloom, so it's very old and very special. I never take it off."

"Not even when you sleep?" Kip asked.

"Nope."

"Not even when you wash your hair?"

"Nope." Tami offered a small shrug. "It doesn't come off."

Harrison stepped in. "Will you all remember Princess ... I mean *Principal* Reaverson if you see her?"

The kids chorused their assurances, and Kip finally straightened and offered her his arm. As he escorted her to the door, he asked, "How long have you worn that necklace, Tami?"

"Always," she replied, touching the familiar weight. "My brother and I each inherited something from our great-grandparents."

Kip opened his mouth, closed it again, then solemnly asked, "Is he also royalty?"

Tami smiled. "A prince among men."

11

TRUE

Melissa suspected she was pushing her luck by showing up at Founders Coffee before sunrise, but the lights were on and the door unlocked. She checked to see if the hours were posted and found a discreet bronze plaque beside the entrance, emblazoned with two words—ALWAYS OPEN.

Inside, she spotted evidence of early morning activity—faculty meetings and what appeared to be a men's Bible study. Once the semester was well underway, she had little doubt that the place would be clogged with students pulling all-nighters.

Rook was the only one behind the counter, and his smile widened at the sight of her. "Oh, I hope you really do rise this early. This shift is the hardest to cover."

"My mom always started us training before dawn." Melissa demonstrated the first several forms of a battler's warmup. "And

73

the members of my host family are up with their chickens."

"I'd hire you twice if I could. Jiminy's no use in the morning." Rook scanned the room, then beckoned for her to join him behind the counter. "I know I promised to introduce you to True this morning, but stuff happened in the overnight."

"Stuff?"

He lowered his voice. "Werewolves are in the news again. There's a girl missing, and it was bad. The two boys who were with her didn't make it."

"Where did it happen?"

Rook bared his teeth. "Close enough that we're playing host to a score of trackers. Do you remember the way back to my place?"

"Yes."

"Good. Go on back. Watch for a wide, white door. We have guests in True's shelter, and I let them know you'd be dropping by. Torloo is quite capable of handling introductions."

Melissa excused herself and wended her way to the enclave's private section. Jiminy's barrier let her through with a funny little burst of gladness, as if the hallway was happy to see her.

She was still puzzling over the combination of sigils that might be used to achieve the trick when she located the entrance to the Kith shelter. With a light rap for courtesy, she stepped inside.

Immediately, a low growl began in the central alcove, where a large black wolf with silver eyes glared at her, hackles raised.

"True," admonished a young voice. "That is no way to greet a guest."

The she-wolf lowered her head to her paws, surly in her silence.

Melissa immediately took a deferential stance. "Should I go?"

"No. You are expected. May I offer the first introduction."

Easing to a seat on a golden straw bale right inside the door, Melissa extended her palms to one of the youngest Amaranthine she'd ever encountered. He appeared no more than eleven or twelve, his voice untouched by adolescence, his eyes large in a face still rounded by childhood.

Still, he addressed her with the poise of a diplomat. "I am Torloo-dex Elderbough."

Melissa looked more closely. "You're part of Adoona-soh's pack?"

He drew himself up. "I am her son."

Adoona-soh Elderbough was one of the Five, the leaders of the Emergence who had introduced the Amaranthine clans to the world. Melissa could see similarities in some of the boy's coloring—tanned skin and dark brown hair. But his eyes were the clear blue of skies. She tried to think back and realized she'd never seen or heard anything about Adoona-soh's bondmate.

"May I ask about your name?" she inquired, matching his seriousness.

"In the language of my people, my name means 'petal moon,' because my sire's den overlooks a flowering meadow. I was born at full bloom."

"That's lovely."

He blushed and mumbled, "It's kind of girly."

Melissa shifted her hands so they supported his. "You bring strength to the name your sire chose by taking pride in it."

Torloo smiled shyly, revealing two dimples, and bent to kiss her forehead. "May I know your name?"

"Melissa Armstrong, newest employee of Founders. Rook suggested I make myself available to True if she needs tending."

"That would be good." He turned to the black she-wolf. "You know it would calm you."

True pointedly shut her eyes.

"Maybe you could start with my brother's Kith," Torloo suggested. "They are trail-weary."

A matched pair of dark brown wolves lifted their heads, ears pricked, tails swaying. Melissa had to smile, for they showed no sign of weariness.

Torloo crooked his fingers. "Risk and Dare are my brother's companions." His chin lifted proudly. "I have been traveling with Naroo-soh, and he asked me to watch over them."

Melissa knew *that* name. Naroo-soh Elderbough was Adoona's firstborn and leader of the Elderbough trackers.

"Brother said it was for their safety, but I think it was probably for mine." The tip of Torloo's tail tucked. "He thinks me too young for this trail."

"He doesn't want you to see the crime scene?" she guessed.

Torloo sighed. "Brother is cautious, and for good reason. I have much to learn before I can be useful to him."

"You could be useful to me." In Melissa's experience, Amaranthine of the same clan always seemed especially perceptive when it came to the likes and dislikes of their Kith. "Will you help me understand what True wants?"

The young wolf hesitated. "What did Rook tell you about her?"

"He implied that it might take some time for her to accept me." She addressed herself directly to the she-wolf. "But he did think we could get along."

Torloo hummed. It wasn't a very encouraging hum.

Melissa sighed. "Can I do anything to make you more comfortable, True? Other than leaving?"

"What if that is all she wants?"

"I would bow to True's wishes, of course. But I think Rook would be disappointed in both of us. And I can't help wanting to please him."

True growled deep in her chest.

"Why?" asked Torloo. "Why are you courting Rook's favor?"

Melissa opted for honesty. "Because I miss my mothers."

Torloo's brows drew down in obvious confusion, but True grumbled and lumbered to her feet. She was leggy and large for a Kith, her muzzle higher than Melissa could reach on tiptoe. Suddenly, that muzzle was all she could see. But True was no longer growling.

A nudge. A snuffle. A sneeze.

Torloo asked, "Your lineage, please?"

Melissa held her ground. "My biological father's name is Christopher Armstrong."

True swung around and pawed at a stack of hay bales—pale green and smelling like summertime.

"More bedding, I think," said Torloo.

"I'll help," Melissa quickly offered.

His claws sliced easily through twine, and she shook out armfuls of dried grasses until they were waist deep.

"Are there herbs you favor?" Melissa looked to True and explained, "Back home, we add mint to feline bedding. And our avians have been on a lavender kick. The scents are soothing."

Torloo turned expectantly to True. After several moments,

he said, "Fallen leaves. She likes the scent of autumn and the way they rustle."

"It may take me a little while," said Melissa. "Not many trees around here are dropping their leaves yet. But autumn isn't far off."

"How soon?" Torloo reached up with both hands high above his head. When the she-wolf lowered her muzzle, he stroked her inky fur. "Are you counting the days? The season will turn in a matter of weeks. Is that why you are so restless?"

Melissa gently laid her hand beside Torloo's, adding her support. "Is there something special happening in autumn?"

"Doon-wen promised to return before the falling of leaves." The boy chuckled. "If he is late, she wants to recline upon a bed that gives proof of his lies."

"That would serve him right," said Melissa. "And if he's late, I'll definitely help. But the way Rook described his brother, I get the idea that he keeps his promises. And that means your wait is almost over."

Silver eyes slowly closed, and the she-wolf let her head droop lower. Torloo was quick to stroke her face, crooning comfort. His growls weren't deep enough to rumble, and they reminded Melissa of purring. She added her own caresses, sifting her fingers through the thick fur framing True's face. "May I tend you, True?"

With a grumbling whine, the Kith backed up and sagged onto her bed of hay.

Torloo caught Melissa's hand and led her over, all smiles. "True is ready for tending."

"Where should I sit?"

"Here." The boy indicated the space between True's forepaws.

"For Rook's sake and for Christopher's and for Jiminy's, she will take you to her heart."

Melissa gladly curled up between soft fur and fragrant hay, but she muttered, "What's Jiminy got to do with anything?"

If True answered, the only translation Torloo offered was a soft giggle.

12

NO RUNNING IN THE HALLS

Within a week of school starting, Tami quickly realized that *every* child at Landmark Elementary knew Ash and Kip. A slightly guilty snoop through their personnel files showed that yes, the two janitors had worked at the school long enough for all the kids to have been introduced to the duo during kindergarten orientations past. And the students *adored* them.

Was it strange for janitors to have so much influence? Maybe. Then again, she remembered Joe being fond of one of the old janitors who'd worked at Landmark back when they were kids.

Not every role model had to be a teacher.

Since she was already being nosy, she gleaned a few more facts. For instance, Kip really was short for Kipling—Alder Kipling. She was shaking her head in sympathy for a young Kip, only to realize that *Alder* was possibly the lesser evil, at least, from a kid's point of view. Ash was short for Ashishishe. Tami could only assume this was a traditional name, a mark of his Native American heritage. A quick search on her phone brought up a meaning.

Crow.

A second surprise came with the unexpected realization that Ash and Kip lived together. Their address was indeed out in Nocking, which meant their commute was even longer than hers. They weren't only always together ... they might *be* together. Tami had no experience with that sort of thing. Maybe if she watched for signs, she'd be able to tell if they were the best friends she'd assumed them to be or ... more.

Tami whisked the folders away without reading any further. If she wanted to know anything more about the two, it would be from them.

Her phone chimed, alerting her to a new comment on her inquiry about their mystery tree. With everything else going on, she'd half-forgotten about her forum post.

Stumped by Your Orphan
Cannot possibly be native to N. America.
Forwarding your query to a colleague
in Europe who is the last word in trees.

Progress! She could hardly wait to tell Joe.

Tami was hurrying along the hallway, bound for the library. She needed a few snapshots to accompany a full listing of their catalog to attach to her request for an Amaranthine librarian. Coming toward her along the wide hall was Ash with a push broom, giving the floors his usual careful attention. Only he appeared to be dragging a couple of third-graders along behind him. The boys, who'd been released for morning recess only a few minutes ago, lay on their bellies, their hands locked around his ankles. With every step Ash took, they slid forward.

"Morning, Principal Reaverson," Ash calmly greeted.

"Good morning, Ash. Gentlemen," she returned evenly. "On your way to the playground?"

"Yes, ma'am." He stopped to lean on his broom handle. "On your feet, boys."

They scrambled up, flushed and fidgeting. Ash poked them, and they mumbled, "Yes, ma'am."

Eyebrows lifting, Ash said, "With your permission, Principal Reaverson?"

"Carry on, gentlemen."

The boys made their escape, trying to run without actually breaking the no-running-in-the-halls rule in front of the principal.

"Those two tend to loiter in their classroom. Probably so I'll come find them." Ash's gaze didn't waver from the retreating figures. "They're all right."

Tami tended to agree, but she wasn't going to let him off easy. "I can't believe you called me *ma'am*."

Ash seemed startled. "My manners are becoming their manners."

"That's ... very true."

The janitor shuffled sideways and ambled on, calling back, "Just teaching the boys to respect a lady."

Tami had the strongest sense that she'd just been complimented.

September was rushing toward October when Tamiko had the urge to convene her special committee of three. Only Ash and Kip weren't in the maintenance room or any of the hallways. She popped in on Mrs. Dabrowski, who was typing up their next column for the *Bowshot*, Archer's local paper.

"Have you seen either of our janitors?"

Flootie checked the time. "At this hour, they're always on the playground."

"They really do oversee recess?"

"Like champs. You should go see." The woman took a second look at the clock. "Let me grab some coffee, and I'll come with you."

Mugs in hand, Tami followed Flootie along the hallway and out the side door into the playground. It hadn't changed much since Tami was little—swings, slides, and a dome-shaped jungle gym. There were also basketball hoops and two goals on a half-size soccer field, which is where they spotted Kip.

Tami shook her head in disbelief. "Is he taking on the whole class?"

"Singlehandedly." Flootie cradled her coffee cup. "He gives those wiggle-monsters a real work-out. It's a big help to the teachers, I'm telling you."

She watched a little longer, enjoying the redhead's athletic leaps and comical ball-handling. But Flootie was right about Kip's showboating. This wasn't so much a soccer match as a game of chase, and the second-graders were being run ragged. "This is better than Phys. Ed."

"No idea where he gets his energy." Flootie radiated approval.

"And Ash is good at coaxing the reluctant ones into quieter games."

Tami didn't notice Ash right away because he was in a tree. "How in the world does he get up there?"

"He makes it look easy, but I never could do it." Flootie gestured broadly with one hand. "He does this vertical leap and catches that narrow lower limb, then does a few chin-ups for the crowd. From there, he swings his legs up and climbs to his favorite branch."

Below his perch, boys and girls were embroiled in a complicated game of hopscotch. A winner was declared, and Tami's amazement doubled when Ash swung down in order to lead the whole group in a game of follow-the-leader. He looked like the Pied Piper of Hamlin.

Of course, the janitors weren't the only playground monitors. Three women—parents who volunteered—looked on with indulgent smiles, and Mrs. Connell, their Phys. Ed. teacher, was taking all comers at the tetherball pole. They even had two interns from the university, a couple of girls who were paying more attention to the janitors than the children.

Tami pointed them out.

"I'll give them a bit of a scolding later. Or better, have Harrison do it. He'll strike the right balance since he's all about the kids. Can you blame them though?" Her secretary hid her smile behind her blue-patterned mug. "Men like Kip and Ash are hard to come by. They'd be quite the catch."

Tami tried for a noncommittal hum.

"Which one do you prefer?"

"I've never given it a thought," Tami hedged. "Don't they come as a pair?"

"They do at that. And they work together to make sure every

84

one of our kids is noticed and known. Thanks to them, we don't have many troublemakers here." Pointing to a cartwheeling Kip, Mrs. Dabrowski cheerfully added, "One could argue that he's our worst—and best—one."

"We're lucky to have them," Tami murmured.

Flootie's fondness was plain on her face. "Landmark would fall apart without them."

13

HOW TO TREAT A LADY

The maintenance room was about the only place on school grounds where Ash was sure he was safe. But Tami had started dropping by for their "special committee" meetings, which were really more like extended coffee breaks. He did try to focus on the business aspects of these sessions, but it was *distracting* having her in a place he considered private—and therefore intimate.

What troubled him most was the fact that he was getting used to her little invasions. Maybe even looking forward to them.

"... they keep doing it, and it's driving me crazy. Whatever they're giving him, it's too small for me to see from a distance."

Kip burst out laughing, and Ash snapped to attention. He'd lost track of the conversation about the same time he realized that Tami had pierced ears. Her hair was usually down, but an upswept style exposed faceted stones that dangled from each lobe. They drew his attention to the shape of her ear, the curve of her jaw, the line of her neck.

"Do you want to tell her, or should I?" asked Kip.

"Go ahead," he murmured, not even sure what they were talking about.

"Paperclips." Kip spread his hands wide. "The kids are passing him paperclips."

Tami's gaze swung his way. Ash sighed and fished in the pocket of his coveralls, coming up with half a dozen paperclips—two silver, one gold, a pink, a green, and one with black and white stripes.

"But why?" she asked.

Ash said, "It's Kip's fault."

The redhead held up both hands. "Hey, it was an accident. Sort of."

Tami settled back in her chair. "This should be good."

"Could be worse," Ash conceded.

Kip rolled his eyes. "You love it, and you know it."

Ash simply grunted.

"As principal, I need to know what's happening on my campus."

"Pulling the principal card?" Kip made a helpless gesture. "What can I do, Ash? She's the boss."

He sighed. "Stop making a big deal out of nothing."

Kip jumped right in. "Okay, so this was a few years back. I *may* have given a couple of first-graders the impression that Ash likes shiny objects. Was it at Christmastime?"

"Valentine's," Ash corrected. As if he didn't remember.

"But that was a mistake, because for first-grade girls, *shiny* means glitter. And Ash has an unholy dread of glitter."

"Gets everywhere." The stuff was almost impossible to banish.

87

"So to spare my good friend from hallways doused in sparkle-dust, I thought fast and offered a more palatable alternative—the humble paperclip. Word spread. Fast." Kip shrugged. "The kids have been giving them as tokens of affection ever since."

Ash shifted restlessly. "It's harmless."

Kip leaned over to tug at Ash's sleeve, revealing a bracelet made from linked paperclips.

"Oooh, very stylish."

The approval in Tami's tone sent Ash's pulse flying.

She said, "It's a cute idea. And paperclips are easy to come by."

"I'm their number one supplier." Kip bounced up and crossed to the workbench. Pulling down a blue plastic bucket, he brought it over for her to see. "Plenty of love to go around."

Tami sifted her hands through the thousands of paperclips they'd accumulated. "Do you have a favorite?"

Ash frowned. "A favorite paperclip?"

"A favorite color."

Kip cheerfully revealed, "He can't resist blue."

She fished out a sky blue paperclip. "What about you?"

"Oh, I've always been more of an acorn guy." Kip admitted, "The whole paperclip thing is really just a spin-off on something my dad started. He'd sneak acorns into my mother's apron pockets. When I asked him about it, he started including me. Acorns in my pockets, under my pillow, in my favorite mug."

"So tokens of affection are a family tradition." Tami was nodding thoughtfully. "One you've shared with your Landmark family."

Kip touched her shoulder and returned the bucket to its shelf.

Ash struggled with unaccustomed envy. Kip had always been

his buffer, helping keep him—and his secret—secure. Ash was all high places and safe distances, but Kip was all shoulder pats and hand-holding and hugs. He was affectionate with everyone from the cafeteria ladies to the bus drivers. It wasn't as if Ash had an aversion to touch. Not by a longshot. But his dual heritage had left him with something even harder to hide than excess fur.

He had to be careful.

"... should be getting back," Tami was saying.

Out of habit, they both rose to their feet. The old courtesies were too well ingrained to shake.

"I'll have to keep an eye out for acorns," she said. "But in the meantime ...."

And she was coming his way. Ash backed up a step, but there was no graceful way to evade her approach. He bumped against a work bench and froze. Tami had him cornered.

"Hold out your hand," she ordered.

He obeyed, and Tami dropped her blue paperclip onto his palm. "For you."

Kip was talking, and Tami laughed. The door shut, and Ash was still standing there, staring at his hand, no sure how to interpret the tangle of urges that were as confusing as they were exhilarating.

"Ash?"

He grunted.

Kip asked, "What's up?"

"She gave me a paperclip."

His best friend nodded. "She totally did."

Ash's throat was tight. "What do you think it means?"

Kip smiled faintly. "I'd wager it means what we told her it means."

89

"What did we say it means?"

"You know the answer." Kip gently placed his hands under Ash's. "They're a token of affection."

"Are you sure?"

Tapping his own nose, Kip touched Ash's. "Unfair, friend. You made me promise not to mention those yearnings of yours."

"I'm not yearning." It was a feeble protest.

For just a moment, Ash could have sworn his best friend looked sad, but Kip leaned close to whisper in his ear. "Ashishishe, I'm not the only one who talks in my sleep."

Ash couldn't sleep.

He lay on his stomach in the bed that took up most of his loft, blankets askew, thoughts as tangled as his sheets. This was a mess. A misunderstanding. Yes, Tami had given him a paperclip, but more than half the kids at Landmark had done the same. And she'd mentioned finding an acorn for Kip. It was a *friendly* token. Hers was a *friendly* affection.

But something about her gift was making his instincts go haywire.

Denying them didn't exactly stop them. But he couldn't act on this sudden attraction, even if it was mutual. Tami was only giving him a second look because she couldn't see him clearly. He looked like a lab experiment gone awry. Disfigured. Awkward. Inhuman.

He might have a handful of friends in the human world, but only because Kip kept them in ignorant bliss. They both had to be careful. Either of them could be labeled a monster.

What would Tami think if she found out that the Amaranthine

she was so eager to welcome to Landmark Elementary were already there? Maybe she'd be glad. But maybe she'd feel betrayed.

It's why most clans remained in hiding. Humans and Amaranthine might be compatible, but they didn't always mix. Ash had no idea who his biological father might be. Or if he even knew he'd impregnated a human. Cyril occasionally renewed his offer to make discreet inquiries, but Ash refused to give up any details that might help locate his kin and clan. Cyril was the only father he needed, and Rook was as good a mother as any.

All he could do was keep from making the same kind of mistake.

He needed to hold off, to hold back ... and to be held.

Halfway out of bed, he paused to place the blue paperclip on its center—safe within his nest. Then he dropped to the ground floor and crept into Kip's bed.

Putting aside his book and pulling him into a loose embrace, his best friend made comforting noises. "Why so miserable?"

"She's wonderful."

"*Such* a problem," Kip said seriously. "How dare she?"

Ash simply clung tighter.

Hands smoothed and soothed. "What do you want to do?"

"Things I can't."

Kip chuckled. "You're a big boy, now, and I'm fairly confident all your pieces and parts are functioning normally. *And* responding favorable whenever she's in the general vicinity."

"Shut up," he groaned.

"Seriously, Ash. She likes you."

"She only thinks she does. The person she sees isn't real."

Kip asked, "Have you been false with her?"

"I haven't been practicing full disclosure for a lot of years." Ash began to relax in spite of himself, taking much-needed comfort from closeness. "Same as you."

His best friend hummed. "I may mess a little with perceptions, but the personality Tami is drawn to ... that's all you."

"But it isn't *all* of me." Ash arched his wings and beat the air. "I'm not human."

"Not gonna matter." Kip cupped his cheek and spoke slowly. "Once I open her eyes, she'll like what she sees. Trust me on this. You're irresistible."

"It can't work."

"Made up your mind on that score?" Kip flopped back. "Okay, you win. What was I even thinking? Guess it's just you and me. Together forever. Sad fate."

"Hey!"

"Kidding, kidding." Kip snickered and hauled him over, tangling their legs together and wrapping his tail around Ash's shoulders.

"I don't want to be in love," Ash whispered.

"That's practically an admission."

He grunted.

With experienced strokes, Kip settled ruffled feathers and kneaded away Ash's tension. "Can I say something as your friend?"

He sighed and nodded.

"Talk to Cyril."

"Guess I better," Ash conceded.

"*And* ...."

"And?"

Kip bussed his cheek. "You're an idiot, and I love you."

14

FOUNDLING

October was the busiest month of an already busy season, and Joe had been up extra late cleaning the cider press. Even so, he was awake before the sun, escaping into the orchard with a sack of day-old applesauce doughnuts and a thermos of hot milk. It was easier to face neighbors and strangers alike if he faced himself first.

Otherwise, he'd spend all day out of step and falling behind.

Joe wasn't sure why he needed this so badly. Not really.

True, it first started when Tami left home—school and internships, jobs and conferences. He didn't like losing sight of his twin, but she had places to go, things to do. At least she still always came home. His sister was part of his balance, but he had to stand on his own two feet.

Maybe that's what this was.

His mornings in the orchard and oak glen—the relative hush of a waking world, the peace he found in puttering among the trees—helped him find his own balance. He needed this little reminder that he was all right, even if he was alone.

Joe's breath puffed in the chill morning air, and his boots scuffed through heavy dew. No frost yet, but it wouldn't be long now. He paced along the boundary, checking fences and keeping an eye out for trouble among the trees.

He paused to nip dead branches and new suckers, watching for signs of pest or blight. Grandad always said dealing with little problems kept them from becoming big ones.

When the oak glen came into view, he swerved toward the shining dome that glittered beckoningly. Almost overnight, their mystery tree had turned to gold. He'd bring a few leaves to show Mom. And hadn't Tami mentioned something about needing an acorn?

Eyes on the glory of autumn overhead, Joe stuffed his hands in his pockets and slowly circled the tree. "Beautiful," he decreed, though the word fell short.

Someone giggled.

Joe caught a flash of movement, but it vanished behind the tree. Was someone there?

He hadn't imagined it, but he couldn't explain it. Maybe it was something other people couldn't see, like his air ribbons and gem snakes. Or maybe even a fairy. The laughter had been small and light, like a person's. A *small* person's.

Taking care to step softly, Joe edged closer, thinking to come up behind whatever was with him in the glen. His first glimpse took him completely aback. A child sat among the roots of the tree, a little girl with her knees pulled up to her chin.

"Hello there, little one," he called softly.

"Sister?" she asked.

"I'm not a sister, but I have a sister." He took a few more steps. "Are you lost?"

She smiled, and he found himself smiling back.

Part of his mind was trying to reason out the presence of a child in the middle of their orchard. They were miles from any other house, and the migrant workers had finished with this section more than a week ago. It was too early for customers or tour groups to arrive. So where had she come from? And why wasn't she wearing any clothes?

Shedding his jacket, he swung it around her thin shoulders. She was small, no bigger than a kindergartener, and her wide eyes held no trace of worry or fear. In fact, she lifted her arms in a silent plea.

He picked her up, tucking his jacket more snugly around her while trying to make sense of what he was seeing. This had to be a Rivven child. Her skin was unusually pale, and her thickly-lashed eyes were dark green. Her ears came to points, but it was her hair that threw him for a loop. Well, not hair, really. Joe tentatively touched the golden leaves that rustled softly on her head. Delicate as tissue and definitely attached, the leaves were growing on her head just as surely as they grew on their mystery tree.

"Are your mommy and daddy close by?"

Her brow puckered in confusion. "Sister?"

"Were you with your sister?" Joe shook his head. "Do you have a name, chick-a-biddie?"

She giggled and rested her head on his shoulder.

Now what? He'd never been very good with kids in the first place, and he was feeling more than a little panicky. This probably looked really bad. What if the girl's parents accused him of kidnapping ... or worse? Could he start an international incident?

"Maybe we should go to my house. Would you like to meet my mom and dad?"

The girl threw her arms around his neck and cooed, "Joey-boy!"

That's what Grandad used to call him, but how would she know that? He started toward home with long strides. "That's right. I'm Joe. What's your name?"

"Chick-a-biddie!"

He was definitely out of his depth. With luck, Tami was still home. She'd learned about Rivven at her conference, and she was great with kids. As he hurried along, she craned her neck, looking back the way they'd come.

"Where are we going?" she asked worriedly.

"To see my sister."

"Sister?"

"Yes, she's my twin." He offered a tentative smile. "You'll love Tami, and she'll love you."

The girl nodded and nestled down in his arms, an expression of serene trust on her dainty features. She startled him by reaching up to touch his cheek. "Joe?"

"Yeah?"

"Hurry."

Tami turned at the sound of her name and the thud of boots up the porch steps. Her brother rushed into the kitchen, eyes wide and breath coming in gasps. "You're still here."

"Just on my way out." She lifted her car keys.

To her dismay, Joe sank to his knees on the floor. That's when she noticed a pair of eyes peeping at her from the bundle in his arms.

"I found a girl," Joe said, all in a rush. "I think she's … well, with the leaves and her skin. People don't usually have woodgrain, you know?"

Tami set down her keys, travel mug, and lunch bag. Joe was babbling, and Joe didn't babble. Usually he was the one to calm her down when something had her riled.

"You found a girl," she repeated, crossing to the door, which flapped open behind him. "In the orchard?"

A child wriggled free and skipped around the kitchen.

Joe stated the obvious. "She's not human."

"She's not dressed."

"That's how I found her." Joe's gaze pleaded for help. "I couldn't leave her out in the cold."

"Where did she come from?" Tami watched the child tiptoe and twirl from appliance to window, touching knobs and exploring textures.

"She was under our tree." He caught her hand. "She knew my name."

Quite the mystery. But Tami needed to take charge, preferably before Dad and Grandad found a baby dryad frolicking between the oatmeal bowls. "Grab her," she ordered.

Joe obediently scooped her off the kitchen table while Tami ducked into the mud room, where their washer and dryer lived. From the basket on the folding table, she snagged a pink T-shirt and returned. "Hands up."

The girl complied, and Tami gently pulled the soft shirt over the girl's leafy head. "Do you have a name, little miss?"

"Chick-a-biddie!"

Joe winced. "I called her that when I found her. Sorry."

Tami laughed softly and held out her hands, as much to rescue her blushing brother as to get a closer look at the girl. "From everything I've heard, Amaranthine are incredibly protective of their children. What clan are you from, sweetheart?"

"Chick-a-biddie," the girl corrected.

"All right, Miss Biddie," Tami conceded. What was the harm in a silly nickname? "Now where did you come from?"

She caressed the girl's cheek, which was the waxen hue of flower petals. Up close, Tami could detect a faint pattern. Joe was right. Biddie looked as if she'd been carved from wood, but she was warm and pliant and animated as any child should be. "You're beautiful," she murmured.

Deep green eyes sparkled, and thin arms twined around Tami's neck. "Sister?"

Thinking this was how Joe had explained her, Tami hummed an affirmative.

Just then, Grandad scuffed into the room. "What's going on out here?" he grumbled. Catching sight of Biddie, he went very still.

Tami was about to explain, but the girl suddenly framed her face with small hands.

"Joey-boy said you would love me, and I will love you." Biddie pressed her lips to Tami's and declared, "You are my Lisbet."

Grandad make a strangled noise. That had been his twin sister's name.

She didn't like to disappoint the child, but neither would she lie. "That's close, little one. I'm Tamiko Lisbet Reaverson. Most people call me Tami."

Biddie gave a small shrug and a sweet smile. "Love you, my Tami."

And something happened. A whole pile of emotions tumbled over Tami in a cascade—fear and relief, longing and contentment, wanting and finding. The only thing she was sure about was their source—Biddie.

"I ... I think I'd better call in sick," Tami whispered.

"Something's changed," Joe said, pale and frowning. "What just happened?"

Tami had no idea.

A kitchen chair squeaked, and Grandad lowered himself into it. His chin was trembling, and his eyes were moist. "Never thought I'd see the day," he mumbled.

"Grandad?" Tami asked. "Do you know what's going on?"

He hauled out a red handkerchief and dabbed at his eyes, then polished his glasses. "I suppose I do," he said softly. "Where's that cousin of yours?"

"Melissa left already for Bellwether."

"Best get her back here," said Grandad.

"Why?"

But Dad emerged, all astonishment and exclamations, and Mom came to see what all the fuss was about, and Grandad refused to say another word.

15
NEW GIRL

Jiminy smothered a yawn, then grinned sheepishly at his mentor. "Sorry, First-sensei."

"Lessons *have* run long. My fault entirely. What's the time there?"

On the other side of the world, a cup of tea slid into view, and an honest-to-goodness butler eased into camera range to eye Jiminy critically. "Michael, you're a beast, nattering through the wee hours of his morning. There are far more *interesting* ways to wear a man out."

"Hey there, Jacques." Jiminy wriggled his fingers in a friendly wave.

"Mister Foster," he returned with a haughty formality that seemed funny coming from a man in his twenties.

Jacques might put on airs, but he also *always* showed up at some point during Jiminy's lessons. Michael had confided that their French-English butler still didn't know much Japanese, so he was greedy for conversation ... even if it came with an American accent.

Another hand appeared and whisked away the tea cup.

Jacques puffed up. "That was the American's tea!"

Well, now. Jiminy had suspected someone was sitting in on this session. They'd covered a lot of ground, and the range of topics had felt scripted. Like an exam.

From off camera, a voice drawled, "While he can appreciate the gesture, I can appreciate the blend."

Jiminy's stomach flipped. Not just *any* eavesdropper. "Good day to you, Lord Mettlebright."

"*Tsk.*" The spokesperson for the fox clans strolled into view, tea cup in one hand, sleeping child propped against the opposite shoulder. "Argent will do. Here, Smythe. Take him."

Although Jiminy spotted his moue of distaste, Jacques said, "Yes, my lord. Come, Master Arnaud. You are required in the nap room."

The toddler, whose long, spotted tail matched the mottling on his fuzzy ears, babbled something in French, which the butler answered with a crisp, "*Non.*"

Once they were gone, Argent Mettlebright spoke again. "Your sigilcraft is ... interesting."

"Thank you, sir!"

Shaking his head, the Amaranthine said, "Michael should not indulge your tendency for improvisation. Apprentices should apply themselves to the basics; masters indulge in creative application."

Jiminy couldn't have been more surprised. "Are you calling me a master?"

Michael hid a smile.

The fox arched a brow. "There are many things I could call you."

"Now, now, old friend," interjected Michael. "My apprentice has endured enough and needs his rest."

Argent inclined his head and withdrew.

"I'll draw up a written assessment for your file. Your copy should arrive in a week or so." Michael leaned closer to his screen, eyes alight. "Give some more thought to an appropriate challenge for your attainment."

Jiminy wryly asked, "You didn't like my list?"

Michael hesitated. "As Argent pointed out, we're testing your grasp of the basics, not your ingenuity ... impressive though it may be. Now, *rest*."

"I'll catch a nap soon," he promised. "Thanks, First-sensei."

"Until next time, Kourogi-kun."

Jiminy signed off, then stood to stretch. Normally, he would have had to content himself with training under whatever ward was close. The Emergence had revolutionized the In-between, making technology—and overseas apprenticeships—safe. With the danger of accidental outing over, reavers could connect freely.

"An appropriate challenge." Jiminy yawned and stretched and double-checked the time.

He usually grabbed a long nap after sessions with his mentor, but he'd barely make it through his rounds before his shift started. A long shower and a large coffee would have to see him through.

The reaver girl was back.

Rook had warned Jiminy off, so he watched her from a safe

distance. Miss Armstrong, battler class, was taller than average, but not so much that her height made her stand out. If anything, she was blending in more than a newbie should. She worked carefully, quietly, and with a seriousness that would probably endear her to Doon-wen.

Her blonde hair had been hacked short, fanning out around her head in disobedient waves. He had to wonder how her hair found the courage to appear in her mirror in such an unruly state. Did she disapprove of its carefree nature as much as she disapproved of him?

Jiminy had begun a private tally of stern looks. He'd earned four already, and he hadn't even clocked in.

Leaning against the back counter, sipping an extra-strong coffee, he contemplated her nose. How did someone who never cracked a smile get away with such a pert nose? Its slight upturn belonged with someone sassy or playful. Yet Melissa worked in silence, keeping entirely to herself. Well, *almost*. She'd made one remarkable exception.

Rook.

Many young women were taken by Rook, but this was the first time Jiminy had ever seen Rook take back. The wolf was all soft smiles and fleeting touches and subtle shows of consideration. Most human girls would have been flattered or flustered, for he was as attentive as a suitor, but Melissa seemed to understand that his interest wasn't pursuit.

She was being treated as pack, and Jiminy would have loved to know *why*. But Rook had warned him off.

It was strange, being on the wrong side of Rook's considerable protective streak.

Why her?

Jiminy poured himself a second cup and pondered the possibilities, only to be caught looking. That earned him his fifth stern look of the morning. He was still paying for that disastrous first impression.

"Good morning, Melissa."

"Good morning, Jiminy."

Oooh, he liked that. More than he probably should, since she couldn't grasp the significance of using his nickname. Rather than be embarrassed by the handle, Jiminy had embraced it so fully, they'd put it on his name badge. It was part of his identity within the pack, an endearment that meant he belonged.

Most co-workers and customers shortened it to "Jim," but not Melissa. She determinedly granted him the full measure.

Did she like it? Did she pity him?

She was wholly immune to his usual arsenal of winks and smiles. Every other girl who frequented their shop could be depended on to react, but Melissa was calm, cool, collected ... and disappointing. Not that he was discouraged.

Today, he'd coax for lesser prizes. Like eye contact.

He sidled up to her and said, "I could teach you."

Melissa's grip shifted subtly on her broom, no doubt readying it as a weapon.

"I know all about wolves and pack life." Jiminy pointedly took a receptive stance, yielding the initiative to her. "I could teach you how to respond to Rook."

"I don't need you. Rook can teach me."

"That's true." He nodded even as he countered, "But it would make a pleasant surprise."

Very slowly, her gaze lifted to his.

Eye contact achieved!

Melissa asked, "What would?"

"It's hard to explain," he hedged. "Much easier to demonstrate."

She hesitated, clearly torn. And in her anxious expression, Jiminy saw how much his offer meant to her. This wasn't the time or place for teasing.

"A simple thing," he promised. "I'll only touch your arm."

With a nod, Melissa gave him the chance he needed.

"Have you noticed he does this?" Jiminy asked, lightly pressing the flat of his hand to her upper arm, then sliding downward to give her elbow a squeeze.

Her gaze turned inward, and she nodded again.

"There's a way to answer in kind." Jiminy edged as close as he dared. "You first this time."

She mirrored the contact.

"Just right," he encouraged. "This means something like, 'I'm here. Stay near. Aren't you glad we're together?' It makes sense. Rook's beyond thrilled to have you here, and it shows."

"Oh." Her expression softened and brightened, and she cast a shy glance in the wolf's direction.

As she drew back, Jiminy caught her wrist and slid his hand down to tweak her little finger. "Do that."

Melissa seemed surprised. "That's all?"

Jiminy shrugged. "There are dozens of ways to respond, but that's the most appropriate for Rook. It means something like, 'This is where I want to be. I'm glad you're by my side.' It's used for close kin or trusted friends."

"Let me try?"

He cheerfully obliged, initiating the exchange. Her hands were warm, her touch firm, her gaze locked. She was as serious about this as everything else she did. Jiminy offered a low hum, his version of the customary wolvish rumble.

"Now him," he whispered.

She nodded and went back to sweeping.

Not wanting to miss out, Jiminy grabbed an apron and started work early. Rook patted his cheek in passing, mingling affection and approval.

Nearly an hour passed before any chance came. Jiminy saw Rook's familiar touch and the way Melissa reached back. She managed to come off bashful and bold, and the look on Rook's face was priceless. Without even checking first, the wolf scooped her up and twirled her around.

Good thing Jiminy had been ready to deflect notice.

It made him happy to see Rook happy, but Melissa's reaction, while subtler, buoyed Jiminy. The next look she gave him didn't qualify as stern. Maybe it was just the afterglow of the delight she took in Rook, but it still knocked Jiminy off-balance. For the first time in ever, he wasn't sure what to say.

Melissa stepped right into his personal space and asked, "Teach me more?"

Settling into a receptive stance, Jiminy answered, "Glad to."

16

AIR OF IMPORTANCE

Melissa, your phone."

She shook her head. "I left it in the back."

"I know." Rook smiled softly. "You've been receiving messages in quick succession. It may be urgent."

"Sorry," he mumbled. Maybe she should have turned her phone off during working hours. "May I?"

He shooed her away, and she hurried to her locker in the changing room. Pulling her phone from her pack, she strolled toward the breakroom while opening her messages. They were all from Tami. She must have been texting at regular intervals for the last hour.

Sorry. I'm here.

Something has come up at home. Are you able to get away?

I'm at work, and I
have a practicum
this afternoon.

Can someone
cover for you?
Could you skip class?

A principal is asking
me to skip class?

I'll give you a note
if it would help.

What's going on?

Hard to explain.
Grandad thinks
you'll understand.

Why me?

What came through next wasn't an explanation. It was a snapshot of Uncle Abel holding a child who was clearly of Amaranthine descent. Only, the little girl didn't resemble any clan Melissa was familiar with. But identification wasn't her first concern. When it came to Amaranthine children, protection always came first.

Let me talk to my boss
Might take me a while to
reach you, but I will be
there asap

Thank you.
No rush. Be safe.
We'll be waiting.

Melissa's thoughts were reeling when she came out of the back, just as two gentlemen stepped up to the counter. The African-American was built like an athlete, though he gave an air of maturity that suggested he'd be coaching rather than playing. He spoke softly to a beautiful man with a profusion of artfully disheveled gingery curls. The former was smart with his tailored suit and spectacles, while the latter was arrayed in an ensemble that looked both offbeat and expensive.

They radiated importance, and Melissa wondered how they were affiliated with Bellwether—guest lecturers, board members, wealthy contributors, museum curators, symphony members, patrons of the arts. At the very least, they could be alumni who'd made it big.

Where was Rook? Until she could talk to him, it would have to be business as usual. When the taller man looked up, she said, "Good morning."

Usually, that worked. Customers generally rattled off their order without further prompting. But the man's eyebrows drew together, and he demanded, "Where is your nametag?"

"I'm new," she murmured apologetically.

"I am aware. But that was not my question."

"I don't have a nametag. Yet."

"Ah!" interjected the other man, amusement shining in his tawny eyes. "But you must have a name."

They didn't need her name to order coffee. So she simply asked, "May I take your order?"

The taller man's gaze flicked to the menu board. "What would you recommend?"

Melissa was more concerned about the weight of the phone in her apron pocket than in discussing coffee blends. In her frazzled state, she went off-script, offering her own opinion instead of the stock descriptions Rook had made her memorize. "Cozy Cottage is rich and mellow, good for sipping, and Harvest Herald has hints of spice, a nice reminder that autumn is close. Personally, I prefer Founders Favor, which has a wild bite. It's not for everyone, but it pairs well with the baked goods from next door."

"Interesting." He held out a hand.

She glanced between it and his face. And a distressing idea crept into her mind. The resemblance wasn't terribly strong, for the angles were different, the build thicker, and the eyes behind his glasses frames entirely shrewd.

Rook hurried out, and his arm came around Melissa's shoulder, but his voice thrummed with warmth and gladness. "Welcome home, Brother."

Doon-wen twitched his fingers impatiently.

This time, she placed her palm on his. He leaned forward and said, "Melissa."

"Yes," she whispered, rather glad Rook was there.

He bent to press his lips to the back of her hand. "Thank you for making True comfortable."

Melissa immediately brightened, for Doon-wen's arrival meant the she-wolf's wait was over. "She's missed you terribly."

Rook put in, "And no wonder, with you gone at such a time."

Doon-wen straightened, but he didn't release her hand.

"She's restless in her confinement," added Rook.

Melissa hadn't realized True was pregnant. Perhaps that's why she was being kept separate from the wolves in the main Kith shelter.

When Doon-wen released her, she reflexively caught his wrist and shyly tugged his pinky.

His eyebrows lifted.

"I'm glad you're home," she offered.

He drummed his fingers lightly on the countertop, then excused himself with a small bow.

As he disappeared into the back, Melissa remembered herself. "Rook, may I leave early?"

"What's wrong?"

She wanted to tell him, but the second gentleman was still standing there, watching them with bright-eyed interest.

Rook said, "Cyril is both a friend and a founder."

"Then you probably both know a little something about *all* the clans ...?" she asked.

"Very probable, indeed," Cyril said smilingly.

"Are there Amaranthine with leaves for hair?"

Neither answered, though they exchanged a long look.

Dipping into her pocket, she showed them her phone.

"Well, now," murmured Rook. "That's not something we see every day."

"Been a fair few centuries for me," agreed Cyril.

Jiminy, who'd stolen up behind Rook, offered a soft whistle. "I thought there was a strict ban on photographing ... her sort."

Rook huffed. "My office. And ward it."

He herded them to the back, and Cyril cheerfully crowded in with them. Melissa explained what little she knew, and the two Amaranthine shared another long look, plus a few fleeting gestures.

Decision reached, Rook said, "Go quickly, and take Jiminy."

"Want it warded?" he asked.

"Swiftly."

Cyril asked, "How many acres?"

Melissa wasn't sure of the exact number. "A little over two hundred, I think."

"That'll take some time. And an anchor." Rook rubbed at the side of his face. "Stopgap measures for now. Take crystals from the stores. If you need back-up ... well, take your pick of the Woodacres."

Jiminy rubbed his hands together. "It's been a while since I had a challenge on this scale. I'd really like Kip, if you don't mind my bringing him in. He'd *love* this!"

17
TRUTH BE TOLD

The wheels of a large, black rolling case droned along the sidewalk. How long had it been since Jiminy left the scope of his own wards? As he puzzled through the past several weeks, which had passed in ordinary ways, he eased closer to Melissa until their shoulders bumped.

"Too close." She warned him off with an elbow. "Are you trying to run me off the road?"

"Not at all. Unless you want to take this cross-country." The commuter lot was on the other side of a wide expanse of green lawn. "I'm always up for a bit of a romp. All wolves are."

Melissa frowned. "You're not a wolf."

"Raised by," Jiminy countered. "It's practically the same thing."

"It can't be," she argued. "You're human."

"I'm a person of reaver descent who's been fostered by a wolf pack since birth." Jiminy really couldn't remember any other life.

113

"Rook says I understand wolves better than humans, which makes me an excellent liaison for my pack ... but an iffy barista at best."

Her steps slowed. "You don't have parents?"

His first impulse was to stick stubbornly to his usual rote—*I am a son of the Nightspangle pack.* But Melissa wasn't asking about who had raised him. "All the reavers in the enclave where I was born have especially strong pedigrees. Thanks to certain resources and the support of their Amaranthine partners, they've earned a reputation for producing children with potent souls."

Melissa stopped walking. "I've never heard of such a place."

"You wouldn't have." Jiminy studied his feet. "Reavers in that place are encouraged to halve the usual wait between pregnancies, but they only keep every other child. Even numbered children are fostered out; odd numbered children remain with the enclave."

"You were an even-numbered child?"

Jiminy nodded. "Clans with the right connections can apply for a child, but they never really know what might come their way—gender, rating, aptitudes. The Nightspangle pack needed a ward. They took a chance and ended up with me."

"That's quite a risk. What if you'd been a battler?"

"Both of my biological parents are wards, so the chances were better than fair." Jiminy took a few steps to get her walking again. She followed, but she was focused on him.

"Have you ever met your family?"

"You're not listening, Melissa." Jiminy wagged a finger at her. "My family is here. From my perspective, I'm a wolf of the Nightspangle pack."

"My biological parents are both battlers." She pulled car keys from her pocket and unlocked the car doors. Popping the hatch, she manhandled his case inside. "I was born under contract, but my mother raised me."

Jiminy hadn't expected to learn so much. A rattled Melissa was a talkative Melissa.

Once they were underway, she asked, "Which academy did you attend?"

"Bellwether."

"I meant your early courses."

"I was bought and brought to become this enclave's anchor, and I was raised in the Amaranthine style. They don't send away their children." Jiminy kept his eyes on the road as she guided the car toward the highway. "I don't often leave campus, so this is something of an adventure."

"They don't let you leave?"

"Nothing like that. I go where they go, and I've traveled quite a bit." He slyly boasted, "I've been to a Song Circle four times, if you count the year I was two."

That earned him a look. "You *can't* be that old."

Song Circles convened once every ten years.

"The circles in different regions each mark time differently, probably to encourage visitors from far and away. I've only been to this area's Song Circle once."

Melissa cautiously asked, "How old are you?"

Ah, they were in personal territory now. He smiled and asked, "How old are you?"

He was sure they'd reached an impasse, but she shot him a mutinous look.

"Twenty-four," she snapped.

Jiminy figured his own transparency had earned him the right to ask, but he chose his words with care. "Will it offend you if I ask about the nature of your contract?"

"I don't have one." They were beyond the city limits, speeding through increasingly rural territory. "I paid my late fee last Dichotomy Day, and I'm saving for this winter's fine."

Okay, that was really surprising.

Jiminy ventured, "Are you ... waiting for someone younger?"

Melissa snorted.

"Well, most of the reasons I can think of for a reaver to put off their obligation are either really delicate or really sad ... or both." He quietly added, "I was raised by wolves, Melissa. You have to know how we are."

"I would rather have a Kith partner than a husband." Melissa stiffly added, "I'm aware of how irresponsible that sounds, and I *will* do my part. Eventually. But right now, I'm focusing on the only kind of partner I've ever wanted."

"Oh. That one hadn't occurred to me." Jiminy looked out at passing cornfields. "I'm twenty-six."

Her lips compressed, but she rose to the bait. In a lightly mocking tone, she asked, "Will it offend you if I ask about the nature of *your* contract?"

"If there have been offers for me, I haven't seen them. Doon-wen is very protective." He idly drew a series of sigils on his pantleg. "And ... well ... *wolves*."

"Your pack won't let you marry?"

"Oh, nothing as ominous as that. But when Doon-wen took me

116

in, it was for keeps. Biologically, I'm a reaver. I hold a reaver's rank, title, and classification. But I'm not in the reaver registry, nor am I bound by reaver laws." Jiminy met her startled glance with a small smile. "It's like I've been trying to tell you, Melissa. I'm a wolf."

Joe sat back and watched his family do what they did best—Tami taking charge, Dad befriending the child, Mom asking questions. But Grandad wasn't giving answers. His jaw was set as he hauled out a big, old map that showed their boundary lines. Grandad unrolled it on the center of the kitchen table, and Joe quietly helped him anchor the corners with the sugar bowl and a potted violet.

"What's this for?" asked Joe.

"The ward."

"What's a ward?"

Grandad snorted. "Reaver classification. Hope they're sending a halfway decent one."

Joe waited, but that's as much as he was getting. Unsure what else to do, he slipped outside to take care of the chores. But even being outdoors didn't ease the tension in his gut. Biddie had thrown the whole world off-balance, but the chickens still needed him. And in a couple of hours, they'd have customers. Letting himself into the apple barn, Joe checked the schedule. No school buses, at least.

Back outside, he started his usual routine—feeding, watering, gathering. They'd missed breakfast, and the resulting emptiness was getting to him. He picked a couple of apples and kept moving.

Maybe if he concentrated on setting the farm to rights, he'd find his feet.

He heard the car coming. Melissa was driving a little too fast, and that added to his worries.

She knew what was going on, and that worried him, too.

Nobody had outright said it, but Grandad's scant explanation pointed in one direction. Melissa was some sort of Betweener spy, and she was bringing a reaver to the farm.

Finding a little girl in the orchard really might have set off an international incident. And Grandad was turning the kitchen into a war room.

Melissa hurried over. "Are you all right?"

Joe shrugged and glanced at her companion. He seemed awfully young to be coming to their rescue.

"You must be Joe." Smiling and offering a hand, he said, "I'm Reaver Foster, but everyone calls me Jiminy."

Even though his folks would have been shocked by his rudeness, Joe kept his hands firmly in his pockets and turned toward the house. "Everyone's in the kitchen."

Grandad was waiting on the porch. "Classification?" he demanded.

"Ward, sir," Jiminy reported.

"Battler, sir," added Melissa.

Even though Joe had guessed, it still hurt to have his suspicions confirmed. Their so-called cousin was a reaver. Why had she come?

Grandad actually seemed pleased by Melissa's revelation, like she'd confirmed his suspicions, but he narrowed his eyes at the ward. "Where do you rank?"

"Bit of a personal question," said the young man with a laugh.

"This isn't the time or place for the best intentions of middling whelps. State your digits, or I'll have to insist on a documented replacement."

Jiminy looked embarrassed. "May I ... whisper it?"

Grandad rolled his eyes but waved him forward. Whatever Jiminy said certainly startled him. "Really?"

"Truly." Jiminy indicated the house. "May we?"

He waved them past, then met Joe's gaze. "If he's telling the truth, we'll be okay, Joey-boy."

"What about Melissa?"

Grandad patted his shoulder. "Times like this, it's nice to have a battler in the family."

Joe quietly asked, "Are we reavers?"

"We're Reaversons."

He was getting frustrated. "What does that mean?"

"It means you have as many reasons to be proud as you have reasons to worry. But you can keep everything you care about if we're careful." Grandad squared his shoulders. "Let's get in there. I'm the only one who understands what we have to lose and what we have for leverage."

18

PROTECT WHAT'S PRECIOUS

Tami hung back, holding onto Biddie as if she were the only sure thing left in the world. Which shouldn't be possible, since the girl was so far outside her realm of experience. But they'd become tangled together somehow, and Tami wanted nothing more than to keep her close and keep her safe.

"I want wards," said Grandad.

"You shall have them," said Jiminy, touching the map. "But a property this size can't be warded in one go. I'll need a little time. And a little help."

"What sort?"

"Woodacre ring any bells?"

Grandad nodded slowly. "Nice folks. Nearby?"

"Near enough." Jiminy circled the oak glen with a finger. "Here first. Pushing outward once I have more anchors."

Tami knew about wards. On Ash's recommendation, she'd requested them for the school. Reavers from the Office of Ingress were scheduled for Landmark's initial installation.

All of the sudden, she realized that Joe was standing alone in the far corner. Why was he there when she was here?

"Joe," she murmured.

Biddie turned her head. "Joey-boy."

Tami crossed to him, and his arm eased around her. She leaned into his side and searched his face. Without words, she asked him what was wrong.

He shook his head and tightened his hold.

Their grandfather thumped the table. "How much authority do you have?"

"I'm not sure." Jiminy spread his hands wide. "Some, I think. I have friends with friends."

"Drop a name or two," challenged Grandad.

"Mettlebright. Elderbough."

Tami was stunned. Two of the Five?

But her grandfather's expression was bland as butter. "A bit far afield to be much use *here*."

Jiminy looked away, then looked back. "I was raised by wolves."

Several emotions flickered across Grandad's face. "There's a pack that close?"

"I really couldn't say."

"And normally, I wouldn't press." Leaning forward on his fists, the old man asked, "Would your leader consider sending us an allotment? They'd be welcome—Kith or Kindred. Safe behind your wards."

121

The young reaver's calm gave nothing away. "To what end?"

"I know what we have, and I know what she's worth." Grandad drew himself up. "I propose an alliance between the Amaranthine and the Reaverson family. Red Gate Farm should become an enclave."

The last place Joe wanted to be was alone with the reaver, but it made the most sense for him to serve as Jiminy's guide. Joe knew the orchard and its boundaries better than anyone. He eyed the reaver's rolling case and offered, "I could bring the small tractor."

"No, thank you. I'm wary of the vibrations, and it's really best if I walk the boundaries before I set the barriers."

Joe asked, "Isn't it heavy?"

"Nothing I can't handle," Jiminy cheerfully assured. "Do you remember where you found the child?"

Did this guy think he was stupid? Pointing, Joe said, "Her tree's this way."

"Lead on!"

They walked in silence. Or as close to silence as anyone could walk while dragging their luggage through gravel. Joe pivoted and picked up the case. "Let me."

"Oh, but ...."

"I thought you were worried about vibrations."

Jiminy yielded with a small laugh. "I'm not used to heavy lifting. Most days, I work as a barista."

"But you're a reaver."

"I'm a reaver with a day job."

Joe said, "You look like a college student."

"Pretty much. If I were enrolled in a standard university, I'd be prepping a thesis to earn my degree." Jiminy brushed absentmindedly at his hair. "I have a mentor who lives overseas, so a lot of my classes are online."

Sifting through the wealth of questions he'd never been able to ask Grandad, Joe ventured, "Is there such a thing as a song circle?"

"Yes. It's the name of an Amaranthine festival, a gathering of clans that takes place once a decade." There was a bounce to his step now. "Food. Music. Dancing. Stories. All sorts of solemn traditions and ceremonies and proclamations. They can last for days, even weeks."

He wasn't holding back. Then again, all of this might be public knowledge.

Joe asked, "Do you think my grandfather ever went?"

Jiminy hummed. "The big festivals are only for the clans, but if he was enclave-bred, he'd know about them. Most enclaves have a circle for official gatherings. Same idea, but on a much smaller scale."

"We have one, I think."

"Yes, I think you do, too." Jiminy asked, "Does it have some kind of boundary? Like a wall or a hedge? I couldn't tell from the map."

Could trees be considered a hedge? Joe was saved from answering, because the golden crown of Biddie's tree came into view.

"Oaks!" Jiminy quickened his pace. "Do you know who planted them?"

"Grandad."

"Your grandfather couldn't have chosen better." He touched

the rough bark and beamed with approval. "This will be attractive to many clans."

"You're going to bring wolves here?"

"Only if we're welcome."

Joe trailed after Jiminy, who made a full circuit of the oak glen before approaching Biddie's tree. One more question really needed to be asked. "Is my sister a reaver?"

"She must be, to have attracted an imp's interest. Your whole family will need to be assessed."

"Isn't that why you guys sent Melissa?"

"Hold on." Jiminy turned to him, his face gone serious. "Assessment is always handled by an Amaranthine. And while I don't know any of the details, I'm quite sure that Melissa considers you kin."

Joe jammed his hands deeper into his pockets, feeling chastised. But he didn't like all the mysterious half-truths and hinting. He wanted to *know* something again, and to know it for sure.

"If Tami is a reaver, will they take her away?"

"Even if your sister has a soul to out-dazzle the stars, there's no chance of that." Jiminy patted his shoulder. "From what I recall of tree lore, your sister and her twin cannot be apart for long. In fact, most build a home within easy reach, directly under the canopy if possible. I don't doubt that Biddie will be happiest if a little cabin or cottage wa– "

"Wait! Twin?"

"In a manner of speaking." Jiminy paused in the process of pacing off the base of the tree. "From what your grandfather shared, Biddie's *true* twin was your grandfather's sister, who died young. The sibling bond has passed to Tami, who's become tree-kin in Lisbet Reaverson's place. What I'd like to know is how a family with even the most tenuous of ties to an ancient grove managed to vow out. I can't emphasize enough the secrecy surrounding...."

But Joe wasn't listening anymore.

If Tami was Biddie's twin now, what did that make him?

Melissa came clean. Although she apologized for neglecting to mention her true status as a Betweener, she tried to emphasize their familial connection and its attendant concerns. She even sketched a little family tree to show how closely they were related.

"The Elderbough Initiative?" Tami asked. "As in Spokesperson Adoona-soh Elderbough?"

"Yes, although it was proposed by her son Naroo-soh." Melissa searched their faces. "Wolves are protective of their packmates, so it made sense to him that reavers look to their own. In America, this has been the best way to locate—and protect—unregistered reavers."

Uncle George's gaze was too keen by far. "Protect them from what?"

"I ... really couldn't say."

Uncle Abel indicated Biddie. "Did you know this would happen?"

"No!" Melissa shot a pleading look in Tami's direction. "It's been a complete surprise. A good one, but really kind of crazy. People like Biddie are sort of like fairy tales. I didn't even realize Amaranthine trees were real, but I'll do everything I can to protect you until better help arrives."

Tami laughed a little. "I'm glad I'm not the only one out of my depth here."

Melissa smiled gratefully. "I'd feel better if I could check the perimeter again, and I'll compare notes with Reaver Foster. Tami, I think you should return Biddie to her tree. That way, she's inside Jiminy's wards. Everyone else can go on with business as usual." Running through a mental checklist, she added, "Don't tell anyone about *anything*—the tree, the child, the wards, the wolves, and the fact that some of you may be unregistered reavers."

Everyone was nodding. And then Tami gave a strange, strangled little moan of dismay.

"What?" Melissa asked.

"Her tree." Color drained from Tami's face. "I posted scans of the leaves to an online forum."

19

BETTER TOGETHER

O ver the course of the day, Tamiko's harrowing dread faded into qualms that she did her best to rationalize away. It was no use worrying. She'd used the school's computer. She hadn't posted any personal information. All she had to do was wait for afterhours, drive down to work, log into that dratted forum, and erase her post, her scans, and her account.

Meanwhile, clouds rolled in and a steady drizzle kept all but the hardiest customers from visiting Red Gate Farm. Tami spent most of the day huddled under an umbrella among the roots of Biddie's tree, chatting with the girl and watching Joe help Jiminy arrange and rearrange stones around the rim of the hollow.

Jiminy seemed cheerful enough. Joe was distracted. And each time Melissa passed through the oak glen on her patrol, she was all business—clipped and conscientious.

After the first couple hours, Tami was chilled through and antsy. She'd missed a staff meeting, and Flootie must have had to reschedule her appointments for the day. And there were still forms to file with the Office of Ingress in advance of the warding.

"Miss Reaverson?"

She stirred and looked up into Jiminy's smiling face. "Yes, Reaver Foster."

"I'm nearly finished with the fine-tuning, but it seems you're throwing off my balance."

Tami looked between him and her brother, who was pinched and pale. Joe only offered a shrug. It was hard to follow much of what the younger man said, especially when it came to the mythical intricacies of sigilcraft.

"If I may be so bold," said Jiminy, "that's an interesting necklace you're wearing."

She touched the stones hidden by three layers of thick clothing. How had he known they were there?

"Purple, I gather. All shades. Good size. *Excellent* quality." Rubbing his fingertips together, he asked, "Might I have a look?"

Joe spoke up. "He's been using crystals along the boundaries. They're part of the wards."

"Anchors," Jiminy said. "Bigger, but not so fine. Which is why your stones are throwing me off."

"Sorry?" she ventured, hugging Biddie.

"Nothing to apologize for. I enjoy a challenge!" He shifted his weight and gestured with a flutter of fingers. "They're in the amethyst range, right?"

"Right. Yes." Tami fumbled with fastenings in order to allow the reaver his peek.

Jiminy whistled softly. "Who warded you?"

"I ... what?"

"That's quite an array. I'm willing to bet that with personal wards of this caliber, an Amaranthine couldn't distinguish you from an average human." He cast a glance at their surroundings, frowning thoughtfully. "Interesting. Do you ever remove them?"

"They don't come off."

He rubbed his chin, then grinned. "I wonder who you are under there?"

Tami had no context to offer an answer, but Biddie giggled.

"Someone in a position to know!" Jiminy offered a wink. "What do you think of your sister, Biddie?"

"Wet and cold and worried," the girl said succinctly.

Joe was at Tami's elbow in two long strides. "Let's go in," he coaxed. "Get some lunch. Warm up."

Tami hesitated. "Doesn't Biddie need to stay by her tree?"

Jiminy raised a hand. "It's best to be clear from the outset. This isn't Biddie's tree. Biddie *is* the tree."

"Wouldn't that mean it's even more important? Although, she's been to the house, and that's quite a ways from here. For that matter, is it all right for me to go? I have work."

"I don't know enough to advise you. I'm no expert on Amaranthine trees." Jiminy waved her along. "Go with Joe. I'll wrap up here, then see about finding the expertise you need."

Joe took Biddie and helped Tami to her feet, gruffly saying, "Come home, Tami. You're not a tree."

When he strode off in the direction of the house, she followed.

And when she reached his side, he slowed his steps and took her hand. Tami pulled in a deep breath and found reason to smile. As long as Joe was with her, everything would be fine.

The dreary day was all but over when Melissa hauled a blissfully bedraggled Jiminy into Red Gate Farm's kitchen. Aunt Hiro ladled thick chicken soup into bowls, and Uncle Abel dropped warm towels over their heads before retreating into the next room.

"I'm pleased, but I'm also puzzled." Jiminy roughed up his hair, which stuck out at odd angles until he ran his fingers distractedly through it. "Did you get a look at Tami's necklace?"

"Yes, she showed me."

"Those stones are *exquisite*. Really similar to the ones my mentor wears, so I know. *Nothing* gets past them."

"That's good. It's probably kept Tami safe."

Jiminy hummed. "Granted. But ... have you noticed how many varieties of Ephemera are making themselves at home?"

"They were my first clue."

"Right. *So.*" Jiminy's eyebrows lifted. "If Tami's soul is on lockdown, what's attracting them?"

Melissa stirred her spoon through her soup. "Odds are on her twin, right?"

Jiminy's brows furrowed. "I know Amaranthine trees attract pollinators, but I spotted glimsleek and midivar. They're known mooches with a taste for reaver souls."

"Not Biddie. I meant Joe. Fraternal twins."

He shot a look toward the family room, then quietly asked, "Can I borrow your phone?"

"What for?"

He was nose-to-nose with her, quick as a wink, but her reflexes weren't anything to be trifled with. Melissa had one arm across at his throat; with the other, she prodded him between the ribs.

Jiminy's eyes widened. "Did you just pull a knife on me?"

"Boundaries," she demanded in an undertone.

"Would it hurt to get a little closer?"

Oh, she'd make sure it hurt. Melissa wasn't in the mood for nonsense. "There is more than one kind of pain."

His smile faded. "I know."

"And you're a horrible flirt."

Jiminy said, "I'm just cheerful."

"You're utterly incorrigible."

He sat back, and Melissa sheathed her blade. She glanced around, but the faint murmur of voices could be heard from the other room. Maybe Uncle George was giving his family more explanations. That would be good.

"Melissa." Jiminy kept his voice low. "People come to Founders looking for two things. The coffee may keep them going, but kindness and courtesy give them something to smile about. Even if it's just for a moment."

"Your gift to all the girls on campus?"

"Well, I've tried it with some of the males, but they're generally less receptive to personal remarks." He shrugged. "Doon-wen told me to stop scaring off the clientele."

Oh, he was too much. "I've seen how you operate."

Jiminy held up his hands, pleading innocence. "Like I said, Melissa. The compliments are a service of the shop. I'm not allowed past the counter, so that's all any of them will have of me—a smile, a kind word, a pretty cup. Froth and nonsense."

Melissa stood, crossing to the stove to get another serving of soup. If she was objective, was Rook any different? He was familiar with their customers, and he had his fair share of fans among the college students. Was it the same?

Jiminy followed her, dishing his own second serving. "You're something new. Rook put you on my side of the counter, and that means something."

She frowned. "Rook hired me because I could fend you off."

"Wrong." Jiminy scooted his chair closer to hers when they reclaimed their seats at the table. "Wolves are very protective. It means that Rook trusts you with me."

Melissa knew she was missing something.

Jiminy tried again. "You have the pack's approval. That's never happened before. And since I'm allowed to get closer, I plan to."

This was all turned around.

"You don't think we can get along?" Jiminy asked innocently.

"Maybe. If you kept your hands to yourself." Melissa waved her spoon at him. "Use your words."

"I will. And they won't be empty."

She rolled her eyes. "And they won't be enough. I won't let you paw at me simply because I'm within reach."

Jiminy took a few bites, then asked, "Do you know how wolves communicate?"

Melissa didn't dignify that with an answer. Of course she did.

"Words. Posture. Sounds. Touch," he listed. "We're going to run into all kinds of trouble if you don't let me touch you. Some things don't translate well into words."

"What's the use of trying to communicate through touch if I don't know what you mean? Based on *my* training, touch is a challenge, inviting retaliation."

He smiled ruefully and asked, "May I borrow your phone?"

Before she could ask why—*again*—Tami clattered down the back stairs. "I can't believe I slept so late! Where is everyone?"

Melissa pointed, and Tami disappeared into the next room for a few seconds, then she was back, grabbing things from the coatrack and rummaging around for keys. "I'll be back as quick as I can," she promised breathlessly. "Right after I pull that forum post."

The door slammed, the screen door slapped, and a few moments later, an engine rumbled to life.

Jiminy sighed. "May I borrow your phone to call a friend?" he asked for the third time. "I need his know-how to get the wards tuned, and as an added bonus, he might be able to do a little discreet assessing of the entire Reaverson clan."

"Someone from the enclave?"

"Yes and no. He doesn't live on campus but visits pretty regularly."

Melissa unlocked her phone and handed it over.

Mouthing his thanks, Jiminy pushed his chair back, tapping in a number from memory as he moved to the back door. To her surprise, he beckoned for her to follow. Once outside, where the porch kept the rain off, he switched to speaker.

"Moshi moshi!"

Grinning, Jiminy said, "Hey, Kip. My friend and I need a little intervention."

"Jiminy! Any friend of yours is a friend of mine."

"Melissa, Kip. Kip, Melissa." And without further ado, Jiminy dove straight into a lengthy explanation of the discovery of a tree, the size of the property, the proposed establishment of an enclave, the limitations of his resources, and an earnest plea for back-up.

"How urgent are we talking, kiddo?"

"Is tomorrow too soon?"

"Tomorrow's a school day."

"This weekend then?" Jiminy suggested. "That would give me time to send for another series of crystals. Maybe I can even get them delivered, spare Joe having to tote them for me."

There was a long pause on the other end of the line.

Jiminy raised his eyebrows and asked, "Kip?"

"Where did you say you were?"

"An orchard up in Archer—Red Gate Farm."

"Are we talking about the Reaversons?"

Melissa spoke up, explaining her role. "Tami's definitely an unregistered reaver, and the rest of the family should be assessed. Especially her brother."

On the other end of the line, Kip blew a raspberry. *"Okay, here's the deal. Tami knows me, but she* doesn't, *you know? She's a friend, and I'd do anything to see her safe, so I'll be there tomorrow,* after *she leaves for work."*

"Tomorrow," Jiminy agreed. "Thanks."

"No worries," Kip said. *"I'll clear it with Ash. He's around here somewhere. I'm sure he won't mind making my excuses to*

Principal Reaverson."

Ash. Kip. The two janitors. Melissa grabbed Jiminy's arm. He shot her a baffled look. Leaning into the phone, she asked, "Are you at the school?"

"Uh-oh. Worlds collide. Probably for the best, in this case." A smile warmed his voice. *"Hey, does this mean Tami talks about us at home?"*

Jiminy, who'd caught on, pushed for an answer. "Kip, are you at the school?"

"Yep. It's beauty night at Landmark Elementary. We'll be here 'til all hours, sudsing the terrazzo."

"She's on her way," Melissa warned. "How long have we been talking? She might already be there!"

Jiminy groaned. "Kip, are you ... comfy?"

Something clattered on the other end of the line, and Kip swore softly.

The call abruptly ended.

20

WE ALL FALL

Tami pushed her speed even though she was worried that leaving Biddie would strain their nascent bond. Was this tension a symptom of something going on in her soul, or was she stressed for completely ordinary reasons? Like inadvertently betraying a family secret.

"It will be fine." Joe had promised to look in on Biddie. She could be home again in under an hour. "Ten minutes on the computer. That's all I need."

To her dismay, Coach was still in the parking lot.

What were Ash and Kip doing here so late?

Determined to get in and out with drawing attention to herself, she splashed to the side entrance and paused to tighten her ponytail. She'd be quick. She'd be quiet. The last thing she wanted now was for Ash to see her looking a wreck. She'd dressed in the dark—lavender yoga pants, a shrunken tee promoting a past year's corn maze, one of Joe's quilted flannel shirts in lieu of a jacket, and a battered pair of slipper flats that definitely leaked. Counting on the cover of darkness and a quick getaway, she'd cut every possible corner. Which meant she wasn't even wearing a bra.

Tami rested her forehead against the cold metal of the door. "Please, please, please let them be on the other side of the building," she whispered. Gathering the necessary resolve, she slid her key into the lock, opened the door far enough to assess the long, empty hallway, flung the door wide, and took off at a sprint.

Only after it was too late did it register that the floors were *extra* shiny.

And there were soap bubbles clustered on its gleaming surface.

And that her shoes not only had holes, they had zero traction.

With a yip of surprise, Tami's feet flew out from under her, and she hit the floor with enough force to send her into oblivion

Someone was talking. Were they talking to her?

"–mi? Tami!"

Why was it so hard to open her eyes? Light and dark swirled one way, then reversed. She blinked a few times, and a face swam into focus. Ash. He looked scared.

"Are you okay?"

She could hardly hear his voice over the roaring in her ears and hoped in a detached way that she wouldn't be sick in front of him. Or on him.

He touched her so gently, testing bones, checking pulse. He

shouted something urgent, but Tami was more interested in the warm hand at her shoulder. This might be the first time he'd touched her. So standoffish.

And then Kip was there—all vivid freckles and fur. No, it must be his hair. Red hair. His hand was in *her* hair, gently probing, and she squinted, trying to understand the sensation that whispered for attention. But the pain was louder.

Tami felt bad. Worry looked all wrong on Kip's face. He was supposed to be smiling, and his eyes should be sparkling. Even his eyes were all wrong. What was it about his eyes? She blinked slowly, and the strangeness was gone.

"Trust us," Kip begged, touching her forehead with the tip of one finger.

When she blinked again, her eyes didn't open.

"What did you do?" demanded Ash.

"Encouraged her to sleep. It was just a little nudge. No harm done." Kip pointed to his tail. "Or did you want to help me explain this?"

"Definitely not." He gathered her into his arms, heart slamming, thoughts reeling.

Kip's hand settled on top of his head. "You okay?"

"Definitely not," he repeated. His every instinct—or at least what he understood about them—had fixated on Tami. She was his choice, and the consequences were terrifying. His lifespan was taking the Amaranthine course, so he was doomed. Tami's lifespan meant she'd leave him lonesome. Not that he'd really be alone.

Well, not unless Kip went off with some pretty redheaded squirrel lady and ....

Ash swallowed against the hopelessness of his situation and asked, "Have you ever been in love?"

His best friend offered a bland stare. "If I had, wouldn't you be the first to notice?"

"Guess so."

Kip steered him toward the nurse's office. "Kith-kin aren't exactly in high demand, and besides, my friend needs me."

It had never occurred to Ash that Kip might have put his future on hold in order to keep him company.

"You aren't inconveniencing me, Ash. I don't want any other nest than the one we share."

"But what about ... all the good things that are part of having a bondmate?"

"I haven't met a female yet—in *or* out of the clans—who makes me feel the right kind of frisky. Maybe I will someday. Maybe I won't. What does it matter?"

Ash supposed there was some truth to that. Tami hadn't been something he could have planned for or avoided. She'd just sort of happened. Maybe it would be the same for Kip. A cute squirrel lady could come waltzing into their lives. If she was a good cook, Kip would fall head over heels and go chasing her through the trees, then settle down in a nest of his own, with freckle-faced babies with names like Willow, Birch, and Rowan.

He asked, "Are you sure?"

"Sure, I'm sure. Our arrangement suits me. If I still lived over the bakery, you gotta know my mom would lovingly haul my fluffy tail to all sorts of marriage meetings. *Not* my idea of fun." Kip offered a prosaic shrug. "There's no avoiding the usual festival matchmaking, but I'm a champ at hide-and-seek and hard-to-get."

Ash's head and heart and hands were full of Tami, whose pull on him was impossible to ignore. He wanted her in ways he couldn't fully understand, but he also wanted Kip to be happy. After everything Kip had done to give Ash a nest of his own, he struggled against the possibility of parting ways.

"Geez, you're hopeless." Kip kissed his forehead. "Stop fretting. I'll be here for as long as you need me. Same as always."

She opened her eyes to the barren whiteness of an unfamiliar ceiling and florescent lighting. Random facts skittered through her thoughts, failing to make sense. Joe was unhappy about something. Melissa was a reaver. Biddie was a tree. Her feet were cold. Wards would keep the children safe. Was she late for work?

Someone was holding her hand.

Turning her head, Tami winced. There was a tender spot on the back of her head. But the room was making more sense now. She could remember driving in. This was the nurse's office at school. And the one holding her hand was Ash. He knelt beside the bed, watching her face with big, mournful eyes.

She gave his hand a little squeeze. "Hello."

"Hey. You okay?"

"Never better," she said wryly.

"I'm so sorry."

"Not your fault. I was running in the halls." She laughed a little. "I feel foolish."

"Don't."

Tami couldn't think of a thing to say, not when Ash was so close and still clinging to her hand. If her head wasn't throbbing, she might have appreciated the romantic potential of the situation. "Ow."

He stiffened. "Do you need anything. Aspirin or … something?"

"Yes, please." She propped herself up on her elbows.

Ash took no time at all bringing a paper cup of water and a single dose in a sealed packet. Handing her the former, he tore open the latter. But instead of putting the two white tablets in her waiting hand, he lightly touched one to her lower lip.

She opened her mouth to accept it and self-consciously washed it down.

In the same way, he fed her the second tablet.

Tami was stunned by the intimacy of the gesture, and he seemed similarly entranced. She lay back. Casting about for something to say, her attention was caught by the single blue paperclip affixed to the collar of his coveralls. She gave it a casual poke. "You're as popular as ever."

Ash dragged his attention sideways and fished in his pockets. He silently displayed the day's haul, nine tokens of affection in an array of colors—silver, gold, violet, yellow, and an especially aggressive neon pink.

"But this one's special?"

A quick glance. A firm nod.

All at once, Tami realized she *hadn't* chosen a neutral topic. "Is it mine?"

"Yes."

He was wearing her paperclip, like a knight wearing his lady's token. Why was everything about this man so distracting? She hoped her infatuation wasn't a testament to her age. At twenty-nine, had she fallen hard for the first handsome, unattached man to cross her path?

No. She'd met Kip first, so she'd fallen for the *second* handsome unattached man. Tami wasn't desperate; she was discerning. Very discerning. And at this range, Ash was easy to read. Regret. Reluctance. Helpless longing.

She supposed that meant it was up to her. Taking hold of the clipped collar, she held him still while she brushed her lips across his.

He gasped.

Tami tried another kiss, light and coaxing.

Ash surprised her by wrapping his arms around her. Their positions made the embrace a little awkward—he'd pinned her arms and hidden his face in her hair. But he held her to his heart with surprising strength, and she could feel the way it was pounding.

"I shouldn't," he whispered.

It was little late for that. "You may."

His muscles tensed and trembled. "I want to."

"Well?" Tamiko couldn't imagine why he was holding back. She'd kissed him first.

One of Ash's hands shifted to cradle the back of her head.

142

"You're hurt. And … stuff."

"Kiss it better?" she suggested.

He moved by degrees, little muzzling touches with his nose, a careful brush of lips at her temple, her cheek. Ash drew back enough to meet her gaze—dark eyes soft as his smile. "Kip's coming."

"Oh," she breathed in disappointment.

Ash dipped down to kiss away her pout. "Later," he whispered. "Can we talk?"

"Later," she agreed. Given everything going on at home, Tami knew she'd have a lot of explaining to do. Hopefully, the particulars wouldn't scare him off.

21

SEEING THINGS

Joe took to the orchard long before sunrise, hoping to reclaim some scraps of normalcy. If he could find them. Last night, Melissa had needed to go pick up Tami at the school, then have her checked for concussion at a clinic. For the first time in years, Joe spent the night in her room, holding tight to her hand and listening to a sleepy confession that didn't really come as a surprise.

Ash.

He didn't exactly mind that his sister was in love. Maybe it was a good sign that the guy had a tree-sounding name. Bound to one in the morning, kissed by another in the evening. There was symmetry there, and the balance made it easier for Joe to believe that both were meant to be.

If only he knew what it meant for him.

When Joe returned to the house for breakfast, Melissa and

Tami had already left together for work. Mom was reading to Biddie, and Dad was serving breakfast. So Joe dropped into the chair beside Grandad's and accepted a plate.

Halfway through the quiet meal, Mom called from the family room, "Reaver Foster texted. He'll be here soon, and he's bringing help."

"What kind?" asked Grandad.

"Another ward, I assume." Mom breezed in, depositing Biddie on Grandad's lap. "I'll put on a fresh pot of coffee."

Working together, she and Dad had the breakfast things cleared away and a fresh batch of applesauce muffins waiting when Jiminy rapped lightly on the kitchen door. "Sorry for dropping by so early."

Joe glanced at the clock. It was coming up on seven.

Dad handled the welcome and introductions, and Jiminy returned the favor, introducing a man with red hair. Heavy work boots and a flannel shirt gave him the air of a lumberjack. A big, friendly lumberjack whose freckled face never lost the hint of a smile, as if he was always glad about something ... or he always had a secret.

That notion stuck with Joe, which was probably why he took a longer look than he usually did with strangers. He couldn't have explained what he expected to find, exactly. The redhead seemed more suited to physical labor than Jiminy. His shirtsleeves were rolled up to the elbow, revealing fine red-gold hairs and freckles on his forearms. His lashes were pale, and his eyes were a clear brown. Sideburns left long. Strong jaw, clean-shaven. Eyebrows in motion—an expressive face.

He looked like a nice guy. He looked completely human.

So why was Joe so certain he wasn't?

Kip loved Tami's folks. Good people. But Joe had him a little worried. He'd zoned out during the introductions, then retreated to a corner, stealing glances and avoiding eye contact. At one point, Kip was sure he would escape, but Mrs. Reaverson got between her son and the door and gave him something to keep his hands busy.

Joe sat at the table, shelling a brimming bowl of mixed nuts.

It was like an open invitation.

While Jiminy answered old George Reaverson's querulous questions, Kip eased over and took the chair across from Joe's. Picking up one of the silver nutcrackers in the bowl, he joined the quiet labor.

Joe tensed.

Kip had always gotten along better with the rowdy kids, but he took a page from Ash's book and kept his big mouth shut. Quiet could be companionable. Silence could be shared.

Slowly, the man relaxed.

Interestingly, his calm affected Kip's mood, as if Joe were setting the emotional tone for the whole room. It looked like Jiminy had been right about this one. There was more to Joe Reaverson than met the eye.

He was definitely warded, but not in the same way as Tami. If Joe had been packing crystal, Jiminy would have pegged him in an instant. No, this was sigilcraft—strong, subtle. Kip could tell the ward was anchored somewhere over Joe's heart. A necklace?

A pendant?

At this range, Kip was catching an enticing array of emotions. And something that set his hairs on end, making him wish he'd chosen a closer chair. Curiosity was scurrying under his skin, enough to get him into *so* much trouble.

Take it slow. If things went the way Ash was hoping, Joe would be family. Plenty of time to get used to one another, to let trust take hold. But ... patience wasn't really Kip's area of expertise.

"I'm Kip."

The man stopped breathing. Kip was honestly concerned he was going to pass out.

"I'm ... Joe." His voice was no more than a whisper. "Am I supposed to ... umm ... isn't it polite to ask about your name?"

Cheese and crackers.

For a few seconds, the table played host to a mutual freak-out, but Kip thrust aside his battered ego to quietly ask, "How did you know?"

"Oh ... umm ... umm. I heard about it on the news, I guess. Maybe a show." He shrugged uneasily, eyes downcast.

Kip offered what he hoped was an encouraging smile. "That makes sense, but that's not what I meant."

Joe glanced up, dark eyes filled with uncertainties.

"How did you know I'm Amaranthine?"

His confusion couldn't have been more obvious. Kip actually checked his hands to see if his illusion was still in place.

"Not sure. Sorry." Joe cast a longing look at the door. "I won't say anything."

"Thanks for that. And it's okay if you don't know *why* you know.

You're new to this, right?"

Joe's hand wavered over the bowl of nuts. "Me?"

Kip hadn't meant to blurt it out like that. Tami's twin looked as if his worst fears had been confirmed. "Let's go back to your question," he offered gently. "Asking about someone's name is the commonest of common courtesies. It's how most conversations start if you're meeting someone from the clans for the first time. When two people trade names, it shows a willingness to explore the possibility of friendship. It's the beginning."

"Are you ... are you my sister's Kip?"

"Yes." He traced a sigil on the underside of the table, wanting a bit more privacy.

"Does she know?"

"She knows I'm her friend. I'm hoping that's enough to get us past the little awkwardness my species might cause."

Joe calmed noticeably. With a guilty glance in his mother's direction, he went back to cracking nuts.

"To answer, Kip is a nickname. I'm registered in all the usual places as Alder Kipling, but my true name is Alder Woodacre. My family has lived in Fletching since forever, so I'm a local boy, same as you."

"Woodacre is a clan name?"

"Yep." It was nice to see worry giving way to a spark of interest. Kip fanned the flame with more information than he probably should be sharing. "Woodacre is one of the smaller clans. Red squirrels, to be exact. Which means I'm nothing more than a cute rodent with a big appetite and a fondness for tall trees and acrobatic games of tag."

"And an elementary school janitor."

Kip kept his voice low, soothing. "That's right, and I'd do anything to protect those kids."

Joe toyed with a pecan. "Even human children are important to Rivven?"

Didn't that go without saying? Kip supposed there was no harm in offering some context. "Back when my grandparents were being born, our people were prolific. That was our be-fruitful-and-multiply phase, so twin births were standard, and families had to spread out to make room. We scattered, following the migratory paths of the animals under our protection into new territories and habitats. But during my parents' generation, everything tapered off. My mother has five siblings; my grandmother has twenty-eight."

"What happened?"

"No one knows for sure, but there's been plenty of speculation. Most say that our birth rate is tied directly to our function. Since we're long-lived, there are enough of us. But maybe that will change, now that you know we're here." With a small smile, Kip suggested, "Maybe humanity needs us."

Joe smiled a little.

"So ... kids. Amaranthine children are precious to the clans, but why stop there? As far as I'm concerned, every life is precious. I've always watched out for the kids at Landmark."

"I went there, you know. When I was little."

Kip lay his hands on the table, palm up. "All the more reason to try to get along, Joe."

He set his things aside and reached forward until their fingertips touched. "Jiro," he said. "Since we're being honest, my real

149

name is Jiro Matthew Reaverson."

"Jiro." Kip slid his hands forward so that their palms touched properly. "Do you think we can be friends?"

"Oh. I don't really ... umm ... I'm not good at friends stuff."

"What do you consider *friends stuff*?"

"Going places. Doing things." Color was rising in Jiro's face, as if he were confessing some terrible failing.

"Friends don't have to go far or do much of anything, not if they enjoy one another's company."

No good. Jiro had that cornered look again.

Kip changed the subject. "Getting back to my fondness for children, there's something I've been wondering." He pointed to the ceiling. "I've been hearing footsteps for a while now—small and light and up to mischief."

"I should just ... umm ... check."

"Don't bother. She went out the window a few minutes ago." Kip jerked a thumb toward the door. "Care for a walk? I could stand to stretch my legs."

A grand tour. The lay of the land. A look at the tree. It all sounded so reasonable when Kip announced they were going for a walk. Joe was a little shocked that his parents agreed so readily. Dad looked proud, like he was glad his son had finally made a friend. Mom even packed up half the muffins and a thermos for them.

It was embarrassing. He couldn't wait to get away from the house. Except that once he and Kip were alone, Joe realized that ... they were alone.

But Kip distracted him with questions—about the trees, the tractors, the outbuildings, the cider press. And then Kip begged for a muffin, which he devoured with a happy little moan of pleasure. Joe let him have all the muffins. Somehow, it reminded him of feeding strays.

"How did you know which way to go?" Joe had been hanging back, half a step behind Kip the whole time, yet Kip had taken Joe's usual route without hesitation.

"Some of it's scent. Some of it's basic tracking. But mostly, it's the resonance of Jiminy's wards. They're protecting that tree, for sure, but they're not hiding it yet. So it's easy for me to get a bearing."

"The little girl ... she's already snuck out two other times. She comes right back here." He pointed to where the golden leaves of Biddie's tree were visible.

"In every tree story I can think of, there's usually a little house or hut or traveler's shelter set up under its branches." Kip walked with a spring to his step. "Traditionally, the tree takes root right beside their twin's doorstep. Have you thought about building Tami a little place out here?"

"Not sure."

"A tree in speaking form can't roam. Don't let anyone take her from the farm. And by the same token, don't let anything happen to the tree. They're part of each other.

"Jiminy mentioned that."

"Good." Kip crouched at the edge of the oak glen, his gaze sweeping the circle. "Wow. You've got yourself a regular squirrel paradise here."

Joe stuffed his hands in his pockets and hunched his shoulders.

"I like it here, but I'm not sure I like the wards."

"Are you getting some kind of feedback from them?"

"Not ... umm ... not with my ears?" Joe gestured lamely. "The balance is off."

Kip studied him for several uncomfortable moments, then crossed to the closest of the stones Jiminy had set up the day before. Without ceremony, he picked it up and pocketed it. With an inaudible pop, the discomfiting pressure vanished. "Better?"

Joe nodded.

"We'll reset the line farther from the trees, and I'll make sure you aren't catching any dissonance. You're probably a crystal adept, so you're extra sensitive."

"Joey-boy!"

Biddie stood amidst her roots, waving.

Kip sidled up to Joe and whispered, "Pinch me!"

"What?"

"I've never *met* an Amaranthine tree before. They're straight out of my bedtime stories. For someone like me, she's a myth." He bounced in place and repeated, "Pinch me!"

Joe could only shake his head in wonderment. He'd always thought the inhuman races were more dignified. Kip was almost goofy. Was he being silly to put others at ease?

They strolled downhill, and Biddie met them partway. Kip crouched before her and offered his palms. "I'm Alder Woodacre, and I'm Jiro's friend. May I ask your name?"

"Chick-a-biddie!"

"Are you teasing me?" Kip asked, eyes wide. "That must be your nickname. I have one, too. I'm Kip."

"Kip!" she echoed. "I'm Chick-a-biddie, and I'm Tami's. This is Joey-boy. He named me."

Joe could feel a blush creeping into his cheeks. "We've been calling her Biddie."

"Then I shall call you Biddie," said Kip. "But we must learn your true name. May I explore your branches? I'm a good climber."

The girl poked Kip's nose and said, "Squirrel."

Kip tweaked hers and smiled. "Clever girl."

Joe said, "I thought you didn't know much about Amaranthine trees."

"I don't. But I have two eyes, a nose, and some really old friends." With a grin, he added, "Maybe I can figure out at least part of Biddie's true name. Would you like that, little lady?"

Biddie kissed his cheek. "Kip may climb."

Kip moved so fast, all Joe really registered was the soft thud of his boots, which he'd left behind. Moving closer so he could look up into the branches, Joe searched for some sign of the redhead. Branches swayed, leaves rustled, but he couldn't tell where Kip was.

When his neck began to ache, Joe spread his jacket and lay on the ground, arms folded behind his head. The slope was only a little damp from yesterday's rains. Biddie flopped beside him, her head resting on his shoulder.

"Are you happier out here?" he asked.

"Happier with you here," she replied.

"But happiest with Tami?"

"Yes!" She curled against him. "Tami and Joey-boy."

"Me, too? Even though I'm not your twin."

"You are Tami's twin. Biddie knows." She nuzzled his cheek.

"Love you, Joey-boy."

It put Joe more at ease, knowing that Biddie acknowledged his birthright. He wanted to fit into the new balance, assuming they could find it. He shyly murmured, "Love you, Chick-a-biddie."

She giggled, her gaze fixed on the overhead branches. "Kip is nice."

There was no denying that. "He's one of Tami's good friends."

"And yours?"

Joe wasn't sure about that, so he offered a cautious, "Maybe?"

"I heard that!"

Kip swung into view, hanging upside down from a branch. Or ... was he actually standing on the underside? Joe tilted his head to one side, trying to make sense of their gravity-defying guest.

"We're more than maybe-friends," Kip released the tree, turning his body and landing lightly beside them. "Jiro and I have traded names, and that's as good as a bond."

"Biddie, too?" asked the girl.

"You bet," Kip promised with a wink. "But I'm very curious, Jiro. Have you ever seen strange things while you're out in the orchard?"

Joe sat up and eyed the redhead, whose hands were clasped suspiciously, as if caging something. "Just normal stuff."

Kip's expression turned thoughtful. "You've been here your whole life."

"Since I was born. This is Grandad's farm, and he grew up here."

He nodded. "Then it makes sense that you wouldn't know otherwise."

"What do you mean?"

"Your *normal* is pretty special." He eased to the ground. "As

154

a for instance, what kinds of critters flock around when you're working out here?"

Joe's heart beat a little faster, but he repeated, "Normal stuff. Birds and things."

"Ever try to look them up at the library? Find out their proper names?"

He knew what Kip was getting at. The things he saw, the strange and beautiful creatures that no one else seemed to notice. This person knew about them, too. Joe slowly shook his head. "I made up stuff. Gave them nicknames."

"This place has become an Ephemera sanctuary, and the ones I've encountered are practically tame. Take this little guy." Kip opened his hands, revealing one of the gem snakes. This is a prismatic midivar, and they are getting increasingly hard to find. They're supposed to come in all seven colors, just like a rainbow. I've already spotted three diff–"

"Eight," Joe interrupted, taking the sapphire gem snake, which wove between his fingers. "We have eight colors."

Kip counted off on his fingers, rattling off seven colors and arching his eyebrows questioningly. "And ...?"

"Maybe white doesn't count as a color. That one's probably albino." He lifted the little creature, which was sort of like a snake with dragonfly wings, and asked, "Midivar?"

"Good. If you want, I can teach you more names. Better yet, I'll sneak you a book. Then you don't have to wait around for my days off.

Joe saw his smile reflected in eyes with slitted pupils and quickly looked away, only to notice Kip's feet. They're weren't anything like human feet. Paws with claws, thickly furred.

"Too soon?" Kip asked. "I can hide the truth if you're not ready for it."

"It's okay. I'm not scared." He just wasn't ready to look up.

"It's not a very big change, Jiro," he coaxed. "Hardly anything at all. I'm still Kip."

Joe's gaze darted skittishly over Kip's features. Same freckles. Same pale lashes. Same little smirk. But his ears came to points now, like all the Rivven on television. It was almost anticlimactic. "So you're part squirrel? I mean … you change into a squirrel?"

Kip said, "I'm an Amaranthine from one of the squirrel clans, and in truest form, I look like a squirrel. This is my speaking form. I use simple illusions to look like a human and pass myself off as one."

"Do you like being able to become a squirrel?"

"Honestly? I like to talk, so I hardly ever change."

"Oh." Maybe it had been rude to ask.

Watching him closely, Kip continued, "I'm relatively young, so my truest form isn't terribly large. Well, big for a squirrel, of course, but we fall on the small side of the spectrum."

Joe was picking up on something, and he dared to give it voice. "Are you embarrassed about being … little?"

"Are you asking me to show you?"

"Yes?"

Kip's smile had a hint of fang to it, and the finger that tapped Joe's nose was tipped by a claw. "Don't tease," he ordered, and then he dropped to all fours.

22

CHEEKY BEGGAR

Something indefinable swelled like a song that Joe couldn't quite hear, touching off a case of gooseflesh. Light diffused, dazzling his eyes, and when the need to squint passed, Kip was gone. No, not *gone*. He'd changed.

Large eyes peeped out from under the edge of a puffed tail, and Joe's nervousness disappeared. He'd seen documentaries where Rivven transformed into massive beasts, but this squirrel was no bigger than the dwarf goats in their petting zoo. Only rounder, softer, and possessing an undeniable force of personality.

Biddie laughed and rushed to pet the oversized squirrel.

Joe was pretty sure this was a breach of etiquette, but Kip leaned into her touch. He watched them with a twinge of envy. Suddenly, Kip's tail flashed under Joe's nose—ticklish and taunting.

He extended a hand.

Sitting back on his haunches, the squirrel met his gesture with a clever paw, which fit neatly on his palm. And then Kip crowded close, pulling himself up Joe's shirt and butting him under the chin. Joe's arms quickly came around for support. The red fur was plush as a kitten's, and there were whiskers tickling everywhere the squirrel's twitching nose touched.

"Soft," Joe whispered.

Biddie heartily agreed.

He settled himself more comfortably, crossing his legs to cradle the squirrel who rubbed their cheeks together affectionately. Joe had always liked animals. He chuckled and mumbled, "Gosh, you're adorable."

And then he remembered who he was holding. He froze, face aflame.

Kip's tail twitched into a question mark, and his eyes blinked.

Joe could have sworn the squirrel fluttered his lashes. Then those delicate paws latched onto Joe's ears, and Kip placed a fuzzy kiss on his forehead. Draping his forelegs around Joe's neck, he sagged against his chest and chirred softly. It was a little like purring.

Biddie said, "He likes it."

"I guess he does." Joe stroked red fur and marveled at how light Kip was. Following Biddie's lead, he tugged at tufted ears and played with the pads on one forepaw. And tried not to think about the fact that he'd have to look this man—person—in the eye later.

The sun climbed, and Joe relaxed. Having an animal lolling blissfully under your hands might just be the best cure for stress. For the first time in a while, Joe felt calm, balanced.

And then the squirrel roused itself enough to change positions, scooting so he was sitting between Joe's legs, slouching back into his chest. That's when Kip changed, leaving Joe cradling his speaking form.

He jerked his hands away.

But Kip grabbed his wrists, wrapping them back around his chest in a loose embrace as he slumped further. Eyes closed, a smile on his upturned face, he said, "One of the hardest parts of living away from the enclave is this sort of thing. Touch is a huge part of Amaranthine culture, and I never get enough."

Joe didn't know what to do.

A clawed hand patted his arm. "Don't be embarrassed, Jiro. I've always been a cuddler."

"I'm … not."

"Figured that out. Should I switch back?" Kip tipped his head back, looking at him upside down. "It's all the same to me."

Was it the same? Joe looked away, then closed his eyes for good measure. Trying to ignore the shape of the person sprawled against him, he searched for the sense of calm and found it waiting. It was peaceful, patient, yet somehow playful. Separate and strange, yet a safe place to linger. Tilting his face toward the sun, Joe stopped thinking about much of anything.

Biddie flung herself across Kip's midriff, and he exhaled on an *oof.* "Let's get situated. No sense breaking my tail or Jiro's back."

They stretched out side-by-side, still partly on Joe's spread jacket, with Biddie wedged between them. Joe stubbornly clung to that peaceful feeling and let his mind drift. He'd barely slept last night.

"Jiro?"

He stirred and hummed.

"What do you call that one?"

Joe opened his eyes and followed Kip's pointing finger to one of the little nut-brown birds. "Flutter-nuggets."

"I like it." He shifted slightly, indicating a tangled knot that drifted harmlessly past. "How about that?"

"Umm... I've been calling those air ribbons. What are they really?"

"Your air ribbons are juvenile gossameer, and the flutter-nuggets are dun nippets. But I'm totally calling them flutter-nuggets from now on."

Joe thought it was better, too.

Kip's voice came again. "Jiro?"

"Hmm?"

"May I see what you're wearing around your neck?"

Joe turned his head toward Kip. "I'm not wearing anything."

Rolling onto his side, Kip said, "There must be something. Your sister has that necklace she never takes off."

"I don't."

Kip's brows drew together, and he pointed to Joe's chest. "What's here?"

"Nothing?"

"You're warded, Jiro. I can tell that much. I don't suppose you'd be willing to take off your shirt for a second?"

Joe sat up and slowly unbuttoned his overshirt, then untucked the white undershirt. Kip pushed to his knees and sat back on his heels, watching closely. Self-consciously pulling the T-shirt over his head, Joe hunched his shoulders and waited for Kip to admit his mistake. There was nothing there. So why was Kip staring?

"You've been sealed," Kip announced. "There's a sigil over your heart. Really complicated, really powerful."

Still seeing nothing, Joe rubbed his hand over his chest.

"You know, Tami's ward is really, really strong, but this is ... epic levels. Yet you're still attracting Ephemera. Could be the seal is wearing off." Kip's eyes widened. "Or it's no match for you."

Joe moved to put his shirt back on, but Kip waved his hands. "Hang on. I might be able to figure out what's up, but I'll need to be touching you. How about I change back into truest form? You can hold me and pet me like earlier, which should get me close enough. All you have to do is relax. Stay calm. Is that okay?"

"I guess?"

"You're giving me permission to touch?" The redhead leaned closer. "If you're not comfortable, it can keep. I mean, I'm *good*, but there are plenty of others who are better, and if you're a beacon ... well. Twineshaft himself may want a look."

A beacon. Joe was already shaking his head. "I don't want that."

Kip hesitated. "I could be wrong. Want me to go ahead and check it out?"

"Okay."

"Really, Jiro. Try to relax."

"Okay," he repeated. Even though he was very much afraid that Kip was right.

But then the redhead swore softly, and the rumble of a tractor reached Joe's ears. The big one they used for hayrides. Grandad was bringing Jiminy, and the wards were down, and Kip had a job to do.

Scrambling into his shirt, Joe whispered, "Don't tell anyone about ... me."

"Likewise." Kip ventured, "Want to meet up later? Like, *late* later? I could come to your room, or you could meet me in one of the barns."

"Yeah. I … umm … yeah."

"Shh, calm down," Kip pleaded. Joe's hands were shaking so bad, Kip had to button his shirt for him. "I've got you. Nice and easy."

"I'm scared."

Kip pulled him into a hug. "Nothing to fear from me or maybes. You're one of my Landmark kids, remember? Even though you're technically an alum, I'll still do anything to protect you."

Hiding his face against Kip's flannel-covered chest, Joe took several deep breaths, as if drawing strength from someplace else, someone close. Yes, Kip was strange, but it was also a relief to have someone to rely on.

As of today, courage came with freckles, russet fur, and a teasing hint of nutmeg.

23

A BETTER CLAIM

When Melissa finally made it through the doors of Founders Coffee, Rook was waiting, ward in hand. He pressed the sigil-stamped disk into her palm and pulled her into the nearest alcove before folding her into a lengthy embrace. She wasn't sure how to interpret his greeting. Had he been worried for her? Was something else amiss?

"I'm so proud of you." Rook gave her an extra squeeze. "You answered Naroo-soh's call, and so you were there in your family's time of need. How are your relatives?"

Melissa quietly basked in Rook's approval. "Faring well, but full of questions."

"And the imp?"

"At times, she seems very old and very wise, but she has the appearance of a small child. I can't shake the idea that she's both fragile and vulnerable."

163

"Trust Jiminy to do his part." He leaned back to get a look at her face. "I heard you worked well together."

She didn't like his leading tone. "Are you matchmaking? Because I don't want or need ...."

"Hush." He bumped noses with her. "I'm only glad the two of you are cooperating. You are dearer than any of the possible futures you represent."

Melissa's frown deepened.

"It's not me," Rook soothed. "But a pack—especially its alpha—looks to its needs."

"Doon-wen?"

Rook said, "He wants to talk to you."

She couldn't exactly refuse. "After my shift?"

"Now." Rook chuckled. "You needn't look so worried. My brother can be forceful, but he'll be sympathetic to your priorities. His have defied tradition often enough."

Melissa loved Rook. She wanted to stay with the Nightspangle wolves, to be welcomed, to contribute to the enclave community, maybe even to help them expand their territory to Red Gate Farm. And to find a Kith partner. The only way she could do any of that was to find favor in Doon-wen's eyes. He was their alpha. He called the shots.

She drew herself up, ready to fight for all the things she could so easily lose.

Somehow, Rook understood. He set her at arms' length. "This isn't a battle, Melissa. Doon-wen is not an obstacle. He can and will be your best ally."

"But he doesn't *know* me."

"True does, and he would do anything to please her." Rook turned her and gave her a small push toward the back. "Take heart. My brother was *delighted* when you complimented his coffee. That's put you on the highest of high grounds."

Melissa rolled her eyes at the weak pun, but she hoped he was right. Making her way behind barriers, she drew herself up and whispered, "Lock and load."

Melissa's search for Doon-wen ended in his private Kith shelter, where she found a second wolf, a size or two larger than True, curled around her in the mounded hay and dried herbs. The big male had the Nightspangle coloring—inky black, tipped with a reddish color that gave their wolves a distinctive sheen.

He opened his eyes.

She wavered uncertainly. "Sorry to disturb you. I was looking for ...." Melissa trailed off because there was something unsettlingly familiar about this wolf's shrewd gaze. She ventured, "... for you?"

True's ears twitched, and the she-wolf licked her companion's jaw. He nuzzled her, rose to his considerable height, and transformed.

Melissa had found Doon-wen Nightspangle formidable enough in a suit. The wildly powerful predator before her was an unreckonable force. She shifted into a submissive stance so fast, she lost her balance, landing on her backside.

He was coming closer, and he looked unhappy. She was

embarrassed, even ashamed. Her face burned, and her eyes followed suit. What kind of battler was she?

"Melissa." Doon-wen crouched, balancing effortlessly on the balls of his feet. "Breathe."

She gasped for air and apologies.

His own posture shifted, and her awareness of him faded somewhat. As if he'd put away a little of his wildness, out of consideration for her. She knew the scope and strength of Rook's presence, but his older brother towered over him in terrifying ways.

No wonder they considered her father brave for calling Doon-wen *Daddy*. Melissa wouldn't have dared. "Sorry."

"What are you apologizing for?"

Melissa could have given him a list. For losing her nerve. For falling apart. For being afraid. But his senses were better than her instincts. He already knew. So Melissa rearranged her limbs, crossing her legs and sitting straighter. "I apologize for my lack of trust."

He huffed again. "Even those who know me well are wary."

"Rook respects you. True missed you."

Doon-wen matched her posture, sitting close enough to loom. He was big, and he exuded none of Rook's gentleness. Traces of resemblance were there, but it was like comparing a deep, calm pool with the plummeting roar of a waterfall.

He said, "Rook adores you. True accepts you."

Melissa felt the weight of those compliments and rallied somewhat. "You wanted to see me, sir?"

"Regarding the proposed enclave. How would you describe the territory that encompasses the Amaranthine tree?"

"Green." And since that was meager praise, she pulled out her phone to show him some of the photos she'd snapped for Magda. "The orchard is extensive, but it only accounts for half of their land. I think Uncle George has been planning for an enclave all along. Did Jiminy mention that there's a circle?"

"Repeatedly." He stopped her at one she'd taken from atop the roof outside her bedroom window. "They are willing to host wolves?"

"Yes." Melissa touched his arm. "When Jiminy mentioned the pack, Uncle George immediately asked for an allotment. You are both wanted and welcome."

"I will need to see and sense and run and rove for myself. Learn the bounds and add my mark. Test the mettle of your kin, to foster the necessary trust." Doon-wen's gaze lifted to hers. "To stay within the bounds of current laws, I have need of a reaver escort."

"Take me." She set aside her phone and offered her hands.

His touch was light as his tone. "True would like nothing better. Have you need of a pack?"

Melissa glanced at the dozing she-wolf and back. The terms had changed. "Sir?"

"Rook hints. True rants. But neither will tell me all I need to know in order to pick up the scent I need." Doon-wen's hands closed around hers. "Show me the trail. Guide my courses. While I would foster you for your father's sake, True wants a closer claim."

"What are you asking for?"

He shook his head. "Ours is more of an offer."

Melissa found herself wishing Jiminy was there to interpret. "*Ours*," she echoed cautiously. "Do you mean you and Rook ... or the Nightspangle pack?"

Doon-wen said, "True and I."

"Is she your Kith?"

His nostrils quavered. "I suppose you could put it that way."

Was he annoyed? This was going poorly. Melissa's hands fumbled toward apology, but he cut her off with a huff.

"True is my bondmate."

"I'm sorry. I guess I assumed she was Kith."

Doon-wen's expression didn't change. "She is."

Melissa opened her mouth, then closed it again. The leader of the Nightspangle pack had chosen a wolf for his mate. A sentient wolf, to be sure, but Kith couldn't take speaking form. Was this what Rook had meant by defying tradition?

Finally, she managed, "Nobody told me."

"*I* am telling you."

Melissa really wanted to know their story, but she couldn't bring herself to ask Doon-wen something so personal. She hadn't even asked him about his name. Yet he and his bondmate were making some kind of offer.

Within his grasp, her fingers curled into uncertain fists. "Please, sir. I'm not sure if we're talking about my job, the proposed enclave, my duties as a reaver, or ... or what."

Doon-wen pressed his thumbs into her fists, uncurling her fingers and kneading her palms. "Why do you withhold yourself from marriage?"

He'd changed the subject again? This had better not be a matchmaking session. But Melissa preferred to set the matter straight. She gave him the short version. "I never met anyone at academy who was interested in more than my rank and designation. Rather than entering a pragmatic contractual arrangement in order to produce the requisite three children, I hope to secure the lifelong love and loyalty of a Kith partner."

"You don't want children?"

She fidgeted. "I suppose. I mean, I intend to do my part. But I don't like to think about going through all of that alone."

Doon-wen frowned. "You would have a husband."

He was thinking like a wolf. "Reaver families aren't like a pack. I barely know my biological father. Mom contracted with him to meet her quota, but they never lived together."

A growl rumbled between them. "I did not raise Chris to treat the bonds of blood so lightly."

She wanted to defend him, if only because she'd never expected anything more from the man. Most of her friends at academy came from similar circumstances. "He made sure I knew how to reach him. He made sure I found my way here."

One large hand cupped her cheek. "So you could gain what he could not supply."

Truly? Melissa thought Doon-wen was giving her father too much credit. But she couldn't bring herself to contradict the wolf any more than she could look away.

With a parting caress, he stood and pulled her to her feet. Keeping hold, he drew her over to True, who lifted her head, ears pricked. Doon-wen adopted a respectful posture and addressed his bondmate. "You were right. Like the Nightspangle pack, who remember the songs that bring the stars near, I cannot resist the cry of her heart. Here is one who values love and loyalty. Shall we nurture her hopes together?"

True rolled her eyes and growled. Not in grumbles and snaps, but in something akin to exasperation.

Doon-wen muttered, "Yes, I *know* it was your idea. I only wanted to give our offer a touch of formality."

He guided Melissa to a seat between True's forepaws. When he joined her, he startled her by hauling her onto his lap.

"I *know* she is not a child, but I would do the same for Chris or Ash or *any* of ours." Doon-wen huffed and asked, "Are you discomfited, Melissa?"

"Less than I might have been. Rook likes this for tending."

The hint of a smile tugged at Doon-wen's lips. "If you will entrust yourself to my brother, my bondmate, and me, we will foster you. In becoming a member of our pack, your only obligation will be to us."

"Like Jiminy?"

"Precisely."

Melissa had to ask. "Are you doing this for him?"

Doon-wen leaned back and looked up. "I am doing this for True."

Smiling in spite of her suspicions, Melissa reached up to stroke the she-wolf's face. "Are *you* doing this for Jiminy?"

"She says she is looking out for our cubs." A mellowness entered his tone—paternal, proud. "Not many days remain before this litter makes its way into the world."

Really, Melissa couldn't tell. She patted the Kith. "No wonder you wanted him home."

The she-wolf grumbled.

Doon-wen boosted her to her feet and stood, circling around to kneel at True's side. "Here. Give me your hand."

Melissa knelt with him, and he pressed her more firmly into True's side than she would have dared.

"We aren't hurting her," he promised. "Here … and here. This is the curve of a rump, and their sibling is tucked close. Feel that?"

"Yes," she whispered in wonderment. "How many cubs?"

"Three."

Swallowing against a wistful wanting, Melissa said, "Congratulations. To both of you."

"Thank you." With his gaze firmly averted, Doon-wen asked, "May I see your assessment folio?"

Such a request coming from an Amaranthine was considered a compliment. A higher one than she'd offered. Stroking through True's thick fur, Melissa said, "On one condition."

Doon-wen flicked his hand, inviting negotiation.

"Will you tell me about your name?"

24

NESTING INSTINCTS

Ash was beginning to wish he'd called in sick. As much as he loved his job, Kip's absence cast a pall on the school day. No surprise. It wasn't as if he took his best friend for granted. Ash knew better than anyone how much Kip took on. No, the source of his malaise wasn't the change-up in their usual routine—even though same-old, same-old was his preferred order of business—but in Kip's destination.

Red Gate Farm.

Jiminy had asked for help warding Tami's home. Which could mean anything or nothing, if not for the family's telltale surname. Especially if you reckoned in the family jewels. That necklace. Kip figured that Tami had been heavily warded from a very young age. An unregistered reaver. Which could mean anything or nothing.

Or everything.

Ash ran a rag over his squeegee and hung it from the hook on his belt, moving along to the next set of windows. Was *that* the reason for Tami's appeal? Had his Amaranthine half been subconsciously picking up on some quality of soul, stirring his appetite?

No. At least, Ash seriously doubted it.

He'd been around more than his fair share of reavers—male and female—and none of them appealed to any kind of baser instinct. Ash didn't go in for tending, didn't crave it the way Kip did. So Tami interested him for simpler reasons. She was his choice.

And he'd never felt more vulnerable in his life.

Maybe it was time to listen to Kip, to call in Cyril, to talk to Rook.

Shaking out his rag, he swiped at a lingering streak and stared unseeing at the brilliant blue showing through patchy clouds. He needed to tell Tami. Soon. Before his secret came out another way. Before the reavers made other plans for Tami, ones that didn't involve the confused pinings of an unacknowledged crosser.

Once Tami was back, they'd talk.

Even though his pledge would likely shatter him. The handful of decades would pass, and her human life would fade, and he would be alone with his grief.

If he survived the sorrow, it would probably be thanks to Kip.

But he was getting ahead of himself.

She might reject him as a monstrosity. The reavers might find out and make him a test subject … or a celebrity. The clans could object. Questions of parentage might arise. And even if, by some miracle, Tami embraced the whole of him, his desires might doom her. A child of mixed heritage—surely even one with quarter blood—often ended their mother's life when making their way into the world.

Ash's hand wavered and fell to his side. It was like he'd told her last night. "I shouldn't."

He'd been afraid to tell her why.

Still was.

"I shouldn't," he repeated. Returning his squeegee to its place, he touched the blue paperclip at his collar and whispered, "But I still want to."

He plodded through empty halls toward the security of the janitorial closet to stow his supplies, trying to figure out the best way to steer a conversation along the perilous courses he would need to navigate.

Like not officially existing.

Like being older than America.

Like having a wingspan.

"*There* you are!"

Ash started and whirled, wincing when a backward step turned into a crush of unseen feathers against the janitorial closet door. "Tami! What are you doing here? You should be … home."

Except Kip was at her home. So maybe it was better that she was here.

Fumbling behind for the doorknob, Ash sought retreat. Times like this, when he couldn't lift his wings high and out of the way, he felt crowded, cornered. A flash of uncertainty showed in Tami's lovely blue eyes, and Ash watched her gladness dim into something guarded. His fault. Batting aside old habits and necessary caution, he glanced down the hallway, grabbed her wrist, and tugged.

She followed.

Wrapping one arm around her, he reached out with the other, shutting the door. Her hands settled against his chest, where his heart was hammering. "You shouldn't be pushing yourself," he said, gruffer than he intended. He slipped his fingers into her hair, searching for the knot. "Does it still hurt?"

"I'm fine. Don't fuss."

But he couldn't stop for all the same reasons he should. This was preening.

She was smiling, and there was an expectancy to the tilt of her chin.

Ash bowed to her wish and his want and touched his lips to hers. This time, there was no hurry. Slowly, softly, they explored their mutual attraction, and Ash liked what he found. It was as if his two halves stopped pulling against each other, for they both agreed that Tami was exactly what he needed.

Her interest was straightforward, and he detected an underlying impatience that sent his blood racing. As kisses deepened, he stumbled into a more intimate connection, touching the beauty behind the amethyst wards.

She weakened his knees, strengthened his need, and left him surer of himself than he'd ever been before. There were so many things Ash needed to tell her, but only the essential one made it into the open right then. "I love you."

"I'm making the call," warned Kip.

Ash barely heard him. The room was all wrong somehow. Why

had he never noticed how wrong it was? He pulled his mattress through the room, angling it across one corner, and shoved their battered sofa into line opposite. Stealing its cushions, he barricaded the third side.

"Want my mattress, too?" asked Kip.

Without a word, Ash ransacked his best friend's area, closing off a rough circle with the second mattress. But what about sharp edges, hard corners? And there were too many fragile things lying about.

Kip backed toward the front door. "Calling. Now."

Toting anything glass to the nearest closet, where it wouldn't be in the way, Ash discovered a fresh supply of soft things. He dragged out sweatshirts and flannel, extra blankets and the spare pillows. The bathroom yielded towels, washcloths, and a plush rug. He was still mounding and amending when Kip's voice preceded him back inside.

"... actually, yeah. Now would be good. The sooner the better."

Ash rummaged for dishtowels, disgorged a tissue box, and wished there was more blue.

Then Kip was in front of him, gripping him by the shoulders, and Ash noticed a generous amount of blue in the plaid of his shirt. He tapped a claw against the top button. "Can I have this?"

"Yeah, of course. But not this second." A gentle shake. "Ash, what's going on with you?"

"I love her."

Kip's expression softened. "Yeah, I know."

"I told her."

His best friend nodded. "That must have made her day."

Ash shook his head. "That's the *only* thing I told her. She doesn't know about ... about me."

"Okay, okay. So you left out a few details." Kip reached up, placing big hands on restless wings. "But she must have responded favorably. Her scent's all over you, and you obviously didn't spend a whole lot of time chatting."

"No. Yes." He leaned into Kip. "She's a reaver."

"Yeah, I figured." A soft sigh, a softer voice. "It's going to be okay, Ash. Better than okay."

Ash looked around the wrecked room and doubted him.

Kip took hold, framing Ash's face. "Listen up. There are things she hasn't found the words for either. Tami's not any old unregistered reaver. She's tree-kin."

He blinked. "Like ... like in the stories."

"Auriel and then some. So instead of tearing apart your old nest, maybe think about building a new one under her twin's branches."

"Joe's not a tree."

Kip kissed his forehead, called him an idiot, and patiently explained what was happening at Red Gate Farm.

"You've redecorated!"

Ash hadn't even heard a car. Then again, his adoptive father didn't necessarily need one. Neither did Rook. The big wolf stood just inside the door, surveying the room with eyebrows shot high.

"Tumbledown chic," continued Cyril. "A trifle makeshift, but possessing a charming innocence."

Disentangling himself from Kip, Ash stood wavering in the middle of his mess. Why had he thought this was a good idea? Their home was in shambles.

Cyril strutted along the edge of the room, eyes bright with interest. "Not a bad start, considering what you had to work with. I approve of the flannel. Used the stuff myself last time I was nest-building. Naturally, there was significantly more padding. And an extravagance of silk. My skin is *so* sensitive in this form."

Ash's chin trembled. An instant later, he was in Cyril's arms.

"*Not* a bad start, you hear me? I know many a mated pair who would blush to confess the hasty rummage and rustle that christened their nest. The flocks are teeming with impetuous souls." Cyril pressed their cheeks together and began a soft litany of bird noises in the back of his throat. Low and drawn out, like a coop filled with drowsy chickens. They weren't really words, but they still translated to comfort and concern.

This was how it had always been.

By some strange confluence of events, Ash had been taken in by the head of the Sunfletch clan. Why a fussy pheasant with glorious plumage wanted anything to do with a drab little half-crow had never been explained ... or questioned. Cyril was his first and fiercest advocate, with Rook as his second. The wolf's devotion to a surly, somber winged boy had earned him his pack nickname.

Today was proof that Ash hadn't outgrown his need for his kind-of father or his sort-of mother. He cast a pleading look at Rook.

The wolf waded through the tangle of textiles and lifted Ash. Mindful of his wings, he sat on the blanket-strewn floor.

Slouching into the lumpy slope of Ash's striped mattress, Rook settled Ash just as he used to. Chest to chest, so Ash could lay down his head and listen to Rook's heartbeat.

A low rumble started, as far from annoyance as a sound could be, and Ash went limp with relief, eyes tight-shut against the threat of tears.

Cyril knelt beside them. "I take it you're in love?"

"Maybe."

"Definitely. You're clearly nesting."

Ash rearranged the set of his wings. "All I did was wreck the house."

"You're a bit of a late bloomer, but we can't really judge your maturity by the usual markers. All it takes to initiate a mating dance is the right lady. Or ... gentleman?"

Across the room, Kip paled and waved his hands.

Rook asked, "Does she know?"

Even though confessing meant telling everything to the enclave's second-biggest gossip, Ash rambled on. Rook stopped him from time to time, gently prying for more information. Cyril interrupted whenever his behavior showed some avian instinct at work.

"But you're from a pheasant clan," Ash muttered. "Wouldn't it be different for crows?"

"When my black-winged son first entered the adolescent phases, I took the liberty of informing myself about pertinent rites and romantic inclinations." Cyril caressed his cheek. "Tonight, I will expose you to every delicious detail of my findings."

Ash looked to Rook, who chuckled. "Don't expect too much from me, boy. I never courted anyone, though I know more than my fair share of ribald songs about seducing moon maidens."

He was tempted to refuse both offers. This was embarrassing. He was well past the usual age for the handing down of mating lore. But ... what if there were things he didn't know he didn't know?

Ash turned to Kip for reassurance, only to realize that his best friend had gone.

25

JUMPING THROUGH HOOPS

ompany. How did one go about preparing for a secret guest? Joe didn't have a whole lot of experience with making friends, let alone entertaining them. Having a twin had always meant he didn't *need* anyone besides Tami. He'd spent high school on the fringes of her circle. Even Kip was one of her friends.

Were there things that reavers did for visiting Rivven? He'd only asked about greetings, but what came *after* the exchange of names?

Food. Based on Kip's appreciation of those muffins, food would go over well enough. Hadn't he even joked about his appetite?

Joe watched for his chance. After the dinner dishes were cleared away, when everyone else was watching television, he raided the pantry. With more stealth than was required to assemble meatloaf sandwiches, Joe filled a tray and sneaked it upstairs.

His room didn't have much—bed, desk, rug. Dad called it a

closet, but that was an exaggeration. His stuff fit fine. Still, the slope of the ceiling might cause trouble. Would Kip be too tall to straighten up?

Maybe that didn't matter, since he could just become a squirrel.

Red numbers flicked by on his ancient alarm clock, creeping toward the hour when Joe usually turned in.

They hadn't set a time.

What if Kip forgot?

Joe cast a sheepish glance at the food. Would it look like he was bartering for friendship? Maybe he was trying too hard.

Kip was a nice guy. Friendly. But Joe understood that nice guys had lots of friends. It was honestly embarrassing, knowing that if Kip dropped by to chat, it would mean more to Joe than it would to him. From what Tami had said, *Ash* was Kip's best friend, so the redhead wasn't looking for anything from Joe.

He'd probably offered to help for Tami's sake.

But even if Joe was simply on friendly terms with the squirrel-person, he'd be glad. Why was he even worrying about this? Joe stared at his hands while searching himself. Maybe it was Kip's promise of safety. That had been reassuring. Especially in the face of looming change.

Their farm might become an enclave.

All of them would need to learn about crystals and packmates and the sorts of things that came with being a Betweener.

And if he was a beacon, they'd surely come for him. Weren't two of the Five married to beacons? There might be special rules for those rarest of reavers. Would they force him to leave his home?

Joe's melancholy reverie was interrupted by a soft tapping

against glass. His window was a smallish square, no sash or slider. Undoing the catch, the entire pane swung inward on its hinges. "Hi," he murmured.

"Hi, yourself." Kip measured the frame with a bemused expression. "It's been years since I took truest form, but you've got me jumping through hoops."

"Sorry."

The redhead shrugged. "Clear a route. I'm coming through."

Joe quickly backed away.

Kip tumbled through the window in squirrel form, coming out of his roll in speaking form, one hand braced on the sharp angle of the ceiling. Jiminy winced. He'd been right about Kip's height. He had to keep his knees bent.

Actually, his knees were *showing*. As were his feet—or rather, paws. Was his whole lower body covered in fur? That didn't match what he'd seen on television. Then again, it wasn't as if Hisoka Twineshaft ever appeared in board shorts.

Most distracting by far was the squirrel tail, all billow and flick and fluff as it took up more space than either of them.

"Nice," Kip whispered. "I'm a big fan of close quarters. How likely are we to be discovered?"

"Not very. Unless Biddie gets curious."

"Okay if I work a little magic?"

"Sure." Joe watched in growing amazement as Kip's clawed hands wove through a series of patterns, etching glowing lines in midair—intricate, beautiful, and humming with purpose. "What's that for?"

"These are sigils. Some for illusions, some for barriers. In a sec, we won't have to whisper." With a crooked smile, he promised, "You could jump on the bed and no one would be the wiser."

Joe just nodded and waited for Kip to finish.

It was kind of pretty, the way shapes spun from his fingertips, orderly and extraordinary. They gleamed on walls, door, window, and floor.

"That should do it," Kip announced at a more normal speaking level. "Sorry to keep you waiting."

Joe wasn't sure where to look. Kip's short, loose pants and faded T-shirt made him look less like a lumberjack and more like a were-squirrel.

Kip blinked a few times, glanced down at himself, and groaned. "I always get comfy after work, and I didn't think. Want me to hide the strangeness?"

"I'll ... umm ... I'll get used to it." Joe gestured to the desk. "Hungry?"

"Starved!"

Then it was easy. Joe felt nothing but relief when Kip sat on the rag rug, leaned against the side of the bed, and signaled *gimme* with both hands. He ate with appreciative little groans, interspersed with compliments to the chef.

When Joe unzipped the little six-pack cooler, Kip's hand hesitated over a cola, then grabbed a beer instead. "Might need two," he said in an odd voice. "But stop me if I reach for a third."

"Is something wrong?"

Kip lifted his second sandwich as if making a toast. "Nary a complaint. You're a godsend!"

But Joe somehow knew better. "You're sad. I can *tell* you're sad."

The forced smile slowly faded, and for one terrible moment, Joe was afraid that the tears shining in Kip's eyes were his fault.

"Can you keep a secret?" Kip asked softly.

"Another one?"

He laughed a little. "I suppose you do have more than your fair share."

Joe felt all awkward about the sudden mood shift, but he nodded. "I won't tell."

Kip crammed the last of his sandwich in his mouth, chewed slowly, swallowed, and sighed. "Okay. Here's the thing. My best friend is in love with your sister."

"Umm ... that's not really a secret." Joe quickly explained, "Tami tells me stuff. She loves him back."

"Yeah. I know." Kip pulled his tail around. It was hard to tell if he was hugging it or hiding behind it. "Head over heels. Hearts and daisies. Cute as can be. But I didn't realize it would be this hard, watching him make an idiot of himself."

Joe wasn't sure what Kip meant, but the way he said it made it obvious that he and Ash were really good friends. It made him a little jealous. And then something that should have been obvious finally occurred to him. "Is Ash like you?"

"Yes and no." Kip gestured vaguely. "Those two *really* need to talk."

"He's Rivven?"

"Not my place to say. Also, not really the point."

Kip was avoiding eye contact, something Joe did all the time. Strange how something so small could make you feel both understanding and understood.

"I'm going to be happy for them ... eventually," Kip said. "But that doesn't really make my part in this any easier."

Now they were getting closer to the underlying sadness. Joe asked, "What's your part?"

"Heartbroken."

Joe blinked. "You're in love with my sister, too?"

Kip laughed weakly. "You're kind of an idiot, but that's okay. I clearly have a weakness for idiots."

And it clicked. "You love your best friend."

The redhead snorted. "Who doesn't? A friend loves at all times."

Fine. He could say it clearer. "You're *in* love with your best friend. With Ash."

"I take back the idiot remark. Compared to Ash, you're a genius." Kip tipped back the last of his beer. "He never noticed."

26

SQUIRRELED AWAY

Questions swarmed through Joe's mind, but he swatted them aside. None of them seemed even remotely appropriate in the face of Kip's heartache. So he handed him a fresh can and opened the tin that still remained on his desk.

"Mom made these with the nuts we were cracking earlier." Joe offered him one of the bite-sized tarts, all dark and sugary and rich with butter. "They're my favorite."

Kip popped it into his mouth and went for an appreciative sound, only it came out as more of a whine.

Joe pretended not to notice and passed him another. He couldn't think of anything else to say, so he just repeated, "I won't tell."

Tears slipped down Kip's cheeks.

Another tart found its way into his hand.

"Jiro, would you mind if...." He cleared his throat. "I really need to hold onto something for a little while, 'kay?"

"Sure."

Kip patted the floor at his side, and when Joe sat there, an arm draped across his shoulders. Turning slightly, Kip reached across Joe and linked his hands.

Joe sat very still in the circle of those arms, but nothing else happened. Just an additional closeness. Tami sometimes needed this from him. He'd always assumed they needed to touch because they were twins. They'd been teased for hand-holding all the way into their teen years. At home, nobody thought it was strange when they curled up together. Were Rivven the same, needing that extra connection?

Usually, Tami was the only one he wanted this close. Now there was Biddie. And Kip.

Joe reached up to feed Kip another tart. Then leaned into his side the same way Tami was always leaning into him.

"You're a good kid," Kip mumbled.

"I'm an adult." He pushed another tart into the teary-eyed squirrel's mouth. "I might even be older than you, in human years."

Kip hauled him snug against his side, wrapping his tail around them both. "You are *not* the first person to call my maturity into question."

His smile was soggy, but he was rallying. Joe rewarded his courage with another tart.

"I remember you, you know." Kip pulled up his shirt to wipe his eyes. "I was a janitor when you were at school."

"No," Joe countered. "Our janitors were two old guys."

"Yeah, that was us. You really hit it off with Ash. He was Mr. Black back then." Kip took a long swig of beer. "I remember you, your dad, your grandad. Ash and I have been watching over Landmark for a long, long time. I thought we'd go on like that forever."

Joe calmly played dumb. "You can't be a janitor anymore?"

"It was always him and me. Just us for so long." He emptied the second can and stared at it without seeing. "He doesn't need me the way he used to. The only person he can see right now is Tami."

"Sorry."

The end of Kip's tail fluffed into Joe's face. "Not your fault."

"I'm sad that you're sad."

"You really are a good kid." He helped himself to the last tart. "But enough about me. I'm here for you, and *this* is actually the right sort of close. You still want me to see what's going on under all your wards?"

Joe nodded. "Do I need to ... umm ... my shirt?"

"Nope, not for this. What I'm looking for isn't skin-deep." And Kip tipped his head to one side and closed his eyes.

He probably should have kept quiet, but Joe wasn't ready for a diagnosis. He blurted, "If I'm a beacon, will the reavers make me go somewhere else."

"It's possible." Kip opened one eye. "Unregistered reavers sometimes join the In-between, especially if they show a lot of promise. At your age, it's not like they'd send you to academy, but you'll need the basics of control. Best bet, you'd be assigned a mentor."

"So I can stay?"

Kip's other eye opened. "You know what it means to be a beacon?"

"Highest rank. Most presence or power or something." He fidgeted and quietly added, "And they're rare."

"That's about right, which is why offers will start arriving by the truckload."

"Job offers?" Joe shied away from the very idea. He was a farmer, not a reaver. He didn't want a position in the Office of Ingress or anywhere else.

"Jiro, you carry a rare and coveted bloodline. The offers I'm talking about will be marriage contracts and applications for paternity. The biggest stables will probably enter a bidding war over you." Kip glibly added, "Everyone will want a piece of you and your extra-shiny genetic potential."

Oh.

Oh, no.

Kip's eyes slowly widened. "Whoa, you are really freaking out here."

"I don't want to be taken from my home, and I don't want any kind of assigned wife." He grabbed the front of Kip's shirt. "I don't *want* to be a beacon."

"Calm down," It would be so much easier to slip past Jiro's seal if the man wasn't feeling threatened. Kip automatically pulled him close, then remembered how slow he should be taking things. "You want me to switch forms?"

"Umm ... later?" Jiro wasn't pulling away. "I might have questions."

Kip smiled past his emotional exhaustion. "Ask me anything, but not this minute. I need to focus."

Jiro nodded.

His eyes had barely shut when Kip felt a tentative touch along the sweep of his tail. Totally innocent. Oddly soothing. Sure, Jiro was pushing into personal territory, but Kip had barged into the guy's bedroom—snug as a squirrel's nest up under the eaves. They were past niceties.

And he was past that pesky seal.

On an intellectual level, he was celebrating his finesse, but most of the rest of him felt like all those times his mother had caught him with a paw in the cookie jar.

"Jiro," he whispered. "Please, calm down. Otherwise, this might get dangerous for me."

"I'm dangerous?"

Kip forced himself to back away from a feast bigger than Founder's Day and Thanksgiving combined. Firmly on the safe side of Jiro's wards, he met the young man's tense gaze and told the truth. "You're *beautiful*."

"A ... a beacon?"

"Without a doubt." Kip knew it wasn't what Jiro wanted to hear, but the man needed to know that this was a good thing. "I'm not experienced enough to guess your magnitude, but I know for certain you'd be hard for *anyone* to resist. Least of all me."

Jiro's brows drew together, and his shoulders slowly sagged.

"I know it's not the news you wanted, but we ca– "

"You don't ... umm ... it's only because ...?" The guy looked a little heartbroken himself. "Are you only being friendly because you can't resist?"

"Nooo! No, I *can* resist. I did resist!" Kip took Jiro by the shoulders and gave him a little shake. "I said it all wrong. You've gotta know I'd never cozy up to you just because ... you might ... feed me. Huh. Okay, even I don't believe that."

Jiro cracked a smile.

Right away, the whole mood of the room shifted, filled with a softer, more hopeful radiance. But it put all of Kip's hairs on end. Jiro wasn't only an unregistered reaver, he was an un*trained* one. This was why little reavers learned control from a very young age. Otherwise, they might unintentionally harm your average Amaranthine.

Not that Kip had ever been *average*. Kith-kin were nearly as rare as beacons. But Kip was no powerhouse. With Jiro, he was in way over his head.

Basics. Kip tapped Joe's nose, then tapped his own. "Lesson time."

"Okay."

"You are going to be popular once the clans catch wind of you. Anyone—and I mean everyone—is going to wish they were where I am right now. Because your soul is stunning, and touching it ...." He trailed his fingers through the air around them. "Bliss."

Jiro paled.

"I know you're uneasy about the reavers finding out, but they're your best protection. Only a reaver can teach you how to harness your soul. They can teach you how to defend yourself if anyone gets pushy. And you'll learn when it's appropriate to give us a taste." Kip hoped it didn't sound like he was fishing for another free meal. "I'd *never* just help myself, but I crave a reaver's soul just as much as the next clansman. It's called tending."

"I can give you part of my soul?"

Kip nodded.

"What do you *do* with it?"

"Savor it, I suppose. It's like dessert. I don't *need* it, but it's the best part of every meal."

Jiro asked, "Should I be disturbed that you're talking about eating my soul?"

"Maybe." Kip noticed with concern that he'd weakened the old sigil with his tampering. "We need to find someone with serious pull to protect your interests."

"You."

Kip understood the compliment. And the impossibility. "I'm nobody, Jiro. Just a small-town janitor whose best subject is still recess. You need someone with *clout.*"

"But you said you'd do anything for one of your kids."

"You're not a kid."

Jiro narrowed his eyes.

Kip's expression wavered. "Okay, there *is* something I can do. It's wretchedly old school, but it should work as a temporary measure."

"Thanks. Can we do it now?"

"We'll need to. You're expecting an allotment of wolves in the morning, and they're sharp. If you want to stay a secret, we need to act fast."

"Are you going to hide me with wards like Tami's? Do I need a special stone?"

"Just sigils. Lots of sigils."

Jiro asked, "And nobody will find out about me?"

"I can't promise that. Not universally. I mean, there are a lot of Amaranthine who are stronger than me. But I can make it a whole lot harder for them to notice you. And even if they do, I'll have made a prior claim." He cleared his throat. "Are you ticklish?"

The man raised a hand like a kid in class. "What do you mean by *prior claim*?"

Kip really kind of wanted that third beer now. And not for the usual reasons. "I need to create a series of overlapping sigils directly onto your skin. They'll bolster the existing seal while adding additional barriers—ones to keep you in, ones to keep others out. I'll anchor them to your own soul, which means they'll be incredibly strong. But you need to understand that the sigilcraft is mine. They'll carry my ... my signature. And according to the customs of my clan, that makes you mine."

"So it's a bond?"

"Sort of." He really wished a better idea would occur to him. "It does define a new relationship."

"Umm ... in what sense would I be yours?"

"My personal stash." Kip couldn't quite meet Jiro's worried gaze as he added, "My food."

27

ONE WAY OR ANOTHER

Tami woke before her alarm and immediately missed Biddie. The girl must have slipped out during the night. Abandoning the warm huddle of blankets, her toes brushed chill floorboards in their quest for her slippers. Tami pulled aside the filmy sheers and raised her shade to consider a sky that still showed stars. Mist clung to the orchard, and it wouldn't be much longer before frost added its bite. Biddie was probably back in the oak glen, which was both understandable and worrisome. Should a girl so small be out in the cold? Would she need warmer clothes, or were trees impervious to climate changes?

Every day brought more questions. Every answer proved how many more questions she hadn't considered. "I wish someone could tell me what questions I'm supposed to be asking."

She zipped through her morning routine, mentally reviewing her agenda for a meeting with Dr. Bellamy. The schools in their flagship alliance would be narrowing down their faculty lists, and he'd suggested coordinating their selections to optimize on the opportunity. *And* a team from the Office of Ingress would begin warding the school today, so her presence was absolutely necessary. Even though she'd rather stay home to meet the wolves Melissa and Jiminy were bringing.

So much was happening, and she couldn't be everywhere at once. She'd simply have to trust Grandad to do what was best for the family and the farm.

When Tami reached the kitchen, Grandad sat at the table, a cup of coffee before him. He asked, "Do you have time to talk?"

"I'd like that."

He waited until she poured her coffee and cut a slice of apple bread. After she sat, he said, "There are things you need to understand. About our family history."

"Shouldn't we wait for everyone else?"

Grandad knotted his hands together. "There are things *you* need to understand. *Only* you."

"All right. I get the impression that keeping secrets is a big part of being a reaver."

He smiled thinly, lowered his gaze to the tabletop, and spoke with surprising detachment. "Being a reaver is all about bloodline. My parents were nothing special—midranks at best—but they had good connections. They used them. Only it didn't work out the way they expected. In trying to improve their position in the In-between, they put themselves in something of a fix. They vowed out as quickly and quietly as they could."

Tami wanted to ask for more details, but this wasn't the right time. Grandad seemed to be working his way toward something that was either dangerous or illegal. Maybe both.

"Lisbet and I had different fathers."

She frowned. "I thought you were twins."

"*Everybody* thought we were twins. Truth is, Lisbet was tree-kin."

New terms kept cropping up. Tamiko patiently asked, "What does that mean?"

"My sister was born under special circumstances." Grandad rubbed at the side of his face. "So was I, for that matter. Mother managed to scrape together the paternity fee for a reputable stable, which is how we're kin to Melissa's people. Meanwhile, Dad contacted an old family friend and begged for help. They left together.

"Dad told me a little about his trip, but he never would say where he went. Only that when he came home, he was already carrying her. My folks went into seclusion after that. Twins, they told everyone. Fraternal twins."

Tamiko tried to make sense of what he'd said. "Your sister was adopted?"

Grandad shook his head.

"But you said your father brought her back from a trip."

"In a way." He pursed his lips, then spelled it out. "Mother gave birth to me. Dad gave birth to Lisbet. And like all tree-kin, she was born with a golden seed in her hand."

The pipes behind Joe's wall gave their usual morning shudder, so he knew his sister was in the shower. And that meant he'd overslept. He rolled over to check his digital alarm clock and got a faceful of fur.

Oh.

Right.

Kip.

Easing an arm over the tightly-curled squirrel taking refuge on his narrow bed, Joe fumbled along his bedside table, then blearily studied the time. It took a few moments to register that he wasn't late. Tami was up early. Had something happened?

A tufted ear tickled his chin. Whiskers twitched, and a small paw grazed Joe's bare chest. Where were his pajamas?

Oh.

Right.

The thing with the sigils.

He couldn't see much. Sunrise was a ways off. But he didn't need light to tell they weren't glowing anymore. Joe shimmied out from under his covers and tucked them around Kip, who didn't stir, even when the desk lamp switched on. With unaccustomed stealth, Joe pushed yesterday's shirt against the crack under his door. He didn't need Tami checking on him.

Avoiding the loose boards. Pulling fresh clothes from drawers. Tidying away empty cans and containers. He loitered until he heard Tami on the stairs, then counted to twenty before opening his door. There were no sounds coming from Melissa's room. There wouldn't be, though. She'd insisted on a night watch.

Joe studied himself in the bathroom mirror, twisting and

turning, but nothing looked different. Kip had explained as he worked through the night, teasing beautiful patterns out of thin air, tracing them onto bare skin. They were wards. And they meant that no one could sense his soul. Not easily, anyhow. So if possible, he was supposed to avoid contact with the incoming wolves. Especially their leader.

When Joe stole back to his bedroom, he found Kip taking advantage of the additional mattress space. He'd changed back into speaking form, curled on his side, hugging his tail to his chest.

Didn't he have work? Tami had joked about never managing to out-early the janitorial crew. And what about his friend Ash? Had Joe inconvenienced the both of them with his plea? Come to think of it, how had Kip arrived? Was the infamous Coach parked alongside the road, where Tami was sure to see when she left for work?

Joe gently touched Kip's shoulder. "Hey, there," he whispered. "It's morning."

Nothing.

"Kip?" He gave a squeeze, then a shake. "Time to get up."

The redhead slept on, breathing deep and slow.

Something stirred in the back of Joe's mind. What was that thing about Rivven sleep patterns? They could sleep for days, almost like hibernation. Was he going to have a squirrel in his bed for the rest of the week?

Joe took a firmer tone. "Kip, this could be bad. The wolves are coming. They'll be here in the house, remember?"

Still gone to the world.

Desperation made the necessary leap to inspiration.

Oh.

Right.

Food.

Still mindful of creaks, Joe opened the narrow door to the little-used back stairs, which led straight to the kitchen. They were steep and narrow, and the inside wall was entirely lined with shelves used for dry storage. When he and Tami were little, they'd considered this hidden passage through Mom's pantry to be one of the farm's greatest secrets.

A tiny flashlight hung from a nail just inside the door. Their cohort for infrequent kitchen raids, usually at Christmas, when tins of cookies lined the steps.

Halfway down, he caught the sound of Grandad's voice. Then Tami's. Were they having breakfast together?

Joe adjusted his plan, turning the narrow beam of his light on the shelves. Something here would probably tempt Kip. He was reaching for a box of graham crackers when he caught a thread of what Grandad was saying.

"... from the most famous of the moth clans. Dimityblest."

"I've heard that name. Aren't they clothiers?"

"That and more. My father's friend arranged everything. In less than a week, we were sworn out, swooped up, and sent here. My parents warned me never to speak of the life we left behind, but sometimes we would remember together."

Although he wasn't usually one to eavesdrop, Joe slowly lowered himself to a stair.

Tami murmured something too soft to hear.

Joe scooted down a few more steps and switched off his flashlight.

"Because reavers are meticulous when it comes to pedigrees. The truth would have come out. Our family was in trouble. Maybe even in danger."

"Why?"

"Apparently, there are only two situations that can lead to a tree-child being born to a male surrogate. Either one should have been impossible for a reaver in my father's position. Unless he was involved in the illegal trade of rare items … or a thief."

"Was he accused of wrongdoing?"

"No. And he liked to remind Mother and me that people were missing the obvious."

Tami said, "I'm sorry, Grandad. I don't know the same stories you do. What would people have accused Great-grandad of doing?"

"Eating forbidden fruit."

Joe heard his sister scoff.

"I'm only quoting the old songs. Trees would seduce passersby and feed them. Anyone who ate fertile fruit would soon discover they were pregnant." Grandad said, "That would mean my father broke into a heavily-guarded tree sanctuary and stole the life he carried."

Tami murmured a protest.

Joe eased onto the bottom step, not wanting to miss a word.

"The only other way was to consume a golden seed, and that would be an unconscionable crime. Because that would mean separating a tree-kin from their twin. And robbing them of a tree's blessing." Joe heard Grandad thump the table, rattling the dishes. "Dad never did such a thing! He was no thief, and he was no liar."

Tami's tone was soothing. "Did he tell you what happened?"

"Lots of times, and always with a look that was soft and warm and … just really glad." Joe could hear that remembered smile in Grandad's voice—hushed by awe, touched by wonder. "Your Great-grandad met an angel."

28

FLAGSHIP ALLIANCE

She was running very late. Buses were already unloading at the main entrance by the time Tami pulled into the only open slot in the staff lot—the one usually occupied by Coach. Did that mean Ash and Kip weren't here?

Checking the time, she forced herself to focus on meeting agendas as she hurried to the school door. Dr. Bellamy was the punctual sort, and she was scraping it close.

Tami was only two steps inside when she spied Ash loitering nearby, fussing with the spotless floor. Had he been waiting? Had he been worried?

Abandoning his janitorial equipment, he cut her off. He touched her cheek, checked the diminishing lump on the back of her head, and searched her face. "Can we talk?"

"I have a meeting." She pushed as much apology into her tone as she could. "Dr. Bellamy might already be here."

Ash's shoulders hunched, then relaxed. A slow-motion shrug that was hard to interpret. "Yeah. He is."

"Come find me later?"

"I'll do that."

She didn't like putting him off with another *later*.

Ash smiled faintly. "It's all right, Tami. There's time."

Taking him at his word, she hastened along the hall and into the main office. Flootie sang out, "*There* she is! And just in time. Break it up, gentlemen."

"What on earth?" Tami asked.

Dr. Bellamy and Harrison looked to be in the middle of a bizarre game of charades.

Harrison quickly explained, "He was showing me the steps to a folk dance."

"Just a little something I picked up during my travels." Dr. Bellamy gave a cufflink a twirl, then touched the elaborate knot of his tie. "Would you like to learn, my dear?"

Tami laughed. "If you want a dance partner, I recommend Kip."

"Oh?" Bellwether's president seemed pleased by the prospect.

"He lured Harrison into a tango."

"And I can vouch for his polka," said Flootie. "But he's off today. Harrison, you'd better save some stamina for recess."

"Yes, ma'am." Harrison bowed to their guest. "It was a pleasure, sir."

Dr. Bellamy cheekily dropped a curtsy. "Until next time, my good man."

Tami beckoned for him to follow her into her office. "I'm sorry for keeping you. Today's been a bit strange, but I have my notes ready. If you'll just ...."

"Principal Reaverson. Tami." He put a hand on her arm. "Would you be wholly devastated if we moved this meeting to a different venue?"

"What did you have in mind?"

"I took the liberty of reserving a private room at my favorite coffee shop. Everything is in readiness." He smiled disarmingly. "Will you indulge me?"

Tami couldn't very well deny the man. She owed Cyril Bellamy so much and respected him as both an educator and an administrator. So she gave in with grace and gratitude in equal measure. "Coffee sounds lovely. Let me get my things."

He insisted on driving, quizzing her all the way into Fletching about the Amaranthine staffers she was considering for Landmark.

"We need a librarian. When the last one retired, the school was forced to eliminate the position. Our library still exists, but it's a free-for-all in there. The interns help to shelve and organize books, but it's not the same."

"An obvious need. And your candidates?"

"The list they sent me has three dozen people, all from different clans, all willing to join our staff."

Cyril asked, "Need help narrowing the field?"

"Please." She patted her satchel. "There are resumes, letters of introduction, and even a short video from each. And I liked your suggestion of bringing in people who can rotate between our schools, developing programs for all grades."

"Art, music, languages, applied sciences." He drummed his fingers on the steering wheel. "We should consider basic courses on cultural awareness, etiquette, cooperation, collaboration. That sort of thing."

Tami made a note.

"*And* I've found an unexpected trove of resources. Ah, here we are."

He pulled into a reserved parking place beside one of the big, historic buildings on campus. Coming around to her side of the car, he opened the door for her. Tami gathered up her things and accepted his courtesy with mild exasperation. After working with Cyril for so many months, she was used to his artless of chivalry.

When he bowed her through the door to Founders Coffee, they were met by a tall African-American man, who guided them through a paradise of dark wood, rich aromas, and casual elegance.

"Your usual room, Cyril."

"Thank you, my friend." Bouncing lightly on the balls of his feet, Dr. Bellamy added, "Have you met Principal Reaverson? Tami, Lou is one of the owners of this establishment."

Lou took her hand in both of his. "Tami. I've heard nice things about you."

"Are you sure you can trust your sources?" She shot Dr. Bellamy a bland look.

The coffee shop owner laughed. "Cyril and I are old friends, but I was thinking of Melissa. She's becoming increasingly indispensable around here."

"Oh!" Melissa had always been a little vague about her part-time job, and Tami hadn't made the connection. "I don't think she's ever mentioned this place by name. It's a small world."

"Amazingly so." Still holding her hand, Lou asked, "What should I bring—coffee, tea, sweets, savories?"

Cyril ordered far too much, claiming, "The fare here is worth sampling. You'll thank me later."

Tami was used to humoring Dr. Bellamy's whims, just as she was sure his advice was good.

They made quick work of her agenda, especially when it came to weighing the advantages of hiring each potential staff member. By the time Tami selected the three Amaranthine who were the best fit for Landmark Elementary, she was confident in her decisions.

Since exploring differences was one of the goals of Spokesperson Twineshaft's initiative, Dr. Bellamy had suggested choosing Amaranthine who fit two simple criteria. First, they should not come from one of the predatory clans—*what big teeth you have*. Second, if possible, she should choose people who looked the least human.

Given the current climate, wolves were out of the question, even though it might have been nice to have a staff member with a tail. Instead, she'd chosen three volunteers who readily displayed their unique heritage with antlers, antennae, and fire engine red hair.

These Amaranthine were not in hiding. They were different, but that wasn't bad. And in becoming part of the Landmark family, these Amaranthine representatives would be able to gain the trust of the children ... and their parents.

"That's settled." She shook her head in awe. "How do you know so many little details about the different deer clans?"

"Oh, that? We were building our proposal for months," Dr.

Bellamy pointed out. "Such things require research."

"But I'm quite sure we didn't look into butterfly clans." She studied one of the attached photographs. "And how can you even *tell* that this person is from a woodpecker clan? All it says on his profile is *avian*."

Dr. Bellamy nibbled at a tea cake. "I suppose it's possible that I've heard his clan name before."

Tami didn't want to quibble, especially over something so small. But there had been so many small things in the last couple of hours. Almost as if Dr. Bellamy was dropping hints. "Are you leading up to something?"

"I suppose I am. How could you tell?"

"Nothing in particular." She toyed with her empty coffee cup. "Maybe all those months of proposal-building left me with some insights, as well. We're friends, aren't we?"

Dr. Bellamy seemed pleased. "I did promise you a treat." From an attaché case, he withdrew a sheaf of papers and presented them with his usual pomp. "Opportunities abound!"

Pamphlets. Brochures. Fliers. As Tami skimmed their contents, her excitement mounted. Amaranthine throughout the region had been appearing at state and county fairs, local festivals, and theme parks. There were also street performers who made the rounds of vacation spots and tourist centers.

"Many of their programs are perfect for schools." Dr. Bellamy tapped a glossy flier showing a family of minstrels in the traditional costumes of their clan. "They're making themselves available to schools who apply for Twineshaft's integration programs."

Tami whispered, "They'd come all the way here?"

"They *are* here. Or as good as. This sampling represents Amaranthine in easy traveling distance. If you invite them, they will come."

"The children would love this!"

"*And* their parents," said Dr. Bellamy.

"We could host regular programs! Invite the whole community!"

"Easily."

A uniformed team of Kith handlers who worked closely with police. Forest rangers who monitored wildfires with the help of an eagle clan. A group of jugglers and acrobats from a lion clan whose performers included two cubs not much older than Landmark's students. Folk singers who taught the traditional songs and dances of the cozy clans.

"This is new to me. What are the cozy clans?"

"Gentle countryside clans with a unique perspective because they've always lived close to humans. Mostly rodents and small birds, but many clans that watch over animals domesticated by humanity count themselves among the cozies." Dr. Bellamy was watching her closely. "Their customs are charming."

Tami sat back in her chair. "This is *amazing*. And so generous. I just hope we can present these programs responsibly, so the kids understand that the Amaranthine aren't here for our entertainment. Maybe if we balance off these programs with those by human and reaver guests? Or we could focus on groups who are already integrated, showing how our races can work together in fun and interesting ways."

Dr. Bellamy smiled. "A far-sighted view. I can only approve."

"If my perspectives have changed, it's thanks to you."

"Might I remind you, my dear lady, that *you* approached *me* with the plan that's led to our flagship alliance." He sat forward, then stood, beginning to pace. "Your vision has changed the future. Or at least *my* future. May I share a matter of some delicacy with you?"

Tami left off putting away her notes, giving Dr. Bellamy her full attention. She archly repeated her earlier question. "We're friends, aren't we?"

To her surprise, Dr. Bellamy came around to sit in the chair beside hers. Turned toward her, he said, "I have always known I would need to declare myself eventually, but the current confluence of events ... well! It would seem the time is now."

She adored this man. No one else in her acquaintance shared his enthusiasm for life or his robust vocabulary. But his wording made her a little uneasy—*declare himself*. Was he about to ask her out? That would be awkward.

"Spokesperson Twineshaft must be informed. This may affect his plans, as well."

Okay, she was out of danger. Tami was glad to have misinterpreted his turn of phrase. "Do you mean when we introduce the new faculty and staff?"

"No, it would be best if I came out *before* Dichotomy Day." He cocked his head to one side. "There. Have I shocked you?"

Tami hardly knew what to say. "Why would Spokesperson Twineshaft be concerned about your orientation?"

Cyril blinked.

Tami blinked.

"I have been entirely too circumspect. A longstanding habit, I fear. While I have no wish to embarrass you with regards to your assumptions, I am—as you would say—a happily married man,

210

boasting many daughters and sons, many of whom share my foibles and fashion sense."

"I'm so *sorry* ...!"

He waved her apology aside. "I am what I am, and I am as authentic as I can be under the circumstances. However, my clan affiliation will surely cause a stir."

Tami blinked.

Cyril smiled.

"There," he said gently. "*Now* we understand one another."

"You're Amaranthine?"

"Yes."

This raised several questions. Perhaps her priorities were mixed up, but the first question out of Tami's mouth was, "Is *that* why we were selected for the Twineshaft initiative?"

"No. Hisoka and I are not directly acquainted, and even if he knows *of* me, it would be by my true name." Dr. Bellamy shook his head. "Our proposal's selection was based entirely on its merits."

She was relieved. And then she allowed herself to be shocked. "You're *Amaranthine*."

He offered his palms.

Covering them, Tami whispered, "May I know your true name?"

"Cyril Sunfletch, from one of the pheasant clans." He quietly asked, "Can you bear up under further revelations?"

Tami couldn't help laughing. "If they're as world-tilting as this one, bring them on."

He raised a hand, which was clearly a signal, for the door immediately opened. Lou strolled in, bearing a loaded tray. Then came a tall man with red hair, freckles, and a stack of bakery boxes.

Lou said, "Allow us to treat you to lunch."

She asked, "What's all this?"

"This and that, but mostly us," said the redhead. "I'll get the door. Go on, Rook. You have the years. You first."

Tami watched in fascination as the newcomer sketched shimmering figures on the room's windows and doors. "Sigils?" she whispered.

"A bit of added privacy," he said with a wink.

Pushing back her chair, Tami stood in happy suspense. The men—males—didn't disappoint. All three underwent a subtle transformation, their Amaranthine features becoming readily apparent.

Lou stepped forward, his tail swaying, and spoke with quiet formality. "Tamiko Lisbet Reaverson, principal of schools, proponent for peace, twin of trees, you have become the allotment from Red Gate Farm. Meet with us, learn our names, and take your rightful share of trust."

"The enclave?" she guessed. "You're part of the enclave?"

"Its founders." Lou offered his hands. "I am Kinloo-fel Nightspangle, often called Rook. My brother Doon-wen, alpha of the Nightspangle pack, led an answering allotment to Archer to meet your family and consider our future."

"You're Jiminy's family."

"Yes."

"Does Melissa know?"

"More or less." The redhead offered his hands. "More *more* than less. She hasn't been next door just yet, but we'll coax her into the nest by and by. Linden Woodacre. Squirrel clan."

Rook said, "We are showing our true faces, telling our true names, and meeting with you in good faith, because trust has two sides."

Cyril, whose ears were now showed both points and piercings, spread clawed hands wide. "Your secrets are ours, and ours have become yours. You will join our number as a founder and guide our two enclaves toward a brighter future."

"Me? Wouldn't it be better for you to work with Grandad? He's the one who prepared the way for an alliance."

"You're tree-kin," said Linden, as if that explained everything.

Tami frowned. "Is there some hierarchy at work here?"

"More of a practicality," said Cyril. "It's a matter of lifespan."

She sighed. "I know I'll probably live longer than Grandad, but he's been waiting his whole life for this."

Cyril made a soft noise, a very birdlike noise. "She doesn't know."

Rook's tail bristled. "By oversight or omission?"

"Hey, now," said Linden. "Don't assume the worst. A whole lotta stuff's happened in short order."

Tami took a deep breath and addressed them each in turn. "Cyril Sunfletch. Kinloo-fel Nightspangle. Linden Woodacre. I know your names, and I know I have a lot to learn. What has you concerned?"

"Not concerned, *per se*," said Cyril. "Simply surprised. In nearly every regard, you might consider us heralds who carry good news."

She had to wonder why this latest surprise was setting off so many guarded looks and speaking glances. It was as if none of them wanted to be the messenger.

Cyril must have drawn the short straw.

Heaving a sigh, he explained, "Those born with a golden seed

213

in their hand choose a good place and plant that seed. For many years they guard and tend their twin, and in exchange, they receive their tree's blessing."

"So say the tales, but cut to the chase," urged Linden.

"Tami, you have become tree-kin. You will share your tree's lifespan." Cyril's smile was tight with sympathy. "We want *you* to join our number because you will live as we do, ever onward, evermore."

An Amaranthine lifespan. Hers. That was mind-boggling.

Cyril gently added, "You and I will never have to say goodbye."

It took a few heartbeats for his underlying meaning to sink in.

She would have to face many, many other goodbyes.

29

ALLOTMENT

Jiminy was up all night discussing the challenges of warding Red Gate Farm's acreage with Michael, who would express ship a set of ward stones to give him a start. More crystals would have to be ordered from Glintrubble—at great expense. *If* Doon-wen approved. Scrawling the grand total on a scrap of paper, Jiminy went to find his alpha ... and a cup of coffee.

Founders was hushed. The pre-dawn lull.

He distractedly went through the familiar motions of brewing, liberally tempering extra strong coffee with steamed milk. He needed to be awake. Melissa would be there soon to escort an allotment to the Reaversons' place.

Melissa.

What was he going to do about her? She was all barriers and bare blades, and he was on the wrong side of both.

Leaning back against the counter, he cradled his coffee and

closed his eyes, inhaling the aroma. How was he supposed to get closer when she held his friendliness against him? Customer service meant paying attention, and women welcomed his little attentions. They sipped at them like the coffees they ordered, but they were gone as quickly as his foam art.

Jiminy liked the beauty of an artfully poured cup, and he favored the quickening pulse that came from a strong brew, but what he really needed was something more lasting. The cup itself.

He considered the big, white ceramic cup—its weight, its durability, its simplicity. With something like this, anything was possible. He could pour himself into it, warm it from the inside, lavish it with all his artistry, making something beautiful and heartening. Something shared.

A heavy hand landed on Jiminy's shoulder. "Is this contemplation?"

Doon-wen wasn't the subtlest of presences, but he could be stealthy when he wished to toy with the youngsters of their pack—of which Jiminy was one.

"Why are you so absorbed, you would allow your coffee to go cold?"

Jiminy murmured, "This is a good cup."

"Not many notice." Doon-wen's eyes narrowed. "You are beginning to understand what is most important. You must be growing up."

He felt both complimented and teased.

"You have not slept." The wolf stepped close, caressed Jiminy's cheek, tested the air, and growled softly. "Coffee is not a substitute for rest."

"First-sensei helped me weigh the options for warding the new enclave." Jiminy shyly added, "He has decided that managing the warding of the acreage—from start to finish—will be an effective test of my abilities."

"Your attainment?"

"Yes."

Doon-wen sniffed lightly. "Traditionally, when a young male reaches his attainment, he looks to the establishment of his den."

"If I can find the right ...."

A warning finger lifted. At first, Jiminy thought he'd been caught in a near-lie. Doon-wen didn't tolerate guile. But then the shop's front door opened, and Melissa came hurrying forward.

"Good morning," she said briskly, joining them behind the counter. "Is there anything I can do?"

To Jiminy's utter astonishment, Doon-wen reached for her and repeated his earlier actions—touching, testing, and scolding. "You have not slept."

"I should hope not," she grumbled. "I was on patrol."

Doon-wen growled.

Melissa's stance was respectful, but she didn't back down. "When my family is safe, I'll sleep long and well."

The wolf huffed, and Melissa relaxed against him.

Jiminy let his confusion show. Doon-wen's behavior had a proprietary nuance, and Melissa's acceptance suggested a prior understanding.

"Have you eaten? Jiminy, pour her some coffee." The pack leader added a non-verbal message—*Take heed. The trail is at your feet. Look no further.*

Reaching for a fresh cup, he crisply replied in kind—*My nose works*.

Doon-wen's smile was hard to interpret. Jiminy couldn't decide if it was peer pressure or approval. But even if the pack leader approved of Melissa, her quick glance promised a swift rebuff.

The wolf rolled his eyes and returned the message—*My nose works*. With an added flourish that implied superiority. And the kinds of subtext with which wolves were conversant.

Jiminy took extra care with Melissa's cup and offered it with a simple, "Good morning."

She murmured thanks and paused to admire the pattern he'd poured into the foam. Her smile was small, but soft.

Doon-wen watched over the exchange and offered his assessment with a confident flick of fingers known by every wolf on the hunt. *Patience. It is within our grasp.*

Melissa's presence was largely incidental. She needed to be there since she was Doon-wen's escort. But the pack knew its business, and they took care of their own. Roonta-kiv oversaw the loading of eight sizable Kith into two horse trailers. She and her bondmate would drive the trucks.

Doon-wen had gone off to bring around his car, leaving Melissa alone with Jiminy, who had—thus far—been behaving himself. She should have known it couldn't last.

His shoulder nudged hers.

"Boundaries," she muttered.

Jiminy asked, "Has something happened between you and my pack's illustrious leader?"

Melissa wasn't sure she wanted to answer. Then again, did she *know* the answer? Jiminy was still her best resource in demystifying wolf mindsets and behavior. "Doon-wen and True took me in."

"In what sense?"

"Fostering." She searched his face, hoping for fresh insight. "He said my only obligation will be to the pack."

"You're okay with that?"

"Is there something I should know?" she asked in a tight voice.

Jiminy checked over his shoulder, then pulled her into a dead-end alley between the coffee shop and the secondhand clothing store next door. She let him.

He stood too close.

She poked his chest.

Rubbing the spot—and easing back a step—he said, "First and foremost, you're in an enviable position. Doon-wen would never offer to foster you if he hadn't set his heart on it. And a wolf's heart is just about the safest place anyone could belong."

Melissa nodded cautiously. What was the catch?

"In a way, you've already gained what you've always wanted. Fostering is a pact. You can claim Doon-wen Nightspangle as your pactmate."

She'd never presume. And fostering had never been her goal. "But ...?"

Jiminy lowered his voice. "This is Doon-wen. He has plans for you."

"Maybe I have plans, too." After a moment's consideration, she added, "He didn't set any conditions."

"That would go against wolf nature. But it won't stop him from encouraging you in my direction."

"We've been over this. I'm not interested in marriage contracts. I want a Kith partner."

"I know. I've been listening, Melissa, and I do understand. I just want to make sure you do, too. Because the Nightspangle pack will see your addition to our number as a sign of interest, if not intent."

"Then we'll defy them by remaining indifferent."

Jiminy looked worried.

"Doon-wen can't force me to accept you, can he?"

"No. That also goes against wolf nature." His gaze dropped. "What is it you want from a wolf?"

Melissa had no trouble reeling off a list. "Complementary strengths. Shared purpose. Mutual trust. Lifelong loyalty. Unwavering devotion."

He muttered something. Too soft to hear.

"What?"

Jiminy met her gaze. "I can give you those things."

Hold up. "I want a *wolf*."

"I *am* a wolf."

"You know what I mean! I want a Kith partner."

Jiminy went on, more serious than she'd ever seen him. "And *because* I'm a wolf, there are things that I want, conditions that have been set, obstacles to overcome."

Melissa tried to listen. Tried to understand. "What do you want?"

Without hesitation, he matched her word-for-word. "Complementary strengths. Shared purpose. Mutual trust. Lifelong loyalty. Unwavering devotion."

"Wanting the same things isn't the same as wanting each other." She returned to her previous point. "Doon-wen will ease up once he realizes we're not interested."

"That won't work." Jiminy's posture shifted, and he made a weary gesture with his hands. "I can't take refuge in indifference because I'm *not*."

Not.

Not?

It took another few beats for Jiminy's meaning to strike. He was not *indifferent*. And that was ... different. Now Melissa was worried. "Maybe you should stop."

He laughed a little, but in a humorless way. "That also goes against wolf nature."

That morning may have been the proudest of Melissa's life. In her role as reaver, she took a position between two races, offering introductions, assuring peace.

George Reaverson stood tall, gaze fierce, surely battler-born and more than ready to fight for his own. But at Doon-wen's approach, his expression wavered toward a wanting Melissa understood all too well. She had to wonder what the wolves would make of Uncle George and his hopes.

"An enclave." The old farmer's voice cracked with urgency. "I have the acreage. I prepared a circle. I know which secrets to keep. The tree alone should be leverage enough to ...."

Doon-wen cut him off with a soft growl. "You do not need

leverage, George. You called out, and we came. The wolves of the Nightspangle pack are here, and we will stay."

Uncle George quietly asked, "You will?"

"Let us speak of the future as those who will share it." The wolf's tail swayed as he matched—even outstripped—the Reaversons' generosity. "Let us run freely across your acreage, and we will protect it. Let us sing within the circle you prepared, and we will welcome your generations to our feasts. Let us exchange names in the manner of friends and live as neighbors."

30

OVERRUN

Mindful of Kip's warnings about the keen senses of wolves, Joe skipped out on the formalities. He'd made short work of caring for the most essential of his responsibilities, then holed up in his room, where the door, the floor, and even the ceiling still shimmered faintly with Kip's sigils.

One wall now boasted a modest stockpile—cereal boxes, bread, peanut butter, apples. He'd even smuggled in one of the coolers for items borrowed from the fridge.

Kip showed no signs of waking, so Joe settled in with the rest of his contraband. Grandad kept a stack of tabloids next to his recliner. Flashy, sensational headlines screamed from their front pages, promising insider information and tell-all tales. Mom found them distasteful, referring to them as gossip rags, but Grandad read them religiously. Because ever since the Emergence, they were riddled with shocking revelations about the Rivven races.

The headlines were incredible.

My Neighbor Howls at the Moon

Rescued! Beast Saves Avalanche Victims

Girl Born with Demon Horns

Top Ten Signs Your Neighbor is Rivven

One Woman's Unicorn Encounter

Joe flipped to see pictures of the unicorn's love child, but they were more confusing than conclusive. It might all be nonsense. Then again, some of it must be true. Why else would Grandad bother?

Slightly more credible were the articles following the movements of known Rivven. And the people closest to them.

Inside Lord Mossberne's Mountaintop Retreat

Cats vs. Dogs: Twineshaft and Starmark Tell All

Adoona-soh's Surprising Fashion Statements

Joe was halfway through an article entitled "This Year's Must-Read Rivven Romances" when he realized that something was out of balance. With the farm overrun by wolves, he'd been adjusting like crazy. He could tell Jiminy's packmates were nearby, which was unnerving. But this was slightly different. Could Jiminy be fussing with the wards again? Nope, this didn't feel quite like the harmonic dissonance that had been bugging him the other day. This was something new. Someone new?

He shook Kip's shoulder.

Still no response.

Joe only hesitated for a scant minute before opening his bedroom door and listening. The house was quiet. Everyone was elsewhere. Hurrying downstairs, he donned jacket and boots and slipped out a little-used side door. Circling the house, he aimed for the road, sure that someone was there.

The house was warded. Jiminy had seen to that. But the driveway wasn't, since their customers needed access to their barns, the pumpkin patch, and the corn maze. The orchard and its produce were available to everyone, no matter their species.

There. Someone was standing among the trees at the end of the driveway. Even though the gate was shut and the banners lowered.

Steeling his resolve, Joe walked down the drive.

Their lurker had black hair and eyes, and he watched Joe's approach without remark or retreat. His corduroy shirt was a weathered gray, and he stood with hands stuffed into the pockets of faded jeans.

"Are you Ash?"

"Hello, Joe."

"Kip's here." He could feel color rising in his cheeks. "He won't wake up."

Ash nodded a few times. "Did he ... say anything?"

"Umm ... yeah."

"How much?"

Joe didn't even know where to start. "Most of it, I think."

The janitor shifted restlessly. "I'm going to need you to be more specific."

A wave of shyness caught Joe by surprise. "Umm ... are you really Mr. Black?"

Ash's eyes widened.

Joe fumbled for something else to explain how much Kip had revealed. "I like his tail. And the claws aren't so bad. And when he's a squirrel, he's ... cute."

Incredulity faded into exasperation on Ash's face. "Okay, yeah. I think that's most of it. Did you get him drunk or something?"

"He stopped at two beers." Joe shuffled forward another step. "Are you here to get him?"

Rubbing at the side of his face, Ash asked, "How safe is he?"

"Umm ... he put sigils everywhere in my room."

Ash eased closer. "That alone means he's safe. And Jiminy's wards don't hurt. What about your sister?"

"She doesn't know. I won't tell."

Joe searched the young man's face, looking for traces of the old man he remembered from his childhood. The eyes. His build. Something in the set of his mouth. It was as if time rolled backward, revealing a stranger who was—and wasn't—his childhood friend.

"Warding this place must have taken it out of him. Kip will probably sleep for a day or two." Ash asked, "Are you willing to keep an eye on him for me?"

"You could come in," Joe offered. "Nobody else is in the house right now."

Ash shook his head. "Did Doon-wen see you like this?"

"Like what?" Joe rubbed uneasily at his chest. Weren't Kip's sigils supposed to be invisible?

"Do me a favor and take a long, hot shower before joining any song circles."

He hadn't washed. Did he smell like Kip? Joe admitted, "I was petting him. His squirrel. Him in squirrel form."

"I'll bet he loved the attention." Ash slowly reached out to touch Joe's arm. "And it's not the end of the world if the wolves find out. But it might get awkward if someone says something in front of Tami."

Joe asked, "Is it the end of the world if Tami finds out?"

Ash's hand fell away. "How much did Kip say about me?"

"Not much. Only that you and my sister really need to talk."

"We do."

"Come up to the house," Joe offered. "She'll be home soon. You can talk."

Ash retreated a step. "I can't just *be here*."

"Yes, you can." This was his old friend. This was the person Tami loved. This was the right thing to do. In a cautious echo, Joe reached for Ash. "Be here and tell her."

For a long while, they just stood there, Joe holding Ash back with a firm grip.

Finally, Ash muttered, "You know what it means ... if I'm Mr. Black."

Joe said, "You're not human. Maybe you're like Kip?"

"And that doesn't bother you?"

"When I was little, I had friends because Tami made them. But you were *my* friend." Joe mumbled, "Thank you for being my friend."

Ash exhaled a funny, fluttering breath, just the way Mr. Black used to, then dredged up a small smile. "Guess I need a friend right now, and my usual cohort is having a long nap. Are you

227

sure you're okay with all of this?"

He took Joe's hand and pressed his knuckles into it. Slowly, he opened his fingers, and Joe could feel the smooth backs of long claws against his skin. He glanced down, but Ash's fingers looked normal.

"Close your eyes," Ash directed.

Joe did, and that was less disorienting. He explored the truth with his fingertips and accepted it. Eyes still firmly shut, he offered his palms. "Are you a squirrel like Kip?"

"No." Warm hands covered his. "I'm different. I'll show you later. After your sister, okay?"

He nodded. Belatedly, he opened his eyes again.

Ash said, "I'm going to accept your invitation, Joe. Is there someplace private. Someplace the wolves won't be?"

"Umm ... sure. I know a good spot."

31

CLOSE YOUR EYES

omplaining would be silly. Tami had every reason to be amazed, delighted, and grateful. There were Amaranthine in Fletching, and they had welcomed her as a friend. She had their support, both as a principal and on a personal level. Inclusion in an enclave. Plans for the community.

She'd been building toward a brighter future without realizing she'd be part of it. Possibilities multiplied by years. She could truly see this through. Make a difference. Change lives. Promote understanding, peace, and cooperation.

Her smile only lasted until Cyril escorted her back to his car. Because the dizzy swirl of good news kept circling back to one horrible, terrible truth.

"What about Joe?" she whispered. "I can't leave Joe."

Cyril made no move to put the key in the ignition. Eyes fixed on the hands loosely folded in his lap, he asked, "You and he are close?"

"Twins."

He measured his words before answering. "You'll always be there for your brother. That doesn't change."

Tami knew what people thought, that Joe needed her. But it was really the other way around. Always had been. Always would be. And that scared her. "I need Joe. That doesn't change."

Cyril didn't contradict her, didn't offer platitudes. He simply asked, "Will he be at home?"

"Yes."

"Shall I take you there?"

"Please?"

"My pleasure."

Tami hardly noticed the passing of familiar landmarks as Cyril played chauffeur. But just outside of Fletching, her wheeling thoughts hit a fresh snag. She'd outlive everyone she loved, and that included Ash.

The only fair thing to do was break it off. And she couldn't even explain why.

"Here, my dear." Cyril pressed a silken square into her hand.

When had she begun crying?

Joe was still mumbling reassurances when his head came up, his attention gone. His priorities shifted, and he made for the ladder. Halfway down, he blurted, "Gotta go. Tami needs me."

Ash's face appeared above him, tense with concern. "Is something wrong?"

"Something's wrong." Joe's boots hit the barn floor.

"Should I get out of here?"

Hurrying for the door, he ordered, "Stay!"

He didn't have time to explain something that had always defied explanation. Maybe it was a twin thing. Maybe being reavers was a part of it. Joe didn't really care about the whys and wherefores. All that mattered was getting to Tami.

A sleek black car had parked in front of the gift shop, and a stranger was helping Tami out of it. She'd been crying. Joe's wariness evaporated. Striding forward, he inserted himself between the strange man and his sister, and Tami collapsed into him with a sob.

"I'm here," Joe whispered.

Her arms tightened around him.

"You would be Joe?" inquired the man politely.

Paying attention now, since this guy might somehow be responsible for Tami's distress, Joe gave him a quick once-over. City boy. Probably rich and important. But radiating compassion. "Who are you?"

"Perhaps your sister has mentioned me. Dr. Bellamy of Bellwether College. You may call me Cyril." With a lazy wave toward the orchard, he asked, "Mind if I take a stroll?"

"We're closed."

"To the public, certainly." The man's eyes were bright with anticipation, his smile coy. "These are exceptional days, and I really would like to catch Doon-wen in the midst of a proper romp. Trust me when I say it would be a *rare* sight."

He knew about the wolves.

"Dr. Bellamy is part of the enclave." Tami pulled back, dabbing at her face. "I'm going to freshen up. Thank you for the ride, Cyril."

"Shall I arrange for the retrieval of your car?"

Tami wavered, nodded, and hurried up the porch steps.

Once she was inside, Joe tried to think what to say. Then an uneasy notion came to him, since he had been advised to wash. "Are you a wolf, sir?"

"Nothing of the sort. I'm not half so rangy or rugged." He cocked his head to one side. "You know, for a twin, you are very *un*like your sister."

Joe guessed that meant Kip's sigils were working. He shrugged and muttered, "We're fraternal."

Cyril laughed lightly, then changed the subject again. "Is there any truth to the rumors of a corn maze on the property?"

He gestured to the sign propped against the barn. "We have one every year. It opens this weekend."

"The squirrels will want to play havoc with your customers." Easing into conspiratorial closeness, Cyril added, "They're one of the trickster clans, you know."

"I didn't know."

"Illusory expertise. Games and mischief. Harmless fun, to be sure. Always coaxing for a laugh, but trustworthy and true of heart."

Joe was uncomfortably certain that this person knew about Kip.

As if reading his thoughts, Cyril said, "He's a good boy. Pick of the litter in more ways than one."

Joe dropped his gaze in time to watch a slender hand pluck a long, red hair from his sleeve. Busted. "Don't tell. He ... he doesn't want my sister to find out ... before ... just *before*."

"You may trust my discretion." Cyril beckoned with both hands. "Once all is revealed, you'll understand my part in this delicious muddle. But we should begin at the beginning."

Joe took the cue and shyly offered his palms. "Sir, can I ask about your … umm … your clan."

"You may." Radiating delight, he announced, "Lord Cyril Sunfletch, a pheasant by clan, a scholar by trade, a founder by choice, and an aficionado of fashion by destiny. Your sister and I met some months ago when she approached me with regards to the Twineshaft Initiative."

"Because you're Rivven?"

"Funny little coincidence, that." Cyril's hands slipped under Joe's, supporting them from beneath. "I revealed myself earlier. Tami's had a good day and a bad day, all bundled into one."

"Why?"

He pursed his lips, then sighed. "Some blessings seem a burden. Comfort her as best you can."

Joe stole upstairs and tapped on his sister's door.

"Come in." Her subdued reply was better than more crying.

Tami's room was a cheery accumulation of mismatched furniture that only made sense together if you knew her. Because she loved everything in there. Like the tall, carved cabinet from their grandparents' house in Kyoto and the old rolltop desk that used to sit in the front hall. Back in the day, it had been where the Reaverson family kept track of all the orchard's accounts. Then

233

there were the vintage apple crates that served as her bookcases. And the antique bedstead that was as old as the farm. That's where Tami sat, in a spot that meant she'd left room for him.

Clad in flannel pajama pants and a hoodie that was technically his, even though she wore it more than he did, Tami looked more comfortable … and in need of comforting.

The featherbed sank with his added weight, pushing them together. Same as always. Joe wrapped his arm around her shoulders and waited.

Tami took a deep breath and blurted, "I don't want to spend forever without you."

He mulled that over for a few moments, then nodded his agreement.

"Nobody told me. Probably an oversight." Tami looked him in the eye and said, "Biddie changed my life."

Joe had to smile. "No kidding?"

But Tami's eyes were brimming again. "She changed how long I'll live."

As she regaled him with this new twist in tragic tones, he listened with increasing amazement. Because this was huge and happy. Only she didn't know it yet. And he didn't want to be the one to spoil the surprise.

Handing her a tissue, Joe risked saying, "Plenty of women wish they could be twenty-nine forever."

She gaped at him, then shoved his arm. "I don't want to spend forever without you."

"I'll figure something out."

"How?" she asked, less skeptical than he expected. Tami always had believed him capable of anything—in a good way.

"Not sure yet, but I think you're focusing on the wrong twin. Biddie needs you." He smiled at her surprise. "Isn't that why you're bound together? Because she'll need your love and protection for her whole life?"

Tami's attention wasn't on her losses anymore. He could see her mind working.

Joe gave her a little squeeze. "You'll have a sister to look out for, and you'll have wolves and squirrels and pheasants and ... oh. Hey, I almost forget. Ash came by earlier."

Her whole body tensed. "He did?"

"And he's still here."

"He is not." Tami's expression begged him to be teasing.

"Sure, he is. I stashed him in our third best hiding place."

Tami's expression wavered a while, then settled on bewilderment. "You put the man I love in the haymow?"

"He went along with it." Joe shrugged. "He wanted someplace private to talk. I promised to bring you there once you got home."

Predictably, Tami's hands flew to her face, her hair. "I'm a mess!"

"I don't think he'll mind."

"He ... he's." Tami's fluster mounted. "I can't be with him."

Joe frowned. "You love him. You told me so."

"But everything's different!" she protested. "What kind of guy wants a wife who's going to be twenty-nine forever?"

His frown deepened. "Is that a trick question?"

That earned him a flurry of small thumps. "Don't be *mean*."

"He's here, and he's waiting." Joe eased off the bed and made for the door. "Just do me a favor. When it's time to talk, let him go first."

Tami was already pulling things out of her closet, but she hesitated. "*That* would be mean. What if he wants to propose or something? It might be kinder if I ...."

"No," Joe interrupted, more sternly than necessary. "Let Ash go first. Promise me?"

His sister held his gaze and gave in. "I promise."

Tami slowly ascended the weathered rungs of two-by-fours nailed into the old barn's exposed studs. This building wasn't used for much more than storage anymore, but it had once been home to horses and cows. The lower part was divided into stalls, and Grandad still used the upper section for stockpiling the bales they used for seating, displays, and hayrides. She and Joe had often played up here, where pigeons cooed and swallows nested and mama cats hid their litters.

Near the top, she softly called, "Ash?"

"Here."

He sat among the bales, looking worried enough to worry her. Tami tried to smooth over any awkwardness. "This is a surprise. I didn't realize you even knew where I lived."

"Kip mentioned it." Ash stood and shuffled his feet. "Nice place."

"Thanks. I can give you the tour sometime."

"Sounds good."

Tami usually didn't leave conversations to flounder. It was so much easier to take charge. But Joe had made her promise to let Ash go first, so she chose a seat and held her peace.

He came closer, crouched before her, searching her face. "I need to apologize."

She hadn't expected that. "What for?"

"I haven't been entirely honest." Ash grimaced. "I never lied, exactly. But there are vows I can't break, people I need to protect, secrets that aren't easy to talk about."

Tami's heart sank. "Are you trying to tell me you're already married?"

"No! Not those kinds of vows." Ash quietly added, "This is harder to explain without Kip."

Now she was really confused.

"I can't undo the illusion on my own."

A broad hint. As good as a confession. She knew then—at least in part—but she had to wonder how Joe had known. "You're Amaranthine?"

"Half." He lowered himself to his knees and held out a hand. "I wasn't sure how to tell you."

Tami placed her hand in his. "Half?"

"My father was Amaranthine." Ash curled his hand into a loose fist and pressed into her palm, much as Cyril had done earlier.

"You have claws."

"Yeah. I have to be careful." He eased a little closer. "It's easiest if I keep my distance."

Taking his hand in both of hers, she tested each digit. Even though her eyes were telling her that his hands were as human as could be, her fingers traced the tapered points of the truth. "An illusion?"

"More than one, actually. I wouldn't pass for human otherwise."

Tami reached for his face, and he held still while she pushed his hair behind his ear. "No points?"

Some of the tension left his posture, and he cracked a smile. "Sorry to disappoint."

"You're a crosser."

"That's the truth." Ash edged closer and whispered, "Close your eyes."

As soon as she did, something rustled around her, brushing against her shoulders, her hair. An enveloping warmth carried a familiar scent, bringing to mind nesting boxes and roosting hens. "You have feathers?"

"I do." Ash caught her wrist and guided her hand upward.

What she found amazed her. "You have *wings*."

She trailed her hand across fanning feathers, then followed the upper edge to the place where they joined Ash's back. Her fingers found a nest of down there. And bare skin, where Ash's shirt had been altered to accommodate his wings. He shivered and flexed.

Her explorations left her pressed close, and he slid his arms around her waist. "You're not ... disturbed?"

Far from it. She kissed his cheek and murmured, "What color are your feathers?"

"Black." Ash's nose trailed along her jaw. "Crow clan."

"Oh. Like your name."

He chuckled. "Snooping in files?"

"A little. I was curious." Tami paused. "Wait ... you mentioned Kip. Him, too?"

"We grew up together. He's good with illusions." Ash touched her hair. "I think he outed himself to Joe."

Recalling the red hair and passing resemblance to one of the founders she'd met earlier, she asked, "Is he related to Linden Woodacre, by any chance?"

Ash kissed her, and all thoughts of squirrels fled.

She was breathless when he drew back and cleared his throat. "I heard from ... from someone connected to the enclave that you're tree-kin. Is that true?"

"Yes." Explanations tumbled out, mostly coherent, though Ash's constant nuzzling and petting were a distraction.

"I was fully prepared to pledge everything, even knowing it would only be for a short time." Ash's voice was low with emotion. "I'm glad it will be longer."

Tami was embarrassed it had taken this long for her to realize. "Your lifespan."

"*Our* lifespans." He kissed her softly. "My years are yours if you'll have them."

32

FREEZING RAIN

Kip woke to the sound of rain rattling against glass. Stretching and scratching, he sat up and studied his surroundings. Long sleeps always left him sluggish. Where …? Not home, but safe. He could feel the reassuring strength of his own wards. Then he spotted Jiro, curled up under a quilt on the floor. And the stockpiled snacks crammed against the wall.

What a trooper.

A quick scamper to the bathroom. A few extra sigils for the door and floor. Then Kip scooped up Jiro and tucked him into his own bed, crawling right in after him. The man squinted groggily, but he couldn't have been seeing much in the dark. Rubbing at cold arms, Kip muttered, "I'm the worst houseguest ever. Total bed hog. And you're *freezing*."

"Kip?"

"How long was I out?"

"Three days." Jiro turned, and his forehead bumped Kip's chin. "Umm ... tomorrow's Sunday."

"Could be worse. Tell me what's going on."

"Temperatures dropping. Threat of freezing rain. Been picking like crazy since yesterday morning," he reported in a sleepy voice. "Late apples are all in. Kinda worried about the maze, though."

Kip couldn't help smiling. "You're a farmer for sure. Crops and weather. Work with me here! What did I miss?"

"Ash was here."

He stopped chaffing. "Was he?"

Jiro's hand found Kip's chest, but he didn't push him away. "He came looking for you."

"When was this?"

"Friday. After work." He was more awake now. And struggling to know where to put his other hand. "He knew you were here. I guess I smelled like squirrel."

Kip took Jiro's floundering hand and guided it around his waist. "My bad. Should have warned you about scents. Was he upset?"

"Concerned. Careful." Jiro's scent changed. "I did what you said."

"Me?"

Jiro's tone gentled. "You said they should talk, so I made Ash wait and brought Tami to him."

Oh. That.

Kip swallowed hard. "How'd that go?"

"Good, I guess. He makes her happy." The mood shifted suddenly, leaving Kip rather queasy, and Jiro murmured, "Promise me something?"

"What do you need?"

"You're Tami's friend."

"Sure am."

Jiro begged, "Don't let her be sad about me."

"Whoa, now. Back up." Kip eased his arm under Jiro's shoulders, which was much more comfortable. "Why would she be sad?"

"Nobody thought to tell us that Tami will live as long as Biddie." His voice wavered slightly. "I won't."

Kip pulled him close. Sadness keened through the soul hidden behind his wards, a lonesome song that tugged at his heart.

"Promise me?" Jiro repeated. "You can make sure she won't miss me."

Right then, Kip would have done anything to drive away Jiro's worries. Make any promise. Do something reckless.

"Did you know ...?" Kip began, speaking slowly at first. "Ever since the waning of their years, humans have always wished for more. That's why the old groves are gone. Our trees were ravaged by those seeking the very life your sister's found."

"Like the fountain of youth."

"That's the idea." Kip stroked Jiro's hair. "If people thought it was possible, they'd pay anything, promise anything. Maybe do anything, even something selfish and terrible."

Jiro's face lifted. "Is Biddie in danger?"

"Possibly. That's why George wants our wolves and Jiminy's wards. That's why most people—even Amaranthine like me—think the old songs are nothing more than stories." Kip chose his next words with care. "We keep certain secrets to protect ourselves. I can use one of those secrets to give you what you want."

He shook his head. "I don't understand."

"I can make sure she won't miss you," said Kip. "She wouldn't have to be sad."

"Really?"

"Well, I know it's *possible*. There's precedence. And the most famous cases also involve beacons."

Jiro simply shook his head again.

"It's just another kind of bond." Kip was already growing attached to his scheme. Mostly because it would be tricky to pull off. "Tami's life is tied to a tree's. Yours could be tied to mine."

Joe wasn't used to *close*. Tami was the exception. And maybe Biddie, since she was more like a clinging vine than a tree. So he didn't know how to react to Kip's casual crowding. Given all the other important things that needed to be said, Joe didn't want to call attention to the obvious.

Like the fact that they were in bed. Which was much warmer than the floor, but still ...! There was a whole lot of touching. For instance, the hand Kip had pulled around his waist had landed on a boundary line of sorts. Kip's shirt had ridden up, exposing bare skin above, thick fur below.

"Hey, Jiro?" Kip kneaded his shoulder. "You still with me?"

"Right here," he mumbled, trying to relax and focus at the same time.

"I'll admit, what I know is technically hearsay, but my source excels at information gathering. He keeps his ear to the ground and squirrels away facts, rumors, secrets, and gossip.

Sometimes, he dishes the really juicy stuff to me, especially if it has to do with crossers."

Joe asked, "Are you a crosser?"

"In a way." Kip's voice held amusement. "You may have noticed I don't adhere to the standard design. Big old tail. All kinds of lovely, pettable fur."

To his embarrassment, Joe realized that he *was* petting Kip, scratching circles somewhere in the vicinity of his hipbone. He jerked away, but Kip caught his hand and pressed it back into place.

"It's okay. I told you. I like it." Kip quietly added, "This is normal, friendly stuff. And we're friends."

Joe mumbled, "I'm not used to this."

"I know. Want me out of here?" He sounded concerned now. "You haven't crossed any lines with me, and I'll give you the same courtesy."

"Thanks." He wasn't sure what to say, so he just tangled his fingers in fur to hold Kip there.

"I'm a rare breed and something of a secret, so keep this under your hat. Long story short, I'm three-quarters Amaranthine, what's known as Kith-kin. Because my dad's Kith."

"You're part squirrel."

"I'll have to introduce you to my dad. He's even cuter than I am." Kip tangled their legs together. "And I have a sister and two brothers—littermates. And enough nieces and nephews to fill Biddie's branches."

"Your mom ...?"

"A Woodacre. What the international press likes to call a High Amaranthine." Kip chuckled. "I've never been able to tell anyone about myself before, so this is fun. But I'm getting off topic. I was aiming the conversation toward crossers, since they're proof of the possibilities."

Joe knew this one, largely thanks to *Heart of a Dog*. "Biological compatibility."

"And not simply in the procreative sense." Kip blazed ahead. "You know that two of the Five have human bondmates."

"They're the Seven, now."

Kip thanked him for the correction by nipping his ear. Joe guessed he'd been scolded.

"Both Lady Starmark and Lady Mettlebright are beacons. Everybody and their uncle knows that." Kip lowered his voice. "What's less obvious—since their males are canny and cagy by turns—is that their ladies are a little like Tami now. Uncle Linden swears that Lady Starmark entered Harmonious' den more than three centuries ago. It'll be the same for the elusive Lady Mettlebright. The whole matter probably won't come to light until the world realizes that Kimiko Miyabe, soon to be Starmark, is keeping time with Eloquence instead of the rest of humanity."

"Their lifespans changed."

"It's bound to come out, and it'll cause a sensation." Kip sighed. "There's concern over the potential for exploitation."

If people would pay anything, promise anything, all for the chance to live beyond one lifetime, what would happen? And which side would be using the other?

"There are limitations, but those happen to work in our favor. The human partner must be a reaver in order to strike the right balance. Something about synergy or symmetry. I'm a little vague on the details, but it should work."

"*How* does it work?"

Kip hesitated. "I do know tending is involved."

The soul-sharing thing. "You never explained how that works."

"I'm not really sure about the mechanics. I mean, tending is give-and-take—you give, I take. But in my experience, the reaver always initiates a session." He sheepishly added, "Never really thought about *how*."

"So we can't try it?"

There was a long silence, during which Kip's hand kept pressing at Joe's shoulders, coaxing his tension away. Finally, he said, "Better not."

"You don't want to?" Joe's heart sank. What had he expected?

Kip made one of his squirrel sounds, a burring of his tongue that was hard to interpret. But dawn must have been approaching, and Joe could make out a little of Kip's face in the gray light. He was grinning.

"Oh, I want to. You're so tempting, it scares me a little. But I am a very little squirrel, and you are very much a beacon. I might be able to hide you, but I'm not sure I can handle you. Not without safeguards."

"Are you ... afraid of me?"

"Nope. Even if you cut loose, dousing and dazzling the whole farm, I know I'd be safe from harm. Your power is part of you. It would never betray your good intentions." Kip's forehead touched his. "I am trying to be sensible. And respectful. Maybe even gentlemanly. If this was a fairy tale, you'd be the most beautiful person in all the realm, and I'm the poor schmuck who doesn't deserve you."

"But I'm the farm boy."

Kip snorted and nipped his ear again. Definitely retaliation, but it seemed playful. And proof enough to Joe that Kip *wasn't* afraid of him. Either that, or he wasn't afraid of anything.

"We're getting off topic again," he grumbled. "I am *trying* to offer you a happily ever after."

"Why?"

"Why wouldn't I? You're like a treasure hidden in a field. A pearl of great price. Brighter than the morning star, and willing as the wind."

Joe cautiously asked, "What about Ash?"

Kip curled into him, hiding his face against Joe's chest as he clung. "Okay, so I'm being sensible *and* selfish. Because if I make it possible for you to stay with Tami, I'll get to stay close to Ash."

"Won't that be hard?"

"Not always."

Joe was being offered something for which many would pay anything, promise anything, do anything. Maybe he and Kip were using each other a little. Or maybe this was more like pooling their resources. "Okay."

"Yeah?"

Joe awkwardly patted Kip's back. "Yeah."

33

DENNY

Melissa couldn't sleep, even though she should have been able to relax. The burden of secrets, the safety of her cousin, the formalities regarding boundaries, limits, and permissions—everything was now in the keeping of Doon-wen and the wolves of the Nightspangle pack. But she couldn't find her way to the rest her body needed. Giving up, she pulled on jeans and a heavy sweater and braved the wet to get to work.

Rook welcomed her with a soft smile and a hot drink, but he didn't bother with words. Melissa was grateful that none were needed.

Staying busy became increasingly easy, thanks to the weather. A combination of gusty wind and miserable drizzle drove half the campus to seek the shelter Founders offered. Students dragged in, cold, wet, and drowsy. Tables filled and stayed full, with people lingering over second and third cups of coffee.

Melissa collected tray after tray of empty cups and mopped around the clogged umbrella stand. Mid-morning, Rook sent her next door to beg for a full restock of their bakery case. She blinked dazedly at the bright, clean interior of Tough Nut bakery, then relayed Rook's message to the lady behind the counter.

"Shake a leg, Linden!" The redheaded woman bustled into the kitchen and was back a moment later, pressing a slice of pumpkin bread into Melissa's hand even as she cajoled a lanky redhead and two teens—all with vivid red hair and a burden of bakery boxes.

"Yes, ma'am!" they chorused.

"Lead on, Melissa," said the man with a wink. "Can't keep these to ourselves!"

She held the door for them, then hurried ahead to open the one into Founders. Their arrival was met by a patter of applause. Rook's voice carried as he cheerfully announced, "Fresh batch of chocolate chip cookies, courtesy of our friends at Tough Nut bakery."

The man at Melissa's side called out, "Lemon shortbread and gingerbread will be along soon."

Melissa watched the ensuing stampede with a smile. "You do this often?"

"Every rainy day," he replied. "We also turn up on snow days, gray days, Tuesdays, Wednesdays, and Fridays. But *especially* on dreary Mondays."

Nothing in his appearance or presence gave him away, but she knew he must be Amaranthine. "You know my name ...?"

"And you shall know mine!" Offering a hand, he said, "Linden Holloway, this go-around. My sister Holly's the bossy one minding the shop. The young ones doling out cookies are cousins—one from my brood, one from my brother's. We're a peace-loving passel, Woodacres one and all."

Woodacres. Like Kip. She wondered if it would be indiscreet to ask how they were related.

"Are you going to eat that?" Linden indicated the pumpkin bread still in her hand.

"Did you want it?" she offered.

His eyes crinkled at the corners. "Tasty as the tidbit looks, I'll wager you need it more than I do. Eat up."

Melissa mumbled appreciatively around a large bite. The squirrel clan's baking was superb.

"So!" Linden lowered his voice. "*You're* the one who's keeping our Jiminy on his toes. Had him at knifepoint, I hear!"

"Only once or twice."

"Delighted to hear it." His glee couldn't have been more obvious as he guided her to the counter, where the redheaded cousins presided over sales—one cookie for a quarter. "The tougher the nut, the sweeter the meat."

Before she could protest, Rook joined them. "You've met Linden? He speaks for the squirrel clans."

Melissa blinked. She hadn't realized. "Spokesperson Woodacre," she murmured respectfully.

Linden rolled his eyes. "*Denny* will do. Sorry for the delay, Lou. Would have been here sooner, but my nephew dropped by and ate his way through a triple batch of cookie dough before we noticed."

It took a moment for Melissa to remember who *Lou* was. He'd always be Rook to her. And she really doubted she could ever call the spokesperson for the squirrel clans *Denny*.

"You mean Alder?"

"None other. He's been and gone. Work and all." Linden frowned thoughtfully. "He's a mooch, but we don't often see him so ... moody."

"Trouble?"

"Not the dangerous kind. I suspect he's at that age." Linden glanced Melissa's way, and his lips quirked. "The raid on his mother's kitchen probably helped. Chocolate is considered a remedy for the lovesick soul."

Rook's brow furrowed. "You think he's in love?"

"Might not be courting behavior. Asked some odd questions, though. Holly thinks it might be a reaver." Linden pointed up. "He didn't even ask after Jiminy, and he usually does that first thing."

"That's not like Kip," Rook agreed.

Melissa's attention snapped to. She hadn't realized they were talking about someone she knew.

Linden waved the whole matter aside. "See here, Rook. Isn't Melissa due for a break? She's looking a bit frayed at the edges."

Rook hummed his agreement.

Were they talking about her appearance or her endurance? She pushed uneasily at her hair and wondered if she should grab another coffee.

"Jiminy hasn't come down yet," said Rook. "Melissa, would you mind rousting him from his den? He's supposed take the next shift."

"His den," she echoed cautiously. "Couldn't you call him? Text him?"

"Deep sleeper," Rook said dismissively.

Linden nodded solemnly. "Might require manhandling."

"Or more sleep. He's been pushing his limits lately."

"Eager for his attainment." The squirrel clansman's eyebrows waggled.

Rook elbowed him and said, "Rest and regard cannot be rushed."

Melissa knew that saying. Magda used it often, quoting one of her former teachers. "Isn't that a feline proverb?"

The colluders exchanged a glance, and Linden cleared his throat. "Dragon, I believe."

"And it's incomplete," she said.

"True enough." Rook seemed entirely thrown off. "They do favor fours. An homage to the four winds."

Melissa could almost hear Magda's rolling inflection. Smiling at the memory, she quoted the full proverb. "Rest, regard, and revenge cannot be rushed."

A convoluted set of directions led Melissa into the very heart of the enclave, up three floors and along a maze of narrow halls. The door to her destination was plain, yet it seemed to shimmer and dance. Countless sigils decorated its surface.

Jiminy's room. No, Rook had called it his den. And he'd obviously wanted her to see it. Why else send her up here?

Reaching up to knock, Melissa snatched back her hand when the sigils moved. Was she about to trigger some kind of alarm? But the intricate figures only drifted back into their former positions. She extended her hand, and once again, the sigils seemed to scatter before her touch, clearing the way. And when she rested her fingertips on the door, she experienced the same happy burst she'd first experienced at the warded entrance to the enclave.

She was welcome. Here, of all places.

Had Jiminy tuned his personal wards to accept her?

Maybe she was reading too much into it. Melissa tapped lightly. Then rapped. Then tried the handle. It wasn't locked.

Her first thought upon entering Jiminy's private domain was confusion. She'd expected a bedroom, but the space looked like it belonged on campus—part library, part workshop. Tidy bookshelves lined one of the long walls, and judging by the number of ribbon markers, book flags, and sticky notes decorating the tomes, Jiminy was conversant with their contents.

At the far end of the room, opposite the door, cubbies and drawers of all sizes overflowed with crystals. Jiminy's collection would probably be the envy of any ward and every museum in the world. She'd never seen the like. Unless you flipped classifications, because in a way, this was a lot like her mother's armory. Tools of the trade.

A computer stood on the desk that jutted out from the remaining long wall, which seemed to have been lined with cork. Sigil designs, scribbled notes, tables and graphs, star charts, photographs of cloud formations, and annotated maps had been tacked across the entire surface. She recognized a handful of national parks, the crests of a dozen mining cooperatives, and a snapshot of Jiminy as a toddler, cuddled against the broad shoulder of an adolescent Nightspangle. In another, he looked eight or nine, and he was cheesing for the camera with three grinning packmates.

The substantial worktable that took up most of the floorspace held tools and gadgets and chunks of stone. Some of it looked like jewelry-making supplies, which made some sense, since ward stones were usually placed in settings or strung together.

No windows to speak of, since this was an interior room—hushed and secure. Clear, white light filled the space, emanating from a series of crystals suspended at regular intervals. It was bright enough to read by and didn't suggest a sleeping chamber. Which brought Melissa back to her purpose.

Where was Jiminy?

Putting her training to good use, she tracked him to his lair. His den included an inner room, which wasn't obvious since it could only be accessed by a crawl-through hidden behind his desk. Melissa pushed past draping furs, softly calling, "Jiminy?"

He was here. She could hear his slow breathing. As her eyes adjusted to the faint light given off by constellations of tiny crystals embedded in the ceiling, she matched his breathing to calm her jitters. This was a private place. She felt like an intruder.

Fur surrounded her, a deep plush that gave off the same wild scent as a wolf. There were no furnishings, only cushions and folded furs. Clearly, the inner room was intended for sleep, and in true wolf fashion, it was large enough to accommodate a group. Jiminy's lone lump in the far corner looked small.

Strange that Doon-wen and Rook lived in a very human apartment, but Jiminy lived in a wolf's den. Each embracing the ways of another.

What should she do? Interrupting felt wrong. She should go.

But Melissa twisted her fingers into the fur and waited just a little longer. Her head ached, and her eyelids grew heavy. This would be a good place to dream of wolves. Just a little longer.

Her guard slipped, her body slumped, and she buried her face in fur. Hardly any time passed when she felt a blanket settle around her shoulders, and she jerked upright, grappling her attacker to the floor and pinning him.

"Melissa?" Jiminy spread his hands in surrender. "Please, don't kill me in your sleep."

She rolled off him, taking the blanket with her. It was perfect for hiding under. "Sorry," she muttered. "Boundaries."

He chuckled. "Who sent you?"

"A matchmaker and a mischief-maker," she grumbled. "Would you just let me sleep? I haven't had a full night in three days."

"Yes. But not alone. Or alone together. Otherwise, the pack will think we're trysting. Doon-wen could insist I take responsibility which always leads to a general cry for proof of ardor." His hand gently shook her shoulder. "Who should I invite?"

"Does it matter?"

"It can, but it doesn't have to." Jiminy patiently explained, "Any wolf would consider it an honor to be asked."

"Doon-wen?"

"I can certainly ask, but he's been extra growly lately. Apparently, the paperwork for registering an enclave is exceptionally tedious. Anyone else?"

She didn't really know that many Nightspangles. "What about the wolves in the photos in your office?"

"Them? Those three pretty much raised me, but they're away for a while."

Melissa was about to steal his blanket and go bed down with

True when another wolf came suddenly to mind. She asked, "Are the Elderboughs still in town?"

All she'd wanted was to borrow a quiet corner in order to catch up on sleep, forgetting—for obvious reasons—that Jiminy considered himself a wolf. *Of course* he'd make a production out of a nap. Within the packs, sleep was almost as sacred as the phases of the moon. Asking for temporary quarters had probably invoked some kind of wolvish standard of courtesy, generosity, and hospitality.

Melissa would have been furious with herself if she hadn't been too tired to make an effort. And if she hadn't been looking forward to something she'd only ever experienced once before. With her father and his Kith companion. Sleeping pack-style.

She'd dozed off again by the time Jiminy returned with reinforcements.

Torloo-dex Elderbough knelt at her side, tugging at her hand. "Did you really ask for me? Nobody's ever asked for *me* before!"

"I will always ask for you, then." She offered her hand. "You are my favorite Elderbough."

His hands were smaller than hers, but not by much. And Melissa could feel his strength, his potential, and his pleasure in being included.

Jiminy crawled into the room, Risk and Dare close behind.

"Did you *really* almost kill Jiminy when he found you?" asked Torloo.

"Incapacitated," she clarified. "I left my blade in its sheath."

"Progress," came Doon-wen's deep voice. Being on hands and knees did little to diminish the pack leader's air of importance. He prowled to the center of the room, nose high, tail switching.

Torloo looked between her and Jiminy and bluntly asked, "Are you courting?"

"No." She sat up and waved at Jiminy as if shooing a fly. "I'm not here for regard or for revenge. I only wanted to rest."

Scooting closer, Torloo whispered, "It would be a good match."

Him, too? Melissa asked, "Why do you think so?"

"Because," the boy answered solemnly. "He is a wolf."

"So are you," she pointed out.

Torloo's gaze slid to the side. "I am many years from reaching my attainment."

Melissa hadn't meant to embarrass him, so she kept her tone light. "Time will tell. Maybe my granddaughter or great-granddaughter will love you."

His eyes widened, and he showed a dimple. Casting aside all formality, he flung his arms around her shoulders and kissed her cheek. "I will be waiting."

"Melissa." Doon-wen sat with legs crossed, fingers drumming his thigh. "My brother is outside. He is prepared to grovel."

She glanced Jiminy's way in time to see him press a palm toward the ceiling. The crystals brightened at his command. Catching her look, he said, "I may have had a few words with him. Entrapment was never his intention. Apparently, it never occurred to Rook that you'd willingly enter my den, let alone willingly remain."

His words bit. Was he angry with Rook?

Doon-wen growled softly, and Jiminy averted his face.

What could she say? Melissa knew Doon-wen and Torloo could read her mood, but Jiminy needed words. She kept it short. "Rook would never willingly hurt the people he loves. He only underestimated my weariness ... and this den's appeal."

Jiminy covered his eyes with his hand and called, "Get in here, Rook. We can't do this without you."

He crawled through, tail tucked, and he kept right on crawling until he reached Melissa. Pulling Jiminy down beside her, Rook mournfully kissed both their foreheads.

"She likes my den," said Jiminy.

Rook's shoulders relaxed. "I know no finer compliment. A den and its founder are likened to a heart and its beat."

Melissa threaded her fingers into the fur that covered the floor and yawned.

Doon-wen immediately took charge, gesturing to the others and saying, "Thank you for inviting us to guard your rest."

Her battler instincts reared up. "Stand guard? Against what?"

Rook and Torloo pulled furs into a central pile, leaving Doon-wen to answer. "Against solitude and its coldness. Against fear and its doubts. Against time and its passing."

"You can stop time?"

"I can diminish its importance," Doon-wen asserted. "All time spent here is ours. It belongs to no other, just as we belong to each other. Now ... enough words."

With that, he transformed into a large, black wolf. Melissa wondered how much power he kept in check in order to fit the available space.

"Sleep sweet," urged Rook, who also took truest form.

The brothers arranged themselves along either side of the room, their muzzles—and formidable jaws—nearest the door. Intruders beware.

Torloo simply kissed his fingertips, held them out to her, and vanished into his own swirl of light, becoming a lean, leggy wolf, no bigger than his two Kith companions. He, Risk, and Dare curled up between Doon-wen's and Rook's forepaws, leaving a narrow patch for her and Jiminy.

Melissa pulled at the blankets and wriggled down among them.

A few moments later, Jiminy stretched out next to her. He said nothing. Only watched her with a seriousness that she was too tired to deal with.

"Can you turn down the stars?" she asked.

He flashed a quick smile, tapped his nose, and pointed to the ceiling. The crystals slowly dimmed. But Melissa could tell he was showing off, because every so often, individual stars would twinkle. It was pretty.

Jiminy asked, "Will you let me hold your hand?"

For an answer, she poked one out of the blanket, letting it flop limply between them.

He fitted his under hers. With both palms turned upward, it was as if he was offering his support.

And that was all. No banter. No flirting. Just an increasingly sleepy watchfulness. Maybe as host, he was supposed to let her go to sleep first?

When she rolled onto her side—as she usually did when she was about to drift off—she turned her hand, and palms met. Fingers found their fit. And Melissa gave in to the inevitable.

A scuffle and sudden emptiness woke Melissa, and she was up and armed before she was truly awake.

"Peace." Torloo's hands closed around her wrist, holding back her weapon with a force that belied his slender frame. "There is no battle here."

"Where is it?" she mumbled.

The young Elderbough giggled.

A protesting groan sounded from the fur-covered floor. Jiminy was trying to bury his head under a cushion.

Melissa sheathed her blade with a sigh. "How long was I asleep?"

"Six hours. Perhaps seven." Torloo's tail wagged. "Are you rested?"

"Yes, thank you." Both Doon-wen and Rook were missing. She had the impression that it was their sudden absence that had disturbed her nap. "Did they have to go?"

"Yes. You should go, as well." Torloo crawled to Jiminy and shook his shoulder. "Your pack sings."

Jiminy's head popped up. A moment later, he scrambled out of the den, muttering about the wards and fair warnings.

"Come." Torloo beckoned for Melissa to follow him out. "True wants you. So does Doon-wen. Come, and attend the birth of their cubs."

34

AVIAN STYLE

Tami hadn't realized the day was so far gone until Mrs. Dabrowski leaned through her office door and shook her car keys. "There are limits, my dear. Whatever it is you're still working on, leave it for tomorrow."

"Arrangements for the town meeting." She pointed from one pile to the next. "Proposed prize lists for Bingo Night. Our next *Bowshot* column. And press releases."

Flootie wrinkled her nose. "Let me and Harrison help with the above-and-beyond stuff. You can't do it all."

"Maybe I should have requested an Amaranthine assistant for us." Tami leaned back in her chair. "I've heard certain clans specialize in paperwork."

"Which clans would those be?"

"Moth, I think."

Her secretary asked, "Is it too late to apply for a moth?"

"Another application." Tami wearily scanned the mess on her desk. "I'm sure I have the right form *somewhere*."

"Leave it," insisted Flootie. "Moths can be first on your agenda tomorrow. And we'll pitch in until you get extra help. Now, go home!"

"Yes, ma'am." Tami dredged up a smile and added, "Thanks."

After Flootie went, Tami sat for a while, resting her eyes and running through the remaining phases of Hisoka Twineshaft's plans for their schools. If she was struggling, the others must be, as well. She'd have to ask Cyril about adding someone to their team, someone detail-oriented and diplomatic.

"Hey."

"Ash." She quickly corrected her posture and tried to hide her weariness. "Busy day?"

"Better, now that Kip's back. The kids missed him."

Although there'd been no time to explore anything that had been said the night before, Tami hadn't forgotten the detail Ash let slip. That he couldn't undo his illusion without his friend's help. "Is he still here?"

"He needed to go home for something." Ash eased further into the room. "It's just us."

"Kip left without you? Don't you live together?"

"I meant he went to ... to where his family lives."

"The enclave?"

Ash simply nodded.

She stood and came out from behind her desk. "Do you need a ride?"

"Thanks, but ... I don't fit in most cars." He looked away and looked back, clearly flustered. "I wanted to ask if we can meet sometimes."

"Away from work?" she ventured. "Like a date?"

"Yes. No. It's an Amaranthine thing, I think. Or an avian instinct." Ash was having difficulty meeting her gaze. "I'm not entirely sure. Sometimes I feel compelled to do things that don't make sense, even to me. It's … embarrassing."

"If it's important to you, I don't see a problem."

His gaze lifted to hers. "Really?"

Tami smiled. "Have you seen some of the things Kimiko Miyabe has to do in order to court Eloquence Starmark? They don't make any sense until the commentators explain the history behind each gesture or tradition. Of course, he's canine and you're avian, so there are bound to be differences. But exploring them will help us get to know each other."

Ash whispered something.

She missed it, so she stepped closer. "Pardon?"

He reached for her, tugged her into his arms, and repeated, "I love you."

"Even though it may lead to embarrassment?"

"You really don't mind?"

Tami lifted her face. "I'm looking forward to being courted by the one I love. Where did you want to meet?"

"The loft in your barn would work."

Certainly convenient, at least for her. "How often would you be dropping by?"

"Every evening."

She couldn't hide her surprise. "That often?"

"If you'll permit it." Ash sighed. "My father swears it's necessary, and I don't think he was teasing. This time."

"Your father, as in your Amaranthine parent?"

"Not my biological father. My adoptive parent is also avian, but from a different clan. He's been helping me sort through my urges." Ash's fingers sifted through her hair. "Courting and building and nurturing a mating bond. He's very excited, since he likes you so much."

"I know your father?"

"Cyril Sunfletch."

Tami laughed. "Dr. Bellamy is going to be my father-in-law?"

"You sound glad." Ash was smiling more naturally now. "And it's nice to hear you refer to my proposed bond as if it's a foregone conclusion."

"Should I have kept you in suspense?"

"No." Ash's lips brushed hers. "Otherwise, I'm not sure I would have had the courage to try."

"You're welcome to try. Every evening. In the loft. Or in the kitchen. Or the sitting room." Tami asked, "We don't have to hide, do we? My family will want to meet you."

Ash hesitated. "I would be pleased to present myself to your family as your suitor. But I don't want an audience for the courting gifts. Their presentation is too personal ... and potentially embarrassing. Cyril described his mating dances in great detail."

"Privacy, then." She slipped her arms around his neck. "Avian clans use gifts for courting?"

"Many do. There are countless variations, but I chose something simple. We can begin tonight, if you'll meet me in the loft." He glanced around the brightly lit office. "I like the atmosphere there better. It's more like a nest."

"When?"

"Eight o'clock?"

Tami accepted that with a smile. "Are you sure you don't need a ride?"

"I'll be there, without fail." The hint of a smirk appeared on his lips. "Your farm isn't so far, as the crow flies."

Kip had no trouble slipping into the enclave unnoticed. He'd been sneaking around the place since he was old enough to crack nuts, and he'd had more practice than most with illusions. His plan was admittedly reckless, and it depended heavily on good luck, but it wasn't exactly risky.

This was home. Or, it used to be. His family expected a certain level of tricky business. They came by their reputation as mischief-makers honestly ... and dishonestly. But no red squirrel liked to be caught red-handed. Yeah, he could make up excuses. Awkwardness and apologies—no problem. He'd play the fool and laugh off his mistake *if* he made one. But Kip really hoped this would work.

Back halls and crawlspaces. Air ducts and acrobatics. With a bit of a scamper and nary a hiccup, he made his way to the entrance to the enclave's inner sanctum—Jiminy's den. Which was heavily warded.

He stood for a while, simply deciphering Jiminy's sigilcraft. Their little phenom was all about personal touches. To his amusement, Kip found wards that promised a world of hurt to a couple of young Woodacre pranksters, should they be foolish enough to try an infiltration. Tuned crystals suggested that other individuals were welcome.

Kip doubted he was shortlisted for entry. He and Jiminy weren't *that* close.

And then one of the sigils began to change shape. Letters formed a simple question—WHY?

No way.

Fascinated, he stepped up to the door. Its anchoring crystals seemed to hum a question. It was almost as if Jiminy had coaxed the stones into divining the intentions of an unexpected guest. *State your business. Give me your reasons.*

Kip had known going in how little chance he had of cracking Jiminy's wards. So instead of wheedling his way past them, Kip tried honesty. He held the urgency of his mission in the forefront of his mind and reached for the door handle.

A clear note seemed to signal approval, and the sigils scattered, leaving the door bare.

The handle turned. He was in.

For a breathless moment, he listened.

Nobody home.

Wasting no time, he crossed to the desk and turned on Jiminy's computer. It whirred to life. Mercifully, there were no passwords to stymie him further. And the icon Kip needed was right on the desktop, helpfully labeled FIRST-SENSEI.

He clicked.

It connected.

Two faces appeared on the screen, but neither was looking at him. Kip felt as if he'd stepped into the middle of an argument.

"Papka won't mind!"

"*Au contraire.*"

Kip's heart sank. This wasn't the person—or persons—he'd been hoping to contact. Should he back out now? His cursor hovered over the button that promised a quick exit.

The teenage girl's attention switched to her screen. "Oh! You're not Mr. Foster." Her eyebrows lifted in an interested way. "Who are you, please?"

"I'm Kip."

"Is Mr. Foster there?"

"Not at the moment."

She folded her hands on the desk and calmly asked, "Why are you in Mr. Foster's room?"

"I needed some advice, and I thought maybe ...." Kip hesitated. This was ridiculous. She was just a kid. Leaning forward, he asked, "Who are *you*, please?"

"Isla Ward of Stately House. This is Uncle Jackie, our butler."

"Jacques Smythe." The young man, who knew how to gussy, offered a sultry smile. "You haven't answered Isla, pretty boy. Why are you in Jimsy's room? Are your intentions honorable?"

Kip got the distinct impression that Jacques hoped they weren't.

Isla must have agreed, since she rolled her eyes and batted the butler's arm. "Behave."

"He looks decidedly roguish," countered Jacques. "I'm only thinking of dear, sweet Jimsy. Isn't he meant to be a possible suitor for you?"

"No," the girl said firmly, but she was blushing.

Kip propped his chin on his hand, enjoying the unfolding drama in spite of his disappointment. Before the Emergence, when technology was off-limits, Jiminy had been so isolated. Clearly, he'd made friends.

Isla said, "I would be pleased to advise you, Kip."

Cute kid. Kip smiled and shrugged. "I don't think you can ...."

Isla's chin tipped up, and she crisply announced, "I am quite knowledgeable on a variety of topics and sympathetic to the wants and worries of every clan. What is the nature of your inquiry?"

Kip was already shaking his head, partly in amazement. He tried to match her formality. "It's a matter of some delicacy."

"My favorite," murmured Jacques.

What a flirt. Kip had half a mind to mess with him. But the butler's expression underwent a sudden shift. His eyes lit up like Christmas had come, though he quickly schooled his features into an unconvincing air of disinterest.

Another voice carried through, blandly amused. "Why have the two of you commandeered Michael's desk?"

"Language lessons," Isla said primly. "We *have* permission."

"Oh? And is your virtual companion conversant in Japanese?"

Another face loomed into view, both amused and accusing.

"Nope." Kip figured he was in about as much trouble as he could be. Leaning heavily on the manners his mother had harped on ever since he'd found his feet, he gave a little wave. "Good evening, Lord Mossberne."

A bejeweled hand planted itself on the desk, and sapphire eyes narrowed.

He smiled and let his tail flick into view. May as well be memorable.

"And you are ...?"

"Kip."

The spokesperson for the dragon clans hummed. "Are you a Woodacre? You *look* like a Woodacre."

"Yes."

Isla piped up. "Lapis, he says he needs advice on a delicate matter."

The dragon turned away, and dark blue hair swayed across most of the screen. "Whose advice?" he inquired.

"Naturally, I assumed Papka."

"If Kip was in need of a ward, young Mr. Foster could surely accommodate him." Turning back to the screen, Lapis anticipated his answer by stating, "Argent is unavailable."

"Gotcha. Sorry to interrupt. I should probably be ...."

Lapis held up a finger. "Isla, my dear girl, yield your place to me. Kip and I need a few minutes alone. Jacques, if you would be so kind?"

The butler murmured something in French, blew Kip a kiss, and strolled off screen. Isla took a little longer, needing to gather up her books and papers. She smiled brightly and offered a gesture that was pure wolvish—*I'm glad our paths crossed.*

Kip grinned and answered in kind.

Then it was only Lapis, who took the time to arrange himself before the camera. The dragon lord's hands flashed through a series of sigils that Kip recognized. He was securing additional privacy on his end. Grateful for the courtesy, Kip mirrored his actions.

Lapis dipped his head approvingly ... and waited.

Not the audience he'd been hoping for, but Lord Mossberne was one of the Five. He probably knew stuff. Kip blurted, "How can I bind my life to a human's?"

Delight suffused the dragon's face. He leaned forward. "You have found a lady to love?"

"W-well …."

"And she returns your affection?"

"We've come to an understanding. Of sorts," Kip hedged.

Lapis tilted his head, as if trying to hear what was left unspoken. Gently, he asked, "Is she a reaver?"

Gesturing surrender, Kip admitted, "He's unregistered."

Rather than off-put, the dragon seemed intrigued. And his gaze drifted out of focus. Finally, he flicked his fingers. "Any other fascinating little complications I should be aware of?"

With a weak laugh, he confirmed Lapis' suspicion. "I'm Kith-kin."

35

KEEPER

Promptly at seven fifty-five, Tami nudged Joe and whispered, "Will you keep Biddie with you for a while?"

"Something up?" he asked.

"A friend promised to stop by."

Her brother's eyes drifted out of focus for just a moment or two. Nodding once, he sat up a little straighter, kissed the top of her head, and murmured, "He's a keeper."

"He told you?"

Joe gently disentangled Biddie, who draped against Tami like a sleepy kitten. "That he's a keeper? Nope. That's just what I think."

"That he's a crosser."

"So *that's* it."

"You didn't know?" Tami was sure Joe had known. Why else would he insist on that first meeting in the haymow?

Her brother shrugged.

"Joey-boy," Biddie murmured, wrapping her arms around his neck and kissing his cheek.

He gently touched the little girl's leafy crown. "We'll be fine. I'll keep Biddie with me. Or walk her home if that's what she wants."

Tami hesitated, quite sure that her brother was holding out on her.

"He's waiting for you." Emotion flickered through his eyes, and he softly added, "Probably has been for a long while. You know?"

She did. And that thought hastened her steps.

Leaves crunched underfoot when she cut across the yard. The moon lit her way, and she mightn't have given it a second glance if not for the sound of wolves howling in an eerily beautiful chorus. Nightspangles in the oak glen, singing the moon into the sky. She paused to consider its rising. A few days from full, the waxing moon was ringed by bands of hazy color. What her grandmother used to call a moondoggie night.

Letting herself through the door, she blinked and waited for her eyes to adjust. "I'm here," she called softly.

"Here I am," he answered. By the sound of it, he'd been waiting at the base of the ladder.

Still blind, she moved forward, hands outstretched. "Did you see the moon?"

"Yes." He caught her wrists and folded her in his arms. Feathers brushed close, and he asked, "Are you warm enough?"

Murmuring hasty reassurances, she asked, "Did you really fly here?"

"No. I can't actually fly. Too much body mass. But I can jump pretty high, and I've learned to use my wings to get the most out of any airtime. I'm not exactly *graceful*, but I can keep up with ...."

"With Kip?" she guessed.

Ash simply nodded and guided her to the ladder. "Up you go."

She needed to corner Kip, get his side of the story. By the time she reached the top, she had a plan. "We should have dinner together tomorrow, just the three of us. Then Kip can tattle on himself, and we'll be past the awkward stage."

"That'd be good."

It was brighter in the loft, where bands of moonlight stole through shutters that Ash must have opened earlier. He took her hands and drew her along, backing directly into the slanting beams. Their light made it possible to make out what could only be called a nest.

"Did you do this?"

"I'll put it back if it's a problem."

Ash had pulled away several straw bales, leaving a hollow in the stack, around which he'd formed a low wall. Inside he'd mounded loose straw and a couple of blankets. Tami thought they might have been the ones from the back of Kip's jeep.

"Nobody is going to notice, let alone mind," she promised. "We don't come up here very often."

He guided her into the niche and made her sit on the outspread blanket. Using the other to cover her legs, he asked, "Can you see all right?"

"Well enough." Tami glanced between him, the moonbeams, and the floor. "Your wings don't even cast shadows."

"Yeah. The sigilcraft is pretty complicated. Kip knows his stuff." Kneeling in front of her, Ash pulled something from an inner pocket of his denim jacket. "Is it all right if I skip the formal parts and just explain? Or would you feel slighted?"

Tami settled back. "Explain as we go, please. Then I'm free to ask questions."

"Okay, good. Because I'm not sure I can pull off all the grand gestures Cyril demonstrated." His grip tightened around the bundle in his hands. "But that doesn't mean I'm not serious."

She smiled and asked, "Where do we start?"

"Here." Ash extended both hands. "With this."

At first, Tami thought it was a gift in clumsy wrappings. But as her fingers explored the soft folds, she quickly revised her assessment. It was a pouch that fit easily into the palm of one hand. The material was supple, like fine leather, and she could feel patterned stitches and beadwork. Braided cords created a drawstring closure. It was empty.

Holding it up so the moonlight brought out some of the shine to the beads, she asked, "What should I do with it?"

"Keep it. And bring it with you when I visit." Ash rearranged himself, sitting cross-legged. "Courting traditions vary between the different avian clans. Crows are collectors. The gist is … every evening, I bring a gift, and if it pleases you, you add it to the bag before sending me on my way."

"What happens once the bag is full?"

Ash plucked at the edge of her blanket. "You *don't* send me away."

Straightforward. Tami fingered the knot. "What kinds of gifts can the keeper of the pouch expect from her generous suitor?"

"Items with special meaning. I brought one." He huffed softly. "Before I show you, can I ask for one of those hard-to-explain things?"

Tami's heart leapt. This was nothing like the pageantry that accompanied the Miyabe-Starmark courtship, yet she was on the edge of her seat. Because this was *her* courtship. And Ash was her suitor. "Tell me what to do."

"It's driving me crazy that I'm not touching you." He waved his hands and muttered, "That sounded worse than it needed to."

"They covered this at the educators' conference I attended. Amaranthine are tactile."

"Yeah. Any contact is fine, but holding you would be ... really nice. And I apologize in advance if I start preening you."

She pushed up onto her knees. "Where to you want me?"

He settled her in front of him so she could lean back into his chest. There was much shifting and tucking and the faint rustle of settling feathers before he was satisfied.

Tami asked, "How does preening work?"

"Usually, it's fussing with hair or fur of feathers. I find it calming." Ash's fingers were back in her hair, gently tugging until her head rested against his shoulder. He kissed her temple and added, "When an avian is preening someone, it's a sign of affection. Or even devotion."

"Does Cyril preen you?"

"Yes." Ash's arms settled around her waist. "My first gift is about him. I thought you'd like to know how he came to be my father."

"Perfect," she said, relaxing into him. "I'd love to know that story."

"First, this." He let go long enough to fumble in a pocket, bringing out something that swung from a chain.

She caught it, exploring the shapes. It seemed to be a necklace with a heavy pendant.

"Hang on." Ash brought out a pen light, which cast a dim circle upon the necklace in her hands. The chain was silver, from which was suspended a speckled egg—pale green with brown mottling.

"Is this a real egg?"

"Yes." With one fingertip, he traced a hairline crack. "A much smaller crow than me hatched from this egg. They managed it neatly, and so my father had this shell set it in silver. See the catch?"

Tami gently twisted the clasp. The top portion of the egg swung upward on a miniscule hinge, revealing a heart of silver. Inside was single twig, gray and brittle with age.

Ash said, "In the oldest of avian traditions, parents would keep a piece of the eggshell from which their child hatched. These keepsakes were made into ornaments, to be used as tokens for courtship. All avian clans recognize the significance of a gift that includes an eggshell."

"Amaranthine hatch?" She couldn't help the skepticism that crept into her tone.

"Avians do if they find their way into this world while in truest form."

She nodded thoughtfully. "Cyril had this made for you?"

"For himself. At least, at first. He wore it constantly—as proof that I'm his son—until last week, when he approved my choice." Ash closed the egg, then closed her fingers around it. "He has been good to me. I don't think I would have survived without him."

"How did you come to be his?" she asked.

Ash rested his cheek against her hair and began, "I'm half Native-American, but I don't remember my mother. I'm half Amaranthine, but I don't know my father's name or his clan. My earliest memories are of fear and running and hunger and pain, but those are half-remembered impressions and make a poor story. Better by far—at least in hindsight—is the tale of a wretched boy who was caught by a wolf."

Tami turned into Ash, her ear pressed over his heart, her hand tucked under her chin.

"I am told that when she found me, I was a mess of scrapes and bruises, and I'd been pulling out my own feathers. The scent of my blood was in the air, and she ran me to ground. I remember being sure that the big, black wolf would gobble me up, but she didn't."

"Was she a Nightspangle?"

"Yes. A Kith named True." Ash's voice warmed. "She trapped me, but she kept me warm, and when the other wolves came, she snapped and snarled, keeping them away. Then one of the wolves changed into a man with a tail. He tried to talk to me, but I was quite wild, unable to speak."

"How old were you?"

"They guessed I was four, maybe five."

"Too young to be alone."

He hummed his agreement. "The pack camped around me and True, and I was sure they were waiting for me to stray from her protection. I didn't realize that these predators were the only reason I didn't fall prey to other beasts. Or that they were waiting for reinforcements."

"Cyril."

"Yes."

That one syllable was packed with love and gratitude, and Tami's estimation of Dr. Bellamy soared higher.

Ash said, "He sashayed into the clearing, dressed all in gold and draped in a cloak of feathers, shining and proud and fearless. When he spoke to me, it wasn't with words, but with sounds—trills and coos and clucks. And they made sense to me."

"Like a bird language?"

"More like … skipping all the words and expressing feelings instead."

"So you trusted him because he was a bird?"

Ash chuckled. "I'm not sure it was as sensible as that. I went to him because he was the most beautiful person I'd ever seen."

"Then it's fortunate for you that Cyril is so very good."

"I've since learned that it's an avian quirk. We can be slow to trust, yet quickly swayed by a strong first impression. Like love at first sight."

Tami caught the change in his tone and tried to search his face. "You seem more sensible than that."

"I have a sensible side." Dark eyes glittered in the moonlight. "But it mostly picks up the pieces after the rest of me has gone and done something impulsive."

"Like love at first sight?"

"Maybe I'll tell you about that tomorrow." He kissed her lightly. "Will you accept my first gift, Tamiko?"

Few people knew her full first name, and even fewer used it. She'd been *Tami* for so long, it was strange to hear Ash draw out the whole of it, lightly touching each syllable, speaking with sounds that had become feelings.

An intimacy. Another gift.

So she did her best to pack a single syllable with all the hope and delight and desire that were brimming in her heart. "Yes."

36

LITTER

oon-wen's growl stopped Melissa in her tracks, and she backed up so fast, she bumped into Jiminy. "That was for me," he murmured, taking a blatantly submissive stance. "And it wasn't personal. More of a formality. Another male in the den, and all that."

"Why are we here?" she whispered.

Jiminy nudged her toward a seat to one side of the door. "When a reaver runs with a pack, it's traditional for them to attend the births of Kith and Kindred alike."

"So we're here in an honorary capacity?"

"Oh, there's a practical aspect. My new packmates need to understand that I'm neither a threat nor a chew toy. I'm often honored to be the first to learn a cub's name, since I'm granted a formal introduction." Jiminy slouched against the wall, totally relaxed.

"What about Rook?"

279

Jiminy shot her a questioning look.

"Isn't *he* another male? Why does Doon-wen let his brother in here?"

"Rook is Doon-wen's comfort, and Doon-wen is Rook's confidence. They are together in everything." He made a gesture she couldn't interpret. "True is a part of their pact, so they are all a part of each other. You know?"

She didn't. But she was beginning to see. Maybe it was because the brothers never covered the same shift, but she'd rarely seen them work together. They were perfect. Without a word spoken, they readied the den for new arrivals. Doon-wen arranged basins and towels, and Rook checked the boxy setup in the corner that Melissa recognized as a blanket warmer. Tails swaying in perfect tandem, their attention stayed on True.

"Are they twins?" Melissa asked.

Jiminy shook his head. "They are close because they choose to be."

Melissa pulled her legs to her chest, feeling extraneous, retreating into herself.

"Not like that." Jiminy pushed straight through boundaries to press his hands against her shoulders. Before she could elbow his gut, he said, "They know we're here, you know."

A silly thing to say. She tried to shrug him off.

"The cubs. Even before they're born, they can sense our souls." Jiminy carefully withdrew his hands, but he held her gaze. "We are the first brightness they know, even before they can open their eyes."

Nobody had mentioned that in her classes at Bellwether's Kith shelter. Melissa asked, "How do you know?"

"The cubs often have baby names for me. They remember me,

even if they haven't seen me since the day they were born." His eyes danced. "I wonder what they'll call you?"

"But ... what should I *do*?"

Jiminy said, "Treat this like a tending. Calm yourself and think welcoming thoughts."

"I'm a battler," she reminded. "My soul isn't exactly gentle."

"But it can be confident." He bumped shoulders with her. "Leave the comforting to me."

Melissa was fully aware that he'd used the same terms for Doon-wen and Rook. Was Jiminy trying to imply that they, too, could be ... perfect?

"Focus on the cubs, Melissa." Jiminy nodded toward True. "Let them get a sense for all the love and loyalty you've always wanted to offer."

Oh, she wanted to. Desperately. But wouldn't that be taking advantage of the situation? What about her classmates at Bellwether? They wanted this as much as she did. "But ... is that fair?" she ventured.

Jiminy shook his head as if she were being very silly. "That's family."

Even though Jiminy wanted to help Melissa navigate through her uncertainty, he knew his place. Mostly because Doon-wen made it abundantly clear, and Rook—much more politely—reinforced their alpha's message. *Back off.*

So he took a seat and waited to see how she'd fare. In a way, this was Melissa's final exam. Her behavior—unguarded and unguided—would determine her attainment.

Rook paused beside him, tousled his hair, and said, "You're jumpy as a cricket."

"Should I wait outside?"

"No. Doon-wen wants you here. Perhaps you should take your own advice. Focus on the cubs."

Jiminy composed himself as best he could, but his attention kept straying to Melissa ... and the way Doon-wen's gaze lingered on her—keen, critical, calculating. Without really meaning to, Jiminy protested on her behalf, a soft whine, a bid for sympathy.

Doon-wen arched a brow and offered no reassurance. Only commanded him to watch and wait.

Unaware of the subtext surrounding her, Melissa knelt beside True's muzzle, stroking the she-wolf's ears and asking questions. Rook occasionally relayed a response, but Doon-wen watched without comment, taking his time, testing the air.

Melissa's attitude baffled Jiminy.

Here was a battler, sure of what she wanted, ready to vie with her peers for the right to partner with a Kith. Yet when given the chance to make an impression on a new litter, she was holding back. Instead of focusing on the cubs, she gave all her attention to True.

She probably didn't want Doon-wen to think she was after his cubs. As if he didn't know how desperate she was to partner with a Kith. As if the wily old wolf wasn't actively bringing them together.

True had chosen her. Doon-wen had plans for her. All because Melissa grasped the essence of Kith partnership. Some battlers might blunder in, hoping for the pick of the litter. But she wanted to be chosen. Melissa was willing to wait for mutual respect, loyalty, and love.

If the sway of their alpha's tail was anything to go by, she would have it.

"Come here, Melissa." Doon-wen held out a hand—commanding, coaxing. He made her kneel in front of him, in the receiving position. "Into your hands."

"Me?" she gasped.

"True wishes it." He gravely kissed her hair. "I wish it."

Melissa offered a shaky smile, and Doon-wen crouched behind her, his body curving over hers in an unmistakable posture. He was covering her, not with the possessiveness of a mate, but that of a father. And Jiminy rocketed to his feet.

Rook was before him in a blink, a hand on his chest. "Wait and watch. You are their witness."

"Does she *know*?" Jiminy gave his best rendition of a growl. "She should not be ignorant of the rare honor they are bestowing."

Meanwhile, True strained, and the first cub slipped into view, landing in the straw between Melissa's knees. She supported the newborn against her chest while Doon-wen made sure nose and mouth were clear. Damp fuzz wriggled, and Melissa grunted under the cub's weight.

"A son," said Doon-wen. "We will call him High, for the hopes he will answer."

Rook hurried forward with towels and a warm blanket. He said, "A fine boy, and a fine name. Welcome to the pack, nephew."

Jiminy didn't want to steal any of the luster from High's arrival, but he could not remain silent. He was their pack's liaison, and Melissa deserved to know what was happening. So he took a more assertive stance and offered another semblance of a growl.

Doon-wen spared him a glance.

"She should know," he said firmly.

With a careless gesture, Doon-wen allowed his approach.

Melissa's smile was the brightest Jiminy had ever seen. Her happiness overflowed, even to him, and he allowed himself a moment's basking. But only a moment. "Melissa, there's a wolvish custom, and you're becoming part of it."

She glanced between them. "Okay?"

"You have been placed between Doon-wen and his mate, and in receiving their cubs, you're being covered in blood and birthing fluids."

"Hardly *covered*," she argued.

"The scent, Melissa. You have the same scent; you are in the same place." Jiminy could see she still wasn't grasping the symbolism. "You are among the cubs."

Melissa cast a questioning look at Doon-wen, finally registering how near he loomed.

When the pack leader said nothing, Jiminy crouched beside her and explained something that normally required no words. "From this day forward, Doon-wen and True can claim you as one of this litter. This is your birthplace. You haven't been raised as a wolf, but you'll *be* a wolf."

True growled.

Doon-wen rolled his eyes.

Rook quietly reminded, "True is Kith."

"Oh, right." Jiminy tried to hide his grin. "Technically, you'd be Kith-kin."

"What's ...?" she began.

But True groaned, and Doon-wen growled. Another cub was arriving, and the discussion ended in a rush of readying.

Jiminy probably should have moved to a polite distance. This was not his den, neither were these his denmates. Emotions ran high, occasionally resonating with the various crystals he kept about his person. Hardly surprising, given that Doon-wen had shed most of his restraint. His cubs would know the full force of his strength. And of his joy.

Rook's presence might not dominate, but it was no less powerful. He hummed as he roughed and wrapped High in a blanket woven from many brushings, fur gathered from father, mother, and uncle.

For a moment, another presence caught Jiminy's attention. Fleeting. Elusive.

"Another son," announced Doon-wen.

He turned his head to pin Jiminy with a look that was not exactly hostile, although it definitely held a challenge. Jiminy quickly lowered his gaze and scooted backward.

Doon-wen's casual grab ended his retreat. "What do you think?"

Jiminy's gaze swung to the cub occupying all of Melissa's attention. His opinion was needed?

Wait. Doon-wen and True were parents to dozens of Kith, all exceptional. Yet none of their children had ever found speaking form. Kith-kin were rare in a broad sense, but for an established pair, their chances were always one-in-four. It hadn't occurred to Jiminy that Doon-wen might have been hoping.

"Is there any way to tell?" Jiminy asked quietly.

"No."

He lifted his hands. "May I?"

Melissa grunted as she hefted the newborn around. The cub nearly staggered Jiminy. "Even bigger than your brother," he accused.

A soft whine. A questing nose.

Doon-wen bent close, murmuring old words into new ears.

Jiminy wasn't sure he could offer any kind of opinion. Historically, Kith-kin surprised their unsuspecting families by suddenly taking speaking form. While not exactly scandalous, they weren't entirely normal. Clans might embrace their special children, but they didn't advertise their existence. Jiminy would never have known that Kith-kin existed if not for Kip.

Could he assess power or potential?

Reavers needed to be periodically assessed by an Amaranthine in order to be ranked. That was standard procedure. But reavers weren't called upon to quantify the quality of clan members. He doubted such a thing was even possible, since the oldest and strongest personages were usually adept at disguising their true strength, like a fox hiding his flourish.

Although ... lately, there were rumors about a person who could see into the souls of Amaranthine. A new breed of reaver, currently making the rounds of settlements and sanctuaries. The way the communiques went on, he was revered as some kind of messiah, since he could apparently tend to the Broken and make them well again.

Someone like that would probably know. But Jiminy's talent centered around stones and sigilcraft. Even so, he recalled

Michael's mention of a new technique, invented on the fly in order to allow two souls into close enough contact to give each an impression of the other. Wasn't that a kind of assessment?

Eyes shut. Mind open. Carefully, cautiously, Jiminy sought—and found—some sense of the cub in his arms. And since a means of comparison was readily available, he turned his attention to the cub's littermates—one born, one unborn.

"He *is* strong." Resting his forehead against the canine brow, Jiminy asked, "Will we have a proper chat one day, cub? I don't recommend giving your elder sister any sass."

Melissa bristled.

Doon-wen's tail wagged with an extra lift, and the glance he shot Rook mingled triumph and trepidation.

"A fine son." Rook's smile was all affection. "What shall we call him?"

"He will be called Gate, to honor the farm where he can run."

Gate licked Jiminy's chin.

Melissa touched Doon-wen's arm. "Is True all right?"

"Someone is eager to catch up to their brothers."

Everyone hurried to welcome True's third cub. But Jiminy sat with eyes half-shut, because that elusive presence flitted briefly into focus. Not True, nor any of her cubs. Not Doon-wen or Rook. The impression was there and gone so fast, it was frustrating.

"A daughter," declared Doon-wen, sounding decidedly smug. "Her name will be Lace, for the ties binding her life to ours."

Rook cleared his throat. "Two sons, two daughters. True is pleased."

Melissa hugged the black cub to her chest. Her voice quavered a little when she asked, "Really?"

Doon-wen inclined his head. "I have been in communication with Christopher. He is not opposed to sharing paternity. Indeed, he and Cove have promised to attend your Whelping Feast."

37
ENOUGH SAID

Melissa texted both Aunt Hiro and Tami, letting them know she was planning on staying over. Doon-wen had insisted, purportedly on True's behalf. Rook's smile suggested that his brother was exercising some measure of paternal prerogative. No matter the reason, she was flattered and flustered and mostly unfazed when Jiminy showed every sign of lingering in the immediate vicinity.

"Take a picture for me?" she asked, holding out her phone.

Jiminy feigned surprise. "What's the occasion?"

"I need to break it to my mothers that I have another mother."

His brows lifted, and he leaned close to whisper, "Shouldn't you get Rook over here, too?"

She probably shouldn't have smiled. "I've sent pictures of Rook before. Lots of times."

Several pictures were taken before True was satisfied, and

Melissa tried to find words that fit the sudden turn her life was taking. How did you tell your parents that you no longer identified as a reaver?

Magda's response came immediately.

> We know.

Which part?

> All of it.
> One of your Nightspangles
> arrived three days ago.
> Spent the whole day

Doon-wen was there? But how could that be? He'd sworn not to go from True until the cubs were born. And Rook had been covering so many shifts.

I'm confused
Which wolf
was there?

> Lookha-soh Nightspangle,
> Bellwether Enclave

I don't know him

> Interesting. You will.
> We were honored
> by his visit. He left
> with our permission

A wolf she'd never met had gone all the way to California in order to tell her mothers about Doon-wen's plan to bring her into the pack?

> Tell True we'll meet soon

When?

> Dichotomy Day at the latest

290

We're proud, no matter
what you choose

Melissa hadn't realized Jiminy was watching her so closely until he brought over one of the warmed blankets and draped it around her shoulders.

"Something wrong?" he asked.

"Do you know someone called Lookha-soh?"

Jiminy blinked. "Yes. I can introduce you, if you like."

"I think Doon-wen sent him to talk to my mothers. To get their permission or something." She tucked her phone away and shoved straw into a better backrest.

"Melissa, there's another possibility." Jiminy sat beside her and toyed with a piece of straw. "And I swear to you, I knew nothing about it."

She shrugged. "Why would you?"

He stared fixedly at the straw twirling between his fingers. "It's very likely that Lookha-soh carried a message from Doon-wen. Wolves prefer firsthand communication. But I strongly suspect that Lookha volunteered for the journey in order to meet your family."

Melissa was too tired for guessing games. "Why?"

"Lookha-soh Nightspangle is my foster father." Jiminy glanced up at her through the fringe of his bangs. "He's very protective."

He had foster parents. They lived here, in the enclave. She'd known that in a detached sort of way, but she'd been so busy enforcing boundaries, she hadn't looked beyond them.

Another detail sent her stomach plunging. "Do they know about the dagger thing?"

Jiminy chuckled. "If Denny knows something, *everyone* knows it."

"Should I be worried about retaliation?"

"For a straightforward rebuff? Hardly. She-wolves aren't renowned for their gentleness." He shrugged. "I wouldn't worry. My mother likes you."

Melissa drew a blank. "I've met your parents?"

"Sure. My father brings the milk deliveries, and my mother teaches at Bellwether. They went along when we brought the Kith to Red Gate Farm."

"Your mom is Roonta-kiv?"

"When I arrived as a newborn, Roonta had recently given birth to a daughter. I was suckled alongside my new sister. Lookha fostered me, and their son Hanoo had the minding of me. I am theirs in much the same way that you belong to Doonwen, True, and Rook."

"I should have realized," she murmured.

"Don't feel bad." He shifted closer. "Say, Melissa. Can I try something?"

She employed an elbow. "You're *always* trying something."

Jiminy charged ahead. "It was during the births that I first noticed something ... different. A little like a song. A little like a soul. I'd like to rule out the obvious—your crystals, you."

"Me?"

"Well, it's possible." Jiminy took an overtly submissive posture. "I want to talk to First-sensei about it. He'd find it interesting, too."

"So this is for class?" Melissa checked.

"Purely academic."

She gave in with a weary grumble. "I'm still armed."

"No touching. Probably. And True's here."

Melissa asked, "What are you going to do?"

He waved his hands vaguely. "See if I can recapture the moment. Prolong the connection."

"Reavers can't give a true accounting of souls," she reminded. Only an Amaranthine could determine a reaver's quality and issue a grade.

"Who says?"

She shook her head. "Everyone says."

"Not my mentor." Jiminy arranged himself in a comfortable sprawl on the straw at her side, hands behind his head, eyes shut. "First-sensei regularly deals with all kinds of potent souls, and he developed a technique that allows the essence of two souls to touch while he mediates. He makes it safe for both parties. Nobody can be overwhelmed."

"And this works with two reavers?"

"Sensei didn't mention trying it, but *we* could."

Melissa pointed out, "It's not even remotely the same."

"Well, no. But doesn't Sensei's discovery prove that there are still things we can discover?"

What was the harm? "Go ahead. Rule me out."

"Relax. Take the receptive attitude they teach for tending." After a lengthy pause, he murmured, "Your personal wards are serious business."

He was meddling with her wards? Melissa asked, "Should I take them off?"

"Would you mind?" Jiminy's eyes were open, his gaze speculative. "I could get past them, but they'd still limit my access."

"To what? My soul?" Melissa undid buckles and braces. "Isn't there someone else's soul you can mess with?"

"No one I know well enough to want to try. Something like this is rather personal, don't you think?"

"I *do* think." Melissa unfastened the cuff on the shell of her ear.

Jiminy sat up fast. "There were more?"

"These only have sigils. No crystals." She pushed the curls away from her other ear, showing him the other cuff, watching his expression. Melissa preferred underestimation to estimation. It was much more useful in battle and rarely led to personal remarks.

"You rank, don't you." It was a statement, not a question.

"Does it matter?" She turned to True. "Am I making you uncomfortable? This won't harm the cubs, will it?"

"I am here. They are safe." Doon-wen's voice came from his bondmate's other side, where he'd undoubtedly been eavesdropping. "Slip the final ward, Melissa."

Jiminy held out a hand, and she dropped the cuffs onto his palm. He explored each carefully while casting surreptitious glances her way. Ignoring them, Melissa tugged up her pantleg, revealing an ankle chain. She undid the clasp and added it to the collection in Jiminy's palm.

"This craftsmanship ...?"

"Spider."

His low whistle was all appreciation.

True huffed, and Doon-wen grunted his agreement.

From his seat near the door, Rook said, "You admire the settings. We see the star."

She probably made for a very spiky, violent, biting sort of star. Nevertheless, Melissa blushed under the compliment.

"Maybe I'll catch a glimpse." Jiminy carefully—almost reverently—set aside her wards and resumed his place. "It might not work at all, but I'd still like to try. If you're willing."

Melissa didn't want to make this a big production. It wouldn't work.

Jiminy tentatively extended his hand. "I doubt it'll work if you don't trust me at least a little."

She gripped his hand firmly and asked, "Will this take long?"

"No idea." Shutting his eyes, he repeated, "Relax. And trust me."

It wasn't as if she *didn't* trust him. He made sense once you took his upbringing into account. Jiminy had a wolf's perspectives and a wolf's ideology. Admirable things. Useful insights. If only he weren't so ....

She struggled to find a word that fit. Cheerful. Talkative. Relaxed. Persistent. But those weren't necessarily bad qualities. In fact, those were some of the things she loved most about Magda, who never minded that Mother was everything she wasn't. Reserved. Focused. Direct. Competitive. Their skills were a complement to each other's both on the battlefield and at home.

Melissa refused to follow that line of thinking any further.

Her plans may have undergone a slight shift, but the essence remained. She neither wanted nor needed a man to size up her pedigree and schedule a paternity visit. Her partner would be fiercely faithful, a steady and equal companion, accepting her silences, understanding her shortcomings, and choosing to remain.

She would accept nothing less.

If only her inner debate didn't keep cycling back to Jiminy and his ridiculous assertion. *"I can give you those things."*

What a thing to say.

What a nice thing to say.

"Are you all right?" Jiminy's urgent whisper tickled her hair. When had he moved closer?

Her confusion doubled when it occurred to her that somehow, somewhere, a boundary had gone missing. This man for whom the wind danced and stones sang had infiltrated the hidden place at her heart.

Reavers had long been hospitable to the Amaranthine, but this wolf bore little resemblance to Kith or Kindred. They had been described as a vast and formless darkness, longing to be lit by stars. Yet here was brilliance. A star without its setting. A soul in all its splendor. And the brush of a personality that could only be Jiminy.

"Boundaries," she whispered. For there were none. Should she be afraid of this?

"Shh, shh. It's okay." His hands moved, cradling her head, her cheek. "My fault, all my fault. But we've gotten tangled. Can you let me go?"

Melissa lifted her hands to show they were empty. She dared not open her eyes. There was too much light behind her eyelids.

Jiminy threaded his fingers with hers and whispered, "This is beautiful. *You* are beautiful. But if this continues, I'll give in, and you'll be angry."

She couldn't make sense of his words. Why would she be angry when everything about this was luminous and lovely?

"Please, Melissa." Jiminy's lips brushed hers with each word. "It was you all along, and I didn't know this would happen, and I think we need some help, Rook."

A shadow billowed over them, settling like the blanket around Melissa's shoulders—warm and safe and familiar. In reaching for Rook, she lost touch with Jiminy.

Her hand tightened, and Jiminy squeezed back.

"Here I am. Right here." His voice wavered. "Please, don't be angry."

Melissa kept her eyes firmly shut, like a child who doesn't want a particularly good dream to end. "I'm not angry."

"But I ..."

"Hush."

Into the sudden silence, Doon-wen spoke. "Jiminy, perhaps you should go."

Jiminy shuffled awkwardly, then whispered, "Melissa, can you let me go?"

What did he mean? Oh. She had his hands.

Melissa finally opened her eyes. Jiminy looked half-frantic and full of apologies she didn't want to hear. "No," she said slowly. "I don't think I can. Could you?"

Eyes wide, he shook his head.

She loosened her grip and nodded once. Enough said.

38

PRESERVATIONISTS

With firm plans finally in place to have dinner with Ash and Kip, Tami had been hoping to leave work on the early side. But shortly after the last buses were pulling away with homebound children, Harrison rapped smartly on her half-open office door.

"Principal Reaverson?" he called, with more formality—and more volume—than was even remotely necessary. *Something* had him keyed up. His eyebrows were jumping, and he was patting his heart as if trying to calm it down.

Mentally bracing herself for a disgruntled parent or another unscheduled inspection by the Office of Ingress, Tami squared her shoulders and folded her hands atop her desk. "Yes, Harrison? I'm here," she replied, even though he could see that for himself.

"Some people to see you." His voice broke.

Tami couldn't have been more perplexed. He looked for all

the world like a man held at gunpoint. Taking a soothing tone, she said, "Thank you, Harrison. I have time."

His Adam's apple bobbed, and he cleared his throat. Then, as if playing the part of a butler in some scene for which Tami hadn't seen the script, he swung the door wide and announced, "Lady Estrella Mettlebright and Dr. Arno Brecht, along with their escort. Dear, me. I didn't catch your name, sir."

"Reaver."

Tami wasn't sure if the stern-faced man was announcing his name or his title.

The reaver looked like he should be playing professional basket-ball instead of strolling around in a long duster and combat boots. Either way, he entered the office, scanned it without any change of expression, and stepped aside for an unassuming man who bowed his head as he passed through the door.

Next to enter was a dainty lady with an abundance of silver hair all done up in glittering combs. Draped in silver and blue, she possessed the ageless beauty—and pointed ears—of an Amaranthine. "*Thank you* for asking after Ismal." Her English was excellent, but her accent suggested someplace far from Fletching. "We are not allowed to traipse about without an escort, and he has been exceedingly gracious."

Tami noted the *we*, which implied that Estrella's companion was also Amaranthine. She took a longer look at the bespectacled male. Dressed all in tweedy browns, he was squarish, creased, and rumpled, with the healthy tan of a perpetual outdoorsman. Meeting her curious gaze, he rocked up on the balls of his feet, then back on his heels, apparently antsy to be introduced.

299

"Welcome to Landmark Elementary," Tami offered with as much poise as she could muster. "What can I do for you?"

"A small matter of some urgency." Lady Mettlebright indicated her companion. "Dr. Brecht is a professor of botany, quite well known in certain circles. For his protection, he is traveling incognito."

Dr. Brecht stepped forward with a little click of his heels. "May I manifest more fully before you? Not unlike the wolves, my clan retains an aspect of our animal counterparts."

"You have a tail?" Harrison lingered in the door, clearly fascinated.

"Not in speaking form." Dr. Brecht's laugh had a fluting quality. "I belong to what is jokingly referred to as the hoof-and-antler set. My people wear a crown."

So saying, he removed his glasses, slipped them into an inner pocket, and pulled a watch on a chain from another. Flicking it open, he fiddled with its interior. The change was both immediate and startling. His wrinkles smoothed away, his irises lightened to a ruddy amber, and his ears took on the characteristic elfin point. But the showstopper was indeed a crown.

"Antlers!" Harrison edged further into the room and offered his hands to Dr. Brecht. "What kind of clan are you from?"

"Deer." He met Harrison's palms. "You may have heard of my clan, which has recently risen in notoriety. In truth, my name is Arno Silverprong."

Tami made the connection. "Tenna Silverprong was one of the Five's two new appointees!"

"My elder sister." He turned to offer his palms to her and leaned in to inquire, "PrinceTam, I presume?"

She drew a blank, but only for a moment. It was the name she'd used when signing onto the arborist's forum.

"Might we have a private word, Miss Reaverson?" asked Estrella. "We've come a long way."

Tami's smile faded. What should she do? Call Cyril? Try to get ahold of the Nightspangle pack? Reeling through options and their viability, she slowly said, "Thank you, Harrison. I'll take it from here."

"If you're sure." He didn't move to go.

"Head on home. I'll see you tomorrow."

Slipping his phone from his back pocket, the eagerly asked, "Could I get a picture first?"

Tami tucked her chin to hide her smile. He was just *so* Harrison.

"Arno cannot, but *I* should be delighted." Estrella insinuated herself into Harrison's side and posed for the selfie. Tilting her head at a saucy angle to put one pointed ear on full display, she looked every inch a vixen.

Harrison excused himself with a dazed wave.

Ismal moved to close the door behind him, but a booted foot prevented him. A freckled hand closed around the door's edge, slowly pushing it wide, despite Ismal's resistance. Kip's expression was neutral, which Tami found a little scary. Ash shouldered past him and took her arm, tugging her to the corner opposite Ismal's post.

"This is unexpected." Kip tipped his head to one side. "What business do you have with Bellwether Enclave?"

Arno's confusion was apparent, and he looked to his companions for help.

"Undisclosed urban enclave," supplied Ismal.

"Not to those who call it home," Kip countered. "Or to those who live under its protection."

"Our information came through *unusual* channels, and it is far from complete." Estrella's fingers flicked her shoulder in a gesture Tami recognized. "We had cause to believe Miss Reaverson might be unregistered ... or at least ignorant."

"Both," Tami admitted. "Or I *never* would have posted those pictures."

Ash's arm slipped around Tami's waist, and he said, "This is our territory, and you are guests. Bring your manners, and we'll show ours."

Kip still seemed angry. "Even an under-the-table meeting has to have equal sides."

"Granted." Estrella lowered her gaze, but her tone had clipped edges. "But do you boys realize what's at stake?"

Ash and Kip traded looks, and Tami realized they had no idea what was going on. They'd jumped in blind. She blurted, "It's okay. She's safe."

"*She*?" Arno practically pounced on the word. "You've verified that the tree is female?"

Tami nodded, but she wasn't sure how much more she should say.

"May I ask how?" He was practically trembling with excitement.

Kip gave a little nod and pulled out his phone.

Relaxing into Ash's stalwart presence, Tami smiled. "We knew Biddie was a girl because she was naked when my brother found her."

"A *female*!" The Silverprong clansman babbled to Estrella in another language.

The fox lady laughed and patted his arm, then sought Tami's

302

gaze. "This is *excellent* news. And she is safe, the tree and her twin?"

Tami slipped her hand into Ash's and said, "Completely."

Kip flashed a grin that was much more usual and pocketed his phone. "All set. Who wants pizza?"

"Here?" Tami whispered. "Are you sure this is the right sort of place to be taking important people?"

"We planned to take *you* here," said Kip, pulling Coach into an open space.

Their dinner date. With all the excitement, she'd completely forgotten.

"You don't like pizza?" Ash gently disentangled her ruffled hair. Travel by jeep had left her somewhat windblown.

Ricky's Roadhouse was Archer's best—and only—pizza place. A staple of her childhood, but probably not up to international standards. Still, she smiled and said, "Everybody likes pizza."

"*Exactly,*" said Kip. "If they're going to horn in, then they're just going to have to eat where the locals eat."

Kip waved at Ismal, who looked to be on high alert, as if the locals might be staging an ambush. Or at the very least, a protest. Arno's antlers were back in hiding, and Estrella no longer looked Amaranthine.

Inside was dim, and off to one side was a long room with dozens of old arcade games, pinball machines, and an ice hockey table. Blinking lights and a tinny chorus of sound effects had been coaxing quarters from kids for decades.

"Welcome," said a waitress wearing a t-shirt with a tuxedo front printed on it. "How many?"

"Reaverson party," announced Kip. "We have a reservation."

"Oh!" She ogled the group with interest, then singled out Tami. "Didn't see you there. Come on back!"

As they filed through, Rick Junior called a greeting from the pass-through to the kitchen. "Hey-o, Tami. Back room's all set for you. Give a holler if you need anything."

Twice, Tami stopped to greet others she knew. Friends and neighbors. All curious about her guests. And about this year's corn maze. And about the selection of Rivven teachers for their schools.

She didn't mind. This was familiar territory. Both the people and this place.

The back room wasn't decorated any different than the rest of the restaurant—plastic red and white checked tablecloths, matted low-pile carpeting, red glass candleholders, and stained-glass swag lamps over the tables. But the staff had pulled together several tables along one wall, and they were filling up fast with pizzas.

"Since when does Ricky's offer a buffet?"

Kip grinned. "They don't. I ordered ahead."

"All this for us?" she protested.

"Don't underestimate Kip's appetite." Ash hooked his arm through hers, and she could feel the brush of a wing against her back.

"We'll have help." Kip's gaze flew to the door. "And proper representation."

No kidding.

Doon-wen Nightspangle cut an imposing figure in a three-piece suit. His glasses gleamed as he took in the room and its occupants.

Cyril Bellamy strolled in next, closely followed by Melissa.

She ignored the Amaranthine stand-off, hurrying instead to Tami. Pulling her into a fierce hug, Melissa whispered, "Everything's fine. Better than fine. They can help."

Tami sagged against her. "I didn't mess up?"

"Well, maybe a little. But it's going to work out."

Kip tapped their shoulders and cheerfully said, "Added reinforcements. Local representation. Times three."

Tami swiveled in time to see Grandad walk in, followed by her dad and Joe.

Her brother immediately veered her way, and she nearly collided with him in her need to connect.

"Hey," he said. That was all. Yet it calmed her.

"This is it," announced Kip. "All present and accounted for."

Ismal immediately began warding the room. Not with stones, as Jiminy had done with the oak glen, but with strange, shimmering symbols he drew on the walls with his finger.

"Security?" she whispered to Joe, who guided her into line for food.

"Seems so."

How could he be so blasé about something that looked like honest-to-goodness magic? And then there were the greetings still being exchanged by the Amaranthine. It was like a meeting of dignitaries—local and foreign. But Joe seemed more interested in the selection of pizzas.

Kip caught her attention then, not on purpose, but simply because she'd been watching Ismal so closely. So when Kip strolled over, spoke a few words, and began helping the man, there was no discounting the obvious. His sigils were brighter, more intricate, and often spun off into space rather than affixing themselves to the walls. Kip wasn't human. He never had been.

Joe slid pizza onto her plate. "Grandad's pretty excited. That's Argent Mettlebright's mom."

She'd recognized Lady Estrella's clan name, of course, and assumed she was related to the Spokesperson for the fox clans. Estrella chatted easily with Cyril, who looked out of place, yet right at home in their small-town pizzeria.

"Worlds collide," she murmured.

"They connect," countered Joe.

"In surprising ways." Tami turned her attention back to Kip only to catch his wistful glance.

She thought she understood. They'd missed their chance to talk. She'd guessed he was Amaranthine by association. Kip probably would have liked to tell her his secret personally instead of having the truth made plain by circumstances out of his control.

Remembering the gestures he'd coached her through back when they first met, Tami carefully worked through her repertoire. *We're good, right? No worries, friend. Take it easy. Everything's fine.*

Kip's expression softened, and he offered a solemn wink.

Everything was fine.

Doon-wen and Kip rearranged tables so they formed a square in the center of the room. When Tami tried to sit with Joe, Melissa stopped her, explaining, "This is a formal meeting, so you need to remain with your escorts. Although, technically, you're theirs."

"I don't know what to do. Are there protocols to follow? Rules or etiquette?"

Her cousin smiled. "Doon-wen and Cyril have the authority here and will act as hosts. All you really have to do is eat pizza and answer any questions directed specifically to you."

Ash already sat at the table, and when she came around, he gave the chair next to his a little push and pat. "Saved you a spot."

"Apparently, I'm your escort for the evening."

He turned his wrist and placed an upturned hand under his heart. "It is an honor."

"Very authentic."

Ash rolled his eyes toward Cyril. "My manners are *excellent*, if a bit rusty. I don't need them to unstop toilets."

She was a little startled by his obvious calm. But maybe she shouldn't have been. "You understand all this?"

He tugged her chair a little closer to his. Fishing in the pocket of his jeans, he came up with a slim rod of blue crystal, pale as ice and etched with symbols. "This was meant for later, but it'll come in handy now."

Placing the stone on her palm, he covered it with his own. Sandwiched between them, the crystal shivered with a faint note, almost too high to hear.

And then it stopped.

Something had happened, but nothing had changed. Tami whispered, "Well?"

"That's done it," said Ash at a more moderate level. "This stone can ward conversations, making them private. When we use it like this, we can talk without being overheard, even by the sharpest ears."

His courting gift.

"It's safe to talk?" she asked.

"Yep." He tangled his fingers with hers. "You should eat, though."

Eating piping hot pizza one-handed was a challenge she wasn't ready to face. Reaching for the provided water glass, she pulled the torn paper cuff off her straw and took a sip. "Why the assigned seating?"

"This is a friendly council." Ash pointed to each table in turn. "Doon-wen and Cyril represent Bellwether enclave, and you have three generations of Reaversons to represent Red Gate Farm. The professor and the lady emissary came at us sideways. Very bad manners, but how were they supposed to know about an alliance that's barely a week old?"

"And we represent ... Landmark Elementary?"

"We're here for Biddie." Ash gave their joined hands a small squeeze. "Tamiko, if you don't eat something, I might embarrass us both by feeding you."

She searched his face. He wasn't kidding. "You want to feed me?"

"*Really* do, but also really don't. At least, not in front of our fathers."

Her attention jumped to the neighboring table. Kip had taken his place on her other side, and he was crowding the corner, talking animatedly with Joe. Or at least *at* Joe, who said little but smiled more than he usually did in public. Empty plates and even a couple of empty pizza pans stacked haphazardly in front of the redhead, forming a sort of barricade. Over which her father was watching closely.

Tami didn't think he could tell they were holding hands, but she couldn't have been sitting any closer to Ash. Dad might not see the wing curving possessively, but he couldn't miss the arm resting along the back of her chair.

Dad leaned over to ask Joe something.

Both Joe and Kip turned to look at her.

Ash's body tensed, but he didn't retreat.

Joe said something to Dad, and his surprise took a few moments to decide where to go next. The glimmer of interest was promising, and Dad might have come right around the table to introduce himself to Ash, but Cyril interrupted all conversation by clinking a butter knife on the edge of his plate.

He stood and made the same gesture Ash had earlier, if with a bit more flourish. "Tonight's honor may have been unexpected, but it is welcomed on all sides!"

As all attention swung to Cyril, Ash pressed a piece of chicken in alfredo sauce between her lips. "Tamiko, please just take a bite," he begged.

She stifled a laugh, pocketed her gift, and applied herself to her pizza while Cyril rambled through some preliminaries. He introduced everyone at the tables except their esteemed guests, then urged them to take the floor.

"I am Lady Estrella Mettlebright of the winter fox clans, and I am here—in a general sense—at the behest of Spokesperson Twineshaft, who enlisted my aid in all matters pertaining to the old groves."

Grandad asked, "Because of your close familial connection to the Five?"

"No, sir. It seems the old cat learned the secrets of my past."

With a nod to her companion, Estrella said, "There is a remote enclave where rare and unique varieties of Amaranthine trees have been gathered, nurtured, and propagated. I spent my childhood among the trees and their kin, alongside other Amaranthine protectors, including members of the Silverprong clan."

Arno stood then, offering the barest of introductions. "I have often served as a university professor in order to stay current with research and rumors, experiments and exploration. Lone trees, such as your own, do crop up from time to time. Seeds do travel, as is their wont and—I daresay—their design. But such trees cannot be left to languish alone. Would you indulge me, good sir?"

He was talking to Grandad, who straightened in his chair. "Well?"

"How long has your family been orchardists?"

"We've been here four generations, beginning with my parents."

"And before?" Arno leaned forward. "Were they always in the business of tending trees?"

Grandad pursed his lips. "Can't say for sure. What does it matter?"

Tami's heart began to beat faster. They'd grown up on stories about the founding of the farm, of its expansion and their innovations. All their family stories began and ended right here in Archer. Grandad had never—openly—talked about a before.

"You *do* remember where you came from …?" Arno prompted. "By your accounts, you were old enough."

"Sure, I remember," Grandad grumbled. "I'd never forget."

Tami could see how hard this was. Secrets kept this long weren't easily spoken. She glanced Melissa's way, and her cousin offered a small smile.

She knew.

Of course, she knew. She'd looked it all up when researching their family ties. But she'd never said anything.

Her father touched Grandad's shoulder. "Where are we from, Dad? I'd like to know myself."

"Wardenclave." Pride tinged George Reaverson's grudging admission. "We're originally from Wardenclave."

39
FULL DISPLAY

After the wolf dismissed them in order to bring the visiting dignitaries back to his lair—or whatever they called it—Joe accidentally cornered Ash by the pinball machines. "Need a quarter?" Joe offered.

"Next time?" Ash asked, his gaze soft and serious. Like he was worried there wouldn't *be* a next time, but he wouldn't blame anyone for steering clear.

Joe didn't want for things to be awkward, and that meant saying something. But historically, that was just another kind of awkward. Still, it helped that he wasn't seven anymore. "We still come pretty often. Mostly on Mondays."

Ash's head tilted. "Is that an invitation?"

"Sure." Joe hoped that was enough, because he couldn't think of anything to add.

But it was the same with Ash as it had been with Mr. Black. He understood all the stuff that was hard to say, even if Joe never got around to saying it.

Ash reached out to touch his arm. "Eight o'clock. Tag along with your sister. Kip will be there, too."

Joe nodded too many times, but he was excited to be asked. Even so, he couldn't help mumbling, "Are you sure?"

"Of you? You bet. Of myself? Not so much." He sucked in a breath and puffed out his cheeks, only to exhale on a weak chuckle. "One thing kind of cheers me up, though."

"Yeah?"

"If she'll have me, we'll be brothers."

They'd only been home five minutes when Dad announced, "Family meeting! We're past due, and we're all here. Let's do this!"

Joe cringed. Reaverson family meetings were a round-robin affair, during which everyone took a turn revealing information. He'd always suspected that his parents cooked the whole thing up in order to figure out what was on his mind. Because *everyone* had to contribute something. Which meant Joe needed to figure out what to say.

"If it won't take too long," said Tami, her eyes on the clock.

She'd come home with them—making this the third time she'd abandoned her car in town—in order to get ready for whatever was meant to happen at eight. Since Kip was involved, Joe figured it had something to do with sigils.

It was hard not to wonder how much Ash's happiness was

hurting Kip. He'd been nothing but cheerful at the restaurant. Downed enough pizza to feed a family of four. Ran interference with Dad over Ash. Even challenged the fox lady to air hockey. She'd won.

Grandad, who'd grabbed up the television remote, pocketed it with a grumble. "Documentary at eight," he said.

Tami immediately relaxed. "I'll bring Biddie down."

Mom did a doubletake. "How did you know she was upstairs?"

Probably the same way Joe had known. It was a little sad that so many of his ties to Tami weren't really twin-sense. Then again, Melissa was a reaver, and he wasn't nearly as sensitive to her. Grandad, either. And it was pretty obvious now that his grandfather *had* to be a reaver. He'd even been born in the most famous reaver village in the world, the birthplace of the In-between.

"Should I give you some space?" asked Melissa.

"Nonsense. You're family," Mom insisted, then launched into an explanation of how to participate.

Dad and Mom liked *news*, so everyone was supposed to share something that nobody else at the table could know. Plans, updates, events, and gossip. Joe usually stuck to farm-based news—harvest tallies, chick hatchings, tractor repairs, critter sightings. Ever since the Emergence, Grandad had seized these opportunities to regale them with random facts about the Rivven and reavers. They'd always assumed he was quoting some documentary or news report. In retrospect, Joe had to wonder if he'd been speaking from experience.

Joe slid into his usual seat next to Tami, who had Biddie on her lap.

Dad called the meeting to order and launched straight into gossip. "I suspect that our Tami is in love."

Mom laughed and one-upped him. "I suspect that our Melissa is in love."

Tami wrinkled her nose at Dad, but she was obviously happy to report, "He's wonderful, and I can't wait to introduce you properly."

The session took a rabbit trail while Mom coaxed for more details. Tami stuck to basics. Met at work. Good with kids. Handsome and handy.

Melissa had to wait for her chance to refute Mom's claim. "I just attended the birth of a litter of Kith wolf cubs." With an uneasy smile, she said, "I guess that makes it puppy love."

More asides, this time courtesy of Grandad, who wanted to know more about the litter. If this kept up, they might not even get around to Joe. Fine by him. No such luck.

What to tell?

Most of his news—the really interesting details—all pointed to the fact that he was a reaver, too. And he wasn't ready to tell *all* of them. Only Tami. He'd never keep secrets from Tami. "Umm … I made a friend who's always hungry. Any ideas on what to feed him?"

He submitted to Mom's quizzing, since she loved that part. Yes, he meant Kip. Yes, they got along fine. Yes, he was to blame for the missing meatloaf a while back.

Biddie seemed to be enjoying their game. Slipping from Tami's lap, she leaned into Joe's side. "Is Joey-boy in love?"

"Not me, Chick-a-biddie. We'll leave that to Tami." He scooped her up and gravely announced, "I'm a late bloomer."

The tree-girl cuddled right in and whispered in his ear. "Kip is here."

His heart leapt, and her eyes laughed. He hushed her, saying, "It's Grandad's turn."

Biddie turned toward him and crooned, "Georgie-boy."

When the old man actually blushed, Joe hid his smile behind her leaves. Grandad loved Biddie. She was all that remained of his boyhood. She was a lifelong hope, a dream come true. And she loved him right back.

Clearing his throat, Grandad said, "That meeting tonight. They were feeling things out, but both sides looked plenty pleased. And that means Red Gate Farm will be more than an enclave."

Tami frowned, "I must have missed something."

"No," said Melissa. "Nothing was discussed openly."

"Lady Mettlebright told me herself. They're going to arrange for a Scattering."

Dad raised a hand. "I haven't heard that one."

"Anything to do with trees isn't broadcast news." Grandad tapped the table with a finger. "They'll bring a group here. Think of them as colonists. All young—children or teens—and all looking for a good place to plant their golden seed."

"Tree-kin?" asked Tami.

Grandad beamed. "Red Gate Farm is going to become an Amaranthine grove."

Tami tried to slip outside unnoticed, but Joe waylaid her.

"Can I be there?" he asked.

She grabbed his hand, and they escaped the house together. They didn't make it far, though. The door opened again, and small feet pattered along the sidewalk after them. Which was perfect, really. Ash needed to meet Biddie.

"All together," Tami said with satisfaction. Joe swung the little girl onto his shoulders, and they hastened toward shelter. She asked, "Do you like Ash?"

"Not as much as you do."

Hooking her arm through his, she hauled him to a standstill. "Still think he's a keeper?"

Joe's smile was shy. "I'm glad it's him."

As usual, Joe's happiness had a way of doubling hers. Hand-in-hand, they rushed for the barn, all but tumbling through the door in their haste. Only to stop in astonishment, for softly colored light was spilling from the haymow.

"Did you notice from outside?" Tami whispered.

Joe lifted Biddie down and murmured, "We wouldn't have. It's warded."

"How do you know?"

Her brother shrugged. "It's Kip. Did you know he helped Jiminy with the wards for the oak glen?"

She wheeled on him, but words failed.

Touching her arm, Joe revealed, "I could tell he wasn't human, so he showed himself to me."

Tami didn't like that her twin had been keeping secrets from her. Then again, this hadn't been Joe's secret.

"Please, don't tell on me. I don't want anyone to find out I'm a reaver." Joe bent close, his forehead touching hers. "I won't risk them sending me away."

The very idea unnerved Tami. In opening the way for the Amaranthine, had she endangered her brother's happiness? Why had no one mentioned that Joe was a reaver? "Nobody knows?"

"Just us." He glanced toward Biddie, who was halfway up the ladder to the haymow. "Three twins and two janitors."

"Won't the rest easily find out?" Tami's mind raced through their day. Joe had been in the same room as a wolf, a fox ... and Cyril, for that matter. "Why haven't they found out?"

"Kip."

"Kip," she echoed faintly.

Joe stepped back and smiled. Tami marveled at the strength—and simplicity—of his conviction. Without another word, he preceded her up the ladder.

She emerged into a wonderland of fairy lights. Or so it seemed. Kip slouched among the bales of straw, booted feet crossed at the ankles. His hands were busy, effortlessly weaving another of the sigils she'd admired earlier, but these were different, decorative. As he finished the luminous form, he reached for something at his side.

On a square of cloth lay a handful of stones, no bigger than peas. Selecting one, Kip set it on one fingertip, held it in the center of his sigil, and murmured something, as if telling it a secret. The crystal lit from within, and with a flick of his claws, he sent the whole construction spinning toward all the other stones twirling amidst the rafters.

Claws.

Tami cataloged his Amaranthine features, relieved to find that fangs did nothing to diminish the friendliness of his smile. Slit pupils and pointed ears were minor details. Kip was still Kip. But Joe seemed displeased.

He asked, "Aren't you going to show her?"

Kip tucked his chin to his chest. "Tonight's about Ash. He's the one she wants to see."

"Don't be silly. You're just as important as he is."

Tami was a little surprised at her brother. Joe wasn't one to push, yet he was sitting in the straw, attacking Kip's bootlaces.

Ash spoke up. "Like Joe said, it's just us."

"Aww, geez. Give me half a sec," grumbled Kip. "It's not exactly easy to reach the catch."

"Where?" asked Joe.

To Tami's increasing amazement, Kip shimmied partway out of his pants, revealing plaid boxers. He twisted his body around, reaching, and Joe seemed to be pushing at something. Averting her eyes, she met Ash's amused gaze.

He sat on the edge of their straw nest, Biddie perched on his knee. "Don't be embarrassed. He can't actually *be* immodest, even without clothes on."

Joe asked, "Really?"

"*Guys*," Kip sighed. "That is so totally *not* the big reveal I had in mind. Tami's into feathers, not fur."

She asked, "You have fur?"

"Fraid so," muttered Kip. "I warded myself for our dinner. Kind of a hassle. Easier to hide everything under my work clothes."

Tami couldn't picture it. And then she didn't have to, because Joe found the elusive catch. Suddenly, her brother was draped in a luxuriant fur stole. His gaze sought hers, full of messages that didn't need words. *Didn't I tell you? Can you believe it? Isn't he amazing?*

And he had. And she did. And he was.

40

HERS AND HIS AND THEIRS

For a long while now, Ash only had eyes for Tamiko. But something in Kip's manner snagged his attention. He was mostly himself, mostly happy, but Ash could sense a crosscurrent flirting just past his wingtips, a turbulence that wasn't like Kip at all.

Ash would have gone to him, except Joe was right there, a bulwark of quiet and calm. The drape of Kip's tail suggested an intimacy that was only confusing because of its suddenness. Something good must have happened for Joe to take to Kip so quickly. They would have become friends eventually. That's just the way it was. "Everybody loves Kip," he murmured.

"Even you?" asked Biddie, her head tilted back to search his face.

Ash brushed a knuckle over her cheek, awed by the subtle patterning there, like fine wood sanded to silk. "He's my best friend."

Biddie leaned into his touch and said, "My Tami loves you."

"You think?" He couldn't help smiling.

She sweetly declared, "Ash loves my Tami."

"You can tell?" Not that he was very good at hiding things. Not on his own.

"Some." Her brow puckered. "Too many fences. Too many walls."

Ash supposed she was picking up on the overlapping wards and illusions that made it possible for him to stay ordinary. "Kip can trick your eyes, but the truth is right here. Can you see my claws?"

"No. None." But her fingers were already searching. She asked, "What else?"

This was supposed to be his big moment, revealing himself to Tamiko. But maybe a little test run would help his nerves. "I don't have pretty ears like yours. Mine are human."

She patted and pulled, verifying his claim.

"No fangs," he admitted. "Not all avians have them, but my sort usually does. So it's another way I'm like my mother."

Biddie poked a finger into his mouth, and he gently trapped it with blunt teeth. Not shy, this kid. Given what little lore he knew of trees, she was going to be all kinds of trouble when she grew up.

"Eyes?" she asked.

"Classic crow. Or so I'm told."

His attention drifted back to Kip, who'd offered his palms in the Amaranthine way. Getting the honest meeting Ash was still waiting for. Tami went on tiptoe as she searched Kip's eyes, which were tearing up. What a softie. This kind of thing would mean the world to Kip, and Ash was every kind of grateful that there was still something they could share.

Ash murmured, "I guess it makes some kind of sense, nests and trees go together."

"Hers and his and ours," said Biddie, in what he assumed was agreement.

Greetings dropped the formalities when Kip opened his arms, and Tami slid in for a hug. Ash might have been a tiny bit jealous, but Kip met his gaze over the top of her head and mouthed two words. *You next.*

The accompanying smirk almost made it a threat.

What did the everlasting prank-monster have up his sleeve?

Kip kissed the top of Tami's head, turned her around, and gave a little flourish of one hand. In a voice low with emotion, Kip asked, "Isn't he beautiful?"

Her eyes widened and tracked upward.

Ash knew he'd been exposed and wished he'd had a little more warning. He'd figured Kip would go for a bigger build-up, prolong the moment, and shout, "Ta da!" But he was just standing there, holding Tami by the shoulders, hiding behind her like he didn't want anyone to figure out he was losing it.

"You okay?" Ash asked in an undertone.

Kip waved a hand. But Ash wasn't sure if he was answering, because Kip's crystals swung into orbit. This part of the plan was a little embarrassing, but necessary. Black wings weren't easy to see in the dark. And Ash did want to be seen. When an involuntary quiver twanged through tense muscles, he remembered to move. Flexing, stretching, and finally extending, he displayed like the courting male he was.

She gasped and gawked, but definitely in a good way.

Biddie slid from his lap and hurried to Tami, took her hand, and pulled her nearer. Also good.

Ash hurried to his feet, wings stirring up dust and straw, hands reaching until he remembered he wasn't going to rush her. But she plowed right into him, hiding her face against his shirt like she didn't want anyone to realize she was losing it.

He shot Kip a bewildered look, but his best friend was rubbing furiously at his cheeks with a red handkerchief that Joe must have produced.

Joe offered a little half-smile. "You look like an angel."

"You think?" Ash wasn't used to compliments. Most Amaranthine looked on him with pity. He was cobbled together, stranded between forms.

"Those wings are damned sexy," Kip accused, not quite making eye contact. "She never stood a chance."

Arms wound around Ash's waist, which also added up to good. So he nuzzled her hair and whispered, "You're okay with the wings, then?"

A bubble of laughter. A hint of embarrassment. A long look that was really more of an ogle.

"Tamiko," he coaxed.

She asked, "Are you for real?"

Ash's ego was preening. "To quote Kip, '*Fraid so.*'"

"He's right, you know. I've never seen anyone so beautiful."

He could have argued the point. There were plenty of avians between here and the city, all of whom had glorious plumage—pheasants, doves, peacocks. Even the pigeon clans had more to strut about. But if Tamiko thought him beautiful, he wouldn't compare or complain. "I love you."

She shook her head, but not to refuse or rebuff him. Amaranthine instincts and senses assured him that his attentions were welcome and any further advances would be favorably met.

A throat cleared.

He remembered their audience.

Joe said, "We'll just walk Biddie back to the oak glen."

Ash ducked his head guiltily and would have signaled to Kip, begging for more time. But only Joe was there, his feet already on the ladder.

"Kip will be with me." Joe stepped down. "He needs to see the corn maze. We'll go to my room after. Hang out."

That odd crosscurrent nagged at Ash, and he hesitated. "Is Kip okay?"

Joe's expression softened. "Yep. He'll be with me."

Kip might hide certain details behind impressions and illusions, but he'd always tried to be himself. Humans were always saying that looks weren't everything. That the hidden person of the heart was what matters most. That a beautiful soul will always shine through.

Nice ideas. True stuff.

Over and again, he'd been accepted for himself, but always by people who never saw past a careful barrier of misinformation. So Kip couldn't shake the nagging conviction that stripped of his illusions, he'd lose everyone's trust and respect and camaraderie.

Real possibilities. Worst nightmare.

Which might be why Kip had also harbored a perverse longing for exposure.

There was a reason Jiminy had called him in when it was time to ward the Reaverson place. He was the best Woodacre for the job. His sigilcraft was stellar. His illusions might have gained him acclaim … except that nobody ever realized they'd been duped.

Until Jiro.

Kip still couldn't decide if it was a blow to his ego or an answer to some kind of unspoken prayer. Either way, Jiro was very good at keeping him humble. The guy was there at the right times, in the right ways. Propping him up. Wiping his nose. Holding his hand.

"Where are we going?" Kip asked.

Tami's acceptance had half-wrecked his composure. She was so sweet about the whole thing, no trace of hurt or hesitation. But Ash's happiness had become Kip's total wreckage. And Jiro's quick thinking, his salvation.

Not many people would be so glad to have been shoved from the second story.

Kip's fingers twined more tightly with Jiro's. "Why are we in a cornfield?"

"It's a puzzle." He glanced over his shoulder, for the path—such as it was—forced them to walk single file. "Didn't you say squirrels like games?"

"Gotcha. This is your corn maze." Kip forced his attention outward, senses straining. There weren't any wolves nearby. Still, he triggered a couple of readymade sigils to give them some cover. "How far are we from the entrance?"

"I didn't bring you in the usual way." Jiro walked on, towing

Kip like a sluggish barge. "It's harder if you have to start from the middle."

"Where's Biddie?"

"We left her at her tree."

Kip winced. "How long have I been out of it?"

"A while." Jiro stopped and studied him in the scant moonshine. "The lights and everything. Tami loved it."

"Yeah."

"You did good," he said, sounding proud.

Kip swallowed hard. "Did my best."

"I know."

The fact that he really *did* ... sorta helped.

A little farther, and the path opened into a wide circle of hard-packed earth. Jiro marched straight to the center and made Kip spin in place, like for a game of Blind Man's Bluff. Ten different openings led into the area where they stood. Each as likely as the next.

"How many acres does this maze cover?" Kip asked.

"Twelve—give or take."

"How long does it take most people to find their way through?"

"First-timers in daylight, without the aid of a compass, usually take ninety minutes."

Kip frowned. "That's specific."

He waved a hand vaguely, not giving away any particular direction. "We have a few towers set up in case anyone runs into trouble. First aid, water, a guide out."

"Lifeguards in a sea of corn."

"That's the idea." Jiro slid his hands into his pockets. "Whoever's on duty has a line of stopwatches. We time the groups for Grandad. He wants to know if the maze is too easy or too hard. It helps us plan the next year's design."

"You do it all from scratch?"

Jiro nodded. "It's different after dark. Disorienting. It can take people twice as long."

"After hours?"

"It's how we close out the year. The last weekend in October, we do a Halloween special. People come in costume, and even if they've solved the maze before, it's different. We add tricks and traps and obstacles. And people in costume, like a haunted house. We keep it tame for the kiddies for the first few of hours, but after eight, it can get pretty scary out here."

Kip had never heard Jiro say so much in one go. "You enjoy it?"

"It's pretty fun."

"Still looking for volunteers?"

"Sure." Jiro casually asked, "Think you'll need ninety minutes?"

"What's my goal?"

"We have flagpoles at the entrance that teams carry through. It's how they signal for help." He suggested, "Get out, grab one, and get back."

Kip grinned. "Start counting."

Jiro blinked once, then quietly obeyed. "One … two … three …."

With a flick of his tail, Kip scarpered.

He jogged along, creating a small racket as he brushed past dry stalks. Some lanes widened. He found other open spaces, shapes within the larger design. Suspicions grew into certainty that the maze created some kind of picture.

"... eighty-six ... eighty-seven ... eighty-eight ... "

Kip poured on as much speed as he dared, not wanting to damage the maze as he hit dead ends and doubled back. He flashed back through Jiro's circle more than once, and each time, the steady rhythm of his voice would warm.

"... three hundred thirty-two ... three hundred thirty-three ... three hundred thirty-four ..."

Jiro was smiling. And that meant they were each—in their own way—enjoying this.

When Kip darted back into the circle, toting the proof of his success, he may have gotten a little carried away.

Joe yelped when Kip tackled him and immediately lost count. Which was a shame, since the redhead had undoubtedly set a new record. But Joe was caught in a dizzy tumble that never quite turfed them. It went on and on, gradually slowing until all he could hear was Kip's breathless laughter and the soft rattle of the cornfield coming from somewhere below.

That made no sense. If they were on the ground, the stalks should be around and above them.

Opening his eyes, he tried to untangle himself from Kip, who was under him, keeping him out of the dirt and grinning up at the stars.

"It's a cornucopia, isn't it?" Kip angled his head enough to catch Joe's eye. "The maze. If I look down, that's what it'll be."

Look down? Joe tried to ease off Kip, but his foot swung into air. Arms tightened, and a leg casually swept under his, lifting it

329

back in line. Kip was supporting the full length of his body, and Joe was almost afraid to understand why. But he needed to confirm his suspicion. He looked down.

They were suspended in midair, somehow caught between the moon and the maze.

"I'm right, aren't I?" pressed Kip. "The basket-weave section is brutal. Slowed me way down."

Joe managed a nod.

"Hey," he said gently. "You bad with heights?"

"No. Just ... umm ... wasn't ready for ...." Joe faltered, and his hands locked around Kip's ribcage. "Did you jump?"

"More of a glide." Kip propped a hand behind his head. "Defying gravity is one of the less-publicized Amaranthine superpowers. Easy does it. I've got you."

"I'm fine."

"My nose says otherwise."

Joe focused on Kip's face, which was better than looking down.

"Senses vary by clan, but ours are keener than yours. My sense of smell might not be at wolf levels, but I know when someone's not having fun anymore." Kip's smile was apologetic. "Almost there."

And they were. The whole time Kip had been explaining, he'd been slowly sinking from the sky. Joe took a few deep breaths, cautiously adjusted his grip, and mumbled, "A little to the left."

They came to rest on bare dirt, inside the rib of a pumpkin.

Joe just lay there, not ready to let go, not wanting to spoil things.

"Sorry, Jiro," said Kip. "Ash loves it when I carry him up and away. He can't fly, but he can't help wanting to feel the wind in his wings. It was thoughtless of me to haul you so far out of your comfort zone."

"I'm fine."

Kip didn't argue the point. Just patted Joe's back. Like this was natural. Like it was nothing.

Joe mumbled, "I must be heavy."

"Eh. I'm stronger than I look."

A confusing answer, since Kip was pretty built. Joe asked, "How strong are you?"

With a rueful smile, he said, "Scary strong."

Joe had heard of people who didn't know their own strength. Was this the opposite? "You scare yourself?"

"No. But I'm scared of scaring people." Kip's hand left off patting, just rested where it was. "And I don't want to betray your trust."

"I trust you."

Kip's brow furrowed. Like he didn't believe it.

Joe immediately felt bad. Was it because he'd smelled afraid? Did that translate to a lack of trust? "Can we try again?"

"The maze? I could probably run it backward and blindfolded, now that I've figured it out."

"Didn't you want a look?" Joe pointed up. "I want another chance."

His nostrils were quivering.

Joe didn't like being second-guessed. He pinched Kip's nose shut and insisted, "You didn't scare me, you *surprised* me. I want a do-over."

"Okay, sure." Kip gently freed his nose. "I'd like a do-over myself. Let's rearrange."

Joe eased off, and Kip rolled into a low crouch, one knee touching the ground.

"Up you get," he invited.

Was he kidding? "I'm too big for piggyback rides."

"You're only too big if nobody can lift you. And I just happen to be scary strong." Kip's eyes were bright. "I give piggyback rides to kids on the playground all day long. Never lost one yet."

Joe resigned himself to the loss of dignity. It helped to think of it as a trust-building exercise. Because Kip needed to trust that Joe trusted him.

Rising up on the pads of his paws, Kip bounced a couple of times and gave Joe's thighs a friendly squeeze. "Ready?"

"Think so."

Taking him at his word, Kip coiled into a spring that launched them into a steep arc.

As the ground fell away, Joe clamped his arms more tightly around Kip's neck. "Whoa," he gasped.

They jerked to a halt.

Turning his head, Kip asked, "Was that *whoa* as in 'make it stop,' or more like a 'wow, am I impressed'? Because I could see this swinging either way."

"Umm ... the second one, I guess." Joe hoped he wasn't throttling Kip, because there was no way he was letting go.

This was surreal. Kip was simply standing in thin air, like a cartoon character who hadn't yet realized they'd run past the edge of a cliff. Joe really didn't want the next few moments to include the predictable plunge and dust plume.

Kip didn't say anything about Joe's choke hold. Instead, he lifted his chin toward the acreage beneath his feet. "Cornucopia verified. And filled with apples. Nice touch."

"Grandad's idea." Joe pointed—briefly—to the section above the horn-shaped basket. "Mom wanted the pumpkin."

"You do a different theme every year?"

"Yeah. For next year, Grandad wants to design something in honor of the Miyabe-Starmark wedding."

"I like it." Kip asked, "Giddyap?"

Joe nodded, and Kip glided off, swaying from side to side, skimming through the air like an ice skater. The orchard passed by, giving way to empty fields and the forest beyond. Kip drifted lower, weaving between the jutting points of pines, keeping to an easy pace.

Gradually, Joe's mood mellowed. If not for the cold, he might have lasted longer. He pressed his half-frozen nose against Kip's shoulder to stifle a yawn.

"Had enough?"

Joe pointed toward the house. "Window's not latched."

Kip gave the barn a wide berth, and Joe didn't have to ask why. He knew Ash was still in there with his sister, and he knew Tami was happy. He wasn't after details. That was already enough information to flush his face.

"You want to go in through the window?" asked Kip.

"Drop me off at the kitchen door. I'll meet you upstairs."

Joe shed boots and coat and tiptoed to the fridge. From the other room, he could hear the television and glanced at the kitchen clock. His parents and Grandad would stay put for another hour at least, tuned in to the nightly news, followed by the *Rivven Report*.

Loading a tray, he hurried to rejoin Kip, who brightened considerably at the prospect of ham sandwiches and pumpkin pie. He ate as though dinner was a distant memory, chatting about nothing in particular, but especially not about Ash, Tami, and the haymow.

When the food ran low, Joe tried for a different distraction. "Why are you so strong?"

Kip's eyebrows lifted. "You mean ... physically?"

"You're a *squirrel*." Joe wasn't sure how to put it any more delicately. "I mean, they're rodents."

"First off, I'm not a squirrel. I'm a *protector* of squirrels."

Joe nearly choked on a swig of beer. "How's that work? You go around helping squirrels safely cross the road?"

Kip huffed. At least he was smiling.

"Do you help them rob bird feeders? Make them nests in attics? Find their misplaced nut stashes?"

"Are you implying that I am a protector of pests?"

"I'm a farmer. I've never had any great love for squirrels."

"Uh-huh. I have it on good authority that you secretly cuddle squirrels." Kip casually indicated the stockpile of boxes and tins in the corner. "This is becoming a squirrel nest."

Joe set aside his half-empty beer can and crawled to his stash. "Thought you said you're *not* a squirrel." Finding the right tin, he pried it open and leaned over to push a nut tart into Kip's mouth.

Kip chewed. Joe popped a tart into his own mouth, then offered another. Although he accepted it, Kip didn't immediately put it in his mouth. By some miracle, was he actually full?

"You should probably stop feeding me."

"But you're always hungry."

He chuckled. "No doubt. And food is always welcome. But I

shouldn't be letting you hand-feed me. It means stuff."

Joe mumbled, "I didn't know."

"How *would* you if I didn't say something."

"Umm ... sorry?"

"Nah." Kip waved off the apology. "I know you're not flirting. You're trying to comfort me, and I'm grateful."

Great. Now Joe was bleary, slightly buzzed, and blushing.

Kip kindly changed the subject. "While I'm here, can I add a few more sigils?"

"You already put them everywhere." He fidgeted. "Just about."

"Overlapping more would be even safer." Kip started clearing away the remnants of their feast. "Change for bed. This will probably put you right to sleep."

It certainly had the last time.

Within the first twenty minutes, Joe was in a blissful haze, unbothered by little things like the tip of a claw tracing patterns across bare skin. "Is it terrible?" he murmured.

Kip responded with a soft, "Hmm?"

"Being in love."

"Oh." After a few moments, he asked, "Have you ever been?"

"Not really." Joe quietly admitted, "But I've always been afraid to lose Tami to some guy."

"Makes sense."

But that wasn't an answer, so Joe asked again. "Is it terrible?"

"No. Not at all. I gained more than I can ever lose. And I'll keep everything that was ever ours, including a lifelong friendship."

"But you're sad."

His finger stilled. His voice softened. "Only for a little while. My sadness will pass, and their joy will continue. Love *endures*, Jiro."

Joe really hoped he meant *endures* as in 'going on and on forever' and not 'suffering in silence,' but he didn't have the heart to ask.

"Speaking of enduring," said Kip. "This sigil would be stronger if I used blood."

Opening an eye, Joe asked, "Mine or yours?"

"Both would be best."

Kip looked uncomfortable ... or perhaps unsure. Joe tried to make light of the suggestion. "Will that make us blood brothers?"

The redhead took more time than usual to form an answer. "The meaning probably varies by clan," he said carefully. Too carefully.

Joe studied Kip's face.

"As you've probably already figured out, squirrels mostly use saliva. This adaptation puts me in new and unfamiliar territory, but I trust my source."

"Which clan uses blood?"

"Dragons," whispered Kip. "I learned some things from a dragon. But we should talk it over another time, when you're not part-tipsy and half-asleep."

"Why?" asked Joe. "If it's better, why not go ahead?"

Kip scooted backward and rubbed his hands together, almost wringing them. "The seals can hide you, but they can't extend your life. For that, I have to find a safe way to tend you."

Joe couldn't understand Kip's hesitation. Feeling like a broken record, he asked, "If that's what we need, why not go ahead?"

"I made some mistakes." He winced. "It's like ... I started out following a recipe for cookies, only to decide midway through that I'd rather have doughnuts."

Joe looked down at his bare chest and belly, where the faint lines of fresh sigils still glowed.

Kip said, "I've warded you from head to toe and back again."

"Right."

"Which means if I want to tend you—which is absolutely necessary—then I need to get past my own wards to touch your soul."

"Okay ...?" Joe frowned. "There has to be a way in. How else would a hungry squirrel access his stash?"

"Oh, there's one or two." Kip stared at his hands. "I should have thought it through, but I was in a hurry."

Joe nodded. "The wolves were coming. You didn't have much time."

"Right." Kip took a deep breath and puffed out his cheeks. "The way things stand, you're so excellently warded, even I can't get in. Not without resorting to a longstanding Amaranthine tradition."

Kip tapped his own lips, then touched the same finger to Joe's lips.

Mouth to mouth? Surely there was another way. He'd said ways. Joe didn't need long to work out the remaining option.

"I'd like to call it a design flaw, but I've heard enough of the old rhymes to know better." Kip laughed weakly. "Way back when, before the In-between was a twinkle in Glint Starmark's eye, one of my ancestors must have been a frisky trickster who liked mixing power with pleasure."

Joe cast about for anything to say. "Maybe we should stick to manly bloodshed for tonight."

Kip tried for another laugh, which faded into a groan. "Give me a little more time. I need to find out if I can overwrite my first sigils with blood. Or if I need to work backwards and start over."

"Should we stop, then?"

"Let me finish these," Kip said. "It won't take much longer, and I'll rest a little easier."

So they lapsed into silence, each lost in their own thoughts as more sigils bloomed across Joe's skin. Maybe this was more than they could handle alone. Then again, maybe he should be glad there was any chance at all.

Finally, Joe found the courage to admit, "I'd do anything to be here for Tami."

Kip's jaw worked. "Even if it meant outing yourself as a reaver?"

Dread washed over Joe, followed by a surge of panic. His breath came in short gasps, every part of him rebelling at the very suggestion of exposure, of capture, of betrayal.

"Whoa, whoa, whoa." Kip's concern was written plain on his face. "Okay. Not that. Anything but that."

Several minutes of urgent pleas and promises restored Joe's calm, but they did little to ease his embarrassment. He clasped his hands over his face, sure he'd mucked up eight kinds of etiquette. "I have to stay."

"I believe you." Kip doused the light, but he lingered in the dark. His tone was cautious. "Jiro, what *did* you have in mind when you said you'd do anything?"

He didn't want to say.

"Between us," he coaxed. "I want to know where you draw the line."

Which was only fair. But so hard to admit.

"I *meant*," Joe began, every word more awkward than the next. "That I'd let you kiss me."

Kip went very still and remained quiet for several moments.

"You trust me that much?"

"Yeah," he croaked.

"Whoa."

And this time, it wasn't the 'make it stop' kind of *whoa*. Joe could tell it was the sort that meant 'wow, am I impressed.'

41

HERALD

Melissa doggedly collected another armful of posts from the timber that had appeared—as if by magic—in the field from which all the pumpkins had been harvested. Doon-wen was already keeping his promise to the Reaverson family with a steady stream of arrivals.

Daily couriers.

Nightly deliveries.

Fresh allotments.

Scribes to witness the necessary contracts, forms, registries, and chronicles. Preservationists, who pottered with soil samples and fretted about security. Ephemeralists, who set about cataloguing the bounty of rare species that thrived in the orchard. Draftsmen and craftsmen, whose initial drawings left little doubt that the Reaverson family would soon play host to a quaint village.

With an eye toward self-sufficiency, the Woodacres had

proposed the addition of a small dairy and the partial damming of a creek in order to create a fishing hole. Cyril wanted a dovecote, a rookery, and a hatchery in order to increase the population of several varieties of birds in Perch County—including pheasants. Kith shelters were already under construction at the far corners of the property.

Uncle George was in his glory.

Today being a Sunday, the orchard was closed until noon. So dawn at Red Gate Farm found the property overrun. Melissa suspected that the urban enclave was standing empty. Everyone had come to work or to wander.

More shipments arrived by the hour. Thatching and ticking and tents. Cordwood and kegs and case-lot quantities of candles. Several crates of wardstones arrived, many of which would be set into the very fenceposts Melissa was toting.

She snapped a picture of the shipping label and sent it to Jiminy.

He spammed the sob emoji. His double-shift wouldn't end until six.

Officially, Melissa was present as Rook's escort, but she'd insisted on pitching in, as was her right as kin. She knew full well that the Amaranthine builders were humoring her. Rabbits who were shorter and slighter were many times stronger. And bears were grappling beams and shifting flagstones with apologetic ease.

Rook kindly suggested, "Torloo and Sooli seem to have found Ash. Make sure they haven't become a bother?"

Melissa found them in the oak glen, where Ash had marked off a small plot between two of the oaks lining the song circle. Not in any official way. He'd simply cleared the patch of leaves and lined the edges with acorns. Would Tami's suitor build her a home here, within view of Biddie's tree?

Torloo-dex Elderbough and Sooli-fen Nightspangle were indeed monopolizing Ash. He perched on some sort of barrel, the young wolves sitting attentively at his feet. Far from being a bother, the kids were both rapt and respectful, for Ash was telling them a story.

"… and so the wind was granted a magic all its own, for it had always been meant for more than scattering seeds and carrying clouds. But young winds can be fitful and flighty and forgetful, which made them difficult to train."

Melissa joined the youngsters on the grass. From there, she could see that Ash's seat was a cask, marked with the crest of the Merryvale clan, whose honey wine was world famous. No doubt the circle would be filled with song tonight.

Ash went on with the story, spinning it out in the manner of bards. "The avian clans knew the winds best, having learned to loft themselves along their many paths, but as so often happens in this world and the next, knowing is not understanding. And as every youngling is wise to remember, not every wing has feathers."

Torloo clasped his hands over his heart, looking very much like the child he still was, no matter his actual years. Sooli must have been close in age, although Melissa was only guessing. Amaranthine aged at the same rate as humans until they reached their twelfth year. On the cusp of a lengthy adolescence, their time slowed to match the pace of their parents.

Rook had offered to bring her along today as a treat, perhaps because she was the youngest cub of the Nightspangle pack.

But also because Sooli wasn't just any young she-wolf. She was Roonta-kiv's daughter.

Sooli-fen was Jiminy's sister.

"The secrets of the winds might be a secret still, lost even to lore, if not for the patience and passion of dragons." Here, Ash slipped out of his narration to ask, "You know about them, right? Wind is to the dragon clans what the moon is to wolf packs."

"When does the angel come?" asked Sooli. "Bechamel."

"Bethiel," Ash patiently corrected, though his attention was definitely straying. "Bethiel of the Changing Winds. His part's soon."

Melissa turned to see where he was looking. She should have known. Three figures had reached the far end of the oak glen, and one of them was Tami. She and Aunt Hiro were talking around the person carrying a large hamper.

For a few moments, Melissa surprised herself by hoping that the man in the middle was Jiminy. It wasn't.

"Muffins," whispered Sooli. "Are they for us?"

"I believe so." Torloo's tail wagged. "Can we?"

"Better hustle," urged Ash, who wasn't really listening.

Melissa guessed he was eavesdropping on Tami, whose arm was looped through the newcomer's. To be fair, Aunt Hiro had his other arm. Like they were all friends.

Ash slowly said, "He's here for you, Melissa."

"Who?"

"The herald." He stood and signaled to the newcomer. "Nice guy. Local office. Dove clan."

For a moment, Melissa's heart lurched, but a local herald wouldn't be sent with dire news from home. Nor would it be about her biological father, since Christopher and Cove were currently abroad. What, then?

Would Reaver Barr at the local office have sent her a communique? Had something happened with regards to the rogue? The latest threat assessment put him far from here, but they might be summoning support for their trackers. Even moving a whole section for pursuit. But were they likely to call for *her*? And what might Doon-wen have to say if the Office of Ingress tried to assign her away?

A hand appeared in front of her, and she allowed Ash to pull her to her feet. Before releasing her hand, he tweaked her little finger.

Her surprise brought a faint smile to his face. "What? Jiminy isn't the only one who was raised by wolves."

Tami closed the gap. "Here you are! Melissa, this is Remill Whistledown. He's the herald I told you about before. The one who's always lived here." To the dove, she added, "And you must know Ash. He's my fiancé."

Something knocked against Melissa's shoulder, but when she looked, nothing was there. Only Ash, whose eyes were wide, his hands caught somewhere between reaching and retreating. She realized what must have happened and brushed her shoulder. Then arched a brow at Tami. "You're announcing the engagement?"

"I don't see why not." Tami radiated happiness. "There's no reason to keep it a secret."

Melissa had to concede the point. Ash and Tami had met in the public sector, and nobody would question the principal and the janitor becoming a couple. They could go on dates. They could plan a big wedding. They could probably even host a community-wide reception in Landmark's gymnasium. And nobody would ever have to know the whole truth.

Other things were still closely guarded.

For instance, Aunt Hiro didn't yet know that her future son-in-law was a crosser. Nor had she and Uncle Abel been told that their daughter would have a tree's years.

But the biggest secret was still Biddie. Kip and Joe were keeping the girl entertained—and hidden—high in her branches. None of the Amaranthine coming and going from the circle realized the significance of the tree at its center.

Barriers within barriers.

Secrets within secrets.

Melissa now realized that not every reaver knew everything there was to know about the Amaranthine. And enclaves didn't share all they knew with outside clans. There were probably as many private matters as there were persons. Things only shared in confidence.

Like Doon-wen's bondmate being Kith. Or the clandestine arrangement that had brought Jiminy to Bellwether. And the surprising truth to Amaranthine lore—or *some* of it, at least.

"Congratulations," murmured Remill. "If you need a friend to free your hands so you may sing, I would be honored."

Ash shook his head. "I don't have much of a singing voice."

"Joy expresses itself in many ways." The herald dipped into his bag and came out with a small box. "For you, Son of Sunfletch."

He hesitated, confused. "I thought you were here for Melissa."

"As it happens, my duties bring me to you both, each in your turn." Remill stepped so close to Ash, their cheeks brushed when he whispered something in his ear.

Ash nodded.

Remill pressed the box into his hand.

With great care, Ash touched the catch and lifted the lid.

The look he sent Tami made Melissa feel like an intruder, for his eyes were bright with unshed tears. She eased back a few steps, averting her eyes. But she couldn't escape the scene entirely.

"Is it right?" Tami asked.

Ash cleared his throat and muttered something.

Aunt Hiro laughed lightly.

Melissa couldn't resist a glance. Ash had pulled Tami into his arms and stood there, holding her. Like they belonged together. Like they belonged to each other. It was an absolute marvel, given everything that had happened, that these two managed to make falling in love look simple.

"Ah, love," sighed Remill.

Melissa startled, not having realized that the herald had remained with her.

"A favored suitor wears his lady's ornament." His tone dropped conspiratorially. "Signifying her wish to court as she is courted. In the avian tradition."

She saw Tami slip a ring onto Ash's finger. "Rings are an avian tradition?"

"Any gift may do, if its message is clear." Remill cooed quietly, all approval for the couple's kiss. "Hers is clarion."

Since the herald seemed eager to share, Melissa asked, "What does it mean for him?"

Remill's hands fluttered. "When a male courts alone, it is in the hope of a return of feeling. When two souls reach an understanding, gifts are exchanged rather than given. Everything can be shared, for their future is one."

Melissa compared this to one of the only other courtship traditions she knew. "Kimiko Miyabe is claiming Eloquence with kisses."

"Ah, wolves," sighed Remill. "What they lack in public display, they make up for in private affections. Are you interested in lovers' games, Daughter of Nightspangle?"

"How did you know?"

"A guess, since fully half of your stolen glances have a yearning quality."

Melissa took a moment to realize what he meant. "No! How did you know I'm considered a Nightspangle?"

"Because, Miss Melissa Armstrong." Remill withdrew a heavy packet from his messenger bag and offered it with both hands. "That is how you have been addressed."

She recognized the heavy paper, the gleaming seal. It was as subtle as a slap, and pain bloomed with its delivery.

How much money had she paid to remove her name from the general registries? Yet someone had caught wind of her. Some stranger was applying for her. And from who knew where? The sender's name was stamped in red ink, with foreign characters that suggested Asian origins.

Melissa turned to ask Remill where the packet had come from, but he'd vanished.

Uttering an oath, she considered shredding the thing unopened. Although it might be more satisfying to sic Doon-wen on the man audacious enough to apply for his daughter, sight unseen. With that pleasant prospect in mind, she strode to her aunt's side. "Could you look at something for me? Is this kanji?"

"Yes. It's a name." Aunt Hiro touched the intricate characters. "Is there another place that gives the hiragana? That would tell us how the name should be read."

Melissa broke the packet's plain seal and extracted the cover letter.

"Here." Her aunt pointed to another string of characters. "The full name means 'cricket moon,' but it has been simplified to Kourogi."

Recognition dawned. "His name is *cricket*?"

"Yes. Kourogi is cricket." Aunt Hiro nodded approvingly. "Not uncommon. Very cute."

Cricket. As in Jiminy.

42

WE INTERRUPT THIS BROADCAST

Melissa didn't remember most of her walk back to the house. Only that she had kept herself calm, smiled at the right moments, and avoided any further greetings. This was not the time for prying eyes and sharp noses. She wanted no audience when she read the contents of this packet.

In truth, it was not her first offer. They'd been arriving since she was twelve, mostly blind applications based entirely on her pedigree and ranking. But it *was* the first time she was interested in what the sender might have to say.

She'd been avoiding Jiminy since his little experiment. Since she'd let him past her wards. Since he'd called her beautiful.

Avoiding someone wasn't hard when they were never around.

Jiminy's shifts ceased to overlap hers, and Melissa suspected Doon-wen's interference. All week, one of them was at the coffee shop while the other was at the farm. He had wards to construct and lessons with his mentor. She had boundaries to patrol and Amaranthine to escort. And three littermates to adore.

On her afternoons in town, she had Lace, Gate, and High all to herself. It was more than she'd ever dreamed of. All she'd ever wanted. Instead of being one reaver among sixteen others, all hoping for a partner, she was one reaver with three cubs all vying for her attention.

But even more than that, she had True.

Once the cubs were a little older, Doon-wen would establish a secondary den at the farm. They would run together, and he had relayed True's insistence that Melissa run with them—astride True.

She made it to her room and slouched to the floor in the most defensible corner. Safely away from prying eyes, Melissa slid a fat sheaf of papers from the packet.

The cover letter was hand-written, the wording excessively formal. She was being approached in an official capacity by the wolves of the Nightspangle pack, founding members of the Bellwether Enclave, situated for two score and four decades in the human city known as Fletching. Lookha-soh and Roonta-kiv Nightspangle offered greetings and good wishes before expressing their desire to put forward their fostered son Kourogi, whose name was sung as "cricket moon," presenting him as a potential bondmate in the Amaranthine tradition or, should she prefer a more human assignation, as a husband.

Melissa recognized the standard language of a reaver contract. Jiminy's parents had correctly included all the usual documentation—pedigree, hereditary traits, academic standing, and progeny projections. But there were hand-written addendums.

One bore the seal of Doon-wen Nightspangle, documenting Jiminy's unique status as a wolf of his pack. Another also included the signatures of Cyril Sunfletch and Linden Woodacre, making it clear that Jiminy was Bellwether's anchor. Contractually, the urban enclave would remain his home for as long as he lived.

Nothing new. He'd told her as much.

Next came documentation of Jiminy's rank, which had been suppressed in order to protect Jiminy's interests. Although officially a wolf, he'd been privately assessed and personally granted an unofficial ranking by Glint Starmark, whose copper seal gleamed upon the page. Reaver Kourogi Foster Nightspangle ranked twenty-ninth on the worldwide registry and, based on his youth and vigor, was expected to rise over the course of his lifetime.

Double digits. That was … unexpected.

Melissa gently set that paper aside.

On the next page, Jiminy's mentor had included a note, certifying that his apprentice currently ranked fourth among reavers with a ward classification. Melissa groaned. She hadn't realized that "First-sensei" was Jiminy's nickname for Michael Ward of Stately House, world-renowned First of Wards. It was that man's opinion that Kourogi would likely be acknowledged as First of Wards one day.

Someone tapped on her door. "Melissa, it's me. Is everything all right?"

"No," she said dully.

"May I come in?"

Melissa crawled to the door and turned the key to let in Tami.

Her cousin took in the array of documents and perched on the end of the bed. "Is this what the herald brought?"

Waving a hand, Melissa stiffly said, "Behold, the romance of reaver courtship."

Tami slid to the floor, already reaching. "May I?"

Melissa gave Tami the short version, but her questions led to a much longer version. By the end, they'd gone through every page in Jiminy's offer twice, and Tami's understanding increased alongside her incredulity.

"You make babies with the highest bidder?"

"That's one way of looking at it." She sighed and shook her head. "I know reaver couples who are together because they love each other. They had the good fortune to meet at academy or during one of the skill camps. But *this* is more or less standard."

Tami had questions about contracts, stables, and academies. Melissa could tell her cousin was having a hard time with reaver practicalities, but Tami wasn't passing judgment. Only trying to understand a system that existed to protect and proliferate rare bloodline traits.

Nodding thoughtfully, Tami reached for the page with Glint Starmark's seal. "And what do you think of Jiminy's offer?"

"His pedigree is beyond impressive." Melissa frowned. "Nobody in their right mind would turn down an applicant of his rank."

"Excellent numbers, excellent references," agreed Tami. "Is it rude of me to ask about your numbers? Are yours ... lower?"

Melissa rolled her eyes. "Ninety-nine percent of the global reaver community is lower."

Tami smiled. "Granted."

"I rank." It was nice to confide in someone. "My biological father is one of the top ten battlers in the States, and at graduation, I placed high—triple digits."

"That's good?"

"Exceptional."

"So on paper, you're great together." Tami's brows knit. "Does *he* know that?"

Melissa's heart clenched, and her shoulders sagged. "Probably. Doon-wen has my assessment folio. And they've been matchmaking from the beginning."

"But you don't like Jiminy?"

"He's … Jiminy."

Tami laughed. "Okay, but how has he responded to all the matchmaking? Is he being pressured into applying for you?"

Melissa slowly shook her head. "That goes against wolf nature."

"So his adoptive parents wouldn't have sent you this without his knowledge." She shuffled through the stack of papers, selecting one near the bottom. "But what about this? It almost sounds like they're trying to operate outside the system. If you and your children *belong* to the wolves, aren't they actually setting up a private breeding program?"

The document in question was unusual in the extreme.

Written in Jiminy's own hand, he let it be known that any children born to his den would belong to the Nightspangle pack, and that their upbringing and education would proceed according to wolvish tradition. Melissa wasn't surprised. Jiminy wouldn't want to send any of his children away. As he had been.

She admired his foresight, his resolve, his protectiveness.

"Belonging to a pack isn't confinement or enslavement. It's family."

Tami's expression softened. "That part, at least, appeals to you."

Melissa hummed a cautious affirmative.

"So what's holding you back?"

"This." Melissa waved at the offending stack. "Everything is so awkward. It'll seem like I changed my mind once I learned Jiminy's rank."

Tami's eyes took on a shine. "Mom was right. You're in love."

"Reavers don't marry for love."

"According to the paperwork, he's not a reaver." Tami raised a hand, interrupting herself. "Which begs the question, why is he resorting to reaver courtship? Wolf traditions have to be more romantic."

Melissa smiled wanly. What a time for Jiminy to decide to respect her boundaries.

Halfway through dinner, Tami realized something that might be important. The same rules and regulations that Melissa had explained earlier might technically apply to her, as well. Her cousin had been fined for putting off her duty to the In-between. Once Tami's status was confirmed, would they expect recompense? That hardly seemed reasonable.

But what if Joe's concerns bore fruit? What if the Office of Ingress wanted her to do her part and contribute to future generations of reavers? And what if they didn't want her genetic material mingling with a crosser's?

Questions, possibilities, consequences, and countermeasures whirled through her mind. She was already drafting an agenda to spring on Cyril when Grandad lunged for the remote and unmuted the television, which was tuned in to his usual dinnertime gameshow.

" ... interrupt this broadcast for a special announcement," intoned an announcer. "Again, we interrupt this broadcast for a special announcement."

A few seconds passed, and the cameras switched to a familiar panel of newscasters. The banner on the screen held the logo for the Miyabe-Starmark courtship.

"Thought so," muttered Grandad. "They've been dragging their feet over setting a date."

"Exciting news from Keishi, Japan, where Spokesperson Hisoka Twineshaft and Spokesperson Suuzu Farroost have called a press conference. Odds are, this is the long-anticipated announcement of the next kiss, isn't that right?"

"Undoubtedly," agreed the second newscaster, folding her hands over her notes. "Speculations have been all over the calendar, with suggested dates ranging from American Thanksgiving to the upcoming Sixth Anniversary of the Emergence. Reaver Hinman, can you give us some idea of what dates might be considered auspicious from the Rivven perspective?"

"There are several annual festivals observed by the Amaranthine, the most prominent of which is certainly Dichotomy Day, which is marked twice a year—during the winter solstice and the summer solstice. The word *dichotomy* comes from the Greek and literally means 'split in two,' which applies neatly since it is both the shortest and longest day of the year, depending on your locale."

The first newscaster nodded in an interested way. "Do Kimiko's previous choices give us any hints? Let's bring up the graphic."

His partner chimed in. "The most recent was Kimiko's seventh kiss, which coincided with the announcement of two new positions on the Amaranthine Council, expanding their number to seven."

"While that's true," interjected Reaver Hinman, "Kimiko said that the day was chosen to mark a much more personal milestone. She wanted to celebrate becoming an aunt for the first time."

A photograph filled the screen, showing Eloquence holding a bundle while Kimiko cooed over her older sister's first child.

The woman conceded, "Kimiko may have her own reasons for choosing the dates and times, but the Five—now the Seven—are certainly making the most of these events."

"Pardon me," interrupted the first newscaster. "But we have word that Spokesperson Twineshaft is ready to begin. Let's take you live to Keishi."

Once again, the cameras cut to a different location. Tami immediately recognized the twin dragon statues at the foot of the stairs to Kikusawa Shrine, the setting for all the pageantry of the Miyabe-Starmark courtship.

Hisoka Twineshaft stood before a small lectern, which bristled with microphones. He wore an understated gray suit, and he was smiling at someone off to one side. The camera panned, revealing the presence of Harmonious Starmark, Tenna Silverprong, and Suuzu Farroost. Not the full rank of council members, but a decent show of support.

Everyone was relaxed and smiling, as if standing before the

world was no big deal.

Tami found herself leaning forward as Hisoka Twineshaft lifted his hands, calling for quiet.

A few last flashbulbs popped, and the Spokesperson addressed himself to the camera. "Greetings, one and all. I'm pleased to address you today in my role as Eloquence Starmark's go-between."

"Those eyes, though," murmured Mom.

Grandad snorted. He was more a fan of the famed Starmark copper. Tami had to wonder if he'd ever met any Starmarks while he was a boy in Wardenclave.

Poised and personable, Hisoka went on in measured tones. "I know you are all eager for Kimiko Miyabe's courtship to progress. I can assure you that Eloquence, who may rightly claim an even greater share of anticipation, awaits his suitor's call. Suuzu?"

With a gracious nod, Suuzu Farroost, spokesperson for the phoenix clans and avian representative, stepped forward to speak. "Welcome and peace. It is my pleasure to serve as Kimiko Miyabe's go-between. Her pursuit of Eloquence Starmark continues. She will claim another kiss from her intended."

Shouts, whistles, and applause resounded. The couple was clearly as popular in Kimiko's hometown as they were around the world. Tami was amused to see that Harmonious Starmark, Kimiko's future father-in-law, contributed a piercing wolf whistle.

Suuzu waited in bemused silence for the din to subside before announcing, "Kimiko has chosen Valentine's Day."

A buzz of excitement rippled through the crowd. Mom laughed, and Dad forked over five bucks. Grandad's smile was the doting sort.

Once quiet was again restored, Suuzu concluded, "The world

will meet once more in the courtyard of Kikusawa Shrine under the branches of Kusunoki on February 14 for Kimiko's eighth kiss."

Tami was early for her evening rendezvous with Ash, but he was ready and waiting. And impatient, if his swoop, scoop, and leap into the loft were anything to go by. And also happy. Several minutes later, she added affectionate to her list.

He eased back, letting her catch her breath, and softly said, "Thank you. For the ring."

"I had help. Joe made it."

"No kidding?"

"He's good with his hands." Tami trailed her fingers over Ash's, finding her token. "It's carved from one of Biddie's branches."

"Tamiko," he sighed "I love you."

Even if she lived straight on into forever, Tami knew she would never grow weary of those words.

Ash's usual tucking and fussing and nuzzling left off, and he murmured, "Something on your mind?"

She nodded. Little by little, she spilled out her concerns about what might happen once she was officially identified as a reaver.

"I understand. Believe me, I do." He held her close and stroked her hair. "I sometimes worry about what could happen if people found out what I am. Everything could change, but I don't think you need to take such an ominous view. I mean, if Melissa's able to put off marriage and a family simply by paying a fine, then there are allowances for personal preference."

Tami slowly relaxed. "You're right. I was frantic earlier, inventing one outrageous contingency plan after another." She hesitated for a few heartbeats, then admitted, "I did come up with a surefire plan to keep you."

"Oh?" His lips brushed her cheek. "I like the sound of that."

She wondered if he would. "No one could oppose us if everyone's cheering us on."

"Who is this *everyone*?"

"America."

Ash's wings lifted, allowing moonlight to slant across her face. She could see his confusion, but she was confident that her idea was good. No, it was great. A truly grand scheme.

"We have the opportunity to make a difference, and not just for the Amaranthine in Perch County." She smiled and said, "I want peace to flourish. Let's give it a place to take root. That way, it can grow."

"I feel like we've had this conversation before."

"Yes."

"Is this where I'm supposed to ask about consequences?"

"Yes." Tami leaned up to kiss him. "Because if you agree, there'll be a bunch."

Ash's head tilted to one side, and he smiled faintly. "Break it to me gently. What are you angling for?"

"We could become America's answer to the Miyabe-Starmark courtship."

His wings shook and settled a couple of times before he asked, "If people find out I'm a crosser, I could lose my job. Kip, too."

"I don't see why," she countered. "We're already bringing in Amaranthine staff. Why not two more?"

"That's optimistic. Too many people are looking for targets. Exposing the truth could put the enclave at risk. And Biddie."

"Not if there's a plan in place."

Ash was clearly struggling with serious doubts, but he was also listening. "A plan. And you have a sure-fire one?"

"Yes." Tami smiled. "We'll get a go-between."

His brows knit.

She went right on. "Having go-betweens has worked wonders for the Miyabe-Starmark courtship. Do you suppose Hisoka Twineshaft would take us on?"

Ash said, "Hold up. I'm pretty sure a go-between is supposed to mediate between you and me."

Tami shook her head. "And I'm pretty sure that Twineshaft and Farroost are the publicists of the century, marketing the love story of the millennia."

"And you want a spin-off?"

Now he was getting it! She said, "I have a good feeling about this. Something like this will win over more people than all the politicians combined."

After an excruciatingly long pause, Ash said, "It could be dangerous. All those things we talked about before—protestors, bomb threats, paparazzi—they could turn up on your front step."

"I trust our enclave."

He didn't take nearly as long to nod this time.

Tami triumphantly concluded, "And if we can get just the right go-between, they'll take care of the press. All we have to do is show up."

Ash blandly said, "You're over-simplifying."

"A little," she conceded.

"I could talk to my father about comparable avian traditions." He muttered, "But I am *not* doing any of the mating dances."

She laughed and asked, "How about the waltz? Black wings. Black tuxedo. You'd be entirely dashing."

His gaze slid sideways. "I can handle a little embarrassment if it helps the clans."

"Thank you." Tami's mind was racing. "We'd better pool our resources. Is Kip close by?"

"Probably with Joe."

Tami had planned ahead, brought her phone. "Do you mind if I bring in Melissa?"

"I trust her." Ash quietly added, "Remill dropped a bombshell on her earlier. She okay?"

"Melissa will be fine." She began a quick message. "But reaver courtship is baffling."

"Not sure I can criticize." Ash covered her hands, then stole her phone. "Before we rally an American version of the Five, may I bring out my gift? Or are we saving ourselves for the television cameras?"

"If we're going to do any good out there, it has to begin here."

"As you wish, Tamiko," he said, adding an avian flourish. "Hold out your hands."

43

LADY METTLEBRIGHT

ami's plan was already sounding more possible by the time she finished explaining it to her co-conspirators, who actually numbered six, thanks to the addition of Biddie.

Kip spoke first. "You're onto something, but you're going to need some serious influencers in the go-between department if we're going to pull this off."

Joe quietly added, "Someone with clout."

"Doon-wen has influence," said Ash. "But he's also in hiding. We need someone who's already in the limelight, and that limits our options."

"Someone on a level with Hisoka Twineshaft, if not the cat himself." Kip nibbled on the edge of a peanut butter cookie. "He's probably booked, though."

Tami couldn't help hoping. "What if we're the very thing he's been hoping for? What if we're exactly what he needs to shift public sentiment into better favor?"

"If the guy can orchestrate the Emergence, surely he can plan a couple of weddings." Kip cuffed Ash's shoulder and grinned. "America's sweethearts."

Melissa leaned forward. "Do any of you have a way to get a message to one of the Five?"

"Indirectly," said Tami. "Also, the Twineshaft Initiative will bring Hisoka to Fletching on Dichotomy Day. But that doesn't guarantee a private conversation."

Joe lifted his hand. "We met Argent Mettlebright's mother."

Melissa raised her hand as well. "I'm friends with Adoona-soh Elderbough's youngest son."

"I sort of met Lord Mossberne once, but I don't exactly have his number." Kip casually added, "But I *do* know a guy who has a direct line to Stately House."

"Jiminy." Melissa's eyes were wide. "When Uncle George asked him to drop names, he mentioned both Mettlebright and Elderbough."

"We need to talk to Jiminy." Tami's excitement was mounting.

"Who wants coffee?" asked Kip. "I'll spring for doughnuts. Or a pie. Actually, I think this is more of a carrot cake occasion."

"At this hour?" Tami checked the time. "And on a school night?"

Kip took to coaxing. "Founders is always open. And there's the time change to consider. It's morning in Japan."

Tami looked to Ash, who nodded. "Let's go."

"I'll drive." Bounding to his feet, Kip swept into a bow. "Your Coach awaits."

363

Since Joe volunteered to stay back with Biddie, they were back down to four when Kip hustled them along a back-alley to a service door standing in the illumination of a dim bulb. Tami craned her neck, trying to figure out where they were. "Is this Founders?"

"Not quite," said Kip. "This place is next door."

Ash groaned. "Is this *necessary*?"

"Quickest way. Or did you *want* Doon-wen breathing down your neck when you invite an outsider to meddle in what he will undoubtedly consider *his* business."

Ash groaned again.

Tami asked, "Where are we?"

"Isn't this the used clothing store?" asked Melissa.

"Yep. It's called Find Me," said Kip, rapping lightly on the heavy metal door. "And it's another way in."

"You planned this," grumbled Ash.

"I certainly did." Kip grinned at his best friend. "Called ahead and everything. We're expected."

Ash turned to Tami and grimly said, "I apologize in advance."

"For what?"

Kip didn't give him the chance to answer. "True story. Find Me is the most popular clothing store on campus. Small label. Handmade. High end. Upcycled. Utterly unique. And budget-friendly for your average college student. But *nobody* goes into this place without support."

Tami was already smiling. Kip's stories were always funny. "Why's that?"

"If you enter without backup, rumor has it that their very pretty shop boys will corner you in the changing room." Kip played up the drama. "None who've survived has left unchanged."

Ash snorted. "Only because they're wearing their purchases."

"Hey," argued Kip. "I've been the cornered one, and it was certainly an experience. They're brutes."

The door swung open, revealing a young man whose trousers and fitted vest gave him the air of a haberdasher. He even had a tape measure casually draped around his neck With a coy smile, he inquired, "Who's a brute?"

"Faisal and Giuseppe held me down, while you tweezed my eyebrows."

"Pish tosh. They grew back. But what's this?"

His gaze swept over them, leaving Tami feeling uncertain about her clothing choices. But also with the distinct impression that she'd met this young man before. Only she couldn't think where.

Kip elbowed him. "Manners, Tyrone."

He made that little avian flourish with his hand under his heart, then presented both palms to Tami. "It is a distinct pleasure to finally meet you, Principal Reaverson."

When she returned the greeting, he gathered her hands between his, giving them a gentle squeeze. Happiness shone in tawny eyes, which should have been a clue, but it was his smile that gave him away. Tami blurted, "You look like Cyril!"

"I should hope so. Tyrone Sunfletch. My father speaks highly of you."

His son. Another member of the pheasant clan. Tami was so delighted, she didn't really register the fact that he'd ushered her inside, where two more very pretty shop boys waited to be introduced.

"Try to keep it short," urged Kip.

Ignoring him, Tyrone steered Tami into the waiting embrace of a deeply tanned Amaranthine with long, sharp features and eyes of such a vivid shade of electric blue, you had to assume he wore colored contacts.

"This is Faisal. Peacock clan. While we mostly deal in secondhand treasures, any of the firsthand designs we sell are his."

Faisal kissed her cheeks and sniffed her hair. "You've been in Ash's arms. Lucky girl."

Tyrone's hands settled on her hips as he stole her back from a regretful Faisal. Tami checked to see how Ash was dealing with all these casual intimacies. Far from annoyed, he was watching the whole thing with a fond smile.

"And here is Giuseppe. Dove clan. He excels in personal style. When he creates an ensemble, it is an expression, a statement, a work of art!"

Giuseppe seemed barely out of his teens, rakishly thin and resplendent in creams and corals. Without a word, he bent to kiss her forehead and drew her hand into his.

Again, Tami checked to see if Ash had a problem, but he was wholly unperturbed. She ventured, "Are these your friends?"

"Family." Ash came unhurriedly to her side and messed up Giuseppe's pale hair. "I'm not the only one Cyril fostered. These are my brothers."

Kip cleared his throat. "And this is Melissa. Are we done here?"

Tami wavered between embarrassment and indignation. Why weren't they giving her cousin the same affectionate treatment? She asked, "You already know each other?"

"No." Melissa was completely unfazed. "Work keeps me busy. I haven't been here."

Glancing to Kip for help, Tami asked, "Why are the greetings different?"

He nudged Faisal, who fluttered a hand, showing off manicured claws. "Firstly, because Melissa is wary of us. Secondly, because she is armed. But *mostly* because Jiminy wouldn't like it." He rolled his eyes and drawled, "Wolves."

Tami understood, then. And judging by the fresh color in Melissa's cheeks, she did, too.

Somehow, when Tami exited Find Me, it was with a shopping bag under her arm. "Should I be accepting things from your brothers?" Tami whispered.

"Whatever's in there, it's probably perfect for you. Go back to shop anytime." Ash slipped his arm around her waist and casually added, "Put it on my tab."

"You have a running tab at a boutique?"

"Tyrone's been my tailor for more than a century. Everything I wear has to be adapted." Ash patted the front pocket of his jacket. "They loaded me down, too. Your next three courting gifts will be tokens that they've chosen."

"Is that usual?"

"That's what they tell me." Ash nodded to himself. "It feels right, so I think so."

Tami quickly lost her sense of direction. Kip led them through a tile-lined tunnel, up a concrete stairwell, along empty hallways, and past a series of fur-draped alcoves. The whole while, he was spinning out sigils, which she assumed were keeping their presence a secret.

When they finally stopped before an ordinary door, it was Melissa who said, "This is it."

Kip hesitated, then eased back a step. "You all go ahead. I'll just run down, order our coffees, raid the bakery case."

"Why?" asked Ash.

"Let's just say I'd rather *not* be noticed by the powers that be." Kip waved them onward, then disappeared around the nearest corner.

Melissa rapped smartly and opened the door, scanned the room, then waved them through. Tami couldn't help comparing her stance to that of the stern bodyguard, Ismal. Given their plans, it really *was* nice to have a battler in the family.

Jiminy sat at the desk in the corner, where he was obviously chatting with someone via his computer. He waved them in, but he addressed himself to his screen. "They're here now. Do you need to go?"

"May I meet your friends?" A feminine voice in accented English.

"You sure?" Jiminy asked. "I don't want to get into trouble."

This time, the words flowed in Japanese.

Another voice, male this time, said, "So long as you're not selling pictures to the highest bidder, you're safe from Dad's wrath. Probably."

Tami came even with the desk in time to see a young Japanese woman tweak her companion's ear. A silvery fox ear, half-lost in a thatch of messy hair. She pressed a hand to her leaping heart and whispered, "Gingko Mettlebright."

Those ears twitched, and he offered a crooked smile. "Hey."

"Gingko's our translator today, since First-sensei was called away." Jiminy stood and guided Tami into his chair. "Any chance your Japanese is better than mine?"

Tami shook her head but held up her thumb and forefinger. "A little, and clumsy." Switching to English, she added, "I haven't been to visit my grandparents in Kyoto in almost ten years."

"You would be welcome here."

"I ... don't travel far anymore."

She glanced back as Jiminy pulled a stool into position for Ash. He looked much calmer than she felt. A wing brushed against her back, and his hand found hers. With a gesture of greeting, he asked, "Are you Lady Mettlebright?"

"Tsumiko," she said.

Ash touched her shoulder and said, "Tamiko."

Jiminy dragged Melissa from her post by the door and sat her down, then crowded in on Ash's other side. Pointing, he said, "Melissa is a reaver attached to the Nightspangle pack. She can be trusted. And Ash is used to keeping secrets."

Gingko's ears flickered forward. "You're the crosser?"

"Yes."

Tsumiko shook her head, murmuring something in Japanese, before carefully asking in English, "May I see his truth?"

Suddenly, a servant of some sort whisked onto the scene, bearing a tray of tea things. He leaned in between Gingko and Tsumiko, who thanked him sweetly.

Ash said, "Kip's not here ...."

"Allow me," offered Jiminy.

Tami, who was still watching the tableau on screen saw the butler stop and stare. "Kip?" he echoed.

"Friend of ours," said Jiminy. "There, that's done it."

Tsumiko gasped, and Tami recognized the Japanese word for angel. Her wondering gaze gave her the courage to launch into the short version of their proposal. If Lady Mettlebright was on their side, she might be able to persuade her bondmate to help them along.

"I'm an unregistered reaver. Ash is a crosser who's been passing himself off as human. He's been courting me in secret, but we think our story could make a difference for Amaranthine in America." So many hopes, so few words. Would they have any impact? All they could do was offer. "We are willing to make our courtship public if the Amaranthine Council will appoint a go-between."

Tsumiko spoke softly in Japanese. Gingko answered her questions in an undertone.

Ash leaned in to murmur, "Even if they don't need us, I need you."

Grateful for the reminder, Tami rested her head on his shoulder. He kissed her hair.

Across the world, Tsumiko giggled and called them cute.

Jacques said something in French that caused Gingko to roll his eyes. But then he leaned away from the microphone and hollered, "Hey, Dad. Got a sec?"

He was there? Tami had assumed Lord Mettlebright was away. Her calm evaporated.

Several seconds passed, and Tsumiko called, "Argent?"

And just like that, there was another person on screen. Arms closed around Tsumiko, and from over her shoulder, a pair of keen blue eyes studied them critically.

Gingko tossed up his hands. "Oh, sure. *Her* you'll answer."

"*Tsk.*" Without breaking eye contact with his virtual audience, Argent reached over to gently tug his son's ear. "Explain yourself, Jiminy."

He shrugged and said, "The Miyabe-Starmark courtship is the best thing to happen to the In-between since the Five. With careful management, the Reaverson-Sunfletch courtship could mean the world for America."

Argent flicked a finger at the screen. "Crosser?"

Ash flexed his wings in an involuntary display. "Half Native American. Crow clan. Like most Amaranthine in the States, I pass myself off as human."

"And you?" Argent's gaze switched to Tami.

"Elementary school principal, recently selected by the Twineshaft Initiative. Unregistered reaver. Co-founder of the Red Gate Farm enclave. And ...." Leaning closer, quietly added, "And tree-kin."

The fox's brow arched.

Tami nodded sympathetically. "It's complicated."

Melissa spoke up. "We have as much to hide as we do to share."

"We'll understand if it's too much for you to handle," Jiminy added breezily.

Gingko chuckled.

"I do not require baiting," Argent blandly assured. Looking off to the side, he called, "Twineshaft, do you have a moment to spare?"

Tami covered her mouth with her hand, holding back the sudden urge to sob ... or scream.

Ash made a soft, birdlike sound in her ear. Comforting.

"How are you so calm?" she whispered.

His eyes creased at the corners. "I already have everything I need."

When Tami glanced back at the screen, Argent was watching them closely. But then Hisoka Twineshaft strolled into view, a sleeping baby tucked into the crook of his arm. He was closely followed by a man with blond curls and an easygoing smile.

"Kourogi-kun," the man greeted warmly. "Oh, hello! Is that Melissa? I'm Michael. How *are* things?"

Jiminy made a frantic gesture.

"No? Ah." Michael sounded disappointed.

"Yes, I'm Melissa." She awkwardly added, "Thank you for your letter."

Tami stole a look at Jiminy, who seemed to have stopped breathing.

Ash surprised them all by curving his wings around them, effectively hiding Jiminy and Melissa behind a curtain of black feathers. In an even, almost amused tone, he said, "They'll be fine. We're the ones seeking council."

Gingko, who seemed to have surrendered half his chair to Jacques, said, "If no one else wants it, *I'll* be his go-between."

Hisoka's eyebrows lifted, and he inclined his head. "Principal Tamiko Reaverson, Landmark Elementary. I didn't realize we share an acquaintance."

"It's a long story." Tami wasn't even sure where to begin, so she simply said, "It has a happy ending."

Argent Mettlebright waved lazily at them. "These Americans appear to be what my lady would call ... an answer to prayer."

ЧЧ

DISARMING

Melissa found the next few days anticlimactic. Everyone else had grandness to scheme and destinies to fulfill, leaving her to fill drink orders and pull double shifts. Doon-wen hovered with enough menace to keep Jiminy at bay, and Rook confined himself to sympathetic looks and fleeting touches. They seemed to be giving her space, but she didn't care for the isolation.

Restless and dissatisfied, she reviewed her options and reluctantly selected the most efficient path to enlightenment.

She called her father.

Twenty minutes later, Melissa knocked on the door to Jiminy's den.

From within, he called, "It's open!"

She closed the door quietly behind her and waited.

"Be with you in just a sec."

Jiminy stood with eyes closed, hands upraised, as if directing the sigils slowly wheeling around him. While she watched, the intricate patterns aligned, locking over each other in a series of concentric rings, then rapidly diminishing in size. With a gentle tap, he pushed the sigil against the face of a polished stone that had been shaped like an egg. The luminous tracery shimmered on its dark green surface for a few moments, before cooling to shadows.

"I've been finessing this ward for *days*. Third time's the charm!" He gave it a cursory glance, then offered it to her. "Think it'll hold up?"

Melissa didn't see wards like these very often. Power hummed under her fingertips, almost musical in its cadences. "Etching would triple the strength."

Jiminy unrolled a leather carrier, revealing a full set of delicate tools. "We'll go all out."

"What's it for?"

"Ash asked for it." His tone was as careful as his glance. "Tami is being courted with tokens and baubles. It's the avian way."

Melissa accepted the opening. "What about wolves?"

His posture remained studiously neutral. "Traditions vary by clan."

She couldn't believe it. This was exactly how her father had described it—verbal sniffing. Firming her stance, she asked, "How does a Nightspangle wolf pursue his bondmate?"

Jiminy set aside his tools.

Melissa returned the masterful egg. He was very careful not to touch her.

"Are you asking how *I* would go about it?" he asked softly.

"Yes."

"I'd probably be wracking my brain, searching for ways to regain the trust I lost before I ever knew her name." His fingers drummed lightly on the worktable. "*Are* you angry with me?"

She shook her head. "Why did you send me a standard nuptial packet?"

"Full disclosure." Jiminy spread his hands wide. "It's the reaver way."

"I thought you were a wolf."

He blinked. He blinked again. "I am."

Melissa folded her arms over her chest and lifted her chin. "And how does a *wolf* address himself to the one he admires?"

Jiminy eased closer. "I'd probably find any and every excuse to be near you, to talk with you, to run with you. And if you wanted it, I would pursue you, with the intention of bringing you into my den."

"I'm already in your den."

"Well …." He gestured vaguely at the room. "*Bringing in* is used euphemistically to refer to … to …."

He trailed off when she withdrew the dagger hidden in a sheath at the small of her back. Startled and silent, he watched her retrieve another blade from the holster in her new boots. When she placed both on the table, his eyes widened.

Another blade at her hip. The fourth in a clever pocket at her thigh. She laid them beside the others.

Jiminy whispered, "What are you doing?"

Melissa didn't answer as she slid the final blade from her armguard. He probably knew what she was doing better than she did herself. But her father had assured her that any wolf—even a practicing wolf who was reaver by birth—would find meaning in the shedding of weapons. And barriers.

Turning her wrist, she unbuckled the armguard with its trio of wardstones.

Next, her ear cuffs. She absolutely hated that her hands were shaking.

By the time the ankle chain lay on the table, she was barefoot and very much afraid that she was glaring.

Jiminy didn't seem to mind. He slowly straightened, taking a more dominant posture.

She didn't back down, but neither did she contradict him. And when she judged him thoroughly fixed on her every breath, she subtly shifted, adopting a receptive attitude.

And he smiled.

Her biological father officially rocked.

"Did you know," said Jiminy, "that there's a whole language to kisses?"

"Anyone who's been following Kimiko Miyabe's courtship knows that the placement of a kiss can have special meaning."

He nodded once. "Where is important. How is important. There are nuances that anyone can correctly interpret, given the chance."

Melissa saw no reason not to be direct. "Are you offering me that chance?"

"I'm asking for a chance."

She lifted her empty hands and said the words he needed to hear. "I trust you."

At his sides, Jiminy curled his hands into fists. "May I touch you?"

"I'm not armed."

His smile was rueful. "And I'm *still* no match."

Melissa may have smirked.

"This is how a Nightspangle wolf pursues his bondmate." Jiminy brought his hands under hers in a supportive hold. "Instead of claiming with kisses, we cross boundaries. Touch is the first."

"How many boundaries are there?"

Jiminy hummed. "I suppose we could count them up as we go along."

Melissa tweaked his little finger. "You've strayed off topic, Fourth of Wards."

"Where was I?"

"The language of kisses."

"Right. Yes. So." To her surprise, Jiminy released her hands and took a step back. "Wolves place greater importance on non-verbal sounds, gestures, postures, and scents than they do on words. Touch is trust, as basic as breathing. And the most meaningful of touches is the kiss."

She hadn't expected a lecture, but she wasn't about to complain. This definitely wasn't covered in the standard reaver curriculum.

"A single kiss to the center of the forehead can be a show of affection. But it could also be a pledge of protection, an apology, a farewell, a sign of approval, a mark of ownership, or even gentle refusal."

That was a wide range of meaning, and only for the center of the forehead. "How do you know what kind of kiss it is?"

"Context, I suppose. Everything a wolf does involves a combination of all those sounds, gestures, and expressions." He asked, "May I demonstrate?"

She offered her hands again, silently repeating the show of trust.

All Jiminy did was rise up on his toes to press his lips lightly to her forehead. "What do you think that meant?"

Melissa frowned. "Nothing much. That was sort of… perfunctory."

"Kisses never mean *nothing*. A simple kiss can mean simple things. I like you. I'm here. I'm glad you're here." Jiminy had returned to a polite distance. "This time, I'll do it a little differently."

Stepping forward, he took her by the shoulders, gave them a small squeeze, then kissed her forehead with more warmth than the last time.

"Well?"

This was familiar territory. She'd received this sort of kiss from Rook. "That was more like … good job, you did well, congratulations."

"See? You're catching on." Jiminy asked, "Ready for another?"

Melissa waited to see what he would do.

But when Jiminy's gaze softened, the lesson veered out of academic territory. He trailed his fingertips over her cheek and gently caressed her mess of curls, like he'd always wondered about them, and he liked what he found. Jiminy was smiling when his lips touched her forehead, and he lingered just long enough to put her cheeks to flame.

Leaning back to search her face, he offered a small hum of approval. "There now," he murmured. "It's not all that complicated."

She asked, "My turn?"

Jiminy blinked.

Melissa wondered if the wolves had also documented a language of winks and wide eyes and fluttering lashes. She really did like the advantage that came with underestimation. "Is the next boundary taste?"

Jiminy's eyes slammed shut, but he was too late. Melissa had already seen all the things he had not planned to say.

"May I kiss you?" she asked.

He swayed into her, and his lips brushed the corner of her mouth. Inviting. Entreating.

Melissa swept in with a fearless assault that reduced her wolf to words. Ones she'd needed to hear. Ones she gladly returned. For they added up to mutual trust, lifelong loyalty, and unwavering devotion.

45

STAKE OUT

Kip's mind was on nothing more urgent than his current craving for nut tarts, nut pies, and nut loaves when he sauntered through the front door of Tough Nut Bakery, toting a burlap sack that rattled pleasantly with the promise of all the above.

His midnight forage through his fifteen-acre nut grove in Nocking, where he and Ash shared a cabin, would make Mom happy. And when Mom was happy, everyone was happy. Especially when she pretended not to notice when a little of this or that went missing from the bakery case or the cooling racks.

Caught up in his contemplations of filberts and filching and familial affection, he didn't pay any attention to the customers in the little line of booths along the wall. Not until one of them stood and stepped into his path.

Kip didn't know him—at least, he didn't know his scent—but

there was something about his smile. He scrambled for some clue to the nagging certainty that he'd seen the young man before.

He was quite ... picturesque.

Tyrone would probably have raved about the silk count in his suit, the exotic origin of every dye used in his artfully selected accessories, and the audacity required to carry it all off. Giuseppe would likely go on another Regency kick. Faisal would probably steal his pants, if only to get at whatever was on the end of his watchchain. Cyril would—quite predictably—adore and adopt him on sight. And then it occurred to Kip *where* he'd seen the new poster boy for Find Me.

In Jiminy's room.

Or more accurately, on Jiminy's direct line to Stately House.

The French butler's smile was triumphant. "Found you!"

Kip hadn't asked to be found. "Aren't you supposed to be in Japan?"

"His lordship fancied a trip."

At the front counter, Uncle Denny was on alert for trouble. And eavesdropping shamelessly. Kip made a covert sign—*this goes no further*.

His uncle acquiesced with ill-concealed curiosity and a single demand—*leave the nuts*. But it was the sympathy in his gaze that set Kip's hairs on end. This must be how Tami had felt when Lady Mettlebright showed up at school—caught, trapped, and traitorous.

Abandoning his harvest, Kip steered the butler out the door and into the alley. "Why is Lord Mossberne *here*?"

"He isn't. Which is why I'm here. I can identify you."

Kip's dread mounted. "Who's looking for me?"

"Silly question. I am Lord Mettlebright's man." He linked arms and leaned in. "I'm Jacques, by the way."

"Why is Argent Mettlebright looking for me?"

"Who can say? He did not." Jacques was all soulful eyes and soft pout. "His silences are a burden I must bear."

Kip couldn't sense a threat, but that didn't mean it wasn't there. Foxes could mess you up. If he was going to get a clue to *his lordship*'s intentions, it would have to come from Jacques. "You work for Argent?"

"When at home, I am the family butler. When traveling, I am Lord Mettlebright's valet." With obvious pride, he added, "I keep him presentable."

That was surprising. And kind of funny. "He can't keep himself presentable?"

"*Mon dieu*, you have no idea." Jacques rolled his eyes. "He is hopeless."

With little else to go on, Kip was studying scents and gathering impressions. The man was pleased with life, proud of himself, and overflowing with ardor for the fox lord. His flirting had a teasing, almost self-mocking quality, utterly lacking in intent. Something else was missing, too. "You're not a reaver."

"You're not wrong." His hand hooked one of Kip's beltloops. "Where do you keep your tail?"

He chuckled. "You're very comfortable with closeness."

"*Naturellement*. Stately House overflows with crossers, and I am the little beasts' favorite uncle." Jacques exasperation was heavily laced with fondness. "We have a squirrel, you know. Little hellion."

"A crosser?"

"He's not a red. Did you know gray squirrels have gray freckles?"

"Yep." Kip was tempted to drag Jacques to school with him. Ash was missing out.

"Still in nappies, and into everything. We should foist him on you. If you're half as much trouble, you probably deserve each other."

Kip went very still.

Jacques brightened. "You like children?"

Cheese and crackers.

"His name is Jarrah, and he sucks his thumb. Free to a good home, I say. He could probably be crated and shipped by weekend next, but Argent prefers to place our orphans personally." Jacques's gaze strayed to a point just behind Kip. "Isn't that right, my lord?"

Instinct kicked in.

Kip bolted.

Running was really a very stupid thing to do. Argent Mettlebright was a fox of superior skill and intelligence, and Kip really was just a very little squirrel. So when a hand closed around his hind leg and pulled him scrabbling from his near-escape through one of the enclave's attic windows, he went limp.

"Kip, I presume?"

Upside down and mute, he lifted a paw to wave.

"I will thank you to *not* bring attention to my presence so near a den of wolves." Argent's eyes narrowed, but he also righted Kip so that the blood was no longer rushing to his ear tufts. "This is not the time for games, Woodacre."

Kip tucked so fast, Argent received a faceful of tail. The stupid was multiplying.

But the fox's only retaliation was a soft cluck of his tongue. He set Kip on the roof of a nearby convenience store and arched a brow.

Transforming, Kip squared his shoulders, prepared to withstand anything if it meant keeping Joe's secret safe. But while the better part of his brain was churning through tactics, his mouth joined in on the stupid. "Wow. You look taller on television."

Argent Mettlebright sighed.

If Kip's tail hadn't been wrapped three times around his torso, he would have tucked again. He settled for a sheepish smile. "Sorry. You probably get that a lot."

The fox merely extended his hand. A slender rod of crystal rested on his palm. Kip bit his tongue, clasped hands, and waited for the ward to take effect.

Argent didn't waste time on pleasantries. "Lapis confided in me. I am here to assess your beacon."

"He's *mine*." Kip's grip tightened. "I won't let you take him."

Without any change in expression, Argent tapped Kip's nose, then touched his own. "I will say it again. I am here to assess *your* beacon."

"You're going to help us?"

"I am certainly in a position to do so."

Which wasn't any kind of promise, even if it was true.

Kip had no leverage. What's more, keeping Jiro's secret meant he was on his own, with no support from either his clan or the enclave. Contacting Lapis had been a risk. This was all Kip's fault. "My friend … he asked me to hide him. He's afraid of what the reavers might demand. He doesn't want to leave his home or learn any of the arts or be bred in captivity."

Argent's growl took Kip aback. It was the same kind Rook used to chase away bad dreams. A comforting rumble, pitched to soothe. "I will not lead your friend into captivity."

"He ... he's *beautiful*." He swallowed hard. "Anyone would want him."

"I do not." Argent's lips quirked. "You may recall that I am also in possession of an unregistered beacon. Tsumiko also expressed considerable wariness with regards to the reaver way of life. I protect her much as you wish to protect your friend."

"You really will help us?" Kip desperately wanted assurances.

Argent sighed. "I am here to help *him*."

Kip felt the color drain from his face. "I'm not keeping him against his will or anything."

"Then you have nothing to fear."

"*Really.*"

"Too many beautiful souls have been snatched and shattered. Too many lives have been caged by avarice and vice." Argent reached up to place a hand against Kip's cheek. "Lapis believed you both earnest and honest, and I am inclined to agree. But an ignorant promise is an empty promise. Have patience, and you may yet have my pledge."

Kip bowed his head.

Argent kissed his brow.

"Can you wait for tonight?" asked Kip. "I have work."

"When?"

"Eight o'clock."

"So be it." Argent left the crystal in Kip's hand, saying, "That is tuned. Keep it with you. I will find you."

Joe slumped against the side of his bed, knees pulled to his chest. He nodded to himself, then nodded again. "It's probably fine."

"You're sure?" Kip slouched beside him, the very picture of dejection. "Because I still have vast stores of guilt and a recurring desire to grovel."

"Pretty sure." Joe patted Kip's shoulder. "I mean, he already promised to be Ash and Tami's go-between, didn't he?"

"Oh."

Joe tried to read the redhead's expression, but they were both rattled. "Does he know it's me?"

"It's too big a secret. I didn't name names." Kip ventured, "Did you tell Tami about this part—the beacon part?"

"Only that I'm a reaver." Joe winced. "I didn't want to get her hopes up. In case."

"Yeah."

Joe's gaze strayed to the clock. "He's late."

"That's probably my fault." Kip held up a rod of crystal. "I might have laid a few false trails, created a couple of echoes. Added an illusion or two."

"Why would you *do* that?"

"Same reason you took me into the corn maze. I figured a fox would enjoy the challenge."

"There are wards all over the farm and thirty-odd wolves on the property." Joe couldn't believe Kip was mucking with one of the Five. "Aren't those obstacles enough?"

Kip resumed his groveling position.

Someone rapped on the bedroom door.

Joe's heart lurched, and Kip lunged for the knob. A peeved Argent Mettlebright stood in the hall. When Kip fumbled for an apology, Argent silenced him with a look, stepped inside, and stiffly inquired, "May I add to your wards?"

"Yeah, sure. Go for it." Then Kip crept back to Joe's side and curled his tail around them.

While he worked, Argent said, "You might have mentioned that your friend is a Reaverson."

"Slipped my mind," Kip admitted. "Does it change anything?"

The fox waved a hand. "In many ways, it simplifies things. Our acquaintance can be attributed to my role in Tami's courtship. Future involvement will go unquestioned."

Joe was almost ready for it when Argent turned to face him.

He was so much *more* than what the television showed.

Should he stand to greet him? That was probably proper, but Joe didn't think his legs would support him at the moment. So he tangled his fingers deep in the puff of Kip's tail and hoped he wasn't pulling too hard.

Spokesperson Mettlebright sat, right there on his bedroom floor, and offered his palms. "My name is Argent. I am here to confirm your status as a beacon and to ensure that your personhood and rights are being respected. May I know your name?"

"I'm … umm … Joe." He didn't want to let go of Kip, so he didn't. "Joe Reaverson."

Argent graciously inclined his head. "And your relationship to Tami?"

"I'm her twin." No matter what, Joe would always be pleased and proud of that fact. With a little more strength, he added, "She's my twin."

Withdrawing his hands, Argent settled himself more fully, elbows on knees, fingers loosely nested. "I am in desperate need of basic information, so I am going to begin asking questions. Of both of you. If I cross into territory that is too personal, simply decline to answer."

Joe mumbled an affirmative.

Mostly, Argent wanted to know ordinary, expected things—family history, childhood memories, educational background, property holdings, hours of operation. Some questions were decidedly odd, though.

"Do you associate the Amaranthine you've encountered with colors?"

He didn't.

"Are you able to divine an Amaranthine's clan while they are in speaking form? For instance, would you be able to tell a red fox from a red squirrel?"

He couldn't.

"Have you ever seen foxes anywhere on the property?"

Not recently. Unless Argent meant his mother.

Argent cracked a humorless smile.

More than once, Kip wouldn't answer Argent. He refused to speak for Ash or to give details about Bellwether Enclave, its founders, or their plans. But he spoke freely and knowledgably about human politics, reaver placement, police protection, citizen patrols, and the attitude of administrators in their county's Office of Ingress.

The fox asked, "How close was the rogue?"

Joe didn't think the question was as offhand as Argent made it seem.

But Kip answered without a fuss. "One county over. Naroo-soh is in Fletching if you want a firsthand report."

Argent's hum may have been displeasure. But then he said, "Your hand, please."

It took a moment for Joe to figure out that the fox meant him ... and another few for him to unsnarl his fingers from Kip. He'd probably been rude to withhold his greeting earlier. At least he felt a little readier now.

Lord Mettlebright offered his hand in the human manner, and his clasp was firm, like a good handshake was supposed to be, except he didn't do the whole shaking part. Neither did he let go. In fact, he went right on talking as if they weren't holding hands.

"How are the people of Archer responding to the prospect of Amaranthine in their town?"

"Positively. I'd even say we're proud. And that's mostly thanks to Tami's tireless advocacy." Kip ticked off his fingers. "Local paper gave her a column. She and Flootie—that's her secretary—write it together. And she has the PTA and the Office of Ingress working together to offer weekly courses at the community center. But hands-down, the thing everyone shows up for is Bingo Night. Harrison Peck—he's our school's attendance clerk—runs the Rivven trivia portion of the program. It's made him a local celebrity."

"Most of the town shows up," offered Joe.

"Stick around until Saturday, and you, too, could win fabulous prizes."

Argent huffed. "I will have to alert Twineshaft to the unforeseen—and therefore untapped—potential of ... bingo."

Kip sobered somewhat. "We'll get a better idea of what's in store when Dr. Bellamy has his say-so. They timed everything so Hisoka Twineshaft and his entourage will be on hand for the last day of classes before winter break. At that time, Dr. Cyril Bellamy, beloved president and Amaranthine in hiding, will come out as a Sunfletch to Bellwether's staff and students."

"Trust *can* inspire trust," said Argent.

Joe was sure the fox gave his hand a small squeeze. And come to think of it, wasn't he closer than before? Had he been inching nearer under the cover provided by Joe's lapful of squirrel tail?

But then Argent shared a little about his bondmate. Tsumiko had been similarly ignorant, not only of her status as a beacon but of the existence of Amaranthine. Wrapped up in her studies, she'd entirely missed the Emergence. "Like yourself, she was moderately isolated and well-warded."

"They didn't bother her?" Joe dared to ask.

"Who? Reavers?"

"The wards." He looked to Kip for support. "I didn't like them at first."

Kip shrugged. "Fine-tuning fixed it."

Argent's brows slowly ascended. "Perhaps we should discuss aptitude. Woodacre, what is your assessment?"

"Jiro's gotta be a beacon," said Kip.

With a flat look, Argent began listing classifications. "Ward. Pinion. Kilter. Battler. Candor. Reach."

"Not sure. I only had the smallest peek. It was enough to know I'm out of my league."

"You have not … indulged?"

Kip reddened. "I'm not an idiot."

Argent's hum hit a skeptical note. Turning his full attention on Joe, he inquired, "May I?"

Joe's gaze dropped with his stomach. "There are wards."

"I am aware." When the silence grew awkward, Argent sighed. "It may interest you to know that you have been safe. Even at this proximity, even with hands joined, I detect nothing unusual about you. You have been effectively … stashed."

"But there's no way in …?"

Argent's gaze slanted toward Kip. He mildly said, "There is a way."

"Isn't there another way?" asked Joe.

"Certainly, but that would require more preparation." Argent smiled thinly. "I understand your discomfort and will not linger any longer than necessary."

Joe mumbled, "If you think it's best."

"May I?" he repeated.

"Yes."

A hand cupped his cheek, then caressed it. If it was meant to calm Joe down, it wasn't working. Kip made that soft chirring noise—sympathy and support.

Argent rolled his eyes and said, "Say, *ah*."

Joe missed a beat. What came out was really more of a "Huh?"

With that, Argent eased his forefinger into Joe's mouth,

carefully pushing past teeth. Which was weird, but also a relief. Joe closed around the intrusion, felt the tip of a claw against his tongue, and held very, *very* still.

Kip slapped his forehead and swore under his breath. "I didn't think of *that*!"

"No?" asked Argent. "I *do* wonder why not."

46

DISCLOSURES

Argent hadn't expected to find anything more than an unusually potent soul and immediately regretted his cavalier attitude. Salvaging the situation required all his poise.

"Trust for trust, Joe," he murmured, as if he had any choice in flashing tails.

Let them think it a diplomatic gesture.

Now that Argent was past the squirrel's wily net of sigilcraft, three things became abundantly clear. The first he could readily admit—Joe Reaverson was certainly owed a beacon's rank. By the ninth tail, he *out*ranked them. Shuttering such a soul might require his full flourish.

This alone was reason enough for Argent to wish Twineshaft was here. The cat's discreet support would have left him feeling less harrowed. Because Argent's second realization might be nothing more than coincidence. But what were the chances? He *knew* this bloodline, was bound to it still, though by choice rather than compulsion.

Joe was a Hajime.

Uncovering descendants in America might have been incidental, even innocuous, if not for the third matter. This young man had been branded by the same style of seal that had once shackled Argent to the Hajime line.

While not exact, each small difference could be accounted for in any number of ways—adaptation, refinement, intent. But the basic structure was so sickeningly familiar, Argent felt threatened. Cautiously, he probed the pattern, which could easily have been a trap.

Another two tails thrashed into the open.

He gently withdrew his finger from Joe's mouth. Resisting his first impulse, which was to taste, Argent hesitated over his second, which was to wipe it on his pantleg. Giving in to a mildly fiendish impulse, he thrust the finger into Kip's mouth.

The squirrel's eyes crossed.

Oh, yes. Teasing him was vastly better than dealing with the repercussions of this discovery.

"Two perfect gentlemen, fraught with maidenly qualms," drawled Argent. "I commend your decision to wait."

Kip leaned away, pulling free. "I was right, wasn't I? He's a beacon."

"Without a doubt." Argent dried his finger on the hem of his tunic. "In my capacity as a member of the Amaranthine Council, I have personally met sixteen of the world's beacons."

"How many are there?" asked Joe.

"Officially? Twenty." Argent inspected his claws, though he

394

was actually focused on calming his tails. They felt as puffed as a squirrel's. Far from dignified. "By longstanding tradition, only the twenty brightest souls alive can attain the title. However, Glint Starmark recently redefined and expanded the classification to account for perennial members ... and to respectfully retire reavers who have reached the limit of their legacy."

Kip leaned forward. "Perennial members?"

"More than half of the beacons alive today are either tree-kin like Joe's sister or bound to an Amaranthine partner." Argent smiled thinly. "The former still do their part, if sporadically, but the latter muddle Glint's precious pedigrees by mingling species. He has opened the rank to new blood, provided they are adding to their legacy."

"Umm ... legacy?" asked Joe.

"Kids," said Kip. "Let's hope the venerable Glint Starmark never finds out that Ash and I are on the verge of wrecking the Reaverson family's progeny projections."

Argent was inclined to agree. "You would not be the first unofficial beacon. My own bondmate is unregistered, yet she has been acknowledged as both beacon and bastion."

He arranged his tails, and Joe's gaze followed. Argent would have caught the young man's straying hand, but Kip was quicker.

Catching Joe's wrist, he offered a mild rebuke. "No touching, Jiro. Tails are personal."

Joe was all contrition, but also confused. "You never said."

Kip flushed guiltily. "I've never minded."

"You *should* have said," grumbled Joe, who turned to Argent next. "I don't feed him anymore. He told me about *that*."

"Then you know more than you did. And you will learn more as you go." Argent wondered how far this boy's ignorance extended. "You know that tending will be required to sustain your life?"

"Yes, Kip told me."

"How much did he tell you?"

Joe shrugged. "Something about sharing a part of my soul."

Argent favored Kip with a hard look.

The Kith-kin offered pleading palms. "I could hardly go into more detail when he doesn't have the grounding and I don't have the know-how. It's why we needed help. It's why we're confiding in you."

Having been in close quarters with them for nearly two hours, Argent had formed his opinions, mostly based on scent and guesswork. The simmering tension between them was an endearingly innocent blend of want and willingness. What made the whole mess interesting was Joe's confidence. His decision was more than made.

In contrast, Kip reminded Argent of some of the children they brought into Stately House. Frightened by the pull of instincts they hadn't learned to trust. Desperate to belong anywhere, to matter to anyone. Awed by their good fortune. Sure there must be some mistake. Cautious to give in. Helpless to resist.

Argent enjoyed secrets and strategies, especially when they netted a prize. In large part, it's why he'd taken on Tami and Ash. The Reaverson-Sunfletch courtship had the potential to redefine public opinion in America and—of greater personal importance— add strength to his ongoing campaign to protect crossers. All he had to do was maximize on an established relationship.

But Joe and Kip actually *needed* a go-between. In the traditional sense. Hardly Argent's forte, yet a very personal prize hung in the balance. Answers.

"I have intimate knowledge of the bond you hope to nurture, and I am willing to teach you what you need to know. I have the necessary strength and scope to handle a beacon, and I have sufficient influence to protect your privacy. However ...." Argent sat a little straighter. "I have a condition and a request."

"What's the condition?" Kip asked warily.

"Beneath your own wards, there is a very different seal upon his soul." Argent didn't bother to hide his distaste. "I want it gone."

"I'll have to remove all the other sigils first." The squirrel cautiously added, "He'll be exposed."

"Fortunately for you, I have considerable experience shuttering beacons." Argent casually added, "With your sigilcraft and mine, this room is now sacrosanct. You will retreat here for tending, as well. Especially early on, when inexperience is bound to leave you awash."

Kip acquiesced with a nod. "And your request?"

"May I bring in Hisoka Twineshaft?"

Joe seemed a little dazed. "Umm ... if you think it's best."

With a hint of a smile, Kip said, "Even an under-the-table meeting has to have equal sides."

Joe opened his eyes in a strange place. Starlight cut through beveled glass, sigils wheeled slowly in midair, and he could hear the trickle of water nearby. A fountain? Crystals like the ones

Kip had lofted sparkled like fireflies, and more details slowly came into focus—trees and trellises, ferns and forget-me-nots. "Where am I?" he murmured.

"This is a fox dream." Argent joined him on what seemed to be a stone bench. "You fell asleep. I am taking advantage."

"Is this real?"

"No. But fox dreams are more true than false." His gesture encompassed the glassed-in garden. "At home, this is my haven. Like your room, my garden is sacrosanct."

"Why am I here?"

"Kip will require another hour or more to undo the rest of his sigilcraft. Then I will help him remove your original seal."

"Do I have to be awake for that part?"

"No. I will keep you company here. You need the sleep."

Little creatures rustled in the foliage. He recognized one or two, like the gem snake that Kip had told him was a midivar. But he had no words for the blue bird about the size of a chicken that wobbled past or the curious mouse-like critter with eensy antlers. He smiled when he recognized a gossameer.

"Do you know what these are called? Kip's been teaching me their names, but I don't know most of these."

"You like Ephemera?"

"Yeah." He reached for the creature that puffed along like a tiny, translucent jellyfish. "Doon-wen invited some specialists to study ours. I guess some are pretty rare. The orchard has already been declared a preserve."

Argent blandly remarked, "So you *can* talk."

Joe shrugged. "I like Ephemera. They're one of my favorite

parts of home."

"And doubtless, you are theirs." He raised a hand and clucked his tongue. "Have you ever tamed them?"

"Yes." To his amazement, a tiny winged monkey zipped from a nearby shrub and darted to Argent's palm. Joe put two and two together. "You like them, too."

"My collection is extensive." Argent set the tiny creature in Joe's hands. "This is a quisp, culled from the sizeable flock at Kikusawa Shrine in Keishi."

Joe had never seen the like. "So cute."

Argent hummed.

Joe felt safe here. Everything was in perfect balance. Of course, if Argent had brought him into a dream, didn't that mean they were inside Joe's own head? Cuddling the little monkey to his cheek, he shyly asked, "Is this like tending?"

"No. We are two friends on a bench, discussing a shared fondness for small creatures." Argent lifted his face toward the starry sky. "Tending is more than a meeting of minds, it is the touching of souls."

"Are you going to teach me how?"

"If you are so inclined. But *first*." Argent turned to face him. "Please forgive my caution, but I must ask if you are under any duress."

Joe drew a blank. "Sorry?"

Argent simplified. "Have you been led to believe that this is your only course? Are you being pressured by anyone into forming a pact with Kip?"

"Oh ... umm ... it's okay. I'm doing this for my own reasons."

"May I know them?"

Joe opened his hands, releasing the quisp. Some of his reasons were mixed up with Kip's feelings toward Ash, which were none of Argent's business. So he stuck to basics. "Kip's nice."

Argent chuckled. "Would that more nice people were so amply rewarded. You are a beacon, Joe. You could easily secure a pact with one of the Five. Twineshaft is difficult to pin down, but Lapis is an affectionate soul."

"No, thank you. I've already secured a pact with one of the Five." Joe tried for a grateful smile. "We're counting on you."

"Very well." Argent arched a brow. "The good news is ... if you can tame Ephemera, you can tend Woodacre."

Joe ventured, "Is there bad news?"

"Are you aware that tending is even more intimate than touch? Many describe the connection in terms of elation, exhilaration, and pleasure."

"Kip and I are helping each other." Joe wanted Argent, at least, to understand. "He isn't in love with me or anything."

"The exchange is not inherently romantic or erotic, but it is intensely personal. Absolute trust is at its very foundation, and mutual consent is essential." Argent touched Joe's burning cheek. "Before my bonding, I was tended by a male friend. If you wished it, I would find a way to bring Michael to you. He tends beautifully, and he is a patient teacher."

"You promised not to tell."

"True, but I will not pretend there is only one way to proceed. You have options. You have a choice."

Joe whispered his thanks.

Argent resumed. "Kip needs your strength in more ways than one. Tend to him, and he will gain in both power and stature. But be wise and firm. Impose limits. Because he may lose himself in your vastness."

"Stop him from taking a third beer."

"Figuratively speaking." With an amused twitch of lips, Argent said, "Something tells me he would be an affectionate drunk."

Joe was inclined to agree.

"Since I know firsthand, I must also speak on Kip's behalf. Your sway over him increases exponentially because of your magnitude. He will want you and no other, for nothing can compare to a beacon's brilliance." Argent gravely said, "It would be the worst kind of cruelty to abandon him."

"Tend and keep. Got it."

Argent reached for Joe's hands and cradled them all the while he talked. Giving information and examples. Outlining customs and courtesies. Reinforcing trust and secrecy.

Joe eventually had to ask, "Aren't you going to *show* me?"

"Yes. If you wish it."

He said, "Help me find my feet, and everything will be fine."

"So be it." Blue flames bloomed over Argent's heart, quickly spreading over his skin as more tails flickered into existence and fanned out on all sides. "Time for your practicum."

Kip hardly heard Argent, even though he was probably saying something important. He was too busy watching blue flames lick across the tracery of sigils decorating Jiro's skin. All signs of "manly bloodshed" were vanishing, yet Kip could feel their hold tightening, their bond strengthening.

"He is unharmed." The fox's gaze slanted toward the bed. "He has never been safer."

"I get it. I'm grateful. But I can't help wanting to ... make sure."

Argent spoke with exaggerated patience. "You can go to him once I am certain you understand Lapis' gift."

"Is that what we were talking about?" Kip felt something lock into place around his wrist, and just like that, Jiro vanished. "Wait, what? What did you do?"

"Calm down. Pay attention." Argent's hold on his wrist was gentle, his gaze attentive. "They appear to be working properly."

Around Kip's wrist was a strand of small, irregular black stones. Their unfamiliar weight was putting his hairs on end. While his other senses didn't seem to be affected, it was definitely messing with his perception. His connection to Jiro had narrowed to a pinprick, and he didn't like it.

Twirling the bracelet, Kip's heart sank. There was no catch. There would be no release. "Why?" he asked.

Argent sighed. "From the beginning, then?"

Kip nodded sheepishly and took a receptive stance.

"Those closest to Lapis Mossberne know that he has long struggled with addiction. Until quite recently, he was numbered among the Broken. So he was naturally concerned for your wellbeing." Argent touched the wardstones at Kip's wrist. "These are tuned to Joe, which will allow for tending. They also provide a formidable damper. You have ready access, but your take will be little more than a trickle."

"Rationing."

"Yes. During future visits, as your reserves grow, I can widen the gap. In due course, you will have no need of such safeguards."

Kip murmured, "Gotta admit, I've been worried about that part."

Argent touched his arm and mildly reiterated, "You have never been safer."

"Thank Lapis for me?"

"Certainly." The fox's hand settled, and he asked, "May I speak plainly?"

Kip dredged up a weary smile. "Go for it."

"You will hamper your progress if you waste time waiting to be given what Joe doesn't know how to offer. Assert yourself, appeal to him directly, and then abide by his decision."

"Communication, huh?"

"He responds well enough."

Kip knew coy when he heard it and would have called Argent's remark into question, but he breezed on.

"The more time you are together, the better. Spend your nights here. Hold him while he sleeps. It is the safest, simplest way to achieve saturation."

That was a big change. He wondered how Ash would react. "And ... I need to reciprocate?"

"Eventually. Tend to yourself first. You need greater gains before you can hope to contain him." Argent stepped around him in the cramped room, moving to the door. "I will assess your progress in December."

"You're leaving?"

Argent smirked. "You are welcome."

Kip had every intention of thanking him properly, but in a blink, the fox was disconcertingly absent. He rubbed at the back of his neck, which was prickling. Had he been drawn into a fox dream? Kip checked the door, its wards, his wrist, and then the bed.

Jiro's eyes were open.

Hurrying to his side, Kip eased the blanket over him and whispered, "Hey."

"He left?"

"Yeah. Just now."

"The dream suddenly ended." Jiro propped himself up on elbows. "He showed me a garden, talked to me there, told me things."

Kip sat on the edge of the bed. "He never let on. You okay?"

"Sure." His gaze was so calm, his scent both settled and serene. "What about you?"

Now that he was paying attention, Kip could feel the drag on his senses. Hardly surprising, given his long night of complicated sigilcraft. Edges fraying, focus fading, he was dangerously close to collapse. "Tired," he admitted. "You okay with me crashing here for a while?"

Jiro scooted over, making room.

Kip was only too glad to climb in next to him. Maybe it was the weariness. Maybe it was the sudden release of tension. Whatever the reason, Kip was embarrassed by how much he was shaking. He tried to hide it by grabbing hold of the only steady thing within reach—Jiro.

"Umm ... you okay?"

"I take back everything I ever said about being scary strong.

Argent is scary strong."

"I know what you mean." Jiro's voice was mild and mellow. "But he came a long way to help us."

"Well, my squirrel quarter needs a moment." Kip gave in to the need to shudder.

"Argent likes you. I think he secretly enjoyed the challenge of finding us."

Kip lifted his face. "He said that?"

"Not with words." Jiro gave a little shrug. "I could feel it when he was showing me how to tend."

Three kinds of envy cropped up, but Kip swatted them aside in favor of an honestly impressed, "Whoa. You tended Argent Mettlebright?"

"No. He kind of … showed me the door, but left it shut."

Kip pulled the blanket over their heads, grumbling when it left their feet out in the cold. Curling his tail around foot and paw alike, he burrowed his nose against Jiro's neck. "Guess it worked out."

"Guess so," Jiro agreed.

There was a little fidgeting as Kip coaxed Jiro into a more compatible position. And a lot of silence, which was surprisingly comfortable, given Kip's fondness for chatter. The tremors eased and his mood lazed contentedly. It felt good to hold Jiro, whose happiness was a subtle thing, but no less real. Kip found himself orienting toward it, pulling into it. How had Argent described his bondmate—both beacon and ballast. That sounded about right.

"Is it working?" murmured Jiro.

"M'wha–?" Kip was so limp, he left it at that.

"Argent said I should try taming you. I think it's actually working." There was an edge of amusement to his tone. "This is how I attract Ephemera in the orchard."

Kip turned his head enough for eye contact. Normally, it would have been too unrelentingly dark for Jiro, buried under covers in the middle of the night. But Kip's sigilcraft was still fresh, so his bare skin gleamed with a hundred patterns that spoke of possessiveness and protection. "Ephemera, huh?"

"Yep."

"And what do you do once you get the little critters into your clutches?"

Jiro's expression turned thoughtful. "It's hard to explain. I guess ... umm ...."

Kip was suddenly aware that a door had opened somewhere inside Jiro. Even narrowed by wards, it touched off a yearning need that was much more complicated than greed, yet infinitely simpler. And utterly safe.

Jiro awkwardly petted his hair and finally answered, "I guess I give them a reason to stay."

47

TELL ALL

More than an hour before Ash was due for his evening's visit, Tami was already in the loft, nestled down with Biddie. The little girl would cuddle up to anyone, which was apparently the nature of trees, but Tami could tell—somehow—when her tree-twin needed her. And *only* her.

So she was stealing this hour to spend with her sister.

Biddie rested her head on Tami's shoulder. Burnished gold leaves tickled her chin as she rubbed gentle circles into the girl's back. Quiet and peaceful.

Their relationship was this odd mix of old and new, much like Biddie herself. Although Tami didn't feel the need to mother her, she certainly felt responsible for the girl. They were on equal footing, each sure they belonged to the other, despite their differences.

Tami relaxed into the contentment that holding Biddie always brought. Despite the bite of winter in the air outside, Ash's nest was snug. He'd added to it nearly as often as he brought his gifts, so that the formerly simple ring of straw bales now boasted a high canopy and cushions.

Branches of all sorts rose around the courting circle, bent and braced, providing support for a fortune in draped velvet. She'd have been more mystified by the extravagance of cloth, which he used by the bolt, if she hadn't already met his fashionista brothers.

Fleeces and flannels were comfortable, but Tami had already noticed that Ash's tastes also ran to sequins and faceted beads, which sparkled in the light of tiny crystal lanterns that twinkled up among the supports.

Blue on blue. Everything was Ash's favorite color, and every part was an expression of his earnest affection and of half-understood avian compulsions. Here, he was completely honest. And completely hers.

Tami's peaceful mood drifted perilously close to sleep, but the soft rustle of feathers stirred the air and with it, her heart. A hand touched her hair, and she opened her eyes to Ash's smile. His lips brushed hers, light with a promise of more to come, and he rested a hand on Biddie's leafy crown.

"Have you been waiting long?" he asked.

Biddie held out her hand, welcoming him into their cozy huddle. Ash's wings were visible this evening, a sure sign that Kip was somewhere nearby. Probably visitingwith Joe. They'd been spending more time together in the last few weeks. Usually, they took charge of Biddie, but Ash eased an arm around both of them, covering her and Biddie under the curve of one wing.

"I have news," he offered. "Well, it's really just gossip, but it's almost impossible to come up with *anything* definitive about Amaranthine trees. Dad's extra sulky tonight because Faisal was the first one to dig up some dirt."

Tami could sympathize. Every question she'd asked about the Scattering had been briskly rebuffed or evaded. The topic was obviously taboo, so any tidbit was bound to be juicy. "What did Faisal find out?"

"There's a grove in Wardenclave, where your family came from."

Interesting, for sure. And probably part of the reason her great-grandfather had needed to leave town. They—whoever *they* might be—would have assumed he'd been in among their trees. A thief in the garden, after forbidden fruit.

"It's seldom discussed, out of respect for Glint Starmark, who is fiercely protective of Waaseyaa."

Tami knew that name. "The boy Glint befriended. The co-founder of the In-between."

"That's the guy."

"But that was hundreds of years ago."

"More like thousands. Long before the place where your history books pick up the story."

She missed a beat. "How old *are* you?"

"Not *that* old." He kissed her cheek. "Anyhow, out of respect for Glint, reavers don't talk about Waaseyaa unless it's to brag on their pedigree. Because he's very much alive, thanks to his twin Zisa. They're brothers, just like you and Biddie are sisters."

They weren't alone in the world. Others knew about Amarathine trees and knew the importance of keeping them safe. But it wasn't such a deep, dark secret that *nobody* knew about it. People—at least those immune to Faisal's charms—were circumspect about the subject.

Ash tapped Biddie's nose. "Apparently, Zisa's hair—if we can call it that—changes with the season. Flowers in springtime. Leaves in summer. And Waaseyaa doesn't age, but his hair never stops growing."

Tami waited for more, but all Ash did was gently touch her hair, as if imagining it at Rapunzel lengths.

She asked, "That's all you know? *Hairstyles*?"

"This is Faisal we're talking about." Ash shrugged a shoulder. "His connection is apparently a cosset in Radiance Starmark's cortege. As far as I can tell, they only gossip about clothing design and hairdressing."

"Well, it's something we didn't know before." Tami hugged Biddie and asked, "Will you bloom for us in the spring?"

The girl smiled a secretive smile.

Touching Biddie's autumn-hued foliage, Tami tried to picture buds and new leaves. But then she frowned. "What happens in winter?"

"Uh-oh, Biddie," teased Ash. "If you lose all your leaves, you'll be bald."

Tami was quick to defend. "If you lose all your leaves, we'll just have to bring you several pretty hats."

The girl's eyes widened. Then she reached up with both hands and pulled out two handfuls of leaves.

Tami gasped as they fluttered onto their laps. "Biddie! No!"

Ash grunted. "Look, Tamiko."

He lifted aside a few leaves. Under the rustling crown of foliage, soft brown ringlets clung to Biddie's head.

"No need to rush through seasons," Ash said firmly. "If you can be patient, I'll bring you a hat tomorrow evening."

"A gift for Biddie?" She sounded almost wistful.

Ash's expression softened. "I'm glad you're with us tonight, because my gift for Tamiko is also for you. I hear you like to look through your sister's treasures."

She looked up through her lashes, as if unsure of Ash's reaction. "I keep them safe while Tami's at school."

With an encouraging smile, he asked, "Which are your favorites?"

Biddie lost no time in spilling out the small trove of courting gifts. And with that, she shed her temporary shyness like a pair of too-tight shoes. She told him snatches of the stories behind some of the gifts, often paraphrased in amusing ways. Or she had her own stories behind what made certain tokens special, displaying a vivid imagination. Watching the girl sort and arrange brought back fond memories. Tami used to spend hours sifting through her grandmother's button jar.

The girl lifted a tiny silver bell. Its bowl looked like a swirl of trailing feathers, and from its crown rose the distinctive figure of a calling bird—a peacock. The work of art was no bigger than Biddie's little finger, and its peal was a small, sweet *ting*.

"One of my brothers gave that to me." Ash was all patience and pride, as if he liked the bell's story too well to mind repeating it. "Faisal is my peacock brother. The bell is an old joke between us. If he ever courts a lady, I'll choose a bell for him to give to her."

The girl peeped under the peacock's train at the bell's clapper, which was egg-shaped. "Because it is funny?"

"Neither of us is what you'd call a songbird. Bells and chimes are traditional courting gifts among avians like us. They're said to summon Bethiel, whose sweet voice can make plain the truth of any matter. If he were to sing on my behalf, your Tami would know me in ways that defy words."

"I know my Tami."

"I'm so glad you do."

For a moment, Biddie held his gaze, as if weighing his words. Then she reached for another treasure, holding it up in silent command.

Ash obligingly began, "Giuseppe is my dove brother."

"Can he sing?" asked Biddie.

"His voice is lovely. He has a gentle soul—hopeful and hopelessly romantic." Ash gently touched his gift with a clawtip. "Doves believe in love letters."

Tami liked the dainty message tube as well. Clear glass allowed one to see the pale pink scroll within, and a pearl stopper kept it safe. When he'd first presented it, Ash would only say that it contained a traditional blessing. But his manner made her curious.

So she'd quizzed Tyrone on the matter. He'd cheerfully read off the enclosed poem, which only served to stump her, since it was in some kind of bardic language. Striking a pose, he translated all three verses, which involved the delights to be found in nests of down … and a rather suggestive line about duets and dawn.

According to Tyrone, doves were affectionate by nature and none too shy in their approval of the intimacies of the nest.

Biddie gently lay the slender message carrier beside the bell before seeking out a pair of circular silver cases, each no bigger around than a quarter. They were a matched set, yet subtly different, for their domed tops had been taken in a shallow cut from crow's eggs. Soft green, speckled with brown.

"Twins," said Biddie, holding them out to Ash, one on each small palm.

"Once upon a time, Amaranthine nearly always came into the world two-by-two." His brows lifted a little. "Cyril has a twin. So does Rook, for that matter."

Tami liked this part of stories. With each retelling, fresh nuances came to light.

Ash said, "Tyrone is my pheasant brother, and his gift is another avian tradition. He's saying he wants me and Tami to multiply. Kind of like saying, 'Hurry up and make me an uncle.'"

Tyrone's gift was quite practical, by avian standards, because he'd provided for the potential future of two nephews, who might one day wish to begin their own courtships. Tami had been startled to learn that Tyrone was not only bonded, but already three times a father. He had two sons of his own.

"It's for a tooth." Ash showed Biddie how to unscrew the top. "An egg tooth, for those born in truest form. But they'd work just as well for baby teeth."

Biddie selected other gifts, and Ash seemed pleased by her interest. If Tami had ever entertained doubts over her plans to publicize their relationship, he banished them that evening. Ash's gifts were no more secret than his feelings for her. How many times—and in how many ways—had he said it plainly? *I love you.*

Sitting up, Ash asked, "Would you like to see what I brought tonight?"

From the pocket of his jeans, he brought out something with a length of glittering chain. Uncurling his fingers, he showed Biddie an egg that had been carved from dark green crystal. Its entire surface was etched with intricate sigilcraft.

"I'm courting Tamiko, so this is from me to her. But it's also partly from Jiminy, who has a way with crystal. And it's also mostly for you, Chick-a-biddie." Ash undid the clasp. "Even though it means my present won't help to fill up you sister's bag, I would be happiest if you'll wear this."

"For me?"

"Yes. Do you understand why I've been bringing so many gifts for Tamiko?"

The girl kept her eyes on the necklace as he fastened it around her neck. "Ash loves my Tami."

"That's right. And sometimes, I want to keep her all to myself." He lifted her chin. "But I also know how much your Tami loves you. I would never try to take her away. And I would never try to keep you apart."

She traced the sigils, quiet once more.

"We'll share a home, Biddie. My wings are wide enough to shelter you both within our nest." He wafted his wings demonstrably.

Biddie said, "A promise for me?"

"I promise to be your brother." He lightly touched the three courting gifts from Faisal, Giuseppe, and Tyrone. "You'll have three of us, you know. A crow brother, a squirrel brother, and a twin brother."

Small fingers closed around her very own treasure. "Brother," she said, as if conferring a title.

Tami's heart swelled, and because she wasn't sure if she'd ever said it plainly enough, she touched Ash's shoulder and said, "I love you."

Days passed with a veneer of normalcy. Argent regularly sent Tami books to read, links to follow, and checklists to complete. Cyril made a present of Faisal, whose energy and efficiency were nothing short of miraculous, and Lord Mettlebright—for lack of a better word—retaliated by assigning both his son Gingko and a pleasant young diplomat named Isla to Tami's team.

Cooperation. Coordination. Everything was humming along, right on schedule. Almost.

As December neared, one item had been sitting at the top of Argent's checklist for two weeks—*inform next of kin*. Tami was almost sure this was evidence of the fox's dark sense of humor. Either that, or he was teasing her. Because she kept finding ways to put off the conversation, even though she was sure it would go well.

Her parents were far from dense, but Tami got the impression that they thought all the secrets were on the Reaverson side.

Quite literally in passing—since they were in the upstairs hall—Tami confided in Melissa.

She should have realized that a battler was more about strategies than sympathies.

"Tonight. I'll create an opening. You take it." Melissa clapped her shoulder. "Lock and load."

It wasn't as detailed as the schedules Isla drew up, but Tami had a feeling it would get the job done.

That evening, Tami realized that Melissa must have involved Joe in her plans. All he did was raise his hand, but by the time he lowered it again, Melissa was out the kitchen door. And when she returned, she hustled two janitors into the house ahead of her.

"I'd like to call a family meeting," she announced. "Now."

Tami flashed her a grateful smile and helped Mom find extra chairs while Joe helped Dad add a leaf. Greetings floated around, and snacks made their way onto the table. Biddie went straight to Ash, who lingered by the door. Not out of reluctance to join in, Tami realized, but because his wings would be in the way.

They were part of him, and they forced him apart. But only from those who didn't know his secret. Why had she left this so late?

She touched a chair on the side of the table that left the most room. Ash kissed her cheek, and she sat beside him. Kip claimed the chair on Ash's other side, casually shielding his best friend, just as he'd always done.

Melissa lead out. "I'm being pursued by a wolf of the Nightspangle pack. Which is like courtship. If Jiminy had his way, I'd already be part of his den, but my adoptive father is making me wait until after my whelping feast." A small smile touched her lips. "I think Doon-wen is using a technicality to tease Jiminy."

Dad rallied first. "It sounds like congratulations are in order!"

Mom asked, "Jiminy's a wolf? I thought he was a reaver."

"He's human, but he was raised by wolves and is considered one by the Nightspangle pack." Melissa quietly added, "Actually, I'm considered Kith-kin. By adoption."

"Get out!" exclaimed Kip. "Me, too! Except not the adopted part."

Ash asked, "True?"

"True." Melissa's smile warmed and widened. "If you count Rook, I'm up to four mothers."

"He's mine, too."

Tami eyed her parents. Dad was utterly bewildered, and her mother was barely holding back a burgeoning inquisition. So she jumped into the next gap and announced, "Argent Mettlebright has agreed to be go-between for Ash and me."

Joe calmly banished the sudden silence. "I like Ash."

Biddie giggled. "And *I* like Ash."

"Not as much as I do," said Tami.

"Hold up." Grandad pointed at Tami. "Say that again."

"I like Ash?"

"Argent. Mettlebright."

"Oh, him." She rallied like a Reaverson. "Lord Mettlebright agrees that America needs a love story to soften their hearts toward the Amaranthine. Ash and I volunteered. With the help of the Amaranthine Council, we'll be going public with our engagement."

There. It was out.

All eyes swung to Ash, who recognized his cue. "I'm a crosser."

"I'm hopping the bandwagon," said Kip. "I *also* like Ash, but that's never been a secret. Is that what this is? A chance to spill secrets?"

"Yes," said Joe. "This is your chance."

"Awesome." Kip spread his hands on the table, taking the proverbial floor. "I'm pretty sure you have to have realized by now that I'm not even a little bit human. Only you've been too polite to let on."

"What?" asked Dad.

"Wait. No?" Kip was playing it up. "You guys saw me make with the wards at the pizza parlor, right?"

Dad said, "I thought that meant you were a reaver. Like Mr. Ismal."

"Oh, that does make sense. I wasn't sure how much Jiminy told you when he brought me in that first time. Guess it's out." His glib tone softened slightly. "Who wants to play Guess My Clan?"

Grandad shook his finger at Kip. "Woodacre ring any bells?"

Kip held up his hands. "Guilty as charged."

Joe cleared his throat. "I like Kip."

"Who doesn't?" asked Ash. "He and I have been keeping each other's secrets for a good long while. Even longer than we've been janitors at Landmark."

"How long's that been?" Kip asked, as if he didn't know.

Tami had to appreciate the way they played off each other. It was kindergarten orientation all over again.

Ash stole a look in Grandad's direction. "Hit our eightieth anniversary a few years back. Hoping to make it an even century if they'll keep us around."

Dad was tapping his fingers on the table, the way he did when figuring in his head.

"You know," said Tami. "Landmark Elementary has *always* been fortunate in the custodial department. Dad, by any chance, do you remember who had that post back when you were attending?"

He rubbed at his chin, his eyes never leaving Kip's face. "Haven't thought of it in years, but sure. Hard to forget Mr. Reynard, the juggling janitor."

Kip did a little smile-and-wave.

Dad's eyes cut to Ash, then back to Tami. "But there *was* another one. Are you saying ...?"

"Grandad?" prompted Tami.

He was silently shaking his finger at Kip, a crooked smile on his face.

Once more Kip raised his hands, as if to repeat *guilty as charged*.

Joe asked, "Who was he then, Grandad?"

"Back in my day, it was Mr. Redman, the janitor who always spoke in puns."

Ash groaned.

Kip shrugged.

Joe demanded fur.

Tami coaxed for feathers.

Mom kept slipping into Japanese.

Dad ordered pizzas.

Melissa scooped ice cream.

And Grandad—for the first time since the Emergence—missed his weekly documentary, the nightly news, and the *Rivven Report*. Without complaint.

Tami knew without a shadow of doubt that she was going to make a difference. On her own, that difference probably wouldn't have extended beyond her hometown. With Cyril's help, they'd pushed change all the way to the county lines. Now, Argent would make sure one small town girl achieved national—and international—coverage.

"Having second thoughts?" asked Ash.

"No." She sagged further down into Coach's back seat. Kip had gone on ahead with Joe. She'd begged for five more minutes. Twice.

"What's on your mind?"

"You."

His arm slid around her waist, and his lips brushed her eyebrow. "If that's the case, then why do I have you worried?"

"I'm not Kimiko."

There was a thoughtful pause before Ash asked, "What does that young lady have to do with us?"

"She goes places, does things." When that failed to enlighten, Tami went on. "She makes appearances all over the world, meeting diplomats and giving speeches. She hosts conferences, rallies supporters, and sits in on official meetings with the Amaranthine Council."

Ash hummed. "Kind of a go-getter, I suppose."

"All while courting Eloquence, who pretty much only leaves the Starmark compound if there's a kiss scheduled."

"The press only knows as much as they see. And what they're allowed to see isn't necessarily all there is to know."

Which was true. But it wasn't really her point. "You're Kimiko."

"Not even close." His smile was the knowing sort, a good sign that he understood.

"I have Biddie, and that means sticking close to home. I doubt I can leave the county without distressing her. Which means you have to be Kimiko."

"I'm really much better at being myself."

Tami let his kisses calm her before trying to reason through her concerns. "You might be asked to travel, to give speeches, to be on television, to do photo shoots and interviews and ... and all the things that Kimiko has to do."

"That's true."

"Aren't you nervous? Or bothered? Or ... regretting that I ever suggested this whole thing?"

"No, no, and never." He toyed with her hair. "I've been wondering if I should bring this up. In many ways, it doesn't matter, but if it would set your mind at ease ... Tamiko, I'm really very old."

To Tami, Ash looked like a man in his early thirties. So did Kip, for that matter. But so did Argent Mettlebright. She'd never actually seen any Amaranthine whose appearance surpassed a vigorous forty-something.

"Age doesn't matter. It won't ever matter, now that I'm tree-kin."

"Yeah, which means you'll understand in time." He sighed and said, "I have a slightly different perspective. People will come, and they'll go. Some of them will use paper towels to clog sinks, and some of them will slip paperclips into my pockets. Either way, I'll learn their names, I'll listen to their words, I'll tell the truth, and I'll hold them to a high standard of courtesy." Ash's feathers rustled and settled. "My manners will become their manners."

"You make it sound like all we have to do is be nice."

Ash said, "That's about right."

"But what about all the bullies and brats?"

"Leave them to our go-between. And leave Flootie and Harrison to Kip." His fingers gently sifted through her hair. "By the time he's done, the two of them will be arm-wrestling for the privilege of walking you down the aisle. No holds barred. No hard feelings."

Because tonight they were tackling the next item on Argent Mettlebright's formidable checklist—*choose your allies wisely.*

Ash nodded toward the bright lights spilling from Archer's community center. "Ready to go inside?"

"No holds barred. No hard feelings." She kissed his cheek and said, "Let's play some bingo."

"G-11."

Inside, most folks were too focused on their bingo cards to pay any mind to a couple of late comers, but Flootie had been watching. She waved one arm wildly, pointing at the stage with the other. Kip was up front, already in position for a round of Rivven trivia.

Bingo balls tumbled in their wire cage, and one dropped through the chute. "N-23," called the head of the PTA. She scanned the room over her reading glasses. "N-23."

Ash muttered, "He's always wanted to play. Harrison must have been taking volunteers."

"Unfair advantage, don't you think?"

"B-07."

"Bingo!" shrieked a woman near the concession stands. Her friends all pointed, in case anyone missed her windmilling arms.

One of the volunteers, whose Lions Club vest jingled with pins, made his way over, and Harrison grabbed the microphone. "While Dan confirms Miss Patty's win, we'll have another round of

Amaranthine trivia, sponsored in part by our friends at the Perch County Office of Ingress. Kip's already volunteered for this round. Who's game? We have room for two more!"

Hands went up all over the room.

Tami laughed when Grandad was pulled from the crowd. He could probably give Kip a run for his money on facts, if not speed. This might be funny.

Ash raised his voice. "Over here, Harrison. Let Tami strut her stuff."

Her attendance clerk broke into a wide smile. "As I live and breathe, Principal Reaverson, would you do us the honor?"

Under cover of Archer's very vocal approval, Ash spoke into Tami's ear. "Homefield advantage. *You* can be Kimiko tonight."

She laughed. "I'm really much better at being myself."

"That's the spirit."

The next fifteen minutes was a bizarre cross between a gameshow and a talk show, with Harrison at the helm. Once more, Tami had the sense that she was in the middle of a skit for which she'd never seen the script. And it was fun.

"What's the name of the first headman of the village at Wardenclave, a man whose surname became his legacy to the In-between?"

Bells dinged in near-perfect unison. Kip must be taking it easy on them. He even deferred to Grandad, who answered confidently. "Gerard Reaver."

"Correct!" Harrison straightened his bowtie. "Gerard Reaver is the reason that human Betweeners are called reavers. You may be interested to learn that Wardenclave—the village he founded and the birthplace of the In-between—is currently governed by Gabriel

Reaver, who is Gerard's direct descendent."

The next few questions were easy enough for anyone following the Miyabe-Starmark courtship. What was the name of the ballad Kimiko was using as a basis for her courtship of Eloquence Starmark? What was the name of the tree at Kikusawa Shrine, under which Kimiko always bestowed her kisses?

But current events had their turn. As did pop culture.

"What city's mounted police recently received a gift of six Kith stallions from Spokesperson Dwennon Thunderhoof?"

"Where do most of the world's known crossers reside?"

"On the popular television series *Dare Together*, what famous cryptid did brothers Caleb and Josheb Dare bring out of hiding for an interview?"

"What PBS children's television show announced they'll be adding a puppet of Amaranthine descent to their neighborhood?"

Tami couldn't keep up with Grandad or Kip, but neither did they leave her behind. Winning had never been the point of these weekly games. This was just the rallying point. In varying degrees, to the best of their ability, everyone in Archer wanted to be counted as allies of the Amaranthine. This town was getting ready to be good neighbors.

After bingo, Tami was surprised when Harrison shook his car keys and said, "Meet you there!"

"Right behind you," called Flootie, who was pulling on hat and coat. "First one there puts on the coffee pot!"

Tami shot a look at Kip, who grinned. "I already ordered take-out from Swifties. Let's roll."

Swifties was little more than a counter and two booths at the back of a gas station. But they turned out the best hot pastrami sandwiches in the county, and they boasted six flavors of hand-scooped ice cream—none of which was ever vanilla.

"What did you tell them?"

"Two reubans, two hot ham and cheese, two patty melts. And a six-quart sampler for dessert."

Tami prodded his shoulder. "I meant, what did you tell Flootie and Harrison."

"Oh! That their beloved principal's weekend is imperiled by paperwork. But a late-night push—with tasty incentives—would set the world to rights."

She asked, "At the school?"

"Where else?"

"But ... Faisal is there, setting the world to rights."

Kip was on his phone with greater speed than he'd used when ringing in with answers to Harrison's trivia questions. But all he did was check to see what Faisal wanted from Swifties.

Tami followed the aroma of fresh coffee through Landmark's pristine halls, straight to the break room, one of the few places in the building where all the furnishings were intended for grown-ups. She stashed the ice cream in the freezer while Ash eased bags of food onto the table.

Flootie made a pleased sound and began an immediate rummage for paper plates and plastic utensils. Harrison pulled bottled water from the fridge, then hunted up their coffee mugs.

By longstanding tradition, everyone on staff kept one on the long shelf over the sink. Photo mugs were a popular choice, and Tami counted no less than five with some variation on the theme *World's Greatest Teacher.*

Flootie's was patterned in the distinctive dark blue of Polishware. Harrison's featured one of those math jokes that probably would have been funnier if he didn't have to explain it. Tami's cup was shaped like a squat daruma, a graduation gift from her grandparents in Kyoto. Hers was red; Joe's was blue. Kip's mug boldly announced *Will Work for Food.*

"Where's yours, Ash?" Harrison asked, scanning the shelf a second time.

"Got a new one." With a sidelong look at Tami, he added, "That green one on the end."

"Nice! This looks handmade." Harrison checked for a potter's mark on the base.

Ash shrugged. "Yeah, I know a guy."

Tami eased over to get a closer look, and Harrison passed it along. Heavy for its size, the mug's glaze was an earthy shade of green, and letters had been incised deep into the clay—*tree hugger.* She laughed.

He shrugged again, like it was no big deal. Because it wasn't. Not really. But Tami was looking forward to a future filled with all the little ways he found to show he cared.

"I really wish they'd send you some support staff." Flootie

settled into a chair. "Weren't you going to get us a secretarial moth person?"

Ash's mouth twitched.

"I *did* get some help, but not from a moth clan." Tami casually asked, "Do you like birds?"

"Depends. Is she detail-oriented?"

"Obsessively," assured Ash.

Tami would have liked to make a remark about pots and kettles. "He's proving very diligent."

"Would you like to meet him?" Ash's gaze slid to the door. "Kip went to get him."

Harrison had been about to sit but bounced to his feet again. "He's *here*? There's an *Amaranthine* here?"

"He's been working nights," said Tami. This wasn't really the big reveal they'd planned, but maybe Faisal wouldn't mind being their opener. "Which is why there *isn't* any paperwork for us to worry about."

Flootie's eyes narrowed. "Ulterior motives?"

"More than one," promised Ash, just as Kip strolled through the door.

"Flootie, Harrison, meet my good friend Faisal."

Tami wasn't entirely surprised to discover that Faisal dressed impeccably for an evening of solitude. He greeted everyone with the same poise he used in dealing with customers at Find Me.

Giving Faisal a puzzled once-over, Flootie asked, "Are you Amaranthine, young man?"

"I am. I use simple illusions to hide telltale features." Faisal sidled up to Harrison and inquired, "Would you like to see more?"

Harrison offered his hands and breathlessly asked, "May I know your name?"

With an approving inclination of his head, he slid his palms over the clerk's. "Faisal Longsweep, a fosterling of the Sunfletch clan. Would you be so kind as to help me with my cufflinks?"

Tami watched closely as Harrison obeyed. Faisal murmured something in his ear, and his fingers fumbled at their task. She tried to gauge what was going on by Ash's expression, but he was looking on with nothing more than fond exasperation.

"There. That's done the trick," said Faisal.

Flootie uttered a reverent, "Would you look at that?"

Having never seen Faisal without his disguise in place, Tami was similarly awestruck. The irises of Faisal's eyes had darkened to brown, while all of the blue they'd once contained had migrated into his hair, which had the same lavish, shifting sheen of peacock feathers.

"Gosh," said Harrison.

"That's all? Have I rendered you insensible?"

"Maybe a little. I mean ... gosh." Harrison earnestly asked, "Is there an appropriate way to ask an avian if they want to be friends?"

Faisal slipped a finger under Harrison's bowtie and gave enough of a tug to bring the clerk closer. "Is there an inappropriate way to ask a human if they want to be friends?"

"Oh." Harrison smiled. "I guess the question's silly either way."

"But the underlying sentiment is flattering." Faisal added, "Nice tie."

Ash cleared his throat. "Introducing you to Faisal wasn't really the point to bringing everyone here."

"Oho?" Flootie's gaze swung to Tami. "There's more?"

Tami said, "We wanted to tell you first."

"You're *engaged*, aren't you!" She pointed to Harrison. "Didn't I tell you? Let me see the ring!"

Ash held up a hand.

Flootie chortled in delight. "*She* asked *you*? That's adorable!"

"Hold up." Kip, who'd been shooting longing looks at the bags of food, said, "There's more to that more. And I'll go first."

Harrison immediately frowned. "You're not ... *quitting*."

"I don't ever want to leave." Kip boosted himself to a seat on the table. "I love it here. Landmark is my home, and you guys are my family."

"Here, here," agreed Flootie, lifting her water bottle.

Tami raised the tree hugger mug, matching the heartfelt salute.

"Okay, so, this is kind of nerve-wracking. C'mere, Harrison." Kip beckoned with both hands. "Help a guy out."

Harrison stepped right up, and Kip took his hand. Tami recognized the gentle press of knuckles into Harrison's palm. It was the same way Ash had first revealed his claws to her.

"Oh, man," Harrison whispered.

"Technically *not*." Kip smiled crookedly. "Sorry, friend."

Harrison said, "Flootie, he's trying to tell us he's not human."

"Saints above!" She lunged up and bustled over. "What are you even saying?"

Tami had never been more proud. They always talked about Landmark as family. In moments like this, her staff proved it.

"Kip, you rascal!" exclaimed Flootie. "How long have you been hiding."

"Long while now." Kip's eyes were suspiciously wet. "I remember when you moved to Archer."

The woman gawked. "That was forty years ago!"

"Can we see?" asked Harrison. "Is it all right to ask?"

"Food's getting cold."

And there was laughter and teasing and coaxing and a compromise. Until Flootie remembered the quiet one in the corner. She propped her hands on her hips and accused, "You *knew*!"

"Can't deny it," said Ash.

Harrison asked, "You, too?"

"That's the gist, but not the whole story." Ash pulled out a chair for Tami. "How about we have mercy and feed Kip. We can talk things over while we eat. Because that's where those ulterior motives kick in."

Tami leaned forward. "Like I said, we wanted to tell you first … because we need your support. I want you to help us announce the truth about Ash and Kip to the whole town. On Dichotomy Day."

48

ENTOURAGE AND RETINUE

Ash loved his dad. Cyril liked to blame it on making a dramatic first impression, but Ash figured he was a little more discerning than he'd been as a half-plucked chick, when fascination and adoration were everything and enough. Love was all mixed up with respect and trust and pride ... and at the moment, a desperate wish to go to him.

"Settle your wings, boy." Rook's big hand reached for his. "He knows we're here. He isn't alone."

Three tiers of Bellwether College's auditorium were packed with a standing-room-only crowd, and not simply because attendance was mandatory for students. Their parents had been invited, as had all alumni. And then there were the members of the press. They'd been afforded folding chairs, and the orchestra pit bristled with cameras and microphones.

Because Hisoka Twineshaft had been kind enough to alert

them to his schedule.

Ash couldn't have navigated the crush on the main floor any more than he could have worked his way into the balconies. But what most people—meaning humans—didn't realize was that well-warded box seats overlooked the stage.

Bellwether's academic rigor was noteworthy, but the college was most famous for its dedication to the performing arts. And Cyril was the most generous of patrons. Naturally, his box was large, more of a balcony, really. And it was crammed with his ever-increasing family.

Ash had a place there. One he was glad to own. But when Rook invited him into the relative hush of Doon-wen's private box, he trailed after him as he'd always done.

A light rap sounded on the box door, and Jiminy poked his head in. "Room for one more?" he asked cautiously.

"You can come in if you ward the door behind you." Rook blandly asked, "Aren't you supposed to be part of the welcoming committee?"

"I convinced Himself that I'm more effective if I have the high ground." Jiminy looked only slightly less like a barista in his dark suit.

Rook's brows lifted. "Who modifies that pronoun?"

"Lord Mettlebright." Jiminy added one last sigil to the door. "He's on edge, and that's putting it kindly."

"He expects trouble?" Ash asked.

"He's *ready* for trouble." Jiminy's posture shifted into lines of confusion. "I haven't ever dealt with foxes. Are they all as prickly as he is?"

"You know better than to generalize," scolded Rook.

Jiminy's chin dipped. "I know, but he's their spokesperson."

Rook slowly shook his head. "Argent is … unique."

Ash tuned them out.

He was still so worried about his father.

Honestly, he was also a little ashamed. He'd been so sure of himself when he'd told Tami that he didn't care about bullies and brats. Because leaving things to their go-between no longer seemed like such a good idea. Not because he was afraid of humans. That was the worst kind of generalization. It was because he was afraid for Cyril. And that made his wings jump and his grip tighten and his heart pound a fearful rhythm.

Caring for someone was vastly different than taking care of yourself.

As he sat on the edge of his seat, fingers locked with Rook's, he guessed he owed Tami an apology. How often would he put her in a place just like this—helpless on the sidelines while someone precious stepped into potential danger.

"It'll be okay."

Ash dragged his gaze from the stage.

Jiminy was bending over him. "Hey, he's going to be fine. You know Cyril. He's always been golden."

"Promise it," whispered Ash, who needed words like these from friends like this. "Promise it, so I know for sure. Because a wolf always keeps his promise."

"You may be the only person who takes me seriously." Jiminy's smile was as soft as the kiss he placed on Ash's forehead. "All I am is all he needs. Your father will be safe."

Ash swallowed hard and whispered, "Thanks, kiddo."

"I grew up, you know."

"It shows."

Jiminy fished in his pocket and plucked out an amber stone. Moving back to the balcony railing, he coaxed light into the crystal and began a series of sigils no bigger than butterflies and just as erratic in their flight.

"What are you up to?" Rook asked suspiciously.

"Finishing touches." Jiminy flashed a grin. "I don't take my vows lightly. Not that our dignitaries haven't already covered their bases. Have you *seen* Twineshaft's escort?"

"Hard to miss," murmured Ash.

Picking reavers out of a crowd had always been a popular game when he and Kip were kids. Even incognito, Ash could spot them and usually sort them. The Amaranthine Council's security team weren't even trying to blend in. Dark teal tunics and the dull shine of pewter armbands.

"Where's Melissa?" asked Rook.

"Crowd control." Jiminy angled his chin toward the front. "She brought back up."

Ash brightened. "When did Chris get here?"

"Late last night, along with Twineshaft's retinue." Rook's smile widened. "See the woman beside him?"

An Amazonian blonde was quelling the entire press box with a stern look that was very familiar.

Ash asked, "How did that go, meeting Melissa's parents?"

Jiminy whispered, "The only thing scarier than her mom is her moms together in a room with my mom."

Ash chuckled.

But then the lights dimmed by half, and the stage lights came up. Cyril walked out and stood in the center of a subtle pattern worked into the boards of the stage. Under the right lights, it had the look and luster of a full moon. It had been his gift to the Nightspangle pack at the theater's founding. An urban song circle.

It was rare to see him act without the other founders. But Cyril had insisted on making this move alone. Partly to protect the enclave, the inner workings of which would remain a secret. But mostly because declaring himself made it safer for Ash to do the same. He had a parent, a clan, and their protection.

Movement near the curtain pulled Ash's attention to three figures who moved without fanfare to three chairs arranged off to one side. These were the principals of West Branch High, Archer Middle, and Landmark Elementary—Cyril's collaborators for the selection of the Twineshaft Initiative.

Their presence was little more than a red herring. And an understated fix for some red tape.

According to recent legislation, no Amaranthine could travel unattended. So once Cyril exposed the truth of his species, he would be in direct violation of the regulation requiring a reaver escort. So in a tidy exchange of paperwork, Cyril submitted testimony, confirming a notable brilliance of soul only to be found in a reaver, and Tamiko signed the necessary documents to act as his escort.

If anyone was foolish enough to try and arrest Cyril, they'd have no grounds.

At center stage, Cyril touched his fingertips to his heart and smiled. Then in a conversational tone, he began, "Speculations have been flying about my reasons for calling you all together this morning. I understand there's even a betting pool and that—as ever—the fates and odds alike favor Hisoka Twineshaft."

Polite laughter.

"I am well aware that our students are eager to be done with this final obligation for the semester, so I will be as brief as I can. Let me begin by putting to rest a few of the more outrageous rumors."

Cyril's calm was infectious, his manner poised. If he hadn't been so attached to his role as educator, he would have done well on the Amaranthine Council.

"I am not relinquishing my post. I am not under arrest, nor has my conduct been called into question. I am not running for elected office. I am not releasing a book. However, I didn't gather you and the members of the press together in order to tell you that I have nothing to tell you."

Another murmur of amusement.

"I have always considered myself a scholar. A deep and abiding love of learning can enrich a lifetime. Truth be told, I have never felt more at home than I do on this campus."

He was good at this. Telling the truth without saying too much.

"If you checked my bio on your way over, you probably already know that I've been president of Bellwether College for the past twenty-six years. What I'm here to share this morning is a quirky little aside. I also happen to be Bellwether's founder."

Silence seized the entire room.

Ash groaned softly. Rook huffed.

Cyril lifted a finger. "Take a moment to gather your scattered wits while I welcome our international guests. They hardly need an introduction."

Without any sort of rush, Hisoka Twineshaft and Argent Mettlebright filed out and flanked Cyril, standing at either shoulder in a silent show of support.

And nobody yet dared to break the silence.

"You know me as Dr. Cyril Bellamy. My true name is Cyril Sunfletch, and I'm an avian from one of the pheasant clans. I am Amaranthine, and since this country's very inception, I have been an American."

In the simplest form of greeting, Cyril offered open palms to an audience being multiplied by every camera in the room.

"There," he said warmly. "Have I shocked you?"

On the longest night of the year, the oak glen was alight, and Ash had a pretty good idea Kip had been showing off. Biddie's tree shimmered with colored lights that would have bankrupted the enclave if they'd been real crystals. But Kip was a champ at making do. He'd figured out long ago that while glass marbles didn't cast light, they could be lit.

However, the critters were new.

Ash waited patiently for one to drift near enough for him to confirm that the thing wasn't any kind of Ephemera. Nope, nothing of the sort. They seemed to be entirely made of sigilcraft, but they flitted among the branches like birds and butterflies. He might have written them off as a specialty of the evening's entertainers, but the minstrels all bore the crests of cozy clans. While merriment and music were part of their repertoire, they weren't known for the illusory arts.

"Clever bit of fuss, aren't they?"

"Kind of pretty," Ash agreed. "Are they yours, Uncle Denny?"

"Wish they were, seeing how chuffed our Chick-a-biddie is over them." Kip's uncle rolled his eyes dramatically toward the base of a nearby oak. "Never would have believed him capable."

Sitting in the snow, heedless of his festival attire, was Argent Mettlebright, with Biddie perched on his knee. She wore a bottle green coat Faisal had designed for her, along with a floppy tam o' shanter, into which he'd tucked a single curling peacock feather. Because it matched her eyes—or so he said.

Argent's agile fingers pulled another bit of magic into existence—a midivar this time—and Biddie clapped and laughed and brought the faintest of smiles to the austere fox's face.

"Easier to believe he takes in orphans when you see him like this."

"Have you seen Kip?" asked Ash. He'd need his friend's help to banish the wards that hid his wings.

"Recently?"

Classic evasion. "Do you know where he is?"

Uncle Denny hummed and huffed. "He outdid himself today. Wouldn't surprise me at all if he was tucked up somewhere safe, taking his fill. Where's your lady?"

"The mice have her." Some of the minstrels were teaching Tamiko the steps to a walking dance that had exploded in popularity ever since it led up to Kimiko Miyabe's fourth time kissing Eloquence Starmark.

"She'll lure you into a mating dance yet!" Uncle Denny took possession of Ash's arm. "Since she's well occupied, how about you and I have a little chat with a cat."

"I ... haven't actually been introduced." Ash lowered his voice. "What are you up to?"

The squirrel waggled his brows. "Stick close, and you'll soon see."

"Why do I need to be involved?"

"Might be good to have a witness."

Ash groaned but gave in. He'd been living with a squirrel for so long, a day wouldn't be normal if there weren't some kind of caper involved. And it gave him an excuse to introduce himself.

Hisoka exuded nothing more than polite interest at their approach. "Spokesperson Woodacre. Ashishishe Sunfletch. It is a pleasure."

"Do you have time for a private word? Or would you prefer not to speak of weighty matters on the darkest day?"

"This is both an auspicious time and a hope-filled place." Hisoka beckoned for more. "I would never deny a spokesperson their right to speak."

Uncle Denny gripped Hisoka's hands gratefully, then slid his into the supporting position. "Two things, really. You see, I have connections. All of us in hiding, we find ways to keep in touch. Even before our boy here took to courting, I was pulling this together."

From inside his sash, he withdrew a folded paper.

Ash had no idea what was going on, but he watched Hisoka's face closely. The cat scanned the page twice, then murmured,

439

"This is quite a list."

"Only one of its kind." He tapped the edge of the page. "Every one of them is willing to step forward and represent."

"That is welcome news."

"It's just the beginning." Uncle Denny withdrew a second paper, which was more of a packet. He beamed. "*This* isn't just cake. It's icing."

Hisoka glanced at the pages, his brows slowly knitting. "Tell me what I'm looking at, Linden."

"A proposal for the proposal." Uncle Denny's hand clamped onto Ash's shoulder. "He has a lady to impress, and she wants nothing more than peace. So he makes the rounds, the old whistle-stop treatment. Fifty states, fifty enclaves, each one doing good in their communities, each one willing to be known."

Ash tried to get a look at the papers. "What are you talking about, Uncle Denny?"

All he got was a wink. Denny was too deep in his pitch to stop now. "I know a guy who knows a guy, as they say. Willing and able to give Ash and his courtship a television series. He goes in, gets a bit of history, tries his hand at their stock-in-trade, and brings home some special trinket for his lady. Real. Informative. Entertaining. And every episode brings another clan or enclave into the open."

"Interesting," mused Hisoka.

"Isn't it? A crosser crossing the country. You never know when he might visit your state." Denny was nodding like the deal was done. "Two-hour episodes aired once a month, plus holiday specials, and you'll have Americans on the edge of their seats for

... oh, four years, at least. You'd be giving the world something to look forward to after the Miyabe-Starmark courtship runs its course."

"Very interesting." Hisoka's gaze settled on Ash. "Is this something you would consider?"

It was a crazy idea. And catchy. It would probably take off, but there would have to be limits. "If you can keep my part of the production to one weekend a month, I'd consider it. Because I'm not giving up my day job. And you'd better come up with some *other* reason than courtship for my bringing home gifts, because I'm *not* waiting four years."

Hisoka smiled. "You remind me of your father."

Ash felt ... teased. "I am his son. All is as it should be."

The cat took a conciliatory stance. "Cyril placed similar conditions on his collaboration."

"He wouldn't leave his school?" That was hardly a surprise.

"He wouldn't leave his son."

While the oak glen rang with the songs of bards and the ballads of storytellers, three twins, two janitors, and two wolves slipped away by twos and a trio. The appointed time was near, and the appointed place hummed with enough power to give Ash pause.

"Did you add to the wards?" he asked Kip.

"Should I be flattered? Or was that a joke?" His best friend's tail was puffed double. "Jiminy?"

"Did anybody catch the guest list to this cabal?"

Tami edged closer to Joe. "All Argent said was that the meeting would have the appropriate balance."

"So seven of us, seven of them." Ash dared to ask, "He wouldn't have brought the whole council, would he?"

"No way," said Kip. "They're all over the place, doing their Dichotomy Day thing like good little ambassadors for peace."

Tami nodded. "Harmonious Starmark is touring South America. Lapis Mossberne is in Jerusalem. Tenna Silverprong is in Russia. And Kimiko Miyabe is visiting Wardenclave."

"That leaves Elderbough and Farroost." Melissa asked, "Any whiff?"

Kip, whose nose was twitching nearly as fast as his tail, asked, "Are you kidding?"

"The wards are too strong, but they're also dropping hints." Jiminy indicated several points along the wall. "Fox. Dragon. Wolf. Phoenix."

Joe simply shrugged, opened the door, and walked through.

"Gutsy," muttered Kip.

"Punctual," countered Tami, patting his shoulder on her way past. "Let's not keep our guests waiting."

Ash waved the others inside, then followed, carefully easing his wings through. The apple barn was closed for the season—tables stacked, baskets stowed, floors swept—but the scent of fruit lingered in the air. More sigils wheeled along the walls and amidst the rafters, fainter in here, with the lights switched on.

Argent waited just inside the door. "Allow me," he murmured, solicitous as a butler.

He thought the fox meant to add more wards to the door, but with little more than a touch, he banished Ash's illusions.

Giving his wings a little shake, Ash whispered, "Thanks."

"It was no trouble." With a lift of his brows, Argent suggested, "Brace yourself."

Before he could ask what for, Tamiko blindsided him.

"Can you believe it?" Her lovely eyes were dancing, her happiness adding a squeak to her question.

"I might believe anything on this night."

"He's here, he's here, he's *here*!"

She bounced against him, not an unpleasant sensation, and he spread his wings further for balance. Whose arrival could possibly have eclipsed that of Hisoka Twineshaft and Argent Mettlebright?

Ash's gaze darted to the cluster of strangers surrounding Spokesperson Twineshaft, and he understood. The Starmark clan had sent a representative. With a chuckle, he suggested, "How about we say *hi*?"

Tamiko nodded, but she remained very much locked in place, also far from unpleasant. Ash took advantage of his now-visible wings to hide her with his feathers. "Starstruck?" he teased.

"He's ... he's Eloquence Starmark!"

Chancing a peek, he reported, "And he's coming this way."

"May I beg an introduction?"

"No need to beg." Ash gently turned Tami to face Eloquence. "We're surprised and honored and ... really very happy."

Tamiko leaned heavily into Ash, a position he encouraged by wrapping his arms around her from behind. Her heart was racing, but she rallied enough to say, "Hi."

Eloquence offered his palms. "My father sends both his greetings and his congratulations. He will come to meet you as

443

soon as he is able. In the meantime, he sent me … and a cask of star wine with which to liven the night."

To Ash's amusement, Tamiko thanked him in Japanese, then English, then again in Japanese before blurting, "You're *here*."

"I apologize for unsettling you." Eloquence took a deferential posture. "Sensei thought it best that we meet quickly and make friends. If that's acceptable."

Ash took charge, catching Tamiko's wrists and guiding her hands into place, then covering them with his own. "Friends sounds good. I go by Ash. This is Tami."

She mumbled, "I'm sorry, I'm just …."

Eloquence gently finished, "… surprised, honored, and really very happy?"

Tami shook her head. "I don't even know where to begin, and I don't want to gush about things you've probably heard a million times."

"You can say anything you'd like."

Ash released Tami's hands, preferring to hold her. Some of it was probably instinct, making sure Eloquence understood his claim. But also because he'd never seen her so flustered, and he wanted to lend his support, to be a pinion to her flight.

Tamiko's hands lingered on Eloquence's. "You and she … you're *beautiful* together."

"Thank you." He gently squeezed her hands, then stepped back. "Kimiko has many commitments, but Sensei and Suuzu are clearing her schedule so that we can be here for your nuptials."

"You would do that?"

"Why wouldn't we?"

"You're ... famous."

Eloquence dismissed that with a flick of his fingers. "After tomorrow, you'll both be celebrities. May I offer a word of advice?"

"Please."

He gestured for permission, which Ash was happy to give. Eloquence took Tami by the shoulders and said, "Never forget *this*. Hundreds of people, thousands of people, will tremble and stammer and gush because they've found reasons to thank you, or to admire you, or even to love you. They'll want to tell you things you probably *will* hear a million times. And when they do, remember *this* ... and the enormity of the emotions a single meeting can hold."

Ash could feel Tamiko grow still, then calm.

"I'll try," she said.

"Good. Please, call me Quen." And kissing her forehead, he lifted his face to Ash. "I think, perhaps, you have the years."

"The years are mine," Ash confirmed and pressed his lips to Eloquence's brow.

A staff beat against the cement floor, and Hisoka raised his voice. "While I could not bring the full council without drawing attention to matters best kept secret, I did my best. You have met Quen. These other three are people I trust absolutely. May I keep the introductions brief?"

"The less said, the better, Poesy," said a strapping wolf in faded blue jeans.

"We know how to keep secrets," countered Kip, his arms folded over his chest.

The wolf smirked. "And we know how to bury them."

Argent clucked his tongue—and something formidable flared around them. The posturing quickly ended. Biddie leaned into Ash's leg, quieter than he'd ever seen her. This group was certainly having an effect on the ladies in his life. Without a fuss, he offered his hand, and when she tugged it, he hauled her onto his hip.

At the center of the room, a large cask of star wine stood on end, with a cloth-draped object resting on top. The Amaranthine formed a line on one side. Jiminy guided their group into a line facing them.

Hisoka said, "This is Boonmar-fen Elderbough, son of Spokesperson Adoona-soh Elderbough."

The wolf touched his fingers to his forehead, as if tipping a hat.

"Juuyu Farroost is elder brother to Spokesperson Suuzu Farroost."

The phoenix's orange eyes locked with Ash's, and he offered a small bow and a low warble of sound that sent a thrill up Ash's spine. He arched his wings into a hospitable curve, which Juuyu accepted with a dip of his head.

"Sinder Stonecairne is ... well. You may recall a display of dragons on the day of Kimiko's first televised kiss? Sinder was the green opposite Lapis."

The dragon offered a cheery wave.

Argent indicated the remaining member in their lineup. "And that is Jacques. He has his uses."

The man flushed as if he'd been paid a great compliment.

Hisoka rapped his staff twice more against the ground at his feet. "You called for help, and we are here. We seven share the same vow. You shall have our guidance, our protection, and whatever resources you need. Never fear to ask. Our answer will always be *yes*."

"And this," continued Argent, whisking the drape from atop the barrel. "Shall signify the height, depth, and breadth of our resolve."

Jiminy gasped. Eyes wide, he gesticulated wordlessly, babbling in the manner of wolves. He looked rather like a cub, wriggling on the verge of incontinence.

"*Tsk*. Have you something to say, Kourogi-kun?"

He clapped a hand over his mouth.

Argent rolled his eyes. "That was an invitation for you to display your superior knowledge."

"By all the stars who ever sang," Jiminy said with obvious reverence. "It's pink."

"Oh, well-spotted," Argent drawled. "*Thank you* for clarifying that for all assembled."

Tami raised her hand. "I see a little pink, but most of the block is clear."

"We still call it a pink. That hint of color at the center is stronger than a triple-shot espresso to the system." Jiminy warmed to his topic, talking fast. "The essence of this stone, the power it contains, has been pulled in tight, condensed, and multiplied. *Any* remnant of this size would make a serviceable anchor, but this is ridiculously strong. Size. Clarity. Color. If this rock was a reaver, it'd be a beacon."

Sinder spoke up. "You are in the presence of the Orchid Saddle."

Jiminy broke ranks, pushing right into the dragon's personal space. Hand brushing urgently at Sinder's, he asked, "One of the Four Gentlemen? First-sensei mentioned them in passing, and

I looked for more information. But I only found one reference, barely a fragment of a story."

The dragon begged, "Don't ask."

Jiminy blinked and closed his mouth.

Juuyu reached across and biffed Sinder across the back of his head.

"It doesn't *look* like a saddle." Kip casually picked the rock up and eyed its angles. "Not even close."

"Have a care." Hisoka quickly retrieved the stone, returning it to the cask. "The term is largely figurative."

"What's it supposed to do?" asked Tami.

Juuyu answered. "Harness the wind."

"Kind of like how Pecos Bill saddled a cyclone?" asked Kip. At the various blank looks he received from the Amaranthine contingent, he folded his arms. "American tall tale. It's legit lore, only a little newer."

Argent sighed. "Setting aside the assorted fables, this crystal is Twineshaft's gift to this enclave and its ward, in token of his attainment."

Jiminy swayed. "Yours, Sensei?"

Hisoka shook his head. "Yours, now, Fourth of Wards. May Cadmiel's song and Bethiel's blessing ward the grove you've pledged to protect. And may every tree and all their kin thrive in peace for all your generations."

Tami only left for work on schedule because Joe had hustled her out of Ash's arms and into the house for a shower. And because Faisal had barged in to help her dress. And because Juuyu Farroost had handed her a Founders coffee to chase away the lingering effects of too much star wine before ushering her into a shuttle with blacked-out windows ... and high enough ceilings to accommodate Ash's wings.

"Good morning," he murmured as she slid into the seat beside his.

She hummed around a sip of coffee.

He was dressed in his janitorial coveralls, and his wings were gone from view. Like today was just another workday.

"Where's Kip?"

"Running through things with Harrison." His knuckles lightly brushed her cheek, and he smiled weakly. "If Faisal wouldn't come back here and harass me for undoing your fancy up-do, I'd be preening you right now to help me calm down."

She hadn't realized he was nervous. "Does it work if I preen you?"

Ash's head tilted as he considered. "You're welcome to try."

"Hold my coffee."

Tami pulled the tie from his ponytail and worked her fingers through the length of his hair. He immediately angled toward her as much as his wings would allow. She scratched little circles into his scalp, and he leaned into her, their foreheads touching.

At times, everything about her life seemed to be hurtling toward the unknown, yet times like this, the whole world seemed to pause. If it was Ash's doing, maybe it was some kind of Amaranthine magic. As if having a long life didn't diminish the importance of moments. He definitely had a knack for drawing out the potential of each one. He was always singling them out and slowing them down, so they could linger in them together.

Little by little, she would match his rhythm. Keeping time with the trees, she would true her heart to his. Ever and always remembering just how much power the meeting of a moment can hold.

Landmark Elementary's gymnasium was bursting at the seams, even though reaver tradition meant opening up the school on one of America's national holidays. Although all were welcome, students and their families were being given priority by the teachers at the doors, all of whom were accompanied by a reaver and an undercover Nightspangle or Woodacre.

Press was confined to the back wall, not that there were really all that many. Not when Spokesperson Twineshaft was scheduled to attend the January 1 program at Archer Middle, and especially not after the media learned that Eloquence Starmark would be making a surprise appearance at the opening festivities for West Branch High.

Decoys and diversions. Because the real story was here. And they'd tell it in their own way.

On the stage, five chairs waited to one side of the podium, where Tami stepped up to the microphone. Taking a deep breath, she felt the moment slow and hoped she could help her Landmark family to linger here, at the beginning.

From her pocket, she withdrew one of her courting gifts—

Faisal's tiny bell. The microphone broadcast its sweet note, as if to summon Bethiel to sing on her behalf. A hush fell, and Tami greeted friends and neighbors. As her gaze swept the room, she caught sight of Joe, standing between Cyril and Rook at the back.

Her twin was here. And he looked calm.

Heart light, Tami got with the program and introduced her audience to the first of their new neighbors. "Please join me in welcoming Fossa Craghart, who is a member of one of the deer clans—the American pronghorn. For the rest of this year, she'll rotate through the classrooms, teaching supplemental sciences. By next fall, we'll have added a lab, where students will enjoy more hands-on learning. Doe Craghart will also be working alongside Mrs. Connell in Phys. Ed. and assist Mrs. Wainwright, our school nurse, in encouraging our kids to have active, healthy lifestyles."

Fossa joined her at the microphone—tall and tan, with short hair and black antlers, she wore loose-fitting clothes that resembled scrubs and a lab coat. Tami met her palms, then presented her with her Landmark lanyard. "Please tell us a little more about yourself."

In richly modulated tones, Fossa gave a fuller introduction, then took her seat.

Tami kept the ball rolling. "Now, help me welcome Viv Bellsweet, who is from one of the butterfly clans. She'll be filling a vacancy in our school. We've been without a school librarian for too long. Viv will bring a much-needed boost to our school's literacy program … and come alongside our teachers as we help our kids cultivate a love for books and a respect for the worlds they open."

Viv was a delicate beauty with hair that passed for strawberry blonde in photos but was much more of a peachy pink in person. Most arresting was a set of graceful antennae where most people kept their eyebrows.

"Lady Bellsweet has already brought our collection up to date and is scheduling story times, author talks, and a book fair."

She presented Viv with her lanyard and let her say a few words. Nearly there.

"Next, I'd like you to meet Torrey Highbranch, who is from one of the avian clans. We'll be keeping him very busy because we're sharing him with Archer Middle. Professor Highbranch specializes in history, customs, and community. We'll learn more about Amaranthine culture firsthand, since he'll be bringing in regular guests—both Amaranthine from the surrounding region and students from West Branch High."

The professor grinned when Tami presented his lanyard and eagerly introduced himself to the audience. His energy levels rivaled Kip's, and she was sure he'd gain the trust they needed.

Almost time.

When the professor took his seat, Tami rang her little bell again. "Harrison, where did you get to?" she called. "It's your turn, you know."

"Coming, Principal Reaverson!" And so Harrison Peck, local celebrity, sauntered across the stage in his crossing guard uniform.

He gave her a wink.

She smiled and retreated a few steps, yielding the floor.

"Who here is a student of Landmark Elementary? Let me see those hands!" he asked, squinting past the lights. "Oh, now that's a bunch. But let's add to the number. How many of you used to attend classes here, even if it was a long, *long* time ago?"

Easily eighty percent of the people in the room had their hands up. Even a couple of the journalists. Tami found Joe in the crowd, and they raised their hands together.

"Not bad, not bad." Harrison waved them to lower their hands, then posed a new question. "How many of you—children, parents, and guardians alike—have been through kindergarten orientation any time in the last eight years?"

Half the audience waved.

Harrison addressed himself to the three Amaranthine newcomers. "One reason we have kindergarten orientation is to make sure our students know which grown-ups are part of our Landmark family." He showed them the photo ID on his lanyard. "You have these now, and that means you belong with us."

All three new teachers lifted their nametags.

Harrison turned back to the larger audience. "I'm Mr. Peck, and you can recognize me easily, because I always wear a bowtie, even when I play bingo."

"It's true!" Tami assured, because for once, she'd been given the script. "I've seen him!"

The kids hooted and hollered. They all knew how this was supposed to go.

"And you'll all be able to remember Doe Craghart, who knows all about nature."

Tami offered a helpful aside. "Doe Craghart also has antlers."

"Oh!" said Harrison, as if he hadn't thought of that. "Is that all right to mention?"

Fossa smiled and inclined her head.

"And you'll be able to remember Lady Bellsweet, who always knows the perfect book to recommend."

Tami cheerfully added, "Lady Bellsweet also has antennae."

"Oh!" Harrison blinked at their librarian. "Do you mind if I mention that?"

Viv folded her hands over her heart and smiled.

Harrison went right on. "And you'll remember Professor Highbranch, who can teach us to have good manners with all of our Amaranthine neighbors."

Tami said, "Professor Highbranch also has red hair."

"Oh! Uh-oh," said Harrison. "We may have a problem. Landmark Elementary already has someone with red hair!"

People chuckled, and several kids called out Kip's name.

"You know," said Harrison. "Introductions go both ways. Our new teachers haven't met two important people who are part of our Landmark family. Should we see if they're here?"

The vote was unanimous.

"Ash!" called Harrison. "Where'd you get to?"

"Here, sir!" he answered, striding out from the wings. Lifting his lanyard, he said, "I'm Ash."

Harrison stage whispered, "You're a grown-up, Ash. That means our kids should call you Mr. Fowler."

"No, thanks. I'd rather be Ash."

"I suppose that's all right, since you gave your permission. Now, aren't there supposed to be two of you?"

"Yeah, there's two of us." And like they'd always done, he put his fingers to his lips and gave a shrill whistle.

Nothing happened.

"Kip!" tried Harrison. "Where'd you get to?"

"Coming!" And Kip burst through the back doors, charged up the center aisle, pretended to trip, tumbled into a series of backflips, and put on the brakes right before crashing into the stage. Brushing off his coveralls, he walked slowly up the steps, as if nothing out of the ordinary had occurred. "Does something need fixing? Or ... did you spill something, Mr. Peck?"

"No, no. We're introducing everyone to our new Amaranthine teachers."

"No kidding?" He did a double-take and gave his ponytail a sheepish tug. "Was that today?"

Harrison asked, "Are you teasing us?"

Kip smiled. "I'm *totally* teasing. I'd never forget a day as important as this one."

"You forgot *something*, though. Where's your nametag, Mr. Kipling?"

Patting at the pockets of his coveralls, he said, "Come on, Mr. Peck. You *know* everyone calls me Kip. I'm Kip, the janitor with red hair."

"And that's a problem," said Harrison.

"It's never been a problem before."

Ash pulled Kip's lanyard from his back pocket and helped him put it on while Harrison pretended to whisper explanations into his ear. Hands waved. Eyebrows jumped and furrowed. Kip nodded and shook his head by turns. And in ten seconds flat, he was up to speed.

"I've got this!" he announced. "My name is Kip. I never wear a bowtie, and I don't have antlers or antennae. I do have red hair, but I'm different than Professor Highbranch. And I can prove it."

He made Harrison back up, crouched low, then sprang up, turning a backward somersault in midair. When he landed, some applauded, but Kip held up his hands. "Wait. It didn't work. Gimme another chance. On the count of three ...."

The crowd counted with him. "One. Two. Three!"

After another backward somersault, Kip checked over his shoulder, then scratched his head. "I guess I'm a little out of practice."

Another countdown. Another flip. But this time, when Kip landed in a crouch, his tail bushed out behind him, and his ears made their point.

Gasps and exclamations of awe rippled through the room as Kip slowly straightened. "My name is Kip. I never wear a bowtie, and I don't have antlers or antennae. I still have red hair, but I also have red fur."

Harrison waited for the first wave of excitement to pass, then asked, "Kip, are you Amaranthine?"

"Yes. I'm from one of the squirrel clans." He looked out over the audience, and Tami thought maybe he was looking for Joe. "Is that okay?"

Applause. And more applause.

Archer rewarded Kip's courage with a standing ovation.

He moved to one of the two remaining seats on the platform and sat, unobtrusively bringing the remaining empty chair to everyone's attention.

People quickly settled back into their seats, and Harrison quietly asked, "Ash, are you going to do backflips, too?"

The silence was absolute.

"I'm not much of an acrobat." Ash faced the audience and said, "My name is Ash. I never wear a bowtie, and I don't have antlers or antennae. I don't have red hair or red fur. I've always liked high places, but I've never really told any of you why."

When he paused, Harrison asked, "Have you been keeping a secret?"

"Yes. But my secret's a little different from Kip's. He has fur. I have feathers."

Kip snapped his fingers and Ash's illusion vanished in a little shower of sparkles, revealing his wings. He demonstrated their full span, then stirred the air with slow wingbeats.

Harrison waited out the expected tumult, then asked, "Ash, are you Amaranthine?"

"Half," he said, chin at a confident angle. "My name is Ash, and I'm a crosser. But that's not the last secret for today."

"There's more?"

Tami stepped forward, and Harrison melodramatically clapped a hand over his heart. "Principal Reaverson, are *you* Amaranthine, too?"

"No, but I do have something to share. It's not the same kind of secret as Kip's, and it's not the same kind of secret as Ash's. But I think it's just as wonderful."

"As wonderful as antlers?"

"Yes."

"Aa wonderful as antennae?"

"Yes."

"As wonderful as red hair?"

"Yes."

"As wonderful as a tail?"

"Yes."

"As wonderful as wings?"

Tami laughed and asked, "Mr. Peck, are you stalling?"

"Sorry. Go ahead."

"We wanted to share our good news with all of you first, because we're counting on our hometown's support. Ash has asked me to marry him, and I said yes."

Under cover of all the confusion, Flootie commandeered the microphone. When she could make herself heard, she said, "I *do* hope you can handle at least one more Amaranthine today. Because Ash and Tami have got themselves a top-notch go-between, and he's here to make his first official statement on their behalf."

Argent stepped out from behind the curtain. Taking his place at the fore, he offered a series of genteel nods and gracious bows until the room began to settle.

Flootie beamed approvingly at the crowd, then spoke for all of them. "Welcome to Archer, Lord Mettlebright. We're delighted to have you."

49

EAVESDROPPER

Biddie was in full bloom on the summer afternoon when Joe overheard something that probably wasn't meant for his ears. Not that he was *trying* to eavesdrop. This was his farm. This was his favorite spot. And he didn't doubt that Amaranthine ears were keen enough to pick up the lazy drift of fingers through fur … and the deep breathing of the squirrel draped bonelessly across his lap.

Which meant that he was *meant* to hear the conversation that pretended to be private.

"So this is her!" The voice was new to the farm, yet familiar.

"Why the sudden change of plans?"

That was Spokesperson Twineshaft. He'd turned up—unannounced and under the radar—a few days ago, escorting Isla. Or vice versa. School stuff, mostly. But wedding stuff, too. Turns out, Isla was the cat's apprentice and a diplomatic *wunderkind*.

459

Voices carried clearly. Hisoka, who liked to be called Sensei, asked, "Are you here at your sire's behest?"

"The idea," came an injured grumble. "I'm at *yours*, if anyone's. Why would you think otherwise?"

"There are ties to Wardenclave."

A skeptical snort. "Most reavers in this part of the world can claim ties to Wardenclave. Are you angling for something, old friend? You know I prefer plain speaking."

Joe cringed. This was very bad acting.

Hisoka asked, "Does this variety of tree grow in Wardenclave's grove?"

"No, this is a new scent." In a softer tone, he added, "Pleasant surprise, really. There are not enough new things in the world."

"Not new," the cat countered stiffly. "Not really."

"No? Well, good. You probably needed reminding." Harmonious Starmark, for the voice could belong to no other, gently said, "Nothing is lost forever."

The conversation faltered, and when Hisoka spoke again he sounded weary. "So you can substantiate George's claim."

"His sire never stole from mine. That much I know." The dog hesitated. "What I *don't* know is whether it's wise to leave the Junzi. You've seen the risk reports."

Joe couldn't help smiling. He'd forgotten himself ... and his audience. But this was a safe place for secrets. Especially since Kip's nap was probably the three-day variety.

"Remote. Warded. Secret. Surrounded." Hisoka sounded pleased. "The Gentleman Bandit will not claim this prize."

"Is that what we're calling him?"

"Or her. And there's no harm in letting Sinder have his way in small matters."

Harmonious chuckled.

They exchanged a few murmurs that Joe couldn't make out.

So they'd been checking out Grandad's story. That was fine. Neither sounded like they were searching for evidence of past misconduct. It had almost sounded like Hisoka was looking for something else, something lost.

"You certainly have a way with animals."

Joe was more used to attracting Ephemera than the Five. And he suspected the latter were more difficult to tame. Especially this one. "He's a person, same as you."

"And he's in an enviable place," said Hisoka.

"We all are." Joe forced himself to relax into the tree at his back. "I won't leave this place, even for you."

"I know better than to ask it." Hisoka chose a seat nearby.

Joe focused all his attention on Kip, who twitched a foot in his sleep. Silences had never bothered him, and this one was peaceful.

"Are you wearing something around your neck?"

"No. Nothing."

Hisoka's focus narrowed. "There's something there, over your heart."

Was he picking up on the seals? That shouldn't be possible. Joe brushed self-consciously at the front of his overalls, only to realize something *was* there. Kip's new favorite trick. "Just some acorns. They're probably warded."

"Ah. So that's it." Hisoka's gaze lingered on the sleeping

squirrel for a while. "About Harmonious. He can't speak of Wardenclave to any but the Five, but he wanted to reassure you. I reminded him that a secret that must not be told ... could still be overheard."

"I figured."

"This tree *isn't* from Wardenclave."

"Nope."

"Joe, do you know where Biddie's seed came from?"

"Lisbet was born with it."

Hisoka asked, "And ... before that?"

"Does it really matter? Or are you just curious."

"I won't know until I know." He showed his palms. "How far will you trust me?"

"Probably all the way." Joe gave a small shrug. "Argent asked us to."

"Thank you." After a thoughtful pause, Hisoka said, "I have accumulated so many secrets that there are few mysteries left in the world. You are one. Truth be told, I am another."

While Joe didn't feel mysterious, he'd already figured out where the problem was. "I shouldn't be a beacon. I don't have the pedigree."

Hisoka visibly relaxed. "Yes."

"And you want to know why?"

"Among other things." His posture loosened further. Rubbing a hand over his short hair, he leaned forward, elbows on knees, and ticked off items on his fingers. "Someone arranged for your great-grandparents to leave Wardenclave without Glint Starmark's knowledge. Someone knew that this is where your family resettled. Someone kept enough contact to know of Lisbet's death. And someone took steps to ensure that the buried seed would have a twin."

Joe could see the chain of events, and he could tell where they were headed.

"Someone warded your sister, who is certainly a reaver. Lovely and above average, but not exceptional."

"Wasn't that Grandad? The necklace is a family heirloom."

Hisoka hummed. "Everyone agrees that Tami's wardstones were handed down from Lisbet Reaverson. But no one remembers when the gift was given. And no one finds that strange. Which is really very strange, indeed."

Joe tried to think back. "She's always had her necklace. She always wears it."

"*And* someone sealed you." Hisoka nested his fingers loosely together. "I wish I had seen the seal myself. Argent says it was already beginning to decay—much to the delight of local Ephemera—so certain markers were lost. But Argent believes that the seal was directly responsible for your covert rise through the ranks."

"I'm not ranked."

"Ah, but you *are*. Argent is more than qualified to render an assessment." With a gesture Joe couldn't interpret, Hisoka quietly said, "Congratulations, First of Beacons."

Joe winced. "Why do *you* think that's a bad thing?"

Hisoka's eyebrows lifted. "You can sense my reservations?"

That was one way of putting it. Joe admitted, "I've been trying to calm you down since you came over."

Sensei drew himself up, but in an embarrassed way. Like when you've just told a guy his zipper's down.

Unsure how else to reassure him, Joe said, "I won't tell."

"Thank you." Hisoka ran a hand over his hair again. "We believe the seal was designed to draw upon this tree's power in order to add to yours. In a sense, Biddie has been tending you. It may be why you feel so deeply attached to this place."

Joe said, "But Biddie chose Tami. She's the one who became tree-kin."

"True." Hisoka sighed deeply. "The person who placed your seal may have had the best of intentions. Things certainly worked out favorably. But the possible repercussions of the seal's existence and usage are ... concerning."

"You're worried about the trees?" Joe guessed. "Like when humans raided the old groves, searching for ways to live longer?"

"It could begin again. Only it would be the reavers this time, seeking fresh power, no matter the cost."

Thinking of the protectiveness of the preservationists, Joe's heart sank. "That sounds kind of like it could lead to a Betweener civil war."

Hisoka said, "I doubt it would come to that. But I'm very much afraid that somewhere, someone may be cultivating potent souls. Presumably, for harvest."

That triggered a memory, a fragment from his dream. "Argent said something about people being snatched and caged. Is this what he meant?"

"In part. But there's more, and we believe everything is connected. You represent our first hint as to *how*." Hisoka slipped from his seat to kneel, like a supplicant before Joe's childhood throne. "Can we speak plainly, as one third twin to another?"

Joe felt the weight and worth of that single secret Hisoka allowed him to know.

Keeping a proper balance meant answering in kind. And trusting all the way.

With a shy smile and a sure heart, Joe asked, "Have you ever met an angel?"

THE END

never more than
FORTHRIGHT

a teller of tales who began as a fandom ficcer. (Which basically means that no one in RL knows about her anime habit, her manga collection, or her penchant for serial storytelling.) Kinda sorta almost famous for gently-paced, WAFFy adventures that might inadvertently overturn your OTP, forthy will forever adore drabble challenges, surprise fanart, and twinkles (which are rumored to keep well in jars). As always... be nice, play fair, have fun! ::twinkle::

FORTHWRITES.COM

This summer is his last chance to win his first love.

MIKOTO AND THE REAVER VILLAGE

Wardenclave has always been a place of secrets and sway. For most of the year, the remote mountain village is closed off from the rest of the world, but each spring, they issue invitations to the most promising young reavers of academy age. Summer skill camps provide opportunities for the elite to train with the best. And by longstanding tradition, for teens of the In-between to evaluate the compatibility of their peers.

At seventeen, Mikoto Reaver is the youngest headman in Wardenclave's history. He's had very little time to adjust to his new role before their close-knit community opens its doors to children of pedigree, the specialists who will mentor them, an allotment of battlers, and a celebrity or two.

Glint Starmark's reputation as a matchmaker has been holding true for millennia, but Mikoto can't bring himself to consider any young lady as a bride until he can speak with the only girl he's ever loved.

There's just *something* about her.

MARKED BY STARS

A wolf without a pack and a boy in need of roots become founders.
After a heavenly visitation, one young wolf turns his back on his pack
and on the moon in order to tread a lonesome path. A blaze of stars.
A brand of copper. A burden of trust. First of Dogs, he takes a new
name, makes peace with group of weary humans, and helps to found
the In-between. This is a tale of the Kindred. This is the lore of the
Starmark clan.

FOLLOWED BY THUNDER

*One sister, a pure light that beckons,
the other, a fierce light that burns.*

Fira and her sister are chased out of another village. Fleeing on foot across the empty moors, they're caught by a storm that roars like the monsters ever in pursuit. But the wind changes and the thundering brings a stampede of defenders who carry them off to a secret place. Where mares dance and rabbits mine. Where the lost clans hid a lasting treasure. Where the girls' curse is considered a blessing.